ALL
THAT IS
HOLY

ALL THAT IS HOLY

BOOK 1

JEREMY KNOP

Podium

To Ashley,
in sickness and in health, forever and always. I love you.

Copyright © 2024 by Jeremy Knop

Cover design by Jon Tonello

ISBN: 978-1-0394-5849-9

Published in 2024 by Podium Publishing
www.podiumaudio.com

Podium

ALL
THAT IS
HOLY

CHAPTER 1

Kneeling on the packed earth in front of the flickering shrine, Odessa Kusa imagined herself at the edge of a precipice. Before her was a vast expanse of nothingness, the very future of human history laid bare at her feet. She felt as if she would be sick.

The small hut was dim. A chill early morning breeze rustled through the thatch roof. A tranquil moment, she and her father in the sanctum of mudbrick and thatch, swaddled in its austere comforts. Today was a day of asceticism. The tight braids tied behind her neck bore no beads or cuffs or charms. No bracelets adorned her wrists. No necklace or ring around her throat. Her father had his bare back to her as he kneeled at the altar, a red skirt around his waist and a pair of hide boots all he wore. His skin was the bronze of the western coasts, a shade lighter than her own, yet in the glow of the sanctified fire, their skin was nearly the same shade of burnished copper.

Her father tossed another bundle of sandalwood and palm onto the fire, the pleasant scent mingling with the smell of blood. Her father's head, freshly shaved and oiled, shined as he touched his forehead to the packed dirt in front of the shrine. Beside him, the old hen, its head and neck plucked bald by the other hens, lay with its throat open and its blood soaking into the dirt. The floor before the shrine was stained by a patchwork of such offerings. The palm fronds fanning out from behind the altar like a peacock's tail were wilted and drooping. Broken machetes and knives were arranged around the altar, their dull edges blackened by smoke and stained with blood. The stone bowl of coals upon the altar was stained a rusty shade by years of blood poured into it.

"Ogé," her father said, his face to the ground. "We of Kalaro beseech you. Give us the strength of body and soul to do as we must. Bless our iron, that which you have given to us. Guide me today, great Ogé, for I am your spear. My faith is my shield. Let this blood heal you in your exile. Let these flames close your wounds. And let us hunt in your name so all may know your glory, mortal and divine." He kept his forehead to the dirt for a moment, eyes closed in reverent concentration before rising. From a gourd bowl, he poured a portion of the hen's blood on the scaffolding of burning sandalwood. The fire rose with a sizzling and crackling as if the flames were satisfied with the paltry offering.

Seeing the trickle of blood splash on the coals only made Odessa's discontent worm deeper into her core. A scrawny old hen was a poor offering but it would have to suffice. There had been no dogs to offer up to Ogé's hunting party. The last dog in Kalaro had died nearly four years ago.

For the hunt we're going out on, we need something much bigger. Before the Gray had come, Kalaro would sacrifice a man and woman each year to the High Gods. Despite the taboo, even the Banished Hunter Ogé would be offered a dog or goat in secret. *We should give Ogé a dozen people for something like this.* But famine had burrowed deep into the land, and plague gnawed away at the weak and the infirmed. Isolated in the mountains as Kalaro was, it had not been able to avoid the Gray. Life was much too precious a commodity now. *Ogé will understand. Even High Gods must know how bad it has gotten. Even in exile, he has to know.*

Her father had begun gutting the hen with a small iron knife. He took heaping handfuls of offal and placed them on the coals to sizzle and pop. When that was done, he took the gourd bowl, still half full of blood, and began sprinkling pinches of herbs into it and stirring the mixture with his finger. His voice rose and fell in hushed song as he worked, barely more than a low hum. He squeezed the juice of a small, unripe genna fruit into the bowl. Stirring and stirring, his chant seemed to swirl with the smoke rising from the altar. Repeating and repeating, the name Ogé the axis of the song, upon which each line revolved. "Ogé, god of iron. Ogé, god of the hunt. Ogé, accept this gift from us." With each repeated refrain her father chanted, anxiety—barbed and thorny—wound around her chest tighter and tighter until she thought she couldn't breathe another breath.

When the bowl of blood and iron was prepared, her father wet the edge of each blade on the altar then wiped his fingers clean on the red cloth spread on the shrine. He turned with the bowl cupped between his hands. "Come, Odessa."

She kneeled in front of the shrine and faced her father. His face was stony. His eyes were unwavering, giving her some stability to cling to and regain some composure. He dipped a finger in the bowl, and she did as well. They painted each other's faces, starting with a line of fine dots curving above their eyebrows. Odessa moved slowly, dotting her father's skin with deliberate care. Her fingers were trembling, and it took all her concentration to steady them enough to finish the delicate dots. Next, they smeared the mixture across their bottom eyelids and moved to their arms, smearing thick lines of red down their arms from the shoulder to the top of their hand and then painting twin bands around their biceps to keep their weapons true.

When they were done, the rest of the blood mixture was poured into the fire. They stayed, kneeling in front of the altar for a long while. Her father chanted to Ogé as wisps of smoke crawled along the ribs of the roof and out a hole in the center of the peak. Odessa closed her eyes and tried to slow the racing of her thoughts. She could only think of the abyss. She and the rest of Kalaro were at the threshold of something great and terrible. *I don't know if I can do this.* When the moment came, she did not know if she could take that step into the unknown where no mortal had ever set foot.

She tried to derive some strength from the shrine, to glean some divine strength from the sanctified flame and alleviate the crushing pressure upon her ribs or still the quivering of her heart. The fire gave her no such aid.

This will be like any other hunt, she told herself. *Papa and I have gone on so many, what makes this one so different?* In her sixteen years, she had joined her father on countless hunts. Since she could walk, she had been a second shadow to him. She had been just a small girl when she first followed him into the Night Jungle. But this was different. Her stomach twisted and knotted like a snake with its head cut off. There was no use in denial. This would be the greatest hunt any man or woman had ever undertaken.

They bowed their heads to the dirt and then rose to leave. Her father ducked through the doorway and she followed, bowing her head to pass beneath the overhanging thatch. The sun rose above the hills to the east through a pall of thick haze, a ball of furious red smothered in a damp, woolen gray like a coal singeing the clouds and bleeding thin threads of fire into the horizon. Mist clung to the ground, heavy on sparse and brittle grass. In the shadow of the main hut and away from the shrine's meager heat, a slight chill prickled up her bare arms, and the skin beneath half-dried paint broke out in goosebumps. The paint on their skin dried slowly, a deep, dark red on skin the color of burnished mahogany. Mixed with genna fruit juice, the color seeped deep into her skin, where it would stay for weeks. No longer would they be able to hide their devotion to the banished god. But should they survive, it wouldn't matter anymore.

Dew clung to the hide of their boots as they made their way around to the front of the main hut. There, they found her mother and sisters waiting in the wattle-fenced courtyard. Her mother was in a yellow kaftan, a bright anachronism in the solemn gloom of morning like a sunflower growing from a desolate stretch of saltpan. Her mother held her father's spear in one hand and her infant sister Kimi in the other. Her sister Ayana was four years younger than Odessa and had the same slender, delicate features as their mother and the same rich, dark skin tone. She held a bow as tall as she was and a long leather quiver with five thick arrows in it.

Odessa reached out to take the bow and quiver, but Ayana clutched them tighter to her chest.

"Ayana," her mother said, an edge to her voice. "What did we talk about?"

Reluctantly, Ayana held the bow and quiver out for Odessa to take. "Good luck, Dessa," she said, her downcast eyes unable to reach her sister's. Her voice was thick and husky with the tears she held at bay only because her mother had told her to be strong.

Odessa took the black palm bow and the quiver with a thin, forced smile. "Why such a sour look?" she asked, slinging the quiver across her back. "We'll be back in a few days. It's no different than any other hunt." The words left a bitter taste in her mouth, but she did not let her false smile waver.

Ayana looked at her, bottom lips trembling. "I don't want you to go." Tears filled her big copper eyes. "Please don't go, Dessa. Please stay home."

Odessa's lips curled in a false grin, but her eyes betrayed her façade. She blinked away a bit of moisture. "I'm not going to war, you know."

Without warning, Ayana wrapped her arms around Odessa's waist and hugged her, refusing to let go. Tears soaked into Odessa's tunic as she held her, her own eyes watering. She squeezed Ayana tightly, restraining the sobs swelling in her chest.

After a few moments, she took Ayana by the shoulders and pried her away so she could look into her teary eyes. "No more crying," Odessa said, sniffling. Ayana closed her eyes, tears spilling from long eyelashes. "I will be back. We'll all be back. I promise. Sister to sister, blood to blood. We'll come back."

Ayana nodded, eyes still filled with tears. They hugged once more and then released one another so Ayana could run crying to her father, who stood waiting, his spear in hand, to embrace her in a one-armed hug.

Odessa wiped her eyes and turned to see her mother watching the embrace. Her mother's head was wrapped in a simple silky cotton gele. Thin gold hoops in the shape of a snake eating its own tail hung from her ears, passed down the Kusa line for generations. "Goodbye, mama," Odessa said warily.

She expected cold reproach for her part in this heresy, but her mother turned and gave her a sad smile. "Good luck." She took her in a one-armed hug, baby Kimi between them, and kissed her on the forehead. "Don't get hurt."

"Thank you, mama," Odessa said. Looking into her mother's eyes, she felt a sudden pang of guilt. Her mother was an ardent believer in the sanctity and total supremacy of the gods. To her mother, she was saying goodbye to her husband and eldest daughter forever.

Her father laughed unabashedly as Ayana held tight to his waist despite his attempt to pry her off. Odessa watched her mother's gaze drift away to him. Her eyes grew distant, lost in thought and feeling again.

"I will bring him back," Odessa said. "I promise."

Her mother's lips pressed into a hard line. "You would do better to convince him to cease his foolishness." She shifted Kimi in her arms. The baby cooed quietly and settled in her swaddling cloth. "This will only bring more hardship, you know. When men rise against gods, no good will come of it."

Odessa nodded, agreeing with her mother but unable to stop herself from going over the edge of the precipice now. She had her own reservations about the hunt. But her father was going and he could not go without his shadow.

Before she could say anything else to her mother, the bleating of a horn rose from the eastern edge of the village and echoed through the valley. Her mother hugged her again and whispered in her ear. "I love you."

Another bleat of the horn, this one more forceful. The other huts around them began to rouse. Odessa's father embraced her mother and gave her one last kiss. Their lips lingered together for a moment. Odessa and Ayana glanced at one another and stuck out their tongues in disgust.

Her father and mother held each other a moment longer. "You must trust me, this is for the best," he said. "We will come back triumphant, I swear."

Her mother held on to his forearm as he tried to pull away. Any hard reproach in her eyes had melted away into a misting of tears. "Come back alive. That's all I ask."

"We will," he said. "I love you."

"I love you too," her mother said, her firm voice catching slightly. Her father gave Kimi a kiss on the forehead and told her he loved her. "I do this for you," he whispered to the baby. "We do this for all of you."

Odessa shifted the awkward weight of the quiver on her back. The village was stirring around them. As she and her father left the wattle-fenced courtyard, Odessa looked back at her mother and sisters. A barb of sadness pricked at her heart. A part of her wanted nothing more than to stay with them. To stay and weave or weed the blighted garden. To talk and laugh with them as she always had.

"We must go now," her father said, holding the wattle gate open. She turned away from her home and followed him into the spacious dirt path running between the concentric rings of huts that made up the village of Kalaro.

They followed the circular path north. Through gaps in the huts, she could occasionally make out the Elder's Lodge, a large, rectangular adobe building at the northern end of the central plaza. A few figures bustled in front of the lodge, casting glances to the east. Voices muddled in the morning quiet.

Her father took her hand and led her into an alleyway between huts toward the outer ring of huts. They hurried with their heads down.

Only a handful of huts near the eastern part of the village were occupied anymore. They sat dilapidated, wide holes in thatch roofs and crumbling mudbrick walls letting the elements in. Rot and moldering decay took what the plagues and blight had not already claimed.

They took the dusty path around the last ring of huts north to join the hunting party on the eastern path out of the village. Past the huts and far on the eastern horizon, Odessa could see the jagged, saw-toothed mountains towering high above the land. The Coatlahara Mountains had formed along the back of the World Serpent's corpse when the world was still young and primordial. A long stretch of forest bristled at the base of the mountains. The Arabako Forest. Somewhere in the endless tangle of forest hid Egende, Guardian of the Arabako.

Swept away by the momentum of her father's fervor, she barely had time to think. Before she knew it, the eastern path was in sight. The reality of what they planned to do was heavy on her shoulders now. The survival of the village depended on this hunt. She knew that. But it could come at the sacrifice of her mortal soul. Any reservations she had now had come much too late.

A dozen men and women milled around the path leading out of town, in hide and mudcloth tunics and skirts of patterned red and black. Some men were bare-chested while others, mostly those carrying spears, wore baggy, long-sleeved tunics or flowing ponchos. They stood at the edge of sparse fields. Wilted and withering plants clawed from the dry, sandy dirt in sporadic rows. The spade-shaped leaves of yams curled and turned brown at the edges. Fanned cassava leaves hung limply from their stems, splotches of yellow and brown gnawing holes in them. Even the weeds grew stunted and marred in the tainted earth. A pervasive dullness bled from the smothering gray sky and permeated the earth. The last vapors of morning mist rose from the fields, gray wisps rising among the plants. The stale, cold breath of a dying land.

When Odessa and her father reached the hunting party, low murmurs were running through the clustered groups and a nervous tension kept them moving, shifting from side to side as they whispered, speaking only to keep the silence at bay.

All but one man was affected by the tense, solemn atmosphere. Ubiko, Odessa's uncle on her mother's side, broke off from one of the clusters as they approached, a short throwing spear slung across his shoulder and a long boar spear in the other used as a walking stick. A kudu horn hung from a rawhide strip at his shoulder. He was short and brawny whereas her father was tall and wiry. "Good day for a hunt, no?" he asked with a wide grin.

Odessa smiled but her father's face was stony, his eyes glancing down at the horn at Ubiko's waist and then to the barren land stretching toward the forest. "What's so good about it?" he asked.

"Are you blind, my friend?" Ubiko gestured to the sun over the horizon, obscured by a thick gray haze. "The air is clear, the sun is shining, and you can barely smell the burn pits today." He drew a long, exaggerated breath through his nostrils. "The perfect day to kill a god!"

"You shame us all." Her father's face cracked, a grin peeking through the façade of stony rebuke. "Put your mask on and hide that shameful grin."

Ubiko stabbed his throwing spear into the dirt and left it standing upright to take the bone-white mask from his belt and hold it over his face. In the shape of a skull, the mask left the bottom half of his face unobscured to reveal a broad, foolish grin. "Better?"

Her father shook his head, a grin breaking through the shallow stoicism. "You're a fool."

Ubiko lowered the mask from his face and leaned on his long boar spear. "If I'm a fool, then what does that make you? This hunt is your foolish idea is it not?" Ubiko smirked, a glint of provocation in his eye.

Instead of rising to the provocation, her father laughed. "Shameful, shameful, shameful."

"Shameful?" Ubiko leaned forward on his spear. "I think it more shameful to hide behind all these pretenses of necessity and crisis. You're as excited as I and you know it." Ubiko glanced at the other hunters behind him, still clustered and occasionally glancing at them. "I also think it more shameful to be sulking like a bunch of whipped children on the cusp of the hunt of a lifetime. Man's triumph over the divine! And everyone acts as if we're going to a funeral."

Odessa could not help but be caught up in her uncle's enthusiasm. The tense, sullen atmosphere that had laid so heavily upon her shoulders lessened a bit as she saw him speak these blasphemies so flippantly. If her mother had heard him, she would have had a fit.

"One day, your blasphemy is going to catch up to you," her father said to Ubiko, face still bearing a wide grin.

"It will get you before it comes for me."

Her father laughed. "Hasn't happened yet."

Odessa's smile wavered a bit. Despite all the jokes, they all knew what they were doing was wrong—the gravest of sins. The risk of courting divine retribution hung over all of them. Kalaro could become a smoldering crater in the mountains because of this. But here her father and uncle were joking about it as they might receive nothing more than a scolding. *Men have a strange sense of humor,* she thought; but in a way, she understood why they did it. It was better to laugh in the face of such things than cower before them.

Behind her, two carts drawn by draft goats and llamas rattled along the road toward them. Inside those carts would be food, water, and the tools of butchery.

"I suppose it's time to go," her father said, watching the carts draw near.

"No one's to send us off?" Ubiko asked.

"Send us off? I'm surprised no one is here to stop us. Especially since someone thought it wise to wake the whole village with their bellowing."

Ubiko smiled sheepishly. "I thought you may have slept too late and needed some waking." Watching the scrawny animals draw old carts of warped wood, he scratched his short-cropped hair with a finger looped through the eyehole of his mask. "You would think the Elders would have come though."

"They'd all rather ignore what has to be done. Rather shut themselves in their homes than face reality. They are content with empty tradition and emptier stomachs."

"I expected the ka-man to come and try to stop us at least."

"You know Kunza won't do a thing. He's let this village rot from the inside out and done nothing about it." The good humor in her father's voice had faded. His words were hard and sharp like good iron. "The gods have abandoned us and all he has done is stay in his hut like a hermit and pray. Praying to gods that care nothing for mankind."

"Come now," Ubiko said with a smile, lightly slapping her father's shoulder with his mask. "Let's show them the error in their ways, no? Unblighted forest. Fertile farmland. Lively game. All within our grasp." Ubiko spoke so the other hunters could hear him clearly. "We'll come back heroes! God killers! What man can say he has killed a god, eh? We'll become legends!"

"You make it sound so easy," her father said. The carts came to a stop only a few paces behind Odessa and her father. "Let's not get too far ahead of ourselves." Her father walked toward the rest of the hunting party, putting a hand on Ubiko's shoulder as he passed.

Her father went from cluster to cluster, speaking with the other hunters. Calming their worries. Assuaging the fear of the heretic.

"That's a big bow," Ubiko said. "Are you sure you can draw that thing?"

Odessa scowled, barely able to restrain her smile. "Start running and I'll show you."

Ubiko feigned hurt. "You would put an arrow in your poor old uncle?"

"Nowhere important. Just a leg or arm."

Before Ubiko could respond, the hunting party began to move, her father at the head of the group. Ubiko gave her a playful shove as he put on his mask and pulled his short spear from the dirt. "It's time."

The hunters left the village on a thin strip of dirt between fields. Far across the valley, the foothills rose, a wide swathe of glistening green. Unblighted trees swayed in the breeze. Beyond the sloping hills of greenery, through gaps in the thick, dull cloud cover, Odessa could make out the sweep of crumbling ribs floating high, caught in orbit far away. A piece of the skeleton of a bygone Forebearer, borne from the void of the Cosmos.

To the south, a mountain higher than the rest rose, the Mount of Ascension. A temple sat atop its flat peak and it was there that Kalaro performed its sacrifices, though it had been almost two years since the village had last traversed those stone steps. The stairway up the mountain followed the path the High Gods had taken when they ascended to the heavens. Even from the village, Odessa could see the sharp drop on the far side of the mountain and the long slope that stretched from its bottom. It was there that the stairway to the heavens had been destroyed and the mountainside sheared off. Where Ogé had fallen as he was cast down to the earth.

The hunting party passed the edge of the sparse fields into thick grasses. At the head of the group, her father slowed. "Masks on, everyone."

Odessa untied the loose knot and took the clay skull mask from her belt. Tying the rawhide behind her head, the mask pressed against her skin and squashed the tip of her nose. Beneath a row of teeth, her lips were pressed tight, only loosening to let breath out in long, wavering exhalations—no more smiles. The unease and solemn, sullen gravity of the hunt weighed unbearably on her shoulders. Bile crept up her throat and she felt sick.

A dozen men and women, dressed in tunics and ponchos and wearing masks like skulls, marched away from Kalaro. With sanctified iron in hand, they approached the forested foothills in silence. Hide-swaddled feet padded along the overgrown path. Hooves crunching upon dirt. Carts rattling along behind them. The mountains loomed high above, a majesty and supremacy about them undisturbed by the approach of the blasphemous hunters. Heedless to all, the mountains stood impassive.

CHAPTER 2

Like the shadows of fast-moving clouds sweeping across the open field of knee-high grasses, the hunters sped across the plain in two groups. One group, led by Ubiko, headed toward the southern edge of the basin while Odessa's father led the second band of hunters north. Odessa stayed at his heels. There was no speaking anymore. There were no more words to say.

The ridge of low peaks to the north was a wall of imperious stone creeping westward into the high hills that ringed the basin's western edge. Behind them, the village was nothing more than a cluster of indistinct shapes. Threads of smoke rose from the distant huts to join the dreary gray above. Often, Odessa caught herself glancing back at the shrinking village. She thought it would edify her resolve and reaffirm why she was doing this. But all it did was make her want to go back home.

As they neared the northern slopes, the ground rose and fell in rolling hills, and the village was blotted out. At the bottom of a slight valley, a river flowed westward from the mountains before curving south through the valley past Kalaro and into the lowlands. Grass grew taller and coarser. Drooping reeds choked the edges of the river's babbling current. The northern riverbank was steep, rising into the higher hills before the ridgeline. The hunting party followed the river upstream. Behind them, the cart bucked and rattled across the roughening terrain.

The Arabako grew into view, the trees soon towering over them and blocking out the looming mountains above. The trees were massive, some of them deeper in the forest as thick around as her family's hut. The cart stopped short of the treeline and set up camp while the hunters slipped into the forest one at a time.

Odessa's father disappeared into the forest. She waited at the tree line until she heard him whistle. He had reached his position. She plunged into the forest, following the path trodden by the hunters before her.

* * *

Thin sunlight punching through gray cloud cover drifted through broad leaves and drooping fronds to dapple the forest floor in shallow pools. Odessa waded through these pools of scant morning light, wanting nothing more than to relish the warmth on her skin. It had been more than a year since she and her father had entered these woods and felt the sun splash so brazenly upon their skin. Egende had only let the villagers hunt and forage within the forest for a few scattered weeks in the last five years. As blight gnawed harvests to almost nothing and the ground grew sour, Egende barred them entry into the sacred wood. No matter what goods the village proffered, of which the village had little to give, no sonorous bellow came echoing off the mountainside to invite them in. The peaked archway at the mouth of the forest path remained blocked by a thickening curtain of ivy and vines strung by the forest spirits that dwelled under Egende's protection.

Sick trees dotted the outer reaches of the forest. What few leaves remained on the spindly branches were brown and curled. Bare and gnarled branches extended toward holes in the canopy, moth-eaten holes in a tapestry of greenery. Deeper puddles of light accumulated at the base of these dead trees.

A high-pitched warble above her head. She jumped at the noise and drew her bowstring back, an arrow already nocked. Above her sat a green paradise bird on a low branch, its plumage like an iridescent emerald in the canopy. It watched her, head cocked, then puffed out its chest and let out another shrill, bubbling call.

She sighed and relaxed the bowstring, the shaft of jungle cedar gliding smoothly against the lacquered wood. The bird shook its head and stared at her, one black eye turned to engulf her, a tiny version of herself captured in the glassy stare. The bird let out another warbling cry and Odessa grimaced. *Yes, let the whole forest know I'm here while you're at it.* The bird continued to watch her with a sort of placid intensity. She began to turn and then, in a sudden flapping of shimmering emerald wings, the bird was gone, lost in lush greenery.

She continued deeper into the forest, the footfalls of her hide-swaddled feet no more than a whisper in the woods. The occasional bird squawked in the distance and faraway insects chirruped halfheartedly, yet the forest was unnervingly quiet, seemingly aware of the hunters' ill intentions. She passed less dead and dying trees as she went deeper into the woods.

Whistles came occasionally from in front and behind as the hunters fell into position, a line stretching across the northern rim of the forest. Six hunters spread out in the labyrinth of tree and brush, spans of rough woods separating them.

A long, drawn-out whistle from up ahead and Odessa turned south. She whistled in response, a timid sound from her dry mouth. Whistles moved down the line of hunters, growing more distant. She tried to memorize how near the whistles to either side of her had been but the buzzing drone of the forest and the pounding of her heart made it hard for her to tell. *I'll just have to go by sight and feeling,* she told herself. She began southward, pushing through a curtain of drooping palm leaves. *I don't need their whistling to stay on course. I can cut trail better than most of these old goats.* Her confident thoughts did little to calm the nervous energy skittering across her skin. If she went off course and missed their quarry, that failure would be on her shoulders. Whatever happened to the village would be her fault.

The undergrowth grew thicker around her feet, and she deferred to a game trail cutting through the brush. She paused often, listening intently. Her eyes darted from tree to tree, searching for movement or a break in the pattern of verdant life. Like bugs beneath her skin, anxiety skittered incessantly across her raw nerves.

Egende's wrath was swift and brutal. In the stories, it appeared without warning, despite its great size, and brought the forest's vengeance upon anyone caught threatening the sanctity of the woods. It was nature's rage incarnate. The forest's fury made manifest lurking in every shadow.

Hours dragged on in a blur of indistinct green. Traveling ever southward, through ravines packed with brush and over slopes that made her thighs ache as if the muscles had been dipped in scalding water. The forest floor was covered in ferns and vines, and it took conscious effort to lift her deadened feet high enough to avoid tripping. Her quiet, deliberate footfalls had regressed to a beleaguered tromping through the brush.

A short whistle, rising in pitch, came from somewhere close, muffled by the spans of forest. She paused, trying to calm her panting before she replied with a curt whistle in return, descending in pitch.

The same whistle replied again, two trilling notes cutting through the forest. Odessa cut through the forest toward the whistler. As she darted through the trees, she noticed the forest becoming sparser, the undergrowth less dense and treacherous. Soon she could make out a break in the trees and two figures standing in the break.

The path cutting through the forest from Kalaro to the Serpent's Peak was ancient stone weathered by innumerable years and encrusted here and there with a thin layer of moss and lichen. The scuff of her boots upon the ancient stone seemed so very loud as she ran up the path to where her father and Adura stood.

Adura, leaning on her spear, flashed a thin, weary smile as Odessa approached. Her father remained stone-faced, sparing a moment to nod at his daughter before continuing his discussion with Adura.

"Where is he now, then?"

"Ubiko wrapped him up and took him back to camp." She frowned. "What parts of him we could find, that is."

Odessa slowed, coming to a halt a few paces away. Her throat was tight and dry. "What happened?"

Adura glanced at her and then looked back at her father.

He did not spare Odessa a glance this time, speaking only to Adura. "Have him taken home and then move your camp to ours. And tell Ubiko I need to talk to him."

Adura nodded and left, giving Odessa a squeeze on the shoulder as she walked past. Her grip was firm and reassuring, but the look in her eyes corroded what little mettle Odessa had left.

Her father came as Adura left down the ancient path. There was a darkness in his demeanor, a cold anger. A thousand thoughts raced through Odessa's mind like a hive of hornets stirred in an uproar. But as he stood, looking at her, his cold demeanor faded, replaced with a morose weariness. He opened his mouth and then closed it, searching for the words to say.

"What happened?" Odessa took a step toward him. "Did someone get hurt?" She knew the answer as soon as the words left her lips. *Not hurt. Dead. Someone is dead.*

He sighed. "Akbal. He's dead."

"No," Odessa said, the word slipping out her mouth before she could think. Akbal was a distant relative on her mother's side, only a few years older than Odessa. She had not known him well, but he had always been kind to her. "No, he can't be."

"Someone spooked a duiker his way. He took his mind off the hunt at hand and killed the beast." He wiped a bead of sweat from his brow. "Egende's wrath was swift and brutal. By the time someone reached him, Egende was gone and Akbal was dead." The end of his spear tapped the stone as he looked out into the forest, his countenance darkening again. "I told everyone, 'Don't get greedy.' This is why. This is what I was trying to avoid."

"He's really gone?"

He looked at her as if he had forgotten she was there. "He's really gone. I'm sorry." He put a hand on her shoulder.

She was too stunned to speak. She had seen him just that morning. He couldn't be dead.

"I never should have brought you into this," her father said. "You shouldn't be here. You should be safe at home."

She shook her head, his words sobering her somewhat. "I'm fine. I want to help."

"Want doesn't have anything to do with it. You shouldn't be here. It's not safe. I thought you could at least join the scouting, but it's not worth it. If something happened to you, I— I don't know what I would do."

Odessa hugged him, blinking away a misting of tears. "I can't let anything happen to you, either. I promised Mama I would keep you out of trouble."

His arms wrapped around her and he chuckled, but he said no more. They hugged for a few moments, a breeze rustling through the canopy of leaves above the path. Through the leaves, the sky dimmed a flinty gray as the sun began to sink down the western sky.

They returned to camp a few hours before nightfall. The camp was dour, the depressing atmosphere of the morning a festival by comparison. Sporadic chatter rose in the form of whispers, but Odessa and her father paid it no mind. A pot sat in a bed of coals, a thin mixture of corn meal, water, and ash simmering at the bottom. They each scooped a portion into a banana leaf and ate. The addition of ash filled their bellies and took the edge from their hunger.

The southern hunting party joined them not long after, a band of solemn hunters astride an empty cart.

Ubiko approached her father. "I take it you heard?"

Her father nodded.

"I wish we at least could have brought the duiker he downed, but the vindictive sow stomped it to pieces along with him." Ubiko glanced over to where Odessa sat beside the fire. "Sorry," he added.

"I told him not to do something stupid like that," her father said. "We'll have a whole forest to hunt soon enough. It's so stupid."

"I know," Ubiko said. "He was just young. He didn't know what Egende was capable of."

"Well, now he does," her father said bitterly. From her place at the fire, Odessa frowned. How could he talk like that? Akbal was *dead*.

Adura returned from the village a short time before the sun had fully slid behind the hills. Her tall, broad frame had lost its rigid vigor and seemed to sag as she came into camp. She immediately headed toward the pot of corn mash.

Ubiko was sitting by the fire next to Odessa when Adura came and began scooping out a portion of lukewarm mash. "How was it?" he asked.

She let the spoon drop into the pot with a loud clatter and sat in a huff on the ground across from them. "It was a mess. The Elders are in a panic. Kunza-ka is furious. Everyone is crying, saying Abkal is Forsaken. And your family is obviously distraught." Her eyes narrowed at Ubiko. "You owe me."

Something between a frown and smile touched the corners of Ubiko's mouth. "Thank you," he said. "I'm lousy at things like that."

"Responsibility? Duty?" Adura said with a touch of genuine irritation.

"I'm not a bad news kind of man."

"You don't want to hear what kind of man I think you are," Adura said, scooping a bit of mash with her fingers and putting it in her mouth.

Around the fire, conversation ebbed and flowed, but Odessa could not follow most of it. It swirled around her with the smoke rising from the fire. Strands of conversation as ephemeral as wisps of smoke. She was somewhere else, beyond the talk and chatter. Beyond the trepidation and commiseration.

People in Kalaro died of plague and starvation. But to be stomped to death by an angry god, that she could not bear. Abkal's soul would sink in the River of Souls and slip into perdition for eternity. He would never join the afterlife. Never feel Matara's embrace. Forever segregated from the cycle of life and death, he would languish in the endless void.

She hoped more than anything that he hadn't been Forsaken. No one knew what it took for a god to damn a mortal, but she hoped poaching was not enough to merit damnation.

For the next two days, as the hunters scoured the southern forest for gods, she ruminated about what it meant to be Forsaken. What it meant to be human. No good came of her ruminations. All she was left with was anxiety and a headache.

CHAPTER 3

The sun was at its apex when Odessa stopped beneath a sprawling acacia, a rarity that high in the foothills. It was the third day of the hunt. In the shade of twisting branches and thick shelves of foliage, she leaned against the furrowed bark and caught her breath. Her fingers massaged a knot from an aching leg. Her eyes still scanned the forest around her. The top of the slope she had just climbed gave her no better vantage than the low ground. Deep within the forest, all she could see were straight trunks of ancient ironwoods and skunk trees. Down the slope, she could see the purple-tinged leaves of a hard pear tree. Nothing moved, other than the bushy tree tops swaying high above. Beneath the canopy, the forest floor was still, and that tranquility permeated her body, weighing her down with a numbness she found more disquieting than serene.

A distant whistle, sharp and long, came from the south. Odessa straightened. She listened, unsure if she had really heard it or not. Silence packed her ears like wads of cotton.

Another whistle, also from the south. This whistle was much closer, a subtle melody rising in pitch before it trailed off, swallowed by the silence of trees.

Odessa whistled in reply and padded south, ducking beneath branches and fern fronds and vines, vaulting over fallen trees, rotten and covered in moss. One hand steadying the cumbersome quiver on her back and the other holding her bow, she raced through the dense wood. A swift breeze through the undergrowth.

After a while, she paused and panted a bit, her head cocked and ears alert. When she heard nothing, she whistled—a short inquiring chirp. Deeper in the forest came a trilling reply. She followed the reply over a ridge thick with ferns and false violets.

Halfway down the other side of the ridge, her father and Ubiko were crouched beneath a cluster of soapberry bushes with a half dozen of the other hunters. Odessa padded down the hill and drew close to her father's side. "What is it?"

Her father pointed to wide ruts in the leaf-carpeted ground not far from the bushes. The smell of soft, loamy dirt mingled with the faint vinegary scent of fallen soapberries. "The dirt is freshly torn up. Tracks lead down into the ravine. The two young ones."

"As big as you, they are," Ubiko added. "Maybe bigger even."

"Where's the sow?" she asked, hesitant to even say the god's name in such a sacred place. As if her words would cause it to appear. Even so, her hushed words seemed much too loud in the placid forest stillness.

"No sign of it," her father said.

"We bring it to us, then," Ubiko said.

"What now?" Odessa asked, hoping her jittering nerves had not put a tremble in her words.

Ubiko smiled. "We kill gods."

The hunters spread out along both sides of the ravine. Creeping along the top of the ridge, her steps deliberate and light and an arrow nocked on a taut bowstring, Odessa caught a glimpse of their prey. Two young boars rooted in loamy dirt. Boarlings almost as tall as she was, their bristling backs coming to a hump at shoulders that would reach just under her chin. Their tusks were still short nubs poking out from beneath their lips. In the hundreds of years, they had lived, they had lost the light-colored striped coats of infancy, their hair starting to grow coarse, taking on a mottled shade of reddish brown. The markings of divinity taking shape in their hair. The glimmering, incandescent lines started in a half-moon shape beneath their eyes and ran down their backs with smaller lines branching off and spiraling down toward their bellies. The shimmering lines of pale yellow were still faint and pale, but if allowed a thousand years of maturing, they would be beautiful, golden, and bright as the sun.

Odessa and the other archers hid atop the ridge as the spearmen and spearwomen crept along the ravine basin from either end. The hunters' noose tightened around the twin boarlings snuffling in the dirt for roots and tubers.

Her middle finger played along the eagle feather fletching of the nocked arrow, the arrow pinched between her thumb and the crook of her index finger, as she watched the divine boarlings. One of the boarlings, slightly larger than the other, scampered ahead. The smaller of the two followed, snorting as it bucked and raced after its twin. Odessa's bowstring remained taut but she did not draw it any farther.

The first boarling skidded to a halt. The second ran past it and then stopped, its body tense. They stood staring at the spear hunters crouched in the undergrowth not twenty meters away.

Odessa pulled the bowstring to her cheek. The bow tilted, her eye focused down the shaft of the arrow, at the smaller boarling. For a moment, the entire forest paused. The young gods were frozen and fascinated and fearful of the strange creatures in the bush. An inquisitive snort. The larger of the two boars took a wary step forward.

Her arrow hissed in the air, quick as a snake bite. The forest's stillness, so laden with tension, now broke, shattered by a chorus of hissing arrows. A high-pitched squeal of terror. Her arrow buried deep in the smaller boarling's side. It jumped and turned to run, and two more arrows sank into its flesh.

The boarlings turned and bolted. They were met with spearpoints. The smaller boarling darted toward Odessa's father, its eyes wide with panic. With serpentine finesse, her father sidestepped and his spear snapped forward and met the charging boar. A terrible squealing. Desperate, pitiful squeals. It bucked and jumped.

Two spears met the larger boarling. One in its throat to the crossbar, the other in its side. It charged into the spear hunters, shoving them to the ground, the handles of their spears ripped from their hands. It dashed past them, trampling a hunter who screamed, clutching a mangled leg turned to meat. Odessa, halfway down the ravine, let another arrow loose, catching the boar in its haunch. Its back leg jerked. It stumbled for a moment and spears came down from all sides and pinned it, squealing and thrashing, to the ground. Its eyes bulged white with fear as it struggled to get up. Its front legs dug in the dirt, trying to pull itself free from the spears holding it down. A spear pulled from its back end and snapped forward to ram the point deep in its rib cage. The boarling expelled a throaty wheeze and its body stiffened and shuddered. Then it relaxed, the vigor draining from its body as it slumped over, bleeding into the dirt.

Beneath her father's spear, the smaller boarling kicked its legs in pitiful spasms. The pathetic kicks growing weaker and weaker. A plaintive whine as her father put his full weight on the spear. And then its twitching bulk slackened and grew still, the luster already fading from its coat.

Odessa rushed down the rest of the slope, her mouth half-open with shock. *We did it*, she thought. *We really did it.* In some way, she still had not believed it possible to bring down gods, even young gods. Iron should not be able to pierce a god's hide. And yet there they lay, coarse hair wet with blood, the ground beneath them greedily soaking up the pooling ichor.

"Get back!" her father snapped in a sharp whisper. "Do not get close! Do not touch the blood!" The hunters milling around the boarlings, still numbed by their achievement, backed away from the bodies.

"We really did it!" Odessa said, a bit too loudly. Her heart still pounded and her blood was running hot.

Her father turned and smiled as she approached, a soft smile beneath a ghoulish skull, warm eyes peering through the mask. He was wiping his spear head with a thick cloth, sopping up thick blood that had reached all the way to the haft. "So we did. All these years, I never thought it truly possible." His smile grew. "Yours was the first arrow in the air, I saw."

A rush of warmth came to her cheeks. "I guess so."

"Don't be modest, Odessa. This is too momentous an occasion to be modest." He finished wiping the dark iron point and then tossed the blood-soaked rag on the ground. Her father's strong hand lay on her shoulder and squeezed. "The honor of these kills is yours, first and foremost."

A mixture of pride and love bloomed in her chest, warm and buoyant. She wrapped her arms around him and squeezed. He hugged her back. Her cheek against his bare chest, she could hear the beating of his heart, the steady thump of a heart so full of love for the daughter that should have been a son. He had never resented her for being born a girl. Had always let her join him on his hunts despite the whispered nattering of others in the village. He raised her as he would a son and allowed her to be both a hunter and a woman. And for that, she loved him more than she could ever put into words.

Their embrace broke, a picturesque moment dissipating and dissolving back into reality. "Now the difficult part," he said.

As the youngest and, arguably the fastest among them, Odessa was sent to fetch the goats and the butchers in their aprons and thick gloves and lead them to the hunters' quarry. The hunters melted into the trees at the top of the ravine, watching for Egende, the satisfaction of their victory now loaded with the gravity of what they had done. Tension filled the forest like a flammable gas, settling heaviest in the belly of the ravine where the young gods lay, their bleeding now done and the ground stained dark with ichor.

She raced along the faint game trail that had brought the boarlings to the ravine. Past the copse of soapberries. Descending down the foothills her legs extended, bounding down steep slopes, dodging trees and ducking branches.

They would have to bleed and butcher the boarlings and load up the godlings' meat in the wagons all before Egende learned of their treachery. Godsblood was poisonous, but it would not be as potent in the young boarlings. That was the hope at least. If they could get out of the forest with their quarry without alerting Egende, the village could eat for months. Until the next harvest at least. A harvest that would hopefully be better.

Whipping past her in her flight were more acacias and palms, more bright orchids and trumpet vine. The slopes grew slighter and the descent markedly less breakneck. She slowed to a brisk jog, sweat stippling her skin and beading up beneath the stifling clay of her mask. The sun pouring through thin clouds made the lowland forest sweltering, moisture rising from the lush plant life becoming caught in the thick canopy.

A distant cracking noise. A groan and a heavy thud. Odessa skidded to a stop. Her heart skipped a beat. She turned back, peering back the way she had come, listening intently. Fear tickled her guts. A rumbling far up in the foot-hills. Something massive crashed through the underbrush. Thoughts of coming back to the ravine to an angry god awash in a bloodbath kept emerging from the back of her mind. Her father's mangled body crushed beneath gigantic hooves. Everyone she knew ripped to pieces, disemboweled, and turned to gore in the mud.

She took off back up the hill, legs pumping furiously. Barbs of fear dug into her, spurring her on ever faster. Branches whipped her arms and legs and face. Undergrowth reached to trip her, but she bounded over it all.

Up in the ravine, one hunter lay wounded with a broken leg, the rest unpre-pared for such a beast. Spears needed to be mended and arrows replaced. Without the element of surprise and missing two hunters, they stood no chance against a mature god —a wroth, raging god. *We never should have done this. No good comes of taking on gods. We got greedy. Got greedy and we pay for it now.* The slopes grew steeper. She charged up a hill, pushing off any tree and propelling herself higher. *Not we. Them. My father. My uncle. Everyone I know.*

A booming bellow rose nearby, echoing through the trees, and shaking the earth itself. Birds took flight in a panicking flutter of wings. She clamped her hands over her ears but the cry reverberated in her bones, in her teeth, and rattled her brain. She squeezed her eyes shut and doubled over. Her legs gave out beneath her and she slumped onto the ground. Her palms pressed tighter against her ears. She could still hear it. Hear the pain and the unbridled rage in that bellowing.

Then it stopped and all that she could hear was her own screaming. She blinked water from her eyes, picked up her bow, and scrambled to her feet. Another crash and thud somewhere up ahead. The whole span of foothills trem-bled with booming footsteps. As she crested another hill, she reached back to the quiver flopping on her back and took one of her three remaining arrows and nocked it.

Scaling the hill up to the ravine, a massive stitch tearing at the tender flesh of her side, another thunderous squeal split her head. A squeal like the heavens had split open, a squeal like the end times. She continued running, her head ringing and her lungs struggling to draw breath. Her balance wavered and her stumbling feet slid on leaf litter. Staggering forward and cresting the hill, there was nothing to see but two dead boarlings lying at the bottom of the ravine. She stumbled downhill amid the rumbling, searching for any sign of her father or Ubiko or anyone.

The ground shifted, pitching beneath her feet and spilling her down the hill head first. She tumbled and came to a jarring stop at the bottom of the ravine. The squeal tapered off but a ringing echoed in her head. Crashing footsteps growing closer.

"Odessa!" Her father's voice came from behind her. She lifted her head and saw him farther down the ravine, frantically waving from the top of the ridge. "Odessa!" He came racing down the slope toward her.

A great crash from the other side of the ravine. She scrambled to her hands and knees and stopped, her heart pausing midbeat.

The great boar god of the Arabako, Egende, rose above the ridge. It swung its head and shoved a tree aside in a burst of splinters. Its four long, curled tusks, each thicker than her father's arms were wide, gored the wood before the beast's massive frame shoved the falling tree away to come crashing down the ravine.

It stopped at the top of the ridge, its back snapping low-hanging branches. The streaks of light on its coal-black coat were as bright as a sunburst. Odessa blinked and an afterimage remained, floating in the black of her eyelids.

"Odessa!" her father screamed. "Run!"

The god saw its children, lying slain at the bottom of the ravine. Its eyes burned with grief and rage. A blood-chilling, bone-rattling, skull-splitting scream rose toward the heavens.

Egende charged toward Odessa.

CHAPTER 4

Hunters poured from the ridge, rushing past Odessa with raised spears and battle cries on their lips. Arrows flew over her head. The boar god charged down the ridge opposite her, a few arrows sticking from its body—but most arrows glanced off its hide. Egende plowed through the underbrush at the bottom of the ravine and turned, swinging its head and slashing the air with wicked, curling tusks as throwing spears took flight and plunged into its side. The spears stopped its headlong charge and it bellowed, the sound deep and furious like the groan of the earth splitting and rending in a quake.

The boar swept its tusks and caught a spearman as he raised his long spear. The spearman flew across the ravine, twirling in the air, a clumsy pirouette before landing and rolling, blood and viscera flung in the air, entrails trailing on the ground. The body rolled a short distance then stopped, cast awkwardly on the ground, broken limbs twisted beneath its gored form.

The spearman's body landed not far from Odessa. Aapo's blood-tinged mouth moved slightly, opening and closing as if trying to speak. Odessa had known Aapo all her life. He was a gregarious warrior; her father had joined him on raids in the lowlands. Now he lay gutted before her, his eyes half-lidded and growing dim.

Shock and fear turned her limbs to stone. She froze, half-crouched on the ground, helplessly watching the boar god's rampage. Four spear hunters circled the boar as best they could and jabbed the air with their spears. Egende flicked spearheads away with a tusk and charged. The hunters scattered away from the massive beast.

"Odessa!" Her father's hands took her underarms and hoisted her onto her feet. "Odessa, you must get out of here! Go!" He ushered her away, pushing her up the hill. She dragged her feet, unable to pry her eyes from the boar. Two more arrows planted themselves in its shoulder. It recoiled and swung its body as if to face the arrows buried in her flesh.

The hunters darted in close, daring to plunge their spearheads into the god's flank.

Something ripped her mask from her head. A flat sting across her cheek. Her father tossed her mask to the ground then gripped her shoulders and shook her. Her eyes watered. Her father had not struck her since she was a little girl.

"Listen to me! Go! You should not be here for this!" Peering through the stone-faced skull, his eyes were flinty and serious. "Do as I say!" He pushed her up the hill. "Run!"

She ran up the slope, her feet slipping in the leaves. Sometimes stumbling, propelling herself with her hands. Her mind was clouded by a pall of stupor. She had to run: run from the blood , run from the guts hanging from a torso in shredded ribbons, run from the god—that massive, immovable god, blinded in its rage. Her feet slowed. At the top of the ridge, she stopped and turned back. The hunters looked more like flies pestering a bull. Her father had joined the fray. He jabbed at the beast with his spear, dancing back and forth as Egende raged. Spears poked the sow from all sides. Egende turned at each stab of a spear. It knocked away a spear pulled from its side with a tusk. The hunter fell as his spear was ripped from his hands. The boar charged the hunter's defenseless form as the rest of the spears retreated. The man struggled to get back up. A shrill scream rose as the boar's hooves crushed his spine and legs. Another stomp and the scream was cut short. The boar stomped and stomped. Its front hooves pounded gore into the soft dirt.

They're going to die. There's no way to kill that thing.

The urge to turn and run away darted up her spine like spats of lightning. Yet her deadened legs stayed planted on the ridge. Images flashed in her mind. Her father's belly opened by a great tusk, spilling his guts. Ubiko crushed into unrecognizable gore. In the ravine below, her father and Ubiko side by side, goading the boar with exaggerated spear thrusts toward its foam-mouthed face. Their taunts were drowned out by another earthshaking bellow. They scattered as the boar charged forward.

Without thought, her legs moved. Carrying her down the ridge in long, bounding strides. At the bottom of the ravine, she slid and retrieved her bow and nocked the arrow she had dropped in her cowardice.

From her crouch, she drew back and let the arrow fly. It glanced off the boar's hide. Egende did not even notice as it swung its head away toward the other spearman. Her father and Ubiko had regrouped and darted forward to take advantage of its blind spot. Blood stained the boar's coarse hair and dulled the streaks of sunshine with gouts of red.

Her next arrow missed as the boar turned and charged toward one of the hunters before being stopped by a spear jabbed in its throat. Her last arrow she nocked and aimed, waiting for the boar to stay in one place. The beast was panting, its movements sluggish as it bristled with throwing spears and arrows. And yet still it raged.

Hands trembling, she nocked another arrow and drew the bowstring to her cheek. It just won't die. The tip of the arrow jerked to and fro. Her fingers grew weak. The muscles of her arm ached and twitched. She drew a breath and held it. Steadying herself. The boar turned its head, wheeling around, its eyes wild with frenzied fury. A soft exhale and she let the arrow loose.

The boar turned to meet the arrow. The arrow sunk into the boar's eye, pinning it so the pupil stared upward, half-lidded. Blood poured down its cheek, dousing the sunlight. The boar thrashed and bucked and roared. Its remaining eye spun, white-rimmed, and furious. Then for a split second, it met her gaze.

It charged past the spear hunters, toward her. She leapt to her feet as a great bellow pierced her ears. Tremors shook the earth beneath her. Her legs gave out beneath her and she collapsed to the ground, forced to her knees by an overwhelming pressure crushing her mind. Her ears rang. Booming footsteps shook the very earth beneath her.

She looked up to see the boar's hulking frame looming before her. Her fumbling hand reached for the knife on her belt. Then a force like a tidal wave struck her and knocked her into the air.

With a sharp gasp, her body bounced along the forest floor. Then the boar's gnashing snout forced her into the dirt. A blur of shadow and sunlight above her. She swung her knife, stabbing and slashing, but the blade did not even make a mark. The boar's mouth clamped down on her arm. Bones crunched and snapped, and blood ran in streaks down her arm. The boar lifted her by her arm, shook her, then rammed her back into the dirt. She gasped beneath the massive weight.

Her father's voice rose in a guttural snarl. The boar let go of her arm and raised its head enough for her to see, through tear-filled eyes, a glimpse of her father, spear sunk deep in the boar's throat. Screaming, he put all of his weight, all of his strength behind the spear.

More spears plunged into the boar. It squealed and recoiled above her. She crawled, dragging her broken arm, trying desperately to get out from beneath the boar's massive shadow. The boar stumbled, its front leg giving way. With one last, lurching effort, she hauled herself away from the great collapsing beast.

A tremendous weight crushed her right side. Coarse hair wet with blood brushed against her face, her skin sizzling where the bloody hairs touched it. She sucked air in deep, ragged breaths. The sweet, pungent scent of a forest god was now thick with an iron-tinged stench of blood. The boar's neck pinned her broken arm in the dirt. She pulled her arm, gritting her teeth against a pained scream, but she could not pull herself free. The pain burned and exploded in bursts of agony.

A shuddering groan vibrated through her arm. Egende writhed on top of her as spears plunged into its flesh again and again. Above her, its eye bulged in agony. Its eyelids twitched with every stab.

Hot, scalding blood pooled around her crushed arm, pouring from the dying god's throat and running in the open gashes in her arm. Egende's last breath rattled in its throat. The pained eye glanced at her struggling beneath, its drooping eyelids straining to stay open. It fixed her with its stare as it shifted its body, crushing her arm further. She began to feel faint as her own blood poured along with the gods. With a shudder, Egende groaned and its eye blinked and rolled upward, half-lidded. The boar god's body slumped. Its lifeblood soaked into the forest floor, the forest it had spent centuries protecting.

Her father came to her side and cupped her face in his hand. "Odessa, Odessa. You're alive!"

"I can't move," she said, tears falling freely from her eyes. "My arm. It's trapped."

Her father leaned close, stroking her face. "Don't cry, my sweet. Don't cry. We'll get you out." He turned and shouted for help. Ubiko came beside her father, a slight limp in his gait. The rest of the hunters approached hesitantly. "Lift the beast, damn you!" he shouted. "And mind the blood!"

The light in the boar's hair was fading in effervescent sparks as the hunters, with all their combined strength, tilted its head to the side. Her father pulled her arm out and cradled her in his arms.

Her mangled, disjointed arm was slick with dark ichor that steamed in the open air. The blood boiled on her skin like hot oil and she screamed. Golden flames bloomed along the length of her arm. She rolled off her father's lap and slapped at the flames climbing up her arm. Unyielding, the fire rose to her shoulder, as bright as the sun itself. Holy fire seared deep into the core of her shattered bones. She rolled on her back, writhing on the forest floor. The flames lapped greedily at her skin but not a leaf caught fire. The other hunters backed away. Even her father watched helplessly, his face darkened with terror.

Eventually, the flames burned themselves out, having had their fill. Her entire arm was scorched and bloody, and layers of skin burned away entirely. The air was thick with the stench of burnt flesh. A silence so absolute it hung upon the air itself, an immensely overwhelming pressure upon the entire forest. A palpable silence solidified around the hunters. The only sound in the forest now bereft of its god were the whimpers and screams of Odessa's agony.

CHAPTER 5

"Help!" Omari screamed. "Help her!"

He wrapped someone's sweat-dampened poncho around her arm. Blood seeped through the wool as soon as it touched the charred flesh. Odessa was unconscious. Barely breathing. Cradling her in his arms, he lifted her lolling head. A faint fluttering danced beneath her eyelids like a caged butterfly beating against its prison. His other arm squeezed the damp poncho. There was so much blood. He tried not to think of all the muscle and bone that lay exposed beneath his grip. Charred and bloody. Her screams still rang in his ears.

You brought this upon her. You did this, you miserable bastard. He held her tight to his chest, feeling the racing of her strained heart. An infernal heat radiated from her skin. *You've killed her, you worthless imbecile.*

"Where is that godsdamned cart?" he shouted to the few hunters milling about at a distance. The rest were clearing trail for the carts or taking care of the other injured. The rest stood, stunned and cowering like whipped children.

"It's coming, it's coming," Ubiko said as he ran forward. He kneeled beside her and gave Omari his poncho. The color was gone from his face. "Adura's clearing a path as we speak."

With a slight trembling in his hands, Omari wrapped the second poncho tightly over the bloody one. "She'll be gone by then," Omari said, his voice on the verge of breaking. "She wasn't supposed to be here for this. She was supposed to be gone when we killed the sow."

"I know," Ubiko said. His fingers tapped nervously against his knee as he watched Odessa's face twitch, subtly contorting in unconscious agony. Godsblood tore through her body like a wildfire pouring through her veins.

Omari rubbed his face, wiping tears from his eyes. "I've done a terrible thing, haven't I?"

"It's not your fault."

"It's all my fault! It is!" He clutched her closer to his chest and closed his eyes. Tears dripped down his cheeks. "It wasn't supposed to be like this."

What was it supposed to be like? he asked himself. *I knew people would die. I knew people would be damned. But I didn't care.* All the anger he carried since a boy on the coasts of the Slateseer melted away. Holding his dying daughter, all he was left with was the hollowness of sorrow. *This is what I wanted, right?* He pressed his face into her dirt-flecked braids and let his tears fall freely within her curls.

How could he tell Mutumi he got her eldest daughter killed and damned to an eternity of nothingness? How could he live with himself?

I just wanted to be free. I wanted us to be free.

"I'm sorry. I'm sorry, don't die," he whispered almost inaudibly. "You can't die." His mind splashed, treading in the depths of hopelessness and barely keeping himself from sinking in despair. He strained, trying to remember what Yakun had told him about gods and godsblood. But all he could remember was the ritual. After so many years of agonizing over every detail, it was all that remained.

He opened his eyes. The flickering beneath Odessa's eyelids was growing fainter. Her lips were pale. "Get my bag," he said.

Ubiko raised his eyebrows and then nodded, recognizing what he intended to do. Ubiko was the only one in the world other than Yakun that knew what Omari had planned to do. He rose and ran off toward the rim of the ravine where his bag lay beneath the soapberry bush.

The ritual was of a dark magic Yakun had spent his whole life studying. A dangerous magic, untested for all of time. But he had no choice now. *I've already damned her. This is the least I can do.*

If he could perform the ritual in time, she might still live. If she could somehow survive the consecration. *It is more of a desecration than consecration.*

Ubiko returned and set the bulging sack down. "Put pressure on her arm," Omari said. "I'll hurry." He rose and Ubiko took his place beside her.

"Do you think it will work on her?" Ubiko asked as Omari opened the sack and took out a bundle of white linen turned brown by dirt and age. "We weren't even sure if it would work on you."

Omari said nothing, steeling himself. He took the kritamé from its linen wrap. The virgin iron gleamed with an almost mirrorlike sheen. He had kept the knife hidden since he arrived in Kalaro, buried within his shrine until now. The bone handle was polished, pure white like the pure sands of a faraway beach. He took the blade and, beside the corpse of the dead god, drew a circle in the bloodstained dirt, four paces across, making sure to use the flat of the blade to make a wide channel in the dirt. Then he divided the circle from north to south and from east to west.

"How is she doing?" he asked Ubiko, as he began carving the runes Yakun had taught him into the earth. They were foreign symbols of earth, wind, water, and fire.

"She's holding on," Ubiko said, cradling her limp head.

Hold on, Dessa. Omari finished carving the runes and ran to the sack. *I'm almost done.*

He took from the sack an oil that Yakun had prepared for him years ago. He pried open the seal over the clay pot and found it still full of the thin, clear liquid. It smelled of sulfur and stung his nostrils.

"Put her in the center of the circle," Omari said, hurrying toward the circle with the oil. "Her head to the east and feet to the west."

Ubiko gingerly picked her up and carried her to the circle, being careful to not step on the lines carved in the dirt. He laid her down almost reverently and backed away. Everyone still in the ravine watched them in silence.

Omari bent down beside her and with the kritamé cut her bloodstained clothes from her body. He tossed the singed remains of her clothes out of the circle along with the two blood-soaked ponchos that had wrapped her arm.

He dipped his hand in the oil and rubbed her burned arm, the oil and blood mixing, the smell of iron and sulfur and burned flesh assailing his nostrils. Her arm was a mess of charred flesh and blood, large sections of skin and muscle had burned away along her forearm. He tried to be as gentle as he could, but he had to make sure he fully coated her arm more than any other part of her body. It was paramount he stop the bleeding before anything else.

After he had coated her arm, he anointed the rest of her body in a thinner layer of oil. Her skin still burned, but her pulse was weak and her breathing shallow and irregular. He wiped the oil from his hands and left the circle to take a leather poncho from the sack and two shoulder-length rawhide gloves. Butchery tools fit for a god. He pulled the gloves over his hands and draped the poncho over his bare, blood-spattered chest. In the clumsy grip of his gloved hands, he took the kritamé and pot to the dead boar god.

He shoved the blade into Egende's belly, just beneath the sternum. The boar's hide resisted the blade, but it still yielded to the iron edge as he cut a wide gash along its belly. Blood spilled from the opening, the body still warm enough that the blood hadn't settled. He held the pot beneath the gash and let it fill with blood until it overflowed and then poured it into the channels he had carved into the earth.

With a gloved hand, he reached inside the god's chest, rooting around guts and lungs until he found the heart. He slid his knife-wielding hand inside and carved until the heart was free from its vascular shackles. Dropping the blood-slick knife to the ground, he reached back inside. With a wet sucking sound, he pulled it out from the bleeding gash and held it, cupped in his hands. It was larger than his head and streaked with veins of shimmering gold.

The heart dripped crimson onto the disturbed earth as Omari walked around the circle. Three times he walked around it, letting drops of blood fall into the circle.

After the third time, he stepped into the circle from the western side and stood over Odessa, the heart dripping blood onto her oiled form. The blood sizzled in the thin sheen of oil on her skin.

He chanted the words he did not understand but had memorized all those years ago. The air around him grew heavy and chilled. His chest tightened but he spoke the words loudly, in that strange guttural tongue Yakun had taught him.

A rush of energy flowed into the circle, building and swelling around him. The air pulsed, thrumming with some power just beyond his comprehension.

As he recited the incantation, he squeezed the heart. Blood dripped on her charred arm. The oil bubbled and popped as the binding took hold. He could see her skin begin to prickle, the hairs on her arms began to stand. Her breath began to quicken.

Against his skin, he could feel the energy arc and scatter on its way to Odessa. The blood and oil seeped into her skin, blood vessels swelling as the mixture coursed through her, carving channels for the cosmic energy to flow through.

Smiling, Omari screamed the guttural syllables into the current of energy surging past him. And then the ritual was out of his control and his incantation trailed off. Power roared around him, prickling his skin and making him shudder. Pressure pounded against his temples.

Memories flickered in his mind. An oath. *All that is holy will be undone. I swear it upon my blood.* Steadfast words spoken before familial obligation had distracted him. *No gods and no masters.* Before the banality of living made him forget his true path.

Somewhere, lost in the swell of emotion and strength, he felt shame for such feelings but his shame was distant and easily forgotten amid the roaring din. The chains of a life spent yoked by gods and godly men broke away, and for the first time since he had left the shores of the Slateseer Sea, he was free.

More guttural sounds spilled from his lips, a torrent of syllables never before uttered by man. Buoyed by the uplifting force, he crushed the heart between his palms in a spray of blood and tissue. Flecks of gold hung in the air with droplets of scarlet as the air grew still, everything within the circle frozen in crystalline stillness.

On the forest floor, Odessa shuddered and spasmed. A cry caught in her throat in a gurgling moan. Her eyes flashed open, wide with agony.

Warm elation bled from him in an instant. Cold dread numbed him to the core. Omari knelt beside her to comfort her, but as he did, a flare of rust-colored flames burst from her arm. The force of the flare sent him sprawling on his rear. Another flare of flame rose into the air and dissipated in a cloud of sparks. Beneath the charred flesh, an infernal red snaked its way through her arm in spiderwebbing lines. The lines glowed and burst into flame again as they crept further past her elbow and up her bicep.

She arched her back, the cords in her neck bulging as foaming spittle sprayed from her gnashing teeth and hung in the frozen air. A choked scream came from deep in her throat as the currents of force came pouring in stronger and stronger, a waterfall of energy crashing upon her.

He scrambled toward the edge of the circle and clawed at the line. As soon as his fingers disturbed the circle, the overwhelming force coalescing dissipated in an instant. Blood and spittle and leaves and dirt dropped to the forest floor. A concussive blast surged through the ravine like a strong gust of wind. And then it was gone and the forest was quiet.

Odessa lay silent, her body twitching. Wriggling out of his poncho and tossing his gloves aside, he crawled to her. His hands went to touch her and then stopped short.

"What happened?" Ubiko said as he ran forward. The rest of the remaining hunters were still stunned by what they had seen.

"Odessa?" Omari's fingers touched her cheek and recoiled. Her skin was scorching hot. The lines along the charred remains of her arm pulsated, threading up from her bloody forearm, along her bicep, and to her shoulder where they tapered away. Her skin was flush with color and her breaths were deeper, although quick. "Odessa?"

"Did it work?"

"I don't know," Omari said, gingerly touching her cheek despite the searing of his fingertips. Shame came from deep within himself, bubbling up like some deep spring, frigid and loathsome. "I fear I've made it worse." When the pain grew to be too much, he drew his reddened fingertips away. "There are much worse things than death."

Hell is hot and the daemons many. Yakun had told him of the Hells below the mortal world. Where those who were forsaken by the gods were sent to rot for eternity, drowning in darkness beyond human comprehension and burning in pools of primordial fire. *Fire with no light and pain with no relief.*

"But she's still alive," Ubiko said. "Look at her."

Tears returned to his eyes and his vision blurred, but look he did. He did not take his eyes off her, not even when Adura and the carts came. He had to bear witness. He had to look at what he had done.

CHAPTER 6

Kunza-ka had been the holy man of Kalaro for decades, earning the title of ka-man when he had barely begun to grow facial hair. On the day of the hunt, he had been praying to the Gods for forgiveness since the morning. Kneeling before the altar of the High Gods, repeating invocations and mantras to each of the five. Swaying back and forth on his knees, tossing braided lengths of fragrant herbs on the fire. His back and knees ached and his legs had gone numb hours ago. In all his many years, he had never had to pray so fervently. So desperately. The only time he had stopped was when the warrior Adura had brought the Kusa boy back home in pieces.

In the warm, aromatic smoke that filled the hut, there was nothing. No divine presence brushed against his skin as it had in his youth. All he could feel was the aching of his joints and the exhaustion weighing on his eyelids. But still he prayed. His eyes moved rapidly beneath their lids. His mouth moved in hushed prayer. To even think of hunting a divine, even a Low forest god, was a grave taboo like no other. To atone for such sacrilege would require great sacrifice and repentance. He communed with Matara and Talara, the two sister goddesses. Matara, the goddess of mercy and the most benevolent of all the gods. And Talara, the Sin-Eater, the patroness of the loathsome, and the martyr of the heavens.

He had tried to stop them. Wasted many hours trying to talk Omari Kusa out of it. *I should have had him killed for such talk.* But the village was divided; hard times had brought the village to a precarious position. And they hadn't heard from Noyo since the last conscription last year. Up in the mountains, divorced from the world below, Kalaro had lost the fear of the gods, he had realized. But he remembered. He remembered that terror all too well.

The bleating of the hunters' horn broke his wavering concentration, the threads of smoke in the hut already having dispersed. He sighed, took his walking stick, and hoisted himself onto numb feet. Feeling ebbed into his legs, a slow throbbing sensation moving down them. He shuffled outside the hut; the long, colorful feathers and tufts of fur atop the head of the walking stick rustling as he walked. Midday heat scoured the land, and he sweltered and baked beneath the layers of skins and the cracking white face paint he wore. Seed pods and small bones rattled from tassels at the hems of his clothes as he tottered to the edge of town.

Another long bleat in the distance. He quickened his shambling pace. Passing the crumbling huts, he could see one of the carts the hunters had taken rolling down the path toward him. He saw no quarry in tow and no more than a handful of hunters. *They've failed, then.* He leaned on his stick at the edge of town as the cart roared down the overgrown path. *Such a waste of life. Life all too precious now more than ever.* Akbal already lay in the Elder Kusa's home, cleaned and prepared for cremation. He wondered how many more he would have to beg Talara to purify. There was only so much the Sin-Eater would accept. Their foolishness put the entire village in jeopardy. And yet they expected him to mend whatever they broke. To cleanse whatever they sullied.

In a way, he was glad they had returned in failure, limping home to lick their wounds and bury their dead. It was better to lose a few brave but stupid men and women than arouse the ire of the gods. He did not like it, but these were not the days when there was food to be eaten and children were brought into the world crying and full of life. Kalaro could not afford to lose the favor of the gods. Seeing the half-empty cart draw near, he felt relief like a weight was drawn from his body.

I hope they didn't do anything too stupid. Trespassing in the Arabako was serious, but not egregiously grave. Some of them might have to be banished. Omari, chief among them. But the situation was mendable.

Then the cart rolled to a stop in front of him. Kunza-ka could hear a girl's cries, whimpers, and groans rising into stifled screams. Omari, the hunter who had concocted and spearheaded the foolish hunt, vaulted the side of the cart and rushed to the old holy man.

"My daughter! She's hurt!" His eyes were red and puffy. He bore the marks of the Banished God on his arms, red and bright in the open air. Kunza-ka clenched his jaw at such blatant heresy. *He should be exiled for that alone.*

Kunza-ka was already shuffling toward the back of the cart when a sick feeling settled in the pit of his stomach. The girl, wrapped in a blanket, thrashed in the bed of the cart, clutching an arm wrapped in bloody rags. Her eyes were glazed with agony. Omari's foolish companion, Ubiko, crouched beside the girl, trying to calm her. Subtle on the wind, the stench of death and sulfur came to Kunza-ka. A chill ran through him like ice water in his veins. "What happened?" he demanded.

"Egende's blood. It burned her arm to the bone!" Omari took the old man's hand. "Please, you must do something!"

Kunza-ka pulled away from Omari. *Egende's blood?* He took a reluctant step toward the whimpering girl. The stench grew stronger, the repulsive aura of filth was like putrid scum clinging to his soul. *Oh gods. They did it.* His grip tightened on the walking stick, then he took a step back, unable to stomach anymore. "What did you do?" he snapped at Omari.

"Please, you have to help her!" Omari persisted.

Kunza-ka's mind was abuzz with incomprehensible, half-formed thoughts. *They drew blood? That shouldn't be possible.*

The girl's scream broke his stunned silence. A ragged wail through frayed vocal cords. It was an inhuman scream that sent a chill down his spine. Kunza-ka looked at the wretched thing in the cart and could only think of one thing he could do. "I will prepare some of Matara's mercy for her."

"What do you mean, Kunza?" Omari took him by the arm, the hunter's strong hand squeezing his thin bicep through his many skins, then letting go as quickly as he had grabbed him. *In his grief, the foolish man forgets himself,* Kunza-ka thought.

"Is there nothing else you can do?" Omari asked. A pleading question to which he already knew the answer.

Kunza-ka scowled. The wrinkles in his forehead deepened, the white paint cracking more. "There is nothing any mortal can do for her now. And the gods will spare her no pity. You have damned your daughter, Omari. You and you alone."

Omari's visage darkened, his fists tightening at his sides before he turned and kicked at a cartwheel and hid his eyes beneath a hand. Kunza-ka sighed. "Take her home." The gravelly edge of his voice softened, stony with the softness of bitter herbs. "She should be with family." His walking stick thumped and his shambling feet lurched into motion. "I'll bring the medicine shortly."

The cart rumbled past him as he hurried back to his hut. His legs were still stiff and sore, and he winced every few steps.

In the days of warring gods, lakes of spilled ichor would leave the surrounding land inhabitable for low creatures like humanity for decades or centuries, depending on who had bled. A god's blood was something altogether sacrosanct. Something much too pure for men and women shaped from mud. He could not fathom the pain the Kusa girl was enduring. Pure divinity was pouring through her body like flows of lava. A generous dose of Matara's mercy was all he could offer her. To give her some modicum of relief while the ichor tore her apart, body and soul rent into pieces by pure, unadulterated divinity.

All he could offer her was an escape from the agony and into cold, formless oblivion reserved for those forsaken by the gods. Being Forsaken was an uncertain fate beyond the discerning of mortal men. A lifetime of sin weighed upon each person, and it was never a surety that Talara would cleanse all their sins. But this time, Kunza-ka was certain. To be marked by a god's blood, that was irredeemable. Severed from the cycle of life, an eternity in a pitiless void awaited the poor girl.

Why did I allow such foolishness? He passed the empty huts, his steps seemingly bringing him no closer to his hut. *Whose fault is it they went on that fool's errand? Not Omari's alone, no. I could have stopped them. I could have told them if they went any further than idle fancy and supposition, they would be jailed or executed. If I would have done something about Omari before it got this far, the rest of them would have backed down.*

The wind shifted and brought the smoke of the burn pit south of the village over the abandoned huts of the empty quarter. The remains of plague-afflicted animals smoldered, and the thin thread of smoke twisting westward above the village carried the acrid stench of burned flesh and disease. Kunza-ka turned and followed the path leading away from the abandoned huts. *Why didn't I stop them?* he asked himself, but in reality, he knew the answer. His back to the smoke of the burn pits, the stench followed him. *I feared the Gray more than I feared the gods.*

But now that the impossible had happened, that fear was all-consuming.

He hurried along the path, past the huts neighboring his. The bones of his left knee ground together, bare bone against bone, as he shuffled, sparking pain.

Stupid old man. He passed his gnarled herb garden and through the beaded entryway of his hut. Wisps of smoke still hung among the thatch above, the fragrance of sage and cypress still strong and cloying. In a worn stone bowl at the side of the hut, he ground dried joja leaves and poppy husk. His thin, gnarled fingers moved along the bundles of herbs and gourd bowls of resins and gums on the cluttered low table, as if divining their properties from touch alone like a blind seer. He poured pure water into the bowl and added a piece of dream root to ease the terror of death.

His mind was ablaze with terrible visions of what would befall Kalaro in the wake of this transgression. If the High Gods did not immediately bring righteous fury upon the village, Azka and his Chosen most certainly would. One of the Chosen from Noyo could come at any time. If they learned that his people had made a god bleed, what would he do then?

As he prepared the mixture, a faint smell drifted from the altar. The smell of urine and decay brushed against him and played in front of his nostrils. He stopped grinding the paste in the bottom of the bowl as the last threads of smoke dispersed and the smell with it. Talara's presence was gone as quickly as it had appeared, leaving him confused and unnerved.

Shaken, he continued preparing the merciful concoction as best he could. *What could Talara want of me?* The thought made his skin crawl. He could not even begin to comprehend what the Goddess of Rot and Ruin would want, but he knew it would not be good. The Sin-Eater did not often deal with men unless they were dead or dying.

A syrupy, milky liquid sloshed in the bottom of a clay cup as he shuffled to the Kusa hut. He leaned more heavily on his walking stick as his limping worsened. When he reached the hut, he pushed through the curtain in the doorway without announcing himself. There was precious little time for such formalities.

On a blanket laid in the middle of the dirt floor of the hut, the Kusa girl moaned and writhed, a smaller girl bearing a striking resemblance beside her, holding her hand. Her face was turned down in a deep, quivering frown, her eyes filled with tears. Ubiko sat beside the wall, a plantain half-eaten in his hand. Omari and Mutumi argued at the far end of the hut next to a squat clay oven, their voices rising in bursts of argument and accusation. A small baby cried in a woven swaddling basket.

The holy man lowered himself beside the girl. Her arm was wrapped in new cloth bandages already soaked through with blood. The aura of sin was thick and putrid on his skin. Cold and filthy, it permeated deep into his being. He pulled a loop of bandages from her arm. The skin at her shoulder was scorched a slick red with lines of dark purple running along beneath the thin remaining layer of skin, darkness pouring through veins and arteries and fanning out in branching capillaries. He pulled the twisting loops of bandage farther. Her arm was disjointed, and he moved it carefully so the splintered bones within did not move. Further down her arm, the skin was burnt off entirely, blood seeping from around yellow gobs of rendered fat. The smaller girl stared at him with pleading eyes but said nothing. He covered the burns with the bandage.

Mutumi saw him and rushed toward him. "Don't do it! Don't you give her that! I won't let you kill her!"

"She is already dead," Kunza-ka said. "You know as well as I. There is no life after this, even if she were to survive. All there is to do is give her peace."

As close to peace as the Forsaken are allowed.

The girl rolled on the blanket, woven fabric bunching around her kicking feet. Her lips whispered tiny cries of anguish. He cradled her head with a hand and brought her close to him. Omari, Mutumi, and Ubiko crowded around. Mutumi's fingers ran through the girl's matted hair, picking pieces of leaf from her locks.

He tilted her head back and put the edge of the cup to her lips. Lips that continued moving, muttering in a hushed tongue unknown to man. "Matara be merciful," he said, knowing there would be no mercy for her.

Tears fell all around him as he laid her head back on the blanket. A line of syrupy liquid dripped from the corner of her still-moving mouth. Mutumi and the other girl hugged her.

"How fast does it work?" Omari asked, his voice husky and raw.

"Minutes," Kunza-ka said. "Very few minutes." He put two fingers on the vein standing out of her turned neck. Her skin was unbelievably hot. Beneath the papery skin of his fingertips, he could feel the patter of a furiously racing heart.

In the next few minutes, the beating of her heart slowed, losing intensity and becoming a tremulous fluttering. Omari bent down and kissed her on the forehead then rested his forehead on hers. He whispered to her as her breathing slowed. "I love you. I love you so much. I'm so sorry, Odessa."

Mutumi had stood up and was pacing the hut, back and forth, casting tentative glances at the girl dying on the floor.

Eventually the heartbeat slowed to a thready vibrating, a barely tangible trembling. He stood up with great effort, his knees groaning and ankles popping as he rose. The walking stick braced him as he hauled his lagging body upright. "She is almost gone," he said quietly. "I will pray for her journey," he lied. There would be no journey through the afterlife for her. No journey along the River of Souls. Mito would never ferry her across to join the merciful Matara. The girl was doomed to perdition for eternity. And everyone in the hut knew it.

They all said nothing. Omari and the young girl held on to the girl. Mutumi still paced and Ubiko stood by her, too stunned to speak. Kunza-ka left without another word, leaving them to their grief.

It was only when the rest of the hunters returned that he learned Egende and her boarlings were dead.

That night, in the hills of the Arabako Forest where the clouds were gathering and meshing above the canopy and before the great overgrown archway, the smoke of a god's hastily built funeral pyre drifted in a wide plume against the force of the wind. The thick, black cloud spread out and hung above the village, blotting out the twilit sky. A twirling maelstrom of black upon the heavy, oppressive gray. A dark cloud of smoke fanned out above Kalaro, where the Forsaken girl refused to die.

CHAPTER 7

It was full dark. The only light in the hut came from the flickering of Ogé's shrine. Omari Kusa kneeled in front of the shrine, his eyes glazed from lack of sleep. A few hours of restless sleep a night was all he had been able to get since the hunt. Four days had passed.

He had done it. He killed a god. Proved it possible for man to triumph over god. Yet his victory was not nearly as sweet as he had hoped so many years ago. It left a sour taste like bile in his mouth.

Odessa was not supposed to be there for the killing of Egende. He had wanted to spare her that with a small lie about butchering. The meat of gods would kill any man foolish enough to eat it. The goat-drawn cart was to carry the dead and wounded home. He had not dreamed she would be among the wounded. It should have been him. She never should have been on that hunt in the first place.

The mercy the ka-man gave her had failed, its potency burned away by the fever that scalded any hand placed upon her forehead. For the past four days, the girl had gone from a comatose stupor to thrashing on the floor, screaming in agony like some dying animal.

What have I done? Oh Ogé, what have I done to my little girl?

The fire crackled, gnawing twigs and palm leaves. Omari felt the urge to cry again but knew no tears would come. He had no tears left to shed. His hand rubbed at his dry, tired eyes. His mind was a constant droning buzz of self-loathing and self-pity. He had betrayed his family, his flesh and blood, in some vain attempt at fulfilling an old grudge. *What a poor excuse for a man.* The shameful elation he had felt as his daughter lay dying in the binding circle was a stain he could never wipe away. In that moment, in that small sliver of time when the entire world seemed to be swirling around him, he had been truly happy. He felt sick. *I'm not fit to be a husband. I'm not fit to be a father. I'm still that stupid slave boy.*

He fed the fire more twigs and fronds. In the scrying mirror of his mind, he saw little Odessa screaming as her arm burst into holy flames like sun fire. Burning her to the bone while her useless father stood helplessly and watched.

He stayed by the shrine until threads of dawn bloomed along the hilltops, begging his god for help. But the Banished Hunter was as silent as he had been ever since being cast back down to the earth. Eventually, Omari reluctantly rose, wincing at a pain in his groin, and returned to the hut and his sleeping family and dying daughter.

When he entered the hut, he found Mutumi kneeling before the small altar to the High Gods sitting against the wall near the hearth fire. Even now, with her daughter clinging to life, she clung to the gods, thinking them just and magnanimous. Only because she had lived her life safe, sequestered in the mountain basin. Far from the tyrannies of gods.

Odessa was peaceful in the middle of the floor. Ayana was still sleeping, curled next to Kimi's wicker basket. He kneeled beside Odessa, his hand hovering above her cheek, wanting to caress her poor, pained face, but wary of the waves of heat radiating from her.

Mutumi bowed her forehead to the floor and then rose, smoothing her white kaftan. She had no jewelry and had her beautiful coils wrapped in a pure white gele. Although Odessa still drew breath, the family was in mourning.

"Did you sleep at all?" Mutumi whispered with an edge to her voice. He feared she would never forgive him.

"Some," Omari said, his voice hoarse.

"Nightmares?" she asked, stoking the hearth fire.

Omari nodded. "The same one."

For a moment, Mutumi said nothing. Her face was blank and pitiless. Then she met his eyes. Her eyes were deep brown, warm and kind. As wonderful as the day they had first met, they still made his heart skip a beat. Nothing had changed since he'd first arrived in Kalaro, a ragged, wrathful man emerging from the Night Jungle. When he first caught a glimpse of Elder Kusa's youngest daughter.

"It's still early," she said, the edge of her voice dulled. "Try to get some sleep now."

"I'm fine," he said. She stared at him with a look he knew well. There was no arguing with Mutumi Kusa.

He relented and lay on their bed of rushes. Ayana stirred as he did, rolling away from him and curling in a ball. He closed his eyes and sleep rushed to take and engulf him.

He was back on the coast of the Slateseer Sea, born into servitude to the god Keshekki, an abomination of chitinous legs and bulbous eyes that never slept. Omari was toiling in the cliffside tunnels, chipping through rock to expand Keshekki's palace, an expanse of sprawling tunnels deep in the cliffs leading to ornate atriums of red sandstone and gold. He had been hauling a cartful of slate chips to dump off the cliffside when he heard a terrible screeching that shook his bones and crushed the air from his lungs. He left the cart and ran to the balcony overlooking the dark sea. Another shriek, inhuman and louder than thunder.

Keshekki clung to the cliffs a fair few spans below, its crab legs flailing for purchase, trying to scale the cliff face. Its head at the center of those legs was a mass of bulging eyes, whirling in all directions. A fleshy mass of melting skin and blisters came out of the water and held Keshekki with fatty fins like a stingray. Multiple mouths gnashed through the folds of sloughing flesh, multiple rows of sharp teeth beneath rolls of skin discolored and bloated and covered with barnacles. It bit into Keshekki, who writhed and struggled beneath the weight of the leviathan dragging it from the cliff side.

With a hissing squealing and the crack of chitin, the fleshy leviathan's embrace tightened, snapping some of Keshekki's legs as its mouths dug into the mass of eyes like they were a cluster of overripe grapes.

Omari was stunned, more scared than he had ever been, too afraid to even breathe. And yet, somehow, a part of him enjoyed Keshekki's terrified screeching. Watching as the disturbing sea creature tore Keshekki apart on the cliffs, he smiled, half-mad with fear. The leviathan gorged itself on the dead god, the sounds of cracking chitin and slurping louder than the crashing waves. In the folds of sloughing flesh, there were marks of divinity, lines of light muddled by melting skin.

After it had fed, the leviathan collapsed and died, and the barnacles on its flesh broke open and filled the air with a cloud of spores, gray as the sky. The cloud rose up the cliff face and poured in the halls of the palace like tidal waves.

Omari ran back into the tunnels, running past his fellow slaves and leaping in a water trough. All around him, slaves choked and coughed and spat up blood. From beneath the water's surface, he watched them die. Omari's lungs began to burn, but he pressed his hands against the sides of the trough and kept himself submerged. A man stumbled and struck the side of the trough, then fell over into the water. Falling on top of him. Half the man's face was drooping off his cheek, and the man was bleeding from his eyes and nose and mouth.

Omari shoved the dying man away and burst out from the blood-tinged water. He gasped, then covered his mouth, coughing as he held the gasped breath in his lungs. Around him, his fellow slaves were splayed on the ground, twisted and deformed by the cloud still lingering in the halls like fog. Plumes of gray smoke rose from the tangled corpses like dust motes. Omari hurried through the halls toward daylight, passing some slaves still standing, blindly lashing out at their surroundings and screaming from misshapen mouths.

He kept running, holding his stolen breath. The halls were a labyrinth of stone, twisting and tangling in the cliffs. As he ran, he saw the corpses of everyone he loved. He saw Mutumi. Ayana. Kimi. Ubiko. All of them bloated with their eyes wide in terror, their throats bulging.

He emerged onto the wooden balcony at the water's edge. Keshekki and the leviathan were gone. A row of posts lined the rocky coastline. The dismembered remains of rotted corpses were nailed to some of the posts, the fate of those that could no longer work. Keshekki cursed them and left them to the elements where their cursed souls would attract beasts, eager to feast upon forsaken flesh.

Odessa hung on one such post, kicking and screaming as chonchons fluttered around her, their faces nearly human save for the fangs in their mouth. The wings sprouting from where their ears should be were thin and membranous like a bat's. They sunk their teeth into Odessa's flesh and pushed off with clawed feet coming from where a neck should be, ripping hunks of skin and meat from her face and neck.

He tried to run and stop the chonchons, but his feet would not move. He was paralyzed. Helpless as the chonchons burrowed into her midsection. Odessa's screams filled the air.

A cry woke him. His own choked cry. Mutumi was at his side, holding him. Ayana was holding a discontented Kimi, soothing the mewling infant. Omari wiped the sweat from his face. "I'm sorry."

"It's fine," Mutumi said, squeezing him in a comforting embrace. But her words were hollow. Resentment in her heart stripping them of all emotion.

As morning shifted into day, Omari left to hunt with Ubiko. Mutumi and Ayana would be harvesting the last of their corn and some early sorghum and yams today, and while he knew he should help, he could not bear being with them right now. Even Ayana looked at him differently now. Not with her mother's resentment; her eyes held only hurt and confusion. In a way, that was worse.

The more he stayed with them, the more his guilt grew like a tumorous mass in his chest squeezing the breath from his lungs and crushing his heart.

"How is she doing?" Ubiko asked as they neared the Arabako's gateway. "Is she waking at all?"

Omari shook his head. "No. She hasn't woken up." He readjusted the quiver at his waist as if it needed adjustment. "Her fever has gone down a little. And she mumbles now and then. But she won't wake."

"She will soon," Ubiko said. "She's a strong girl." His sandals scraped against the dirt path. The valley was quiet. The forest eerily still. Behind them, a thin thread of smoke rose from the edge of the village. The smoldering remains of funeral pyres in the burn pit. "I'm sorry for not coming by since then. It's been . . . "

"No, I understand. It's been hard for everyone."

Ubiko rubbed his neck beneath his jaw where a tiny lump had formed. A tired smile came his lips. "I'm just so tired of funerals."

Omari nodded. He had been there when Ubiko's wife, Kimalma, was laid to rest. Ubiko had burned his wife and their stillborn child and never been quite the same. His easy smiles always carried a hint of falseness now. There was a sadness in his eyes that would not leave.

"How are the others doing?" Omari asked.

"Everyone's scared." They passed the high-peaked archway, beneath strands of severed vines hanging from the arch. The sun hid behind thick clouds, and the forest was dim and quiet. "I talked to Adura the other day after Akbal's ashes were spread. She's having trouble sleeping too. And she found a lump." Ubiko reflexively touched the hard lump at the side of his own neck again. "She asked me what we were going to do and I didn't know what to tell her. No one's killed a god before. We're in uncharted territory."

"Does anyone else have lumps?"

"I don't know," Ubiko said. "How bad are yours now?"

Omari stopped, only a few paces from the archway. He pulled the bunched-up fabric of his thin poncho from his neck to expose three large lumps. One small lump behind his ear was swollen like a ripe berry, while the other two were lower and large, almost merging at the side of his neck. "The one on my groin is smaller but it chafes so terribly, I can barely stand it." He pulled the fabric back against his neck.

Ubiko was quiet for a moment. "Are sure that one's a lump? Perhaps your stones finally dropped." He grinned but his eyes were full of concern.

Omari tried to force a smile as he began walking again. "You're a bastard." He wanted to say more but stayed quiet. He wanted to forget about it all and lose himself in the forest, but the dull, wilting leaves and the eerie quiet was a constant reminder of what he had done. And of who he left behind in the village to suffer.

CHAPTER 8

Pain like molten iron poured through Odessa's veins. Fiery blood collected in the singed atriums of her heart, then rushed through her body and back again, the delicate intricacies of her heart charred black. Veins and arteries scorched. Every breath of air in her lungs burned away as soon as it was drawn in.

Hot. Everything was hot. Burning all the time. Her insides liquified, boiling beneath the skin. Sweat evaporated as soon as it came dotting her skin. Pain swelling and swelling but never breaking. Waves of agony crashing over her again and again. Never receding. Just building and building in intensity, a crescendo of fire pouring through her extremities, hellfire still burning along the length of her arm, eating her flesh to the bone, her bones blackening and cracking in the heat so the flames could lick at the marrow. She could feel her flesh cracking and peeling and sloughing off, her innards sizzling and melting as they spilled out into the void. Screams rose inside her but there was no place for them to exit, no way to release the anguish, the agony tearing her apart. Stripping her until there was nothing left but her spirit plummeting somewhere far beyond the world she had known.

Everything was black. And endless void empty save for her. She fell deeper into the cosmic abyss. The darkness deepened, shifting around her. Churning and swallowing her in fathomless nothingness.

Left with only agony—unending, unrelenting torment. Endlessly burning, the void seared her spirit, blackness seeping into the core of her eroding soul.

The deeper she sank, the more the abyss churned, the tides of oblivion battering her even further into the depths. The deeper she sank, the more her agony increased. And yet it would not end. Even when she felt there was nothing left to hurt. When everything had been stripped from her. When her mind was numb to the agony, it continued still.

She did not know when she realized it, but eventually she noticed that the abyss was not complete nothingness. She was not alone in the void. Something lurked in that complete darkness. Vast and formless, it seemed to drink in that pitch-black oblivion. In the periphery of her vision, eyes shone with a pale luminescence in shades no human eye had ever seen—yet when she looked at them, all she could see was the darkness. Shapes without form or definition slithered and writhed through that dark, just outside her comprehension. As if she were in a womb of pure night, peering through the veined and membranous barrier to see the shifted shadows of a world not her own.

A droning, thumping sound surrounded her, enveloping and penetrating her. It lacked any natural rhythm, just an irregular buzzing in a register deeper than anything she had ever heard.

Roiling tendrils probed the darkness. Dread and fear like nothing she had ever experienced filled her mind, a maddening dread overcoming all else. Even her pain was a distant afterthought.

The infernal buzz became deafening, rattling her to her very core. Eventually, her mind gave way, cracking and crumbling in the presence of something unlike anything she had ever experienced.

Tendrils of abyssal blackness worked their way toward her as pressure began tugging at her right arm and dragging her through that oblivion. Away from the abyssal tendrils and the vast enormity of what lurked deep in the depths of nothingness. A current drew her upward where the tides of the interstice would take her in their infernal churning.

She languished there for some time, her mind and spirit slowly mending. The pain dulled in that liminal place between life and death.

She could not tell how much time passed. Where she was, time was an illusory thing like a mirage upon the horizon. Time wore on, stretching and folding upon itself in limbo, the churning tides eventually brought her up from those interminable depths. Drawing her closer and closer to the brink of consciousness where more pain awaited her, before dragging her back into the endless seas of dream and nightmare.

One moment, she could hear her family distantly. Their voices echoed, garbled syllables. She could see them, blurred forms taking shape from the thinning black around her. And then they would disappear. Replaced by images of slaughter and the sound of screaming. The stench of burning flesh. Smoke as black as night. Torsos careening through the air, loops of intestine spinning as it fell. The wet bellow of an angry god choking on its own blood. Blood. So much blood. The smell of it. The taste of it. It would not leave her.

The further she drifted from the edge of consciousness—further from the muffled voices of family and friends and the blurry shapes of faces she knew and loved—the less she felt the boiling heat and mind-rending pain. But the tide continued to turn, bringing her back to the shores of the waking world.

* * *

Eyes barely open, indistinct figures moved around her. Muffled voices so distant, they sounded like echoes off the mountainside. Soft daylight pricked at her narrowed eyes.

"It's a stronger concoction," a husky, brittle voice said.

A figure stood over her. "You're not giving her anything else," a man's voice said. "We've tried all your concoctions and nothing has worked. I won't let you do any more to her. Just let her die in peace."

"I have given her weeks of peace," the brittle voice said. "Refuse this mercy and you will be forcing me to take harsher measures."

"And what the fuck does that mean?" The figure standing over her stepped toward her feet. Her eyelids drooped and then opened a bit wider. She could see her father standing with his back to her. "What are you going to do, old man?"

"Omari!" her mother's voice called from somewhere in the hut.

A large man more than a head taller than her father stepped in front of him and shoved him back a step.

"Don't touch me, Obi!" her father snapped. "You damned bastard. Nothing but a dog on a leash."

"Omari," the ka-man's husky voice returned. "She is in pain."

"But she is going to wake up!"

"Even if she does, she will wish she was dead."

Her mother was beside her father, holding his arm before he could do or say anything in return. Odessa's head lolled to the side as she blinked, her eyelids becoming increasingly heavy. She slipped back into the warm tides of feverish sleep.

The next time she awoke, it was dark. A cool night breeze came through gaps in the thatch-shuttered windows. Poultices of aloe and gotu kola packed on her right arm beneath a layer of taro leaves did nothing to soothe the infernal pain. Her bones were smoldering coals singing the surrounding flesh. The slightest movement shattered the tenuous equilibrium, cracking the surface and sending up plumes of pain like cinders through her entire body. The constant throbbing was fickle. Any breeze upon her skin or the most minute movement stoked the flames from the embers of her bones.

Body slick with cold sweat, she lay as still as she could on a blanket spread on the cool, packed dirt floor, another thin blanket spread on top of her and chafing her oversensitive skin. The chill of the night came from beneath the curtain hung across the doorway, a gentle draft scouring her raw skin.

Her head throbbed as if her brain were beating against her skull. Her family slept soundly across the room, near the coals of the hearth fire. Ayana's mouth was slightly ajar, crusted with drool, and occasionally let escape a soft snore. Kimi was quiet, barely making a sound even when awake. Ever calm and beatific, a byproduct of her weak constitution.

Watching them sleep, Odessa's mind swam. *Is this real?* The pain was real, she knew that well enough. But she still doubted it. *I must be dead. A spirit haunting this place.*

Faintly, in the quiet chirping of faraway insects and the rustling of thatch in the breeze, she could hear the droning buzz of nothing in the natural world. In the dark hut, lit only by the pulsing coals in the hearth, she could see eyes faintly glowing at the edges of her vision, flickering and shifting like afterimages burned in the back of her mind.

This is a dream. A cruel, sick dream. Terror and dread billowed within her like clouds of smoke, choking her. *I'm still there. I'm still in the dark.*

She shifted her body a bit and pain flared within her like a cloud of embers. Her stomach twisted and bile rose in her throat, where a breath caught. Her throbbing head became light and her vision blurry. She pressed her eyes shut against the swell of burning pain and soon found herself in the hold of unconsciousness once again.

In the early hours of dawn, she roused, half-submerged in sleep. Ayana and Kimi still slept, but in the morning dimness she heard voices.

"Do you truly think they would do such a thing?" her mother whispered. "Kalaro is not such a cruel place as that."

"The other families are afraid. The sores and the sickness, they are making everyone paranoid. The other families will follow Kunza's word without question if they think it will absolve them of their part in this."

"But they would not banish us! It's smoke sickness, surely. They would not do anything as stupid as exiling a whole family over smoke sickness."

"Kunza-ka says she is a mark on our family and the entire village. She bears the sins of the village, she and she alone. They say as much already. They say the sores and sickness are her doing," he said.

Her mother sighed and Odessa could hear her collapse in her father's arms. "This is absurd," she whispered.

"Everything is absurd, my love. The sky is gray. The land is soured. And men kill gods. Absurdity is our normal now."

"What can we do?" her mother asked. "Whether we stay or go, she's still suffering."

"Are you really agreeing with that wizened old herb-crusher?" her father snapped.

"What should we do, then? Forget about us, what is she to do now? If she even wakes up, what then? She's doomed. And for what? What did you accomplish that was worth your daughter's life? Not to mention all the other hunters that got killed or maimed. What did you do but take the life from the Arabako?"

"I did what no one else in history has ever done. I proved that men can kill a god. I proved that they are not above us."

Her mother was silent for a moment. "You're mad," she whispered. "You're a godsdamned madman."

"I did this for us. All of us."

Her mother snorted. "You can't lie to me, Omari. I know you don't really believe that. You did it for yourself. You cannot stand authority. You don't like being told what to do. Like when I told you to not take gods so lightly and you ignored me. Now our daughter is cursed for it. All because of your boundless arrogance."

Her father sighed but did not answer.

"The life of the Forsaken is no life at all," her mother said. "You know that as well as I do."

"Don't quote Kunza like he's some prophet. He's a puffed-up peacock," her father said with a certain bitterness.

"But is he wrong?"

"How can you be such a heartless bitch?" Her father stormed past Odessa lying on the floor and stormed out of the hut.

From the corners of her eyes poured tears Odessa could not contain. She stifled whimpering sobs as her mother cried by the cookstove.

Lying alone in the middle of the hut, there was no one to console Odessa. Nothing to stop the maelstrom of abstract thoughts rushing through her mind. Stifled sobs became lodged in her throat or raked at her ribs as tears poured down her face from her eyes shut so tight her brow furrowed. *All I wanted to do was help my papa. My village. That's all I wanted.*

Yet the village was talking about her. The ka-man had said she was better off dead. *It's not fair.* She remembered the unextinguishable flames bursting from her skin. The taint of godsblood. Perhaps the ka-man was right. It would have been better for everyone if she had died. *It's just not fair at all.*

She wanted to scream. To shout and to rage into the quiet night. To let out all her hurt. But she clenched her jaw and let the tears flow. Silently sobbing on her back in the center of the floor. Every ragged breath sending plumes of searing pain up her spine.

Hot tears swept her back into the swelling tides, where she sank to depths where no light could reach, where even dreams did not venture.

CHAPTER 9

She had been moaning in her sleep. Dreams of burning flesh and all-consuming darkness. A tentative hand cradled her head and raised it. Tremors of pain arced from her neck down her spine. It felt as if the vertebrae in her neck had all burst one after another in a shower of splintered bone. Odessa cried out, her eyes flashing open in a panic.

"Odessa!" her mother held her, disbelief upon her weary face.

"It hurts," Odessa croaked. Her throat was parched and raw. Hot tears filled her eyes. But she couldn't move—the pain so debilitating, all she could do was cry. "It hurts so bad."

"I know. I know it does, baby." Her mother's soft eyes watered ever so slightly as she raised a small gourd bowl to Odessa's lips. "But this will help."

Her mother tipped the bowl into her mouth, filling it with bitter liquid that made Odessa cough and hack, but she swallowed most of it. The bowl, lifted from her lips, clattered to the floor as her mother held her to her chest and cried. Odessa gasped, going light-headed. All along her spine, vertebrae screamed with white pain. The tense muscles in her back and shoulders pulled taut and frayed as her mother cradled her and cried.

Odessa's legs twitched and spasmed as pain swelled, consuming her mind. In her mother's arms, she slipped into unconsciousness.

She awoke some time later, head resting in her mother's lap. Ayana was saying something, but she could not understand the garbled words. She was now cognizant of the pain in her bones and organs and that scorching heat that boiled beneath her skin; but the widow's bark made it all seem distant, like a rumbling over the feverish waters. She lay back and closed her eyes, feeling the throbbing of agony like distant thunder. Her head was fuzzy, as if packed with cottony tufts of wool. The bitter taste of widow's bark was thick in her mouth and plastered the back of her throat. Its slight, sedating calm made the hut around her fluid, the smells and sounds and dim shapes all slowly churning around her.

Her eyes blinked lazily, moving slowly from one face to the other. She smiled with a twinge of distant pain. "Hi."

"Dessa!" Ayana was sobbing so hard, she could barely catch her breath. Ayana cried and landed on her. Ayana wrapped her arms around her. Bolts of pain like lightning forced a cry from Odessa's mouth. But despite the waves of throbbing pain that brought black spots to the edges of her vision, she hugged her little sister back. She squeezed with weak, clammy arms and let the tears fall from her eyes.

"I missed you," Odessa croaked. Her throat was parched and raw.

"Ayana! Let her breathe!" Her mother pulled Ayana away and crouched beside Odessa.

Her mother's gentle hand brushed a lock of hair from Odessa's brow. "I can't believe it," she said, her eyes soft and comforting, but also somehow wary. "Are you really here, baby?"

Odessa's mind was still a sloshing mess of half-formed thoughts, and it struggled in deciphering the collection of syllables. She could not tell if her mother was joking or not. She just smiled, glad to see her mother's face.

"Odessa! Are you there?" her mother shook her shoulder.

Odessa blinked the bleary gaze of unconsciousness from her eyes. "Yes, mama. I'm right here."

Tension bled from her mother's shoulders. "I was afraid the fever melted your brain."

She shook her head in exaggerated swings, listening for a sloshing between her ears. "All good."

Her mother unwrapped the bandages from her right arm and gingerly wiped away gobs of poultice. The burned arm was dark red and had a slick sheen dotted by blisters and streaked with faint threads of dark purple and black, spiderwebbing veins from the gash in her forearm down to her fingers, and up her bicep toward her shoulder. Among the scorched and charred skin ran deep furrows like canyons carved in her flesh. At the bottom of those canyons of scar tissue ran fresh scabs that continued to ooze a bit of blood no matter how much the rest of her arm healed.

With fresh poultice packed liberally on her arm, her mother began to wrap it with a short spool of linen bandage. Ayana offered to do it, but Mutumi refused. As she bandaged Odessa's arm from shoulder to fingertip, Odessa wondered why there was no splint or cast of wet rawhide. She could remember the crack of the bones in her arm. She could still feel the bones grinding against one another before they snapped and splintered.

Her arm was still missing hunks of flesh beneath taut scar tissue. A constant itch was beneath those gnarled and furrowed scars. Her marrow was still smoldering coals, but the broken bones in her arm had mended. Despite her healing, the pain remained, sinking within her—a less brash and more pervasive pain. With the widow's bark, molten agony had turned to a caustic acid that seeped deep into her muscles.

When her arm was wrapped beneath the thick binding of poultice and bandage, Odessa moved it, testing it in the drug-softened fog she found herself in. Her fingers danced at the end of the mummified arm with only an occasional twinge of pain from tendons frayed and singed. *Hello,* she thought as her fingers waved. The coals in the marrow of her forearm smoldered and smoked with irritation but did not burst into flames of torment.

After a moment, her eyes drifted from her arm to scan the hut, her mind taking a while to process the sight. To process what was missing. "Where's Papa?"

"He'll be back," her mother said with a faint note of bitterness. She set the sullied bandages beside the washbasin along with the gourd of leftover poultice and an unused taro leaf. She turned, a wan smile on her face. She looked tired. "You must be starving. Let me make you something easy on your stomach, yeah?"

Odessa nodded and tried to sit up before pain shooting up her spine, right through the deafening sedation of widow's bark, laid her back down. At the hearth fire, her mother made her a thin cornmeal gruel. Odessa was starving, but the smell of cooking filling the hut made her stomach turn and a strange sickness seemed to rise in her throat.

When the thin rice gruel was finished cooking and had cooled, her mother and Ayana helped her up into a sitting position. Tears trickled to her eyes as her little sister propped her up. Their mother left Ayana to tend to her as Kimi began crying to be fed.

Ayana held a cup of water to Odessa's lips. Odessa took small sips, letting the water fill her dry mouth and trickle down her raw, inflamed throat, soothing the smoldering coals inside her. The more she drank to slake her overwhelming thirst, the more her empty stomach recoiled. Nausea rose from the sloshing of her stomach and Odessa had to push the water away. She sat still for a moment, damming the nausea.

"What's wrong?" Ayana asked.

Odessa held the nausea at bay a bit longer before relaxing. "Cold water on an empty stomach," she said. "Made me a little sick."

"Here," Ayana said, taking the bowl of warm, watery rice and offering it to her. "You need to eat."

The smell made her nausea swell like a lump, but her mouth watered nonetheless. Queasy, she knew she had to eat something. She swallowed hard and forced the nausea down.

She took a small sip of gruel. It was bland and warm and wonderful. She took another sip, larger this time.

Her stomach lurched. Gruel and bile surged up her throat. She clamped a hand over her mouth. Hot vomit spurted from between her fingers and out her nose.

She vomited until she retched, rolling onto her hands and knees, the pain bringing tears to her eyes.

"Mama!" Ayana cried, but their mother was already rushing to Odessa's side, Kimi in hand and her breast still out. She put Kimi in Ayana's arms and stroked Odessa's heaving back.

"You're all right," her mother whispered. "You're going to be all right."

Odessa could barely breathe in the midst of her retching. Back arched from the force, each gagging retch made her feel as if her ribs were going to crack. Saliva hung from her lips in strands of mucus.

Before her mother and Ayana had cleaned up her mess, Odessa had already fallen asleep again, whimpering and moaning. In her dreams, her skin blistered and peeled, her fat sizzled and popped, as the dark took her deeper and deeper.

In the evening she was half-awake, sipping water from a cup Ayana held, when her father and Ubiko came through the doorway.

"Odessa!" Her father rushed to her.

Without knowing why, Odessa recoiled as he approached, arms spread wide to take her in a hug. His sudden appearance came with visions of blood and flame.

Seeing her cringe, he stopped a stride short and let his arms drop. Hurt hidden in his wet eyes, he smiled. "Is it really you?" He kneeled beside her, tentatively reaching out to touch her shin.

She smiled, the sudden pang of fear evaporating in the warm comfort of reunion. His scalp and face were covered in prickly stubble and his eyes were tired. "It's me."

"I was so worried." His grip was firm on her leg, as if worried she might be lost to him for good if he let go. "I can't believe you're awake. I thought I'd lost you."

In her joy, Odessa barely noticed the swelling around his throat or the pallid cast of his complexion.

Her mother came to stand next to Ubiko, watching the reunion. She whispered to him and they spoke in hushed tones before Ubiko nodded and slipped out of the hut into the night.

Omari sat next to Ayana. His arm wrapped around Ayana and she clung to him like a baby sloth. "How do you feel?" he asked Odessa. "Does it hurt?"

"Mama gave me something to take the edge off, but it still hurts deep down. Like my bones are just smoldering."

"Your mama is taking good care of you, yeah?" He glanced at his wife, his smile crumbling against the hard expression like a reed boat upon jagged cliffs. Odessa's mother wore a smile, slight and thin, but there was stone beneath it.

When her mother's eyes drifted to Odessa's, her expression softened. "You should drink some more, Dessa. And you must try and eat again."

The thought of food made her sick. "I can't keep it down, Mama."

"You have to try. You can't expect to get better if you don't eat."

She looked to her father for support but found him nodding in agreement with her mother. Her stomach reeled in preparation, a viscous nausea rising from her belly to her throat.

Voices outside the hut drew near. Her father snapped upright as Ubiko entered leading Elder Kusa, her grandmother. Odessa sat straighter, happy to see Ubiko had brought her, but her grandmother stayed near the doorway, a strange remoteness in her eyes. Their eyes met and then her grandmother's gaze darted away to her mother. They exchanged glances, a small, distant smile and a nod.

What's wrong? The atmosphere in the hut had shifted without her noticing. The air was heavier, laden with an odd tension.

Her father noticed the change as well, but noticed it too late.

Through the curtain emerged the ka-man. The bones hanging from his skins chittered at his shins as he entered.

"What are you doing here?" her father asked. Her mother gave him a stern glance before stepping in between him and the ka-man.

"Thank you for coming so late, Kunza-ka."

He nodded dismissively and brushed past to stand above Odessa, his flat, cloudy eyes almost looking through her.

"Her bones are mending. Her burns are healing. And now she wakes," her mother continued. "She gets better with each passing day. The gods are good. They've shown her mercy. It's a miracle."

"It's an ill omen." The ka-man stepped around her, his walking stick tapping against the dirt.

Her mother followed him at a distance. "But look at her. She's awake! That must be the work of the gods."

"There is nothing godly about this," he said. "All I see is a girl that is better off dead."

Odessa shrank back, the words sinking deep in her chest and weighing heavy upon her heart.

Her mother stopped. "But . . . she's awake. The gods are merciful and—"

Behind Odessa, the ka-man turned. "The gods didn't show her mercy. I did. I offered her mercy, enough mercy to kill ten men, and she refused it." He made for the doorway, the spotted pelt about his shoulders swaying as he walked past her. "How she lived I do not know, but I know it was not the work of any god. There is nothing holy at work here and I will say no more on the matter."

"Yes, it would be for the best that you say no more." Odessa's father said, an edge of hostility barely hidden beneath mock politeness.

Kunza-ka stopped and stared at her father. Ubiko took a step toward her father to restrain him if needed. "I have nothing to say to you anyway, Omari. My words are wasted upon you."

Her mother interjected before her father could speak. "What does this mean? What happens now?"

"This changes nothing. She is Forsaken. There are only two paths for her now. Banishment or death."

Her father charged forward, shouting. Ubiko grabbed him by the shoulders and hauled him back. Her mother and grandmother followed the ka-man as he left for the doorway, her mother pleading and begging to no avail. Kimi shrieked from her basket.

The scene playing out in front of Odessa came to her delayed and muddled. *Banishment. Death.* None of it seemed real. Everything since they had left for the hunt seemed like some strange fever dream. She focused on Ayana's hand gripping hers. Ayana eased her onto her back and dabbed at her perspiring forehead with a damp cloth. Ayana's eyes were averted from the ruckus near the door. All the raised voices were of little import to Odessa, except those of her mother and father. The others melted into the rhythmic drumming of heat and pain pounding in her head.

She closed her eyes as Ayana wiped the sweat from her cheeks. Odessa drifted to sleep as Ayana squeezed her hand reassuringly and a teardrop fell from Ayana's cheek onto it.

CHAPTER 10

For a week, Odessa lay on the hard-packed floor, whimpering and writhing. Dreams of tusks and blood and screams plagued her nights. Along with the droning buzz like that of a malignant insect caught in the back of her mind. She awoke most nights clammy with sweat, a scream caught in her throat.

Ubiko came to visit most days, sickness and lack of sleep weighing on him more with each day. The holy man himself had come and checked on her progress a handful of times, pacing around her and shaking his head, sometimes even deigning to look at her blistered, scar-marred arm —always careful not to touch her. He would only look at the thin black lines tracing the delicate route of veins and blood vessels and mutter beneath his breath.

Now able to eat thin gruel without immediately vomiting, Odessa had slowly begun to regain her strength. After a week of sleep interspersed with short bouts of wakefulness, she was able to sit up on her own and even walk for short stretches before she either became so winded she had to rest—or so overcome with the smoldering within her body that black dots began to encroach upon her vision. Although she could walk these short distances, she never dared leave the hut. Passions inflamed the village and she was the thorn around which such inflammation throbbed.

Around her, beneath the skins of those she loved, rose boils and lumps and tumors. The entire village was afflicted with the onset. Her father's had grown larger, swelling from the side of his neck and taking a purple tinge. Her mother had found two lumps in her armpit, and Ayana had a small bump beneath her jaw. Even Kimi had a lump the size of a pea in the hollow of her chubby little thigh. Yet Odessa was unaffected.

A warm, gentle midmorning breeze drifted past shutters propped open halfway. Clean air filled Odessa's lungs as she stood in her sick clothes, a long gown of cream linen, her eyes bleary and bagged with lack of sleep. She lifted the shutter to peer outside. Ayana was picking up the few scattered items left by their neighbors through the night: woven totems and devil traps made from twisted wattle and twigs. Her mother scuffed the dirt at the edge of the wattle-fenced yard with a sandaled foot, kicking away a pair of evil eyes dug into the dirt. Everyone in the village was trying to ward the pestilence away from their homes, but some had taken to trying to contain the plague at its source.

Odessa let the shutter drop upon its prop stick. Guilt gnawed at her. She wished she could at least help pick up the pieces left in the wake of her survival. Do something to make up for the pain she was causing her family. But she could barely bend over without passing out from the exertion and the pain. Yesterday, she had tried to help as best she could in her weakened state, but she could not stand the stares and the whispers. Even though the villagers did not say anything to her, she knew what they had been saying. What they were all still saying.

Banishment or death.

She left the window and sat with a pained sigh beside Kimi's basket. The infant was quiet in her swaddling cloth, chin wet with drool. Odessa dabbed the drool with the corner of the cloth. Kimi barely stirred, her small fingers twitching at the commotion.

When her mother found the lump on Kimi's thigh, she did not even cry. She just turned to her father and began shouting. Blaming him for everything.

It wasn't his fault. If I didn't get hurt, none of this would have happened, Odessa thought. *If I hadn't lived, none of this would have happened. If I would have just died, no one would even know what we did.* Her father had told her many times since she woke up that it wasn't her fault. That all the hunters that had been there were equally guilty, they all shared the sin. But she wasn't stupid. She knew what being Forsaken meant. You became a cancer.

A little while later, Ayana came inside, rushing toward where Odessa sat cradling her throbbing arm as she applied a salve to the worst of her burns.

"Look!" Ayana said, holding out two small yellow flowers in her hands. "The mountain lilies are blooming!"

Odessa forced a wan smile. "They're so pretty!"

She hunched over the flower in Ayana's outstretched hand and tried to grasp it but stopped short, withdrawing her raw fingers. Burned hand hidden behind the thin folds of her gown, she pinched the flower's stem between the unblemished fingers of her unmarred hand. Cradled in her slender brown hand, the flower was the muted yellow of the sun filtering through thick haze. "How many are there?" she asked.

"Just a few, but Mama said the rest will start blooming any day!" Ayana said, beaming.

Odessa wore a thin smile. A smile cracked and crumbling at the edges. "Do you want to go flower picking when they all bloom?"

"Yes!" Ayana cheered without hesitation. "Can we go tomorrow? Please?"

"Tomorrow?" Ayana did not seem to see the faltering of Odessa's smile, the distant sadness clouding her eyes. Through the last week, Ayana had seemed mostly oblivious to the inflamed tensions festering in the village or the unease at home—but Odessa knew better. Most likely, Ayana was seeing what was happening far better than she was able to while quarantined at home. Odessa rammed her self-pity down the pit of her stomach. "Do you really think they'll all have bloomed by tomorrow?"

Ayana paused, thinking, and then shook her head. "Yes. Yes, I do."

A puff of air passed through her nostrils, as close to a laugh as Odessa could manage in her present state. "If you say so." She tucked the flower behind Ayana's ear, keeping it in place with a tight coil of black. "But if you wait until the end of the week, I'll make you a crown fit for a fairy princess." With that, she had bought herself some time to regain her strength. She smirked as Ayana's face lit up. Last year, Odessa had braided crowns of sweetgrass and lilies for Matara's Harvest Festival, and she knew how Ayana had loved her crown, keeping it until it was a ring of brittle grass and shriveled flowers.

Beneath her gown, her burned hand tightened in a fist. A spur of pain pressed into her palm like an iron spike. *Even if I'm strong enough to walk, will I even be able to pick flowers with this damned thing?* She could barely pick up a bowl with her unfeeling, leaden fingers. The strength in her arm was coming back to her slowly in throbbing waves of molten heat, but her fingers were clumsy and numb.

The rest of the day, Ayana talked about what she planned to do with all the flowers she picked. Crowns and wreaths and bouquets for everyone in the village. All the while, Odessa thought of how the rest of the village would react, seeing the cause of their sickness and their possible damnation frolicking among flowers as if she had not a single care in the world.

The next day, Odessa busied herself watching her sleeping infant sister while Ayana and her mother harvested potatoes and the few peppers that had grown from their plot behind the hut. Later in the day, her father, mother, and Ayana would be leaving for the communal plots outside of the village and along the stone terraces in the hillsides to harvest corn and potatoes and what few yams and cassavas were ready for harvesting. With only Kimi, quiet in her bundle, to keep her occupied, she sat and wallowed in her misfortune.

"Hello?" a voice called from outside.

Odessa peered through the window to see Ubiko and Adura standing in the fenced-in yard. She dropped the shutter and went out to greet them.

Adura was haggard, her brawny frame thinned like a flowering tree stripped by a summer storm. Odessa smiled at her, happy to see her for the first time since the hunt. Adura gave her a thin, tense smile, an expression lacking the strength and confidence Odessa had once admired and almost worshipped. Adura was tired and beaten.

Ubiko was thinner and his complexion more sallow than last time she had seen him a couple of days before. The lump on the side of his neck was large and dark purple.

"I thought you'd be out in the forest with Papa today," she said to Ubiko. Her father had left before sunrise to hunt a bit before the harvesting. His insomnia was making him restless, and he spent most of his time in the Arabako lately.

"Oh no, not today," he said, wiping shimmering beads of sweat from his wide forehead. A sheen of sweat glistened on his face and bags hung from under his eyes. "Came to check on you. You seem in better shape than the last time I saw you. How's the arm?"

She raised the bandaged arm. "Better than it was."

Ubiko nodded almost absent-mindedly, glancing at the neighboring huts in the circle of huts. "Good," he said. "That's good." He itched beneath his tunic and looked back at her. "Anyone been giving you trouble?"

Odessa's brow furrowed. The last time Ubiko had visited, he had not acted this strangely. "Not as long as I don't leave the hut," she said, trying to follow his gaze to the other huts. "Is it getting bad?"

He crossed his arms and glanced at Adura. "Just talk. Lots of talk."

"What kind of talk?" she asked.

"Why don't we go inside? Is your mother in too?"

"No, she's out back in the garden with Ayana. Why?"

"Just want to say hello. You head inside, I'll be there in a moment."

Odessa stammered for a moment, about to resist, when Adura came and put a hand on her arm. "Let's go," she said. "It's been a while since I've seen you. We have some catching up to do, don't you think?"

Odessa wanted to persist and demand to know what was going on, but standing had made her weary. She nodded and led Adura inside while Ubiko, after casting a few wary glances toward the neighboring huts, went around to the back of the hut.

Kimi mewled weakly from her basket as Odessa entered, stealing her momentarily from her paranoia. A foul odor filled the hut. She hurried to check the baby, fussing with the swaddling cloth to find Kimi had soiled herself. With a sigh, she lifted her from the basket. Holding the mewling baby at arm's length, she turned to see Adura leaning in the doorway. "I'm sorry, she made a mess of herself. I have to . . . "

Adura snorted with faint mirth. "Go ahead, I understand." She leaned against the wall with her arms crossed, watching as Odessa set to cleaning Kimi.

Adura's gaze made her suddenly very conscious of her every movement. She had cleaned and changed Kimi many times but now, with the clumsy way her hands were moving, she would have thought she had never even seen a baby before.

Kimi fussed and whined quietly. Adura's faint smile slowly eroded. Her gaze became distant for a moment. "Did you know I had a baby once?" she asked.

Odessa looked up, Kimi's chubby leg in her bandaged hand and a filth-smeared rag in the other. "You did?"

"A little boy. A long time ago. I wasn't much older than you when I had him." A wistful glint in her eye softened her hard, tired face. "He died not long after you were born, I think."

"I'm so sorry." Odessa didn't know what else to say. Adura had never spoken so openly to her.

"I would have done anything for him," Adura said, not looking at her. "If it had been in my power, I would have damned the whole world to keep him here." Her tired eyes rose to meet Odessa's and then fell away again. "I understand why your father did it. Why he did what he did to save you. I don't blame him for that." A strong, calloused hand wiped the sweat beading at her brow. "But I begin to wonder if we should have followed your father into the Arabako in the first place. I wonder if he was wrong about all of it. I don't think there was ever a chance we could kill a god without consequence. This was always going to happen."

The hut was quiet save for Kimi's soft, murmuring cries. Stunned, Odessa's mouth hung ajar for a moment. "Are you well?"

Adura snorted. "None of us are well. You got the worst of it, but we're all just different shades of sullied." She pushed off from the wall, a harsh solemnity about her. "I wish you hadn't been there on that hunt. I'm sorry for that."

Odessa nodded, her hands working idly to clean Kimi as she tried to gather her muddled and discordant thoughts. The hunt. That damned hunt. She didn't want to think about it, but it was all anyone ever wanted to talk about. The gore and the screams. The weight of Egende's body on top of her as the god shuddered with its last breath. The hate in its glassy eyes as its lifeblood poured out onto the forest floor.

The flames. Those hellish flame bursting from her arm. She would never forget the stench of her own flesh burning. The mind-shredding pain. And then nothingness.

She wrapped Kimi in a fresh swaddling cloth and set her in her basket. Kimi squirmed weakly in the bundle of cloth for a moment before relenting. Before Odessa could stop herself, her disordered thoughts came out in the form of a question. "What did you mean 'what he did'? What did Papa do to save me?"

Adura turned from where she stood before the small shrine to the High Gods. "Shit. You don't know. Of course, you don't know." She took a step forward and then stopped. A finger rubbed along her bottom lip as paused, brow tight with an apprehension that had Odessa sitting with bated breath. With a sigh, she kneeled in front of Odessa, tired eyes soft and overflowing with pity. "I don't know exactly what he did," she said, barely above a whisper. "But Ubiko told me what he saw." She took Odessa's unbandaged hand and held it in her strong, kind grip. A creeping chill grew in Odessa's chest. "Killing a god was a terrible sin. An unimaginably awful sin. But what your father did to you . . . it was unnatural."

Odessa couldn't speak. Her throat was swollen shut, trapping all her questions and denials inside her chest, where they battered her quivering heart.

"It was some dark, twisted blood magic like nobody has ever seen. He carved out Egende's heart and used some perversion of the gods' own magics. You lived, that is for sure. But at what cost, I wonder?"

Before Odessa could say anything, Ayana came through the doorway like a wild animal. The knees of her gown caked in dust and dirt. She ran to Adura, telling her all about Odessa's miraculous recovery, but to Odessa her words were distant and indistinct. Her bandaged hand lay in her lap, throbbing as it always did. *What did you do, Papa? What did you do to me?*

Ubiko and her mother came into the hut not long after Ayana. Once inside, her mother stopped in front of Ubiko, sleeves of her vibrant turquoise gown rolled back from her dirt-stained arms as she carried a basket half-filled with small, pock-marked potatoes. She set the basket down by the doorway, turned to Ubiko, and folded her arms across her chest.

"Now what is all this really about?" she asked plainly. "This is not just a social visit, no?"

Ubiko shifted in the doorway, looking uncomfortable. "I just don't think it's a good idea for you all to be alone right now. Just in case."

Odessa hurriedly bundled Kimi's soiled cloth and took it to the woven laundry basket—to be washed in the river by someone strong enough to carry it through the village without passing out. She dropped the filthy blanket into the basket and replaced the lid with a sleepwalker's torpor. *He wouldn't do something like that. How could he? Papa doesn't know anything about magic.*

Her mother was frowning at Ubiko. "What do you mean?"

"All I mean is with Omari out hunting, someone should be here just in case."

"I'm here, aren't I?"

"Well, yes but —" Ubiko stammered.

"What has you so flustered? Come out and say it already."

"Nothing yet," Adura spoke up. "It's just talk for now."

Her mother whirled on Adura. "Talk of what?" she asked, an edge to her words.

"Just scared talk. But it would be wise to take precaution," Ubiko said, stepping farther toward where his sister stood in the center of the hut.

"The elders fear retribution from the gods," Adura said. And they see it everywhere now. And with this ill-timed illness, others are as well."

Ayana stood beside Odessa, her hands clasped nervously to her chest. Odessa took her by the hand and squeezed.

"I told you and Omari not to take on the gods for exactly this reason," their mother said to Ubiko sharply.

"I know, I know," Ubiko said. "But this will pass. You all must be careful until then, though. A scared animal is a dangerous animal and people are too. They make rash decisions when fear gets to them."

"Rash decisions like hunting a god?"

Ubiko shook his head in exasperation. "Godsdamn it, will you just listen to me?" he said, his voice rising to the verge of a shout. He paused and took a step back, struck by his own sudden outburst. "I'm sorry. I'm sorry, I have not been sleeping well with all the stress. Not even poppy tea helps, I'm up pacing all night and . . . " His words trailed off. "I'm just trying to help keep you safe."

An awkward silence stretched in the hut. "I know that. I know," her mother said, the edge in her voice softened. "I thank you for that. Truly." She sighed and adjusted the plain gele on her head. "Forgive my rudeness, you are still guests in my home. Sit, please." As Ubiko and Adura sat on mats in the center of the hut, she turned her attention to Odessa. "Get a pot of water boiling for chilate, will you? "

Odessa took Ayana and together they set a pot of water on the coals of the hearth. With all the excitement of the day's visit, Odessa's body began to ache and her hands to twitch as she measured cornmeal and old cacao powder and dumped it into the bubbling water. Ayana stirred continuously, with the ardent dedication of a smith at a forge. When the water began to simmer, Odessa hurried to find the few spices they had left.

"How is the sickness?" her mother asked, sitting across from Adura and Ubiko. "Is it getting any better?"

Ubiko shook his head. "Not any better, but not any worse either. A few more have come down with sores and rashes but that's all so far. The elders worry for nothing. There is nothing divine about it. We've outlasted plagues before, this is nothing." Odessa thought she sensed something in his words, something unsaid. He rose, attracted by the fragrant scent of cacao, and stood beside Ayana as she stirred, sniffing the fragrant steam rising from the pot. His attention fell upon Odessa finely dicing one of the last of prior year's dried chilis. "Only one? A bit tight with the chili, yeah?"

"This is how I always make it," she said.

"Then you make it wrong," he said, a selfsame grin shining for a moment through dour weariness. To Odessa, it seemed much too forced.

"You'll drink it and like it," Odessa said, trying to channel her mother's ire in her tone. Trying to force a smile to her lips.

"Yes, ma'am," he said before turning to Ayana and sticking his tongue out in mock disgust. Ayana smiled and he gave her a gentle shove with his elbow as he went back to join the adults in their continued conversation.

"Everyone is at the end of their wits," Adura was saying.

"It's not as if we haven't seen calamity before. The sky's turned gray, for the gods' sake. We've been at the end of our wits for years."

"You have to admit, these sores and such come at a very coincidental time," Adura said.

"Coincidences happen all the time. I had the sniffles the day the Gray came over Kalaro. Does that mean it's my fault?" said Ubiko.

Adura shook her head with annoyance, but Odessa's mother nodded. "I actually think you're right for once," she said. "I think the Gray is your fault."

Ubiko frowned. "Why is it the only time you joke is when it's at my expense?"

"You make it so easy."

"Coincidence or not," Adura said, dispelling any levity. "Kunza-ka has the entire village now. It's only a matter of time before they do something."

"Like what?" her mother said.

"I don't know, but something must be done. I think we all can agree on that, yes?"

Her mother looked at both Ubiko and Adura. "But what can we possibly do to repair all you and Omari have ruined?" Her voice was flat with no edge of accusation at all. The blame had already been placed in her eyes, and there was no need to press the matter further. All they could do was fix what had been broken.

"We killed Low Gods. The lowest of the Low," Ubiko said, ignoring a sharp glance from his sister. "If we can keep Kunza-ka and everyone from doing anything rash, I think we can get through this. Adura and I, we're trying to organize a raid in the lowlands."

Odessa added a pinch of allspice into the simmering pot. *A raid?* No one had left Kalaro for a lowland raid in at least five years. All their warriors had grown dull in the fields. Even Obi had not been immune to the sedative effect of years without bloodshed. He was thinner and quieter like a caged animal finally broken.

"And how many more will die in this raid?"

"Mutumi, I don't think you understand how precarious a situation we are in right now," Adura said. "Even if this sickness is nothing, which I hope it is, Kunza-ka is on the verge of doing something drastic. And who are going to be the first people he comes for when he does?" The question hung unanswered like the stench of smoke above the burn pits, cloying and oppressive.

"If we get enough prisoners," Ubiko said. "I think we can appease the High Gods, Azka, and everyone else. A sacrifice like none other."

Odessa ladled hot chilate into gourd cups, spilling cream-colored liquid down the side of each cup. Nausea bubbled in her stomach, not caused entirely by the strong fragrance of cacao and spices. *A sacrifice. Sacrificing people.* It felt as if all the air had left the hut and she was suffocating. *How many more people are going to die because of what we did?*

CHAPTER 11

Dawn arrived serenely through the haze of twilight. The sun rose from behind the mountains, a ball of pale orange blazing through the gray cloud cover thickening above the Arabako Forest. The basin, still doused in blue tones, was still and tranquil. Barely a breeze to jostle the dry leaves of the forest. Terraced fields along the hillsides stood half-picked, cut corn stalks lying in piles along the edges. Smoke rose from the circled huts of Kalaro in wispy plumes. Dew dripped from the eaves of thatch roofs.

In the dim rays of dawn's first light, a flash of bronze high in the sky above the Night Jungle. Like a speck of gold dust lost in a cloud of ash, it flared and then disappeared in the dreary expanse of soot-dark clouds.

A few quiet seconds passed.

The flash of bronze streaked above the basin like a comet cutting through the clouds. Then a thunderous crack split the stillness. A sharp boom rattled dew from roofs and leaves in the wake of that bronze light.

Kunza-ka jerked awake, ripped from restless and tenuous slumber. The old ka-man rose hurriedly from his bed of reeds, joints swollen and irritated by the sudden movement. Unsteadily, he used the wall to brace himself. The lumps in the hollow of his armpit ached as he pushed himself onto his feet.

"Kunza-ka!" a deep voice, thick with urgency, called from outside his hut.

"I'm coming!" Kunza-ka snapped, his dry throat only able to produce a hoarse croak. Tentatively, he tried to massage the pain from the lumps, but they were tender to the touch. *They've grown.* Another small lump was forming on the side of his neck. He slipped into his jaguar pelt and leaned against his walking stick for support as he exited the hut.

An early morning chill cut through his thin frame. Obi stood, bare-chested in the early morning dimness with a curved sword sheathed at his waist. He bowed his head in deference as Kunza-ka approached, but the beast of a man still towered over him. Tall and wide, dark skin bulging with thick cords of muscle, Obi was truly Kalaro's finest. "I'm sorry to bother you."

"What is it?" Kunza-ka asked.

Obi turned and pointed to the sky above where the Night Jungle and the mountains met. Kunza-ka narrowed his eyes but could see nothing but gray clouds and mountaintops. And then he saw it. Among the clouds, a bronze flash in the faint morning light.

"From Noyo," he said. "It's circled the basin once already and will soon be landing, I think."

His bowels turned to ice. "They're not due to collect from us for months still."

Despite his words, the shape in the sky grew larger. Wings of bronze occasionally flashing like a fish breaking the water's surface. *Gods be merciful, why must this happen now?* "Gather an entourage. The Elders and Ajatunde. And a handful of your men. And have someone with a torch flag the Chosen down on the northern edge of the village." Kunza-ka pulled his pelt tighter around his shivering body, better obscuring the lumps rising beneath his chin. "It must at least appear as if this village is crumbling to pieces."

"As you wish, Kunza-ka." Obi bowed again but Kunza-ka waved him away. There was little time for formality. As Obi hurried to make preparations, Kunza-ka shuffled back inside his hut. Inside, he found he had too many things to do pulling him in too many directions at once. After a moment's indecision, he went about his own preparations. He washed his face and reapplied the white face paint . The skirt he wore was plain and stained with dirt and grime; he hastily changed into an intricately patterned ceremonial skirt of black and red and white, with symbols and images of the High Gods embroidered in the labyrinthian weave. A heavy necklace of multiple beaded strands laden with bronze and gold and small pieces of carved jade chafed against his lumps.

His headdress sat high on the top of his head and was missing a few quetzal feathers along the crown, and the layers of peafowl feathers along the back of his neck had thinned considerably. The feathers that remained had long ago lost their lustrous sheen. He remembered the first time he held it in his hands. The unbelievable shimmering of blue and green. Each feather like a jewel.

Kunza-ka made his way out of the village, his skin crawling and his legs trembling. Behind him the Elders Kusa and Cuchal followed. Elder Kusa wore a matching kaftan and gele of dark orange. Gold bracelets and necklaces clattered faintly as she walked, an absurd show of familial wealth in a village rotting from the inside. Elder Cuchal wore a bright blue dashiki with yellow trim.

I come leading two peacocks, Kunza-ka thought bitterly.

Behind them, Obi and three warriors followed close behind, spears and shields in hand. The three warriors Obi had brought were in full regalia, a suit of red quilted cotton adorned with palm fronds and feathers about the shoulders and waist. Obi was bare-chested still, a loincloth and sandals all he wore despite the chill. His shield was a large oval of wood wrapped in leather and painted in faded streaks of red and black. Obi's face was as inscrutably blank as always. Usually, having Obi at his side would have given Kunza-ka a bit of comfort; but today, Obi's stone face only unsettled him further.

The Chosen had already landed by the time the entourage left the village. As large as an elephant, the leonine shape sat at the top of the slight ridge overlooking the village. It hulked above the poor torch-bearer kneeling before it. Two wings made of sharp bronze feathers folded upon its back. The Chosen sat totally still, haughty and predatory eyes taking in the entire basin. Cold, imperious cat's eyes, glittering with the divinity Azka had bestowed upon it, focused on the hurrying group of villagers as they approached.

Without a word, they prostrated themselves before the beast. Dew seeped through their clothes. Kunza-ka's heart thumped in his chest and he was sure the Chosen could hear it. Could hear the patter of his guilty heart. Could smell the sin on each of them like the palpable stench of body odor. Foreheads against the dirt path leading out of the village, seconds dragged in an indefinitely long silence.

Kunza-ka squeezed his eyes shut and waited, resisting the urge to lift his head. If he was to die, he did not need to see it coming.

Finally, the Chosen spoke, an impossibly deep and throaty sound like rumbling thunder coming from its lion maw. "By order of Azka, Sovereign of the Western Wind, I bring ill tidings." Rote, flat words rolled together like a purr. "Yesterday, as the sun rose, Kutali, third and youngest son of Azka's line, was found dead. After months of valiant resistance, he succumbed to illness as he slept."

Kunza-ka's eyes opened a crack, his forehead still pressed to the dirt. *Illness? What illness could kill a god?*

"His soul is in Mito's hands now. Let them guide him to the afterlife in peace and soon, Matara shall take him in her embrace and bless this world with his presence once again." The Chosen paused and Kunza-ka stiffened, his eyes snapping shut once again.

After a prolonged moment of silence, the Chosen began again. "By divine decree, today shall begin a period of mourning that will last until the end of this cycle. Thirty-five solar years. Each day will begin with a lamentation to the High Gods for the sake of our young god, taken far too soon.

"To honor Kutali, Azka, Peerless Ruler of Mountain and Plain, has commissioned the finest masons and artisans to construct a tomb like no other. As such, along with the yearly conscription, the state of Noyo requires an additional levy of laborers from each settlement within its lands."

Dread ran down Kunza-ka's spine and along his nerves until it had seeped into his every molecule. *We barely have enough able-bodied souls to keep us from starving and they want more? Not to mention the sickness, these damned lumps. Nearly half of us have them now, I'm sure.* This would spell the end of Kalaro. Even with the Arabako open to them, if they had no one to hunt or clear and work the land, then it would not matter.

"In thirty days, a detachment from Noyo will arrive and collect laborers for the tomb's construction, along with a portion of this year's early harvest." The Chosen rose on its four sinewy legs, long talons digging into the earth. "Any attempts to evade these levies will result in harsh punishment."

Silence for a moment as its gold-glinting eyes scanned the village again. There was little movement in Kalaro. Everyone had heard about the Chosen's arrival by then.

"How many do you have in Kalaro?" the Chosen asked.

Kunza-ka did not raise his head from the dirt. "Ninety-three," he said. "Eight of those are children. Seventeen are over fifty-two years." He knew these numbers by heart. They had been on his mind ever since the hunt. The young died so readily, yet the old clung stubbornly to life.

The Chosen stood, thinking for a moment as its eyes moved along the distant forest's edge. "Ten. Noyo will take ten men and women. After the harvest, Noyo will require more but for now, ten will suffice."

Ten? How can we spare ten people during harvest time?

The Chosen shifted its wings, the bronze clinking as they stretched and folded again. "People of Kalaro, I shall leave you to your mourning." It stepped back a few steps. "Noyo will collect its due in thirteen days."

As its departing words were coming from its fang-lined mouth, a southerly breeze blew through the village and over the prostrated villagers' backs. A breeze from the southern seas, smelling of salt and storm.

The Chosen stopped, its mammoth frame gone rigid. It sniffed the gentle breeze, nose wrinkling at the stench wafting from the village below.

"What is that?" it growled. It sniffed again, taking a step toward Kunza-ka and the others. "What is that stink?"

No one spoke. They stayed, frozen in place on the path, as if their stillness would make the Chosen go away.

"What is that stench?" the Chosen boomed. The ground beneath them vibrated.

Kunza-ka swallowed hard and peeled his dry tongue from the roof of his mouth. "A dying girl," he said, raising his forehead from the dirt. "She was forsaken for trespassing in the Arabako." The lie came so easily he had not even noticed it slipping from his lips until it was already spoken.

The Chosen's glimmering eye narrowed, chilling Kunza-ka's blood in his veins. A rumbling came from behind the curled lips of the Chosen. "Thirty days."

A great rush of air shoved him aside as the Chosen took flight.

Before he staggered to his feet, the Chosen had already streaked over the village, circling the basin twice before heading over the southern ridge, a comet in the sky again.

Oh gods. It'll kill us all. It'll see she's tainted. That we're all tainted. And it will kill each and every one of us.

Kunza-ka staggered down the hill, leaving the Elders struggling to rise to their feet. They called after him but he continued, cursing his old legs with each aching step. Obi followed behind him like a massive shadow.

Something had to be done before the detachment from Noyo arrived.

Damn you, Omari. Damn you and your cursed daughter. You'll be the death of us all, you bastard.

When he returned to his hut, he found Adura waiting outside. "Kunza-ka," she said when she saw him near. "I saw the Chosen. What did it say?"

"Why are you here?" he said sharply. Adura used to be such a devout girl; now a god's blood stained her hands. He leaned upon his walking stick, his legs still weak from the encounter with Noyo's envoy.

Adura frowned, obviously hurt by his curtness. But he had no time to coddle those that had threatened the entire village. When the group from Noyo came in thirteen days, they would find out what they had done. If the sickness did not kill them, then Azka and his Chosen most assuredly would.

"I'm sorry, Kunza-ka," she said, quietly like a scolded child. Where was the brave, arrogant warrior that helped kill a god now? She told him of her plan, the mass sacrifice she hoped would appease the High Gods and absolve them of their sins. All the other hunters, even that fool Omari, agreed to make the journey into lowlands and capture a score of suitable offerings.

Would that be enough? How many human lives could equal that of a god? And three gods at that. Kunza-ka rubbed his chin slowly, a rough plan taking shape like the form of a statue hewn from stone. "Gather your other godkillers. We leave immediately. But not to the lowlands. Not yet. We must first prostrate ourselves before the gods and beg that we may offer anything in their names."

He was inside his hut without as much as another glance at Adura. There was much to do. In a frenzy, he gathered what he would need: more than a year's worth of herbs and powders, a collection of bones, and most of all his cauldron, a heavy copper pot stoppered with a thick wooden lid and tied shut with thin hemp ropes. Contained inside was all that made him what he was. What made him the medium between the spiritual and the physical. The mortal and the divine. Inside the stained, patina-mottled pot, his blood mingled with the blood of the many offerings he fed it since he the day he became a ka-man.

"Kunza-ka?" Obi said from the doorway as he was putting a leather-swaddled obsidian knife into a sack. "What will we do about Azka and his Chosen?"

"Have faith, Obi," he said, pulling a small braid of garlic from the ceiling and putting it in the sack. "Just gather your most loyal and come with me on this pilgrimage." Obi's broad face was as impassive as always, but he could tell the big man was worried. The same worry weighed on Kunza-ka's weary shoulders as well, but the plan was all that he had, and he clung to it as if without he would drown in the depths of his own despair. "The gods will provide, my friend. The gods will provide."

CHAPTER 12

In the Arabako, beyond the high-peaked gateway, ran a path paved with rough-hewn stones weathered by centuries of the trodden steps of pilgrimage. Soft moss crept along the edges of the stones beneath a thick layer of leaves scattered across the path. In better times, when the gate had been unbarred year-round, Kunza-ka had spent many early mornings sweeping the path clean. Standing in the gateway beneath a curtain of dead vines, he peered down the winding path, into the heart of the forest, and a profound sadness chilled him. The finality and gravity of what he had allowed to happen weighed on his old limbs.

You stay out of the forest and abandon the spirits and look what becomes of you. An old man in a dying wood.

The forest was dim and lifeless. The shimmering warmth that had once fallen upon the leaves was now smothered and doused by the clouds above. The spirits had abandoned the forest; the lively essence that once coursed through the trees now left a disquieting hum in its absence. The faint scent of decay wafted through the corridors of trees and brush.

Emptiness. The forest had been emptied. A husk remained where gods once walked. Kunza-ka had neglected the spirits he had once communed with regularity, and now they were gone, having left to find new sanctuary.

"Shall we go on, ka-man?" A voice asked from behind him. Adura stood beside Obi. A retinue of hunters and warriors stood behind him. All of the hunters had come, except for Ubiko and Omari and his Forsaken daughter. He had not been surprised.

"Yes," he said, already weary from the walk from the village. The abrupt morning had drained him so much, but he forced his legs onward and began down the path through the forest. They had much ground to cover before the trek up the mountains.

His walking stick thumped sharply against the stone—a slow, awkward rhythm through the eerily quiet forest. The leaves above them showed signs of blight even as they walked deeper into the woods. Brown-tinged leaves, shriveled and dry like discarded cocoons, shells of their former selves although there was no metamorphosis to be had—just death and rot.

Soon, the path grew steeper and twisted through the uneven foothills. Kunza-ka puffed and panted, his pace slowing to a shuffling crawl. His retinue fell behind him out of courtesy, their young bodies unencumbered by the heaviness of age.

But all of them bore splotches of reddened skin and furious sores dotting their bodies and bulging around their necks.

We offered Egende and her boarlings to the High Gods, but that was not enough. Not nearly enough to atone, Kunza-ka thought as the path cut through the heart of the forest. *I will make it right. A Low God's dying curse is nothing to the love of the High Gods.*

The gods of the earth and the gods above were worlds apart. The corporeal were not the same as those that had ascended to the ethereal, though the same ichor ran through their veins. *Faith in the true gods above will spare us the worst of a worldly god's wrath,* he told himself. But a boil in the hollow of his armpit, which chafed against his white gown as he walked, told him otherwise.

The canopy of leaves grew slightly greener and fuller as they went higher in the foothills. The sky above appeared through chinks in the foliage, a hazy slate color.

Shadows beneath the trees deepened as they made their way up to the base of the mountains, where they made camp in an overgrown clearing built long ago for such respite. They built a fire in the center of a circle of stout stone pillars listing to the side or half-buried in a hollow at the bottom of the mountains. The Stairs of Ascension began not far from the clearing, hard stone steps cutting into the mountainside, through the thinning trees and stony soil rising steeply ahead. It ran in the saddle between two high peaks before falling back upon itself over and over as it slithered up the side of the highest peak in the range. The Serpent's Peak.

Kunza-ka sat upon a stone pillar fallen on its side and sunken in centuries of dirt. He peeled the leather thongs from his feet and massaged a blistered sole. At the foot of the stairs, a statue flanked either side and stared at him with eyes of fiery ruby. Two boars flanked the foot of the stairs, each equal in its piercing stare. The four tusks curving from their mouths were made of pure white marble, their brilliance only somewhat diminished over the years.

He had always looked at the craftsmanship of those statues with wonder, but now he looked at them with shame and fear. It had been years since he had made the trek up the stairs. Not since the early years of the Gray. He had forgotten the awesome presence at the foot of the mountains. The statues looming over the path, taller than even Obi. Two twin boars sitting on massive haunches, their backs hunched and their heads tilted down toward the path leading up the stairs. Yet those bejeweled eyes seemed trained on the holy man.

The hunters and warriors sat and ate quietly around a fire started in a pit blackened with the ash and soot of ancient fires. Kunza-ka ate nothing. He had been fasting since the hunt for Egende had begun, drinking only bone broth in between his prayers. His stomach turned on itself and his head floated with airy, dreamlike exhaustion. Sitting on the pillar, he was able to catch his breath and ease the tight stitch in his ribs and remove the searing thorns from his raw lungs.

As darkness collected in the hollow, he kneeled at the foot of the mountains in front of the twin boar statues and prayed. He prayed for strength and he prayed for mercy, but his prayers felt as if they were cast to the gales. Swept away as soon as they passed his lips, gone into nothingness. Lost in a hollow emptiness gaping in the atmosphere.

The fire was little more than coals when he finally lay down to sleep. Bundled in his skins, he shivered as cold unfurled from the mountain tops and poured down the foothills. It felt like hours before he finally fell asleep. No dreams came to him from the ether. The energy of the sacred forest had dried up, a drought evaporating any remaining spiritual essence. At the edge of a great gaping vacuum like a wound in the cosmos, he only tossed and turned in a shallow slumber. The silence. The isolation. The emptiness. It all ate away at him. Eroding the boundaries of consciousness, leaving his nerves raw and exposed to that harrowing void.

The twisting of his empty stomach and the clawing of hunger against his ribs refused to quiet even as he struggled to hide in the solace of slumber. He rolled over, trying to fall back asleep. *Foolish old man,* he thought, pulling the jaguar skin about his shoulders tighter. He knew sleep would not return to him now. His thoughts were too loud in his mind. *Should have come to the gods in the first place. Before Omari had their support, I should have come to the gods.*

A breeze whistled through the trees. A rustling of leaves like the whispers of a thousand dead souls. *I should have never stopped coming to the gods. I should have stayed on that mountain until the gods had rid us of the Gray. Then none of this would have happened.*

But he hadn't stayed. Years before, when the Gray had first begun to gather above the mountains, he had spent countless days on the peak, losing himself in smoke and visions, but nothing had come of it. His prayers had been wasted. The gods had spurned him. When he returned from his failed pilgrimage, defeated and disheartened, more of his people had succumbed to the Gray, their charred bodies lying unceremoniously in burn pits. He had returned, smelling of incense and herbs, to the stench of disease and burned flesh. To a people frightened and clinging to the vain hope that the gods would save them.

At the time, he thought the gods had abandoned them. He still thought that to some degree, though the intensity of his resentment had been muted by the passage of years. Perhaps that petty resentment was the reason he hadn't stopped Omari before he gained the support of the other hunters. Why he hadn't ordered Obi and his warriors to cut them down that morning.

How many years had he prayed to the High Gods? How much faith did he have that it could all be lost so easily? It had been a shallow faith, useful only for ritual and ceremony. Such a charlatan he had become. Weak conviction and soft metal, that was what Kunza-ka was made of. What happened to the boy praying to Aséshassa when the harpies had come? He had truly believed the High Gods were humanity's guardians from the evils of the world. What happened to that belief?

He knew it was weakness that had softened his faith. A weakness that brought him and all of Kalaro to their doom. Now the salvation of the entire village and of himself rested with him. *Am I strong enough to do this? Or am I a craven old man too scared to do what must be done?*

Kunza-ka left camp hours before dawn had even begun to bleed above the mountains. The forest was still damp with shadow when the holy man gathered his bundle and took off up the stairs in that half-dark before the others began to stir.

One step at a time, lifting heavy, chafing, blistering feet, he climbed ever upward. The sun's rays peeked out from behind the mountains still towering above, diffused in cloud cover into an orange halo above the peaks. Sparse trees dotted the mountainside, bursting through the stony soil, gnarled and twisted. Leaves crunched beneath his leather-bound feet. His walking stick struck the ancient stone with sharp, resonant clicks that reverberated into the morning stillness.

He was halfway up the saddle of the ridge when the sun began bleeding into the damp gray, orange suffusing into the clouds, turning the slate-colored sky above him to a steely, ashen blue. The sharp striking of ironwood upon stone echoed in the sweep between mountain peaks like the crack of distant thunder.

His legs ached. His thighs burned with acid fatigue. His breathing was thin and quick. He wanted nothing more than to stop and rest but he kept climbing, hunched over his walking stick. Climbing ever higher. Dense, impossibly heavy feet rising step after step.

At the top of the saddle, the stairs stopped and a platform of stone nestled upon a crag overlooking the leeward mountainside. Crags and bluffs of rock surrounded the platform, softened only by a dry, withered layer of grass and brush. He stopped at the top of the stairs, not willing to look to the right side of the platform where more stairs climbed steeply up the Serpent's Peak. He leaned upon his stick and panted, his muscles quivering from overexertion. His spine was a red-hot wire close to snapping.

Limping to the edge of the platform, he looked out at the eastern side of the mountains. The ground fell steeply into low, sharp ridges of desolate rock. Only a scattering of trees clung to the gravelly stone. Far beyond the harsh land stretched an unforgiving desert, dunes as high as the mountains rolling into the horizon. Beneath the ashen sky, it all looked so bleak. When he made his first climb, the sun beating upon the faraway sands had given the sweeping mountains below a sort of majesty and glory. Through old, clouded eyes, he now saw nothing but a brutal, desolate wasteland.

Two pillars flanked the stairway up the mountain's slope. Eroded by centuries of harsh wind, the twin snakes had lost much of their intricate stonework. The serpent upon which the mountains had formed had been venerated by early man. Now only their handiwork remained; meanwhile, the Serpent was only thought of as a landmass upon which man could pray to the gods it spawned in its death. The gods that climbed its back in their ascension to the heavens. At its peak, where Ogé had fallen to his demise and taken with him the passage to the heavens, the barrier between corporeal and ethereal, that effervescent veil, was thin.

The hunters and warriors behind him could be heard laboring farther down the steps, the path behind him obscured by high bluffs and scraggly trees. Kunza-ka shouldered his bundle again and cast one final glance down the path, over the dense forest of green to the grasslands and then to the village, just a speck lost in the hills to the west. Hills of blighted yellow and brown. He began again, eyes lowered to watch his feet as he trudged up the first steps. The snakes regarded him coldly as he passed between them.

The air grew thin and, with no trees or cliffs, the wind swelled and buffeted him, rushing in his ears, droning furiously and incessantly. He put his head down, chin tucked in his skins. The head of his jaguar pelt flopped in the wind, waving in the blustering gusts rising from the forest. The teeth and bones hanging from strings rattled.

Lightheadedness made his feet clumsy. He could barely fill his lungs with this thin air. Coals smoldered there, and each breath scorched his raw throat. Hunger pangs were driven like spikes in his sides. His thoughts drifted through his exhausted mind.

Halfway up the stairs on the ridge of bare brown sandstone, his leaden foot caught the lip of a step and he stumbled, falling forward, his walking stick clattering on the stone. His knee struck the sharp edge of a step. A burst of pain shot through his leg and kept him on the ground.

"Kunza-ka!" a voice called from behind. A clamor of footsteps as the retinue raced up the stairs. He gathered his walking stick and rose to his knees, clinging to the stick like a drowning man clinging to driftwood. Obi was at his side first, taking him by the arm as the rest of the retinue gathered around him. Kunza-ka imagined vultures would have done the same had he not gotten up. Bodies crowded around him in colorful ponchos, their hands delicately lifting him to his feet.

"You must be careful," Obi said, steadying him with a hand around his thin arm.

Kunza-ka leaned against him for a moment, gathering what strength remained within his haggard old body. Then he pulled free of Obi's steadying hands and continued climbing.

"Come," he said. The rush of the fall had rattled his nerves and his voice was thin and taut. "It grows dark."

The sun hung above the village now, a hazy yellow hole in the Gray growing redder as it descended. The bitter wind was chilling enough in the warmth of the sun; when night came, the upper reaches of the world grew cold enough to freeze the blood in one's veins. The preternatural chill of the cosmos seeped through the fabric of existence, bleeding through the thin air of the mountain's peak.

He pushed forward, his retinue following his plodding pace. *How long since I last took this climb?* He had gone on the pilgrimage alone then, he remembered. *More than a decade, definitely.* He found himself leaning on his walking stick more the farther he climbed. *Fifteen, maybe. How long since the Olmez family died? Must have been at least fifteen years.* In his mind, he was returning from the pilgrimage to find the Olmez hut being emptied. The youngest Olmez girl's body being carried out, bloated and discolored. Her hair patchy and thin. Her face swollen and misshapen by the Gray.

The village grows old and weak. The young all die and the old live on to watch, useless and helpless to stop it. He felt as if he could topple over at any moment, over the edge and down the mountainside. So many children had died in the village, so many bloody stillbirths in the hands of solemn midwives, so many babies choking on their first breath of tainted air. The village's numbers had dwindled, more than halved in the last twenty years. Despite their best efforts, the crops grew stunted and shriveled in blighted fields and the few remaining livestock animals they had—llamas, draft goats, and chickens, mostly—were rheumy and malnourished. Nestled in the mountains, the husk of Kalaro lay slowly rotting away, sullied with the stench of disease and death and the stink of the burn pits. And the presence of the High Gods remained distant. As a young man, he felt their presence everywhere: in the wind rushing through his hair or the sunshine that splashed upon his skin. Yet when he called upon the gods, no one answered.

The stairs grew steeper and the mountaintop came into view. The terraces of the tiered pyramid carved from the mountain's peak loomed overhead. He could just make out the flared, high-peaked roof. Icy fingers sunk into his guts as he climbed. A chill ran down his spine, much colder than the blustering wind buffeting the climbers. Fear like shards of preternatural ice lodged in his quivering heart.

Ajawaya will strike me down before I set foot in that temple.

To come to the abode of the gods after taking part in a god's murder. It was pure arrogance that brought him up the mountain, he realized. Inside his chest, whatever smoldering resentment had been set alight more than a decade ago now guttered out in the blustery mountain winds. Whatever hope he had of saving Kalaro and himself sputtered.

Before the final stretch of stairway up to the pyramid, the steps up the mountains stopped at a small stone platform dug into the rock. A small, conical hut of stone and crumbling mortar sat on one end of the platform, overlooking the desert far on the darkening horizon. Here, the retinue began to set up camp, setting up tents or escaping from the wind in a hut not much larger than the one Omari Kusa kept to worship the Exiled Hunter in secret. Obi set Kunza-ka's cauldron down in front of the stairway up to the pyramid.

"You should rest before you make the final climb," Obi said to him, catching him staring at the temple, an ornately carved building of stone the color of dark jade and weathered by rain and wind. An altar of black rock sat in front of the temple, the slab of rock stained with centuries-old blood.

"No," Kunza-ka said, cursing the word as he said it. His legs were burning and he wanted nothing more than to rest, but he knew there was no time. "No, I must go now."

He started up the final stairway, his legs shaking with each step. The untamed rock on either side of him soon fell away, replaced by wide terraces. The terraces were as tall as a man and made of smooth gray limestone, cracked and crumbling at the corners. With great effort he climbed. Halfway up, a sudden gravity slowed his footsteps, the thin air condensing around his feet like mud. Both his body and his mind screamed for him to stop, but he continued his climb until he hauled himself onto the flat peak.

From the top of the pyramid, the entire mountain range stretched before him. Kalaro and the highlands to his right, blocking the last remnants of sun sinking into the horizon. His fingers traced ancient grooves and nicks in the basalt as he shuffled around the altar. The walls of the temple were a tableau of complex carvings, faded by time but still quite visible. The shape of a snake twisted around the doorway, coiling around the shapes of other ancient gods, its plumed head curled at the top of the wall, fanged maw enveloping another nameless god lost to time—this god a mass of twisting tentacles.

The temple was dark as he entered, only a sliver of twilight entering the doorway with him. Five shrines stood positioned along the three walls of the temple, with a sixth shrine lying on the floor, reduced to rubble and dust hundreds of years ago. Bits of iron and the dried husks of withered palm fronds among the debris. From the five intact shrines came a fluttering glow, faint against the stone walls. A large brazier burned in the center of the sanctum. The eternal flames were now little more than smoldering coals.

Kunza-ka laid his bundle on the floor and rifled through a year's worth of herbs and offerings, gathering a modest offering to each god and placing them upon each bed of coals. The offering bowls were blackened with the soot and smoke of centuries of burnt oblations. Small bundles of dried herbs tied with string offered to each god. Myrrh and sweetgrass to Matara. Verbena and hemp to Aséshassa. Tobacco dusted with phosphorus to Ajawaya erupted in a plume of gold flame. Amaranth and braided reeds to Mito. Sage and garlic to Talara. Calming, fragrant smoke began to fill the temple, thin tendrils rising from the altars to high, smoke-blackened ceiling. He hung a cracked sheet of leather across the doorway as the smoke swirled around the room, with only a small grate in the ceiling to allow its escape.

Whispered mantras mingled with the rising smoke in the cold stone temple. After a while, he heard Obi outside with the two hens they brought along squawking in alarm. He stepped outside the temple and into the torchlight. The hunters stood around the altar while Obi stood by the temple doorway, a hen's leg in each hand. Hanging upside down, the birds flapped and squawked.

Kunza-ka stood at the top of the world. Beneath a blank black sky, he recited a prayer.

"To the Twins of Life, Matara and Talara. To the Sage of Bronze and his everlasting wisdom, Aséshassa. To the Keeper of the Fount and Guide on the River of Souls, Mito the Eternal. And to Ajawaya, the Luminous King, Holiest of Holies, and Lord of Storm and Star. We offer to you all that we mortals have and may hope to have. With all the reverence the soul of men can offer. All the devotion a short, mortal lifespan can offer. To all gods, High and Low, we revere you and devote ourselves to you wholeheartedly. I beseech you, please forgive our transgressions and grant us mercy mortals such as we do not deserve."

Obi held a hen by its legs above the altar. When Kunza-ka approached, hand outstretched, the bird flapped its wings and squawked. His hand was slow and clumsy as it reached for the hen's head, taking a few sharp pecks, but soon enough he had hold of the bird's head. He pulled its neck taut and with a quick, firm motion the obsidian blade opened its throat. Blood poured from its neck and splashed onto the altar, where it ran in swirling channels carved into the black stone.

The other hen did not struggle when Kunza-ka took it by the head. Its body jerked as the blade sliced through its neck but that was all the resistance it offered. Even some animals knew the futility of such struggle. One's life was never one's own. It was given and was taken and there was no stopping that.

Kunza-ka took the dripping bodies into the temple to portion them out to the Gods. The heads to Aséshassa, the hearts to Ajawaya, the blood to Mito, the guts to Talara, and the meat to Matara. The smell of sizzling fat and charred flesh filled the temple. Smoke stung his eyes and irritated his throat. From his pack, he took a slice of dried dream cactus and, kneeling in front of the shrines, he put it to his lips.

"I prostrate myself before the throne of gods and the Heavens themselves, a lowly man before the holiest of all so that you may bless me with your divine presence." He put the wafer of dried cactus on his tongue and chewed, acrid bitterness filling his mouth as he mashed it into a dry paste and forced it down his throat. His tongue fished pieces from the gaps in his teeth. He put his forehead to the ground. "I prostrate myself before the Gods, a lowly man unworthy of the celestial."

A strange boiling started in his empty stomach, which twisted and knotted in cramps. He rose from his prostration and, with his watery eyes shut, breathed deeply and drew smoke deep in his lungs. The more he breathed, the more he could feel the smoke swirling around him, heavy against his skin. With some effort, he cleared his mind of worldly thoughts, banishing them like the sun evaporates early morning fog, and opened his soul to the Cosmos.

Lightheadedness swelled in his skull, buoying his mind high above the mortal plane. His body sloughed from his spirit. A moment of fear rose and then passed. He opened his eyes, serene and at peace. Thick currents of smoke writhed around him, shapes danced behind the curtain of smoke and mist, hidden in the sheer thinness of a veil no mortal would ever pierce. He waited for something to emerge from the maelstrom of smoke, for some figure to coalesce in the fog.

It was morning when the smoke finally cleared and the psychedelic euphoria faded from his mind. He lay on the cold floor, threads of smoke still filtering through the grate in the ceiling. Muted light shone down on him, segmented by the grate. He rose and began preparing more offerings of yams and corn. His dry mouth watered as he placed the offerings on the coals of each shrine, but he ate nothing, choosing to kneel in the middle of the sanctum again and chew upon mantras until his hunger abated. He would commune with the Gods or starve to death. They would not ignore him this time.

CHAPTER 13

The day after the ka-man left for the mountains, Kimi died. She had not suffered. She had not even made a sound. Odessa's mother had woken up to find Kimi stiff in her cradle, eyes half-lidded, lips parted from her last, tiny breath. Her blanket had not even been tousled. Little Kimi had just slipped from this world as one dips into a warm bath.

With no one to perform funerary rites, the family did the best they could to ensure her soul would reach Matara's embrace. Wrapped in a linen shroud and laid in a basket of woven reeds, they prayed Mito would be kind and guide poor Kimi's spirit along the River of Souls.

Odessa's mother and father refused to immolate her in the burn pits with goats and chickens and plague-ridden blankets. Omari built a pyre in the backyard, a small one fit for an infant. Odessa offered to help, to busy herself and distract herself from her grief, but her father told her to tend to Ayana. He alone built the funeral pyre, silently hacking at dead limbs and stacking them. His tears fell without a sound, flowing freely as he worked.

Since Ayana's birth, no one in the Kusa family had died. Ayana never had to confront the unrelenting sting of grief and loss until now. The hole in her, the empty place in her heart that could not be filled—she did not understand it. Death had been a vague concept to her, always present, always taking from other families, but never hers.

Odessa sat on a cushion in the hut and held a whimpering Ayana.

"It's all right," she whispered. "Kimi is in a much better place. Where she's never hungry and she's with grandpa and grandma."

Odessa babbled, trying in vain to keep her voice from quivering.

"You never met grandma and I don't remember her well, but I do remember she always made me laugh. I'm sure she's making Kimi laugh just the same right now." She kept her eyes on Ayana, not daring to look at her mother hunched over Kimi's basket, stroking the baby's face and sobbing hoarsely in long, ragged spurts.

Ubiko came, his face thin and sallow, carrying a bouquet of wilting sweet-grass and amaranth, an offering to Matara and Mito. Usually, an offering to Talara was in order to rid the deceased of their burdensome sin so they would not sink in the River of Souls. But since Kimi was an innocent baby, there was no need for absolution. He set the bouquet on the floor beside the basket and whispered condolences to Odessa's mother. They hugged and for a while, everyone in the hut clung on to someone else, people drowning in grief together.

After a while, Ubiko crouched next to Odessa and Ayana. "How are you girls doing?" he asked, a hand on Ayana's trembling shoulder. "Are you holding up all right?"

Ayana lifted her head and sniffled. "She was my little baby sister. Wasn't even old enough to talk yet."

"I know," he said, voice thick and husky. "I know. It's not fair."

Odessa looked at the lump growing on his neck. She swallowed and spoke the words she had not dared to utter. "Is it our fault? Because we killed Egende. Is that why Kimi died?" Her words shook as they spilled from her mouth. She tried to blink tears away, but they ran down her cheeks in rivers. "Is it my fault?"

Ubiko swept her and Ayana in a hug, squeezing them tight. Crying into his shoulder, Odessa tried to ignore how thin he had gotten and how bony his shoulder had become.

"No, no," he said. "Of course not! It's this damned plague of Gray. This has been going on for longer than you've been alive. How could it be your fault, silly girl?"

Her father entered, dappled with sweat, his white tunic dotted with wood chips and splinters. He knelt beside her mother and laid a hand on her shoulder. "It's time."

Another harsh sob bubbled from deep within her mother's chest, her very soul, and Odessa had to bite back a sob herself. Her father hugged her and she clung to him, if only to stop him from taking Kimi's funeral bundle for a moment longer.

They followed her father out of the hut and into the backyard, a procession in all white, ignoring the neighbors watching and whispering. Her father laid Kimi in her basket atop the pyre and set the bouquet of sweetgrass and amaranth inside with her, then began to cover the pyre in long, dry reeds. Ubiko held Odessa's mother, rubbing her back as she stifled cries in her hand.

Odessa could not stop crying. No matter how much she scolded herself and told herself to be strong for Ayana, the tears came. She tried to tell herself that this was not her fault. That Kimi had always been a sickly baby. But deep down, in the core of herself, she knew her curse had killed her. The evil she harbored in the dark lines throughout her arm had brought this sickness. The god's blood that had spilled and mixed with her own now radiated evil, and it was poisoning the entire village. Poor Kimi had just been the first to succumb to it.

Before he lay the last few reeds on the pyre, her father parted the leaves and stalks and gave Kimi a final kiss on the forehead.

"I'm sorry," he said, the words coming out choked and cracking. "I love you."

He laid the reeds over her face.

From the hearth in the hut, he put a few hot coals in an earthen firepot and brought it to the pyre, carefully laying them atop a bed of soft tinder at the base of the pyre. One gentle puff of breath coaxed the coals to life and he stepped back, flames leaping to embrace the wood. He took Odessa's mother from Ubiko and hugged her tight.

When the flames had engulfed the base of the pyre, her mother let go of her father, wiped her eyes, and stepped to the pyre.

"Please gods," she said, low and hoarse. "Any gods, High or Low, please forgive us. Please bring my little Kimi to Matara's side. She didn't do anything wrong. Whatever we did, she didn't do anything."

The reeds atop the pyre caught flame, curling as fire crawled along the length of them. Her mother's hands crept to her face, almost covering her eyes. "She didn't hurt anybody."

It was not the first child she had lost; Odessa had seen a mother's pain before, the despair of a stillbirth or a plague death. A mother's heart was never hardened by the death of her child. It never got easier to bear.

"Please," her mother whispered. "Please, gods above." Her words faded into stifled cries and whimpers. Her father was at her side, holding her around her shoulders, the both of them watching the fire consume the pyre. Soft smoke rose to the heavens, Kimi's soul drifting to the stars far above the clouds.

The river issued from the northern foothills of the Arabako Forest and ran down along the northern edge of the village to the hills of the south where it poured into Lake Nahbe. Walking slowly along the river path with a clay pot of Kimi's ashes, Odessa's family reached the riverbank. The water was cloudy and slow-moving.

Her mother crouched at the edge of the clay riverbank, the urn cradled against her breast. "Mito, guide my little Kimi." She kissed the glazed clay and then tipped it out over the river. Ashes caught in the wind, somersaulted in the air, flakes of mortality rising to the aether. Most of the ashes landed in the water, to be swept away in the current, bobbing along and churning into the silt below. Back to the earth from which she had come.

On the shore, Ayana wrapped her arms around her mother's waist and her mother embraced her. Odessa went to hug her mother, to feel the comforting touch and the maternal warmth that had soothed her so many times in her life.

Yet when Odessa touched her mother, she could feel her mother's body stiffen. The tension in her mother's body as she hugged her lessened but did not entirely dissipate. When she stepped away, Odessa noticed a strange look in her mother's eyes as they quickly darted away from hers. Odessa stood on the riverbank, watching her mother take Ayana by the hand and lead her to the gentle consolation of the Kusa elders.

When the funeral procession returned to the hut, it seemed empty and lifeless. Ubiko and another of their extended family went to the hearth, the same hearth that had served to send Kimi to the heavens, and began preparing yam soup with onions, garlic, and chilis, trying to fill the hut with comforting scents to mask the misery permeating the air like dank mildew. Ayana helped make a doughy mixture of corn flour and cassava starch to dip in the soup, busying her small hands with kneading.

Her father and mother sat together on the far wall, leaning against one another, holding hands and supporting each other like two felled trees staying upright through mutual effort. Occasionally, they whispered to one another, grief heavy on their faces. More than anything, they comforted each other in their shared misery.

As the soup simmered, other villagers began trickling in to give their condolences to the grieving parents. The noise in the hut grew louder. All around her conversations rose, but no one spoke to Odessa as she sat by Kimi's empty cradle. No one so much as glanced in her direction. A barrier she had not been aware of had been erected, an invisible wall separating her from everyone else. Beneath the long, billowing sleeves of her white kaftan, her fingernails dug into the bandages around her arm.

After a while, Odessa could take no more. Ostracized in her own home, left alone with a tumult of grief and guilt, she was falling apart. Emotion came surging through the cracks of her brittle mind state. She stood up and walked to the door. Conversations quieted as she passed. She felt a lump growing in her throat again and her eyes misted. She went outside, sidestepping a pair of elderly villagers walking to the door.

She stumbled to the backyard, half-blind with tears, and hid in the small hut next to their shrine to Ogé, head in her hands. She could still feel her mother's body tensing at her touch. She could still see the accusing look in her mother's eyes. The aggrieved resentment. *She thinks it's my fault. I killed Kimi.*

Set around the shrine were small wicker totems. Fresh blood was drying in the dirt in front of the shrine. Superstition had infected her father as well, it seemed. Evil eyes carved into the walls watched her cry all alone, consumed by guilt and grief.

CHAPTER 14

A third day atop the mountain arrived, and Kunza-ka could put it off no longer. The hunters were getting restless. They wanted to be in the lowlands, raiding and gathering offerings. But he had to make the gods hear his prayers. He had to get their attention.

After two straight days of prayer, days spent drifting in the smoke of visions to find nothing but specters moving beyond the veil of the Cosmos, Kunza-ka had nothing to show for it. Smoke wafted through the leather flap as he stepped outside into the tremulous light of dawn. Obi stood outside, waiting.

"Nothing?" Obi asked.

"Nothing." Kunza-ka walked to the altar and pressed his hands against the blood stained stone. The altar's surface was still tacky with blood. They had dragged a goat up the stairway last night and its blood had not dried completely.

"Then—" Obi started.

"Yes," Kunza-ka interrupted. "I'll start the preparations. Get your men ready."

Obi nodded and left down the stairs. Kunza-ka leaned against the altar a moment longer, letting the cold morning air take the smell of smoke and blood from his skin. With a sigh, he pushed off the altar and went back inside the temple.

Morning had spilled into the mountain valley by the time Kunza-ka emerged again, a small calabash bowl in his hands. He descended the steps as the camp was rousing. The hunters crowded around the bottom of the stairs before he even reached the last ten steps. Questions filled the air. Some of the hunters were looking especially sick, the lumps and sores on their body inflamed and angry.

"Calm down, everyone. Calm down."

The hunters parted, assisted by the warriors in their red quilted cotton suits, and Kunza-ka descended the last few steps.

Adura stepped forward as Kunza-ka made his way toward the fire flickering in front of the small hut. "What's happened? What are we doing?"

Kunza-ka stopped, his back turned to the crowd. His breath was caught in his throat. He swallowed, working some saliva into his dry mouth.

"I don't know how to say this." He turned to face them. "The gods—" His voice failed him and he swallowed again. "The gods are silent. I'm sorry."

The hunters began to chatter, complaining that they had wasted precious time that could have been spent in the lowlands. Kunza-ka loudly cleared his throat.

"Prayer has failed and I apologize for that. It is clear we must get their attention another way. Adura, you were right. The gods require blood."

He raised the calabash, milky brown liquid sloshing inside. "But first, we drink in the name of the High Gods above. The blood that is to be shed is for them alone. May they be merciful and bless us in the days to come." He took a small sip from the gourd, the taste of fermented corn and cacao strong and overwhelming to his dry palate. After he swallowed, a bitter note lingered on his tongue. He held the bowl out to the hunters.

Adura took it and glanced inside before taking a sip and passing it along.

"Be strong, my friends. Be brave. The gods will smile upon us again."

Everyone took a draught, letting the thick drink nourish them. Obi was the last to take a small sip and returned the bowl to Kunza-ka. From a pouch in his skirt, Obi took a bundle of coca leaves and tucked a few in his mouth. Kunza-ka took a few as well and turned his back to the crowd of hunters still milling about, readying themselves for war. He stuffed the leaves in his mouth and chewed, grinding them until they were paste, sucking the bitter juice from the pulpy wad.

Obi strode through the crowd, handing each one of his warriors a few coca leaves.

In a few minutes, the hunters were stumbling about, confused. A few minutes more, and they began dropping to the floor, their eyes fluttering shut beneath the weight of Matara's mercy. It had been a relatively potent dosage. With the small sip he had taken, even Kunza-ka was feeling the sedative draw of unconsciousness upon his limbs. He took a few more coca leaves from Obi and chewed them sluggishly, like a goat chewing cud. They did not have many coca leaves since it only grew at lower altitudes, too close to the Night Jungle to safely cultivate any more. The other warriors stood among the falling hunters, shoving them away when the hunters stumbled toward them asking what was happening. Obi and his warriors had barely wet their lips, so they stood wide awake as everyone else slumped upon the stone.

Once all the hunters had sunk deep in the murk of unconsciousness, the warriors, in pairs, began hauling the them up the steps to the altar.

Obi steadied Kunza-ka as he tried to stagger toward the stairs. "Are you well? Did you take too much?"

He shook his head. *I only drank enough to assure them,* he told himself, but still his feet dragged, unbelievably heavy. The coca leaves were reviving him, gradually overwhelming the sedative calm of Matara's mercy.

It was not long before the warriors had finished carrying the hunters up to the altar. With Obi's help, he ascended the stairs. His heavy feet caught the edge of a step with nearly every step. His mind was clearing but his body was numb and deadened. His thoughts were still muddled, but in a vague sense, he was glad for it. It cushioned him from the harsh reality of what was to come. What he had to do.

The altar stood before him now. The massive slab of rock cold to the touch. His head hung as he leaned upon it. He had barely enough strength in his numbed body to stay upright. On the face of the altar lay the obsidian knife. The glassy surface of the knapped blade looked like the waves of a pitch-black sea. He picked it up, the carved jade handle smooth and comforting in his hand.

Obi laid Adura's nude body on the altar. Her skin prickled with goosebumps. Her eyelids fluttered in whatever dreamscape she found herself in. Kunza-ka blinked and swallowed hard, trying to focus on the knife in his hand and nothing more.

"May Talara cleanse your soul," he muttered, words slurring together in a smeared mumble. "And may Mito guide you to Matara's pleasant shores. We give your soul to the gods so they may forgive us our sins. The cycle of life continues. This death begets life. May the gods watch over you once more. Be brave, young warrior."

The blade hung over her, his hand trembling. Her breathing was soft, whispering through her lips. He placed a gnarled hand on the smooth skin of her arm. Her pulse was strong. She was warm.

The blade was so wickedly sharp that it took almost no effort to open her throat. He dragged the blade from one side of her neck to the other in one fluid motion. For a split second as the blade parted her skin, no blood came out. Then it poured from her open neck in throbbing pulses. Her body jerked. A wet gurgling as she choked on blood and wheezed out the slash in her neck. Blood sprayed in the air, propelled by her last breath.

After few moments, the throbbing pulses of blood slowed. Her body was still. Hot blood ran in the channels of the altar, winding grooves along the smooth stone surface, draining off the sides into channels that ran down the pyramid tiers. Blood dripped in small, sporadic drops on the stone around the altar.

Her eyes were still closed, giving her an almost peaceful air about her despite the bloody gash in her neck. He poised the blade above her chest, the tip dancing in his trembling hand.

The point plunged between her breasts, in between the ribs and sternum. He carved, careful not to pry with the brittle blade. Hesitant fingers reached into her warm chest cavity. Prying with all the strength his faint, frail arms could muster, he cracked her rib cage open.

Heat radiated from her open chest. It still quivered in sporadic spasms. He carved it from her chest, the blood pouring over his wrists as he pulled it out and held it cupped in both hands. He held it out to the heavens, dripping blood on the altar.

"I offer this heart to you, gods of all and everything. I offer this life to you as proof of our devotion. Forgive us our transgressions, and take this heart as recompense."

With heavy feet and heavy heart, he carried Adura's heart into the temple and placed it on the coals of the large brazier in the center of the temple. Tongues of flame lapped greedily at the bloody lump, swallowing it whole.

By the time he emerged again, Adura's body was gone and another hunter's had replaced it. He took up the knife again and repeated the process. Stabbing and cutting over and over.

The sun was high in the hazy sky by the time he finished. His arms were stained with blood up to the elbows. The warriors had retreated down the steps, silent and sullen. They were no strangers to death, but this was unlike anything the young men and women would have seen. But to Kunza-ka, the blood drying on his hands was a familiar sight.

In the smoke-filled room, he could hear the rustling feathers of vultures outside coming to dispose of what was left of the hunters. Their bodies remained strewn around the altar, gutted and drained of blood. Everything of value burning in the fires of the shrines. A lonely funeral in the sky was all Adura and the rest could be afforded. A gruesome and greedy procession hissing outside.

Kunza-ka took a piece of dream cactus in his bloody hands and ate it, tasting the hunters' bitter sacrifice. Their blood was on his tongue, the taste of iron mixed with acrid cactus. Mumbled chants and slurred mantras tumbled from his mouth, exhaustion and sedation fogging his mind. Faint tendrils of delirium crept in through the black spots growing in his vision. The dream cactus swirled like smoke in his skull, euphoria wrapping around the delirious thoughts, silken and intoxicating.

The smoke grew thick and heavy and dark. Swathes of smoke hung above the stone floor like mists rising from an icy lake, swirling around the ka-man as his head drooped in drug-addled prayer.

The temple was dark, almost pure blackness. Shapes moved in the shadows through the pall of smoke. Through shifting, churning curtains of mist, the fires of the shrines shone like flickering suns, each so far away that barely any light could filter through the thick smoke. In the periphery of his vision, figures danced. Figures so mockingly clear in the corner of his eye, only to disappear when he turned.

The smoke against his skin was cold and damp. The rank stench of decay. A gust of wet wind brushed against the back of his neck. The hairs on his neck rose at the touch.

"Ka-man," a raspy voice like metal dragged on stone spoke behind him. "Do you fear death?"

CHAPTER 15

Kunza-ka stammered soundlessly, mouth opening and closing with no voice. Suddenly, his mind was blank. He licked his dry lips and worked some moisture into his mouth, the taste of blood and coca leaf now a dry film on his tongue.

"My goddess." He put his forehead to the frigid stone. "With the gods to guide me in the afterlife, I fear nothing." Even he could hear the insincerity in his choked voice. The quivering of his words as they left his lips.

"You would be wise to fear death, ka-man." Another gust of wind, putrid breath from a gruesome maw just inches from the back of his neck. The hair there stood on end. His skin prickled. "The gods guide you no longer. Your soul is burdened with great sin. When you die, you will sink like a stone."

Frozen, unable to move, the smoke coalesced and slithered. The smell of decay constricted around him, choking the air from his lungs.

"You think you know pain," the goddess said. "You do not. But you will. When you sink into the maelstrom and your soul is ripped and rent and torn asunder. When your mind finally crumbles and you become yet another drop in that swirling, seething ocean of torment, that is when you will truly know pain. That is when you will truly know fear. That fear you should have afforded the gods, you will know it then. All of you godkillers will know it then."

Dank smoke slithered across the small of his back, a tentacle of dampness causing his skin to ripple in gooseflesh. It grew heavy across his back and he buckled beneath its weight, pressed against the cold floor.

"Cleanse me then, great eater of sin. Take the sin from my people, I beseech you, and I will serve you for the rest of my days. "

"A human's lifespan is but a fleeting moment to a god such as I. And an old man's days are fewer still. What use are you to me, ka-man?"

His eyes squeezed tight, his mind scrambling for an answer. What could a man possibly offer a god?

"You have much hubris to come before the gods and make such demands. You ask for absolution? There is no salvation for godkillers. Your people will die. There is nothing you can do."

"Talara, my goddess." The words trembled like a cornered mouse. "Please, I gave you the hearts of the godkillers. The rest of my people are innocent."

"Innocent?" The smoke swelled above him, crushing the air from his lungs. "Not one of your people is innocent. Not only were you all complicit in the murder of a god, you allowed a man to profane the sacred, the divine, with black magic. You allowed a man to steal that which makes the gods divine."

"I-I don't understand."

"The Forsaken girl," Talara rasped, voice echoing off the temple walls obscured in shadow and smoke. "Her father took the boar god's lifeblood and stole its divinity with profane magics. It festers within his daughter's tainted blood now, a catalyst for all manner of wickedness. He created an abomination and you have allowed it to pervert and defile your people."

"I thought she would die on her own."

"But she did not. She lived. Even now, she grows stronger. Her corrupting influence spreads. A disease gnawing through your people."

"What can I do, my goddess?" Kunza-ka croaked, the pressure on his back squeezing the air from his lungs. "I will do anything. Please."

"You dare lie to me, ka-man?" Talara's voice was sharp and brittle like obsidian scraped along bone. "Your faith is weak. Your dedication vacillates at the slightest resistance. I see what you are, ka-man. I know what you are. You would forsake each and every one of your people if it means you would live."

He shook his head, forehead scraping the floor. "That's not true. Everything I do is for the sake of my people. I— " His words were cut short in a pained wheeze as the tendrils of coalescing smoke flattened him to the floor.

"Liar," Talara hissed.

Black spots burned at the periphery of his vision as he kicked and clawed at the floor. Feebly, piteously squirming. Primitive, animalistic fear flooded his mind, black and frigid. Fear eroded all that he was, washing away the superficial trapping that made him who he was. He was no ka-man. He was no man. He was a boy. A frightened boy.

"No more lies," Talara whispered. "You blind yourself. Your eyes deceive you, turning away from the truths of the world." The goddess's presence bore down on him a moment longer and then relaxed a bit. "Your lack of faith, your worldly attachments, they sit upon your eyes like cataracts." Her voice was softer like coarse sand ground against the back of his neck. "Open your eyes. Speak the truth."

A whisper came, softly against his ear. "Do you fear death, Kunza of Kalaro?"

"Yes," he blurted without a thought. "Yes, goddess. I don't want to die."

The weight upon his back lifted and he sucked in a deep breath, hacking and coughing as smoky air rushed into his lungs.

"Good," Talara said, the word seeming to surround Kunza-ka, comforting him as he coughed and wiped tears from his eyes. "Good. When my brother and my sister and I conspired to make humanity, we gave you short lifespans for a reason, ka-man. And that reason, that is why you should be very afraid of death." Kunza-ka was on his hands and knees, retching and heaving. "Death is my domain and, let me assure you, it is something to be feared."

"Please," Kunza-ka said, his voice hoarse. "Please spare me. Spare us. Cleanse us of our sins."

"That is not something done easily. There must be recompense."

"I will give you Omari. And the girl." He rose, eyes searching the smoky void around him, a hand nervously scratching at a burst boil on his neck. "I will give you everyone if you just take this damnable curse from me."

"If you want absolution," Talara's voice, like the rumble of an opening tomb, moved from behind one ear to the other, "then you must rid yourself of that weakness that allowed this abominable disaster to occur in the first place." Shivers ran down his spine and icy fear poured through his guts. The goddess drew close. The damp cold against his skin tightened deeper in his flesh like frostbite. "Rid yourself of such weakness. Give me your sin, ka-man. Give me those eyes that have deceived you so. See clearly once more, Kunza of Kalaro."

His mouth was dry again. Cold sweat leaked down the small of his back. "What do you mean, goddess?"

"Cut out those eyes that have led you astray. Those eyes that were blind to all that was holy around you. Pluck them out and cast them into the fire of my shrine."

He didn't remember picking up the knife, yet there it was in his hand. Still wet from the hunters' sacrifice. Protests rose to his quivering lips and died unsaid. Smoke curled around him, dank and smelling of decay. It slithered around his body and guided him to his feet before melting away and retreating to the shadows residing in churning whorls of smoke.

Stumbling feet carried him forward to the flickering light of Talara's shrine. Like a distant star, it shimmered in the pitch black. Smoke swirled about him.

He leaned against Talara's shrine, a gnarled stone pillar with a bowl set in the top. Around the bowl coiled a pile of stone entrail, and from the back of the shrine a stone ribcage rose, flaring around the bowl like a scalloped shell around a pearl. A bed of coals burned red in the bowl and lit his white-painted face a deep orange. Smoke boiled up the sides of the bowl and down to the floor, pooling at his feet. On trembling legs, knife clutched in a trembling hand, he let out a quavering breath. *Oh gods, give me strength.*

Hesitantly, his thumb and index finger rose and pried his eyelids wide despite their twitching protests. His eye watered. The tip of the razor-sharp blade came unsteadily toward it, the glassy surface of knapped obsidian reflecting the hellish glow of coals. The eye quivered and jerked and spun wildly in its socket. The cords in his neck stood out through his thin, wrinkled skin, resisting the urge to pull away from the knifepoint wavering a hair's breadth away.

"Do it," Talara said. Talara's form hid half-obscured in the dark, massive in the spacious sanctum of smoke and shadow. Writhing tentacles made of entrails were coiled on the floor, slick with mucus and mold and lichen. A filth-stained bat's head with an upturned nose and rows upon rows of sharp yellowed teeth sat almost out of sight atop the tangled mass of slithering entrails. Talara's body, from which the entrails spilled, lay shrouded in the darkness, a spongy, serpentine body, putrid and half-decayed. "Cut out your eye, ka-man and you will be forgiven. Your sins will be mine to bear."

As soon as the knife's point touched the delicate pink membrane of his eye socket, Kunza-ka screamed, hoarse and inhuman. Blood welled from around the very tip of the blade and poured down his cheek. His eye tried to roll back into his skull, but he rammed the blade in deeper. He wheeled back from the altar but would not pull the knife out. He dug the blade into his eye, slicing around the circumference of it. His eyelids fluttered, trying to blink away his fingers and the blade. Blood ran down his neck and chest in a river of crimson. After he had cut around his eye, he pulled the knife out and collapsed onto the floor in front of the altar. The knife skittered across the floor. Smoke spun around him, swirling greedily as blood fell on the floor in fat drops.

"Put it in the fire," Talara said. "Burn it in my name."

He shook his head in short, weak jerks. Pain lanced through his skull, white hot agony filling his brain.

"Rid yourself of your weakness or you and the rest of your people die for it."

With a sobbing moan, his fingers, clumsy and slick with blood, reached up to his face and pushed past his drooping, half-closed eyelids. He dug in the socket and pulled at the gooey remains. His body shook and spasmed as a long cry came through his gritted teeth. A squelching, sucking noise, then a tear as he pulled free the eye from its moorings. Another scream rose to fill the temple, echoing off the walls as he rolled on the floor. His consciousness ebbed, melting into darkness, but he clung to it, resisting the reprieve. Fist squeezing the sinewy clump of bloody eye, he rolled onto his knees and crawled toward the shrine.

Pulling himself up to the shrine, fingers burning on the hot stone, he tossed the gob of eye onto the coals, where it sizzled and popped. His knees gave out and he slumped against the shrine, crying as he held onto consciousness with a loose, tenuous grip. Raw pain radiated from the pit of gore in his head. Strands of bloody viscera hung from his lashes. Between ragged panting, he sobbed.

"Good," Talara whispered. Her bat head drew nearer, her eyes obsidian-hued in the glow of the shrine. Slick entrails brushed his legs. "Good, ka-man. Now the other."

"I can't !" he howled.

"But you must."

"I can't do it !"

"You wish to be a half-blind fool with a tainted soul and no village?"

Collapsed against the floor, he could only weep, blubbering and gasping for air. The pain was too much.

A tentacle slithered up his chest and brushed his cheek. It was heavy yet gaseous, made of smoke and magic. The entrail gingerly caressed his face, easing the pain pounding through his skull. "Fear not, ka-man. You will not be without reward. Do this for me and I will make you whole." Another tentacle slid across his lap and dropped the knife in his limp hands. "Now cut the other eye out and regain my favor."

He nodded, whimpering as he lifted the blade to his teary eye. Still numb with shock, he plunged the knife up into the center of his eye and was swallowed up in total nothingness. Pain lanced like a spear through his head as he blindly sliced around the eyeball. When the eye was loosened from its socket, he let the knife clatter to the floor again. Clumsy fingers felt around his bloody face before reaching into the socket and pulling the stringy pulp from his head.

Guided by slick tentacles, he hauled himself up to the shrine and dropped his second eye in the coals. A sizzling droplet spat out by the heat landed on his cheek. He could barely stand. The stink of his own eyes rendering on the hot coals stung his nostrils and made him lightheaded. He clung to the coiled rim of the bowl, using all his strength to remain upright.

"Now," Talara said. "As a boon for your devotion, take from the coals your new eyes."

Hesitant hands ventured out, patting the scorching rim of the bowl and slowly working their way down to the coals. His own voice came, eerily distant from himself. "Where are they?"

Two thin tentacles wrapped from his elbows went down around his hands and led them into the searing hot coals. His skin reddened. He tried to pull away, but the tentacles were unyielding.

"Here," Talara said, forcing his hands into the coals. "Take them."

His eyes had rendered into a puddle on two round coals, both burning impossibly hot. His fingertips scalded, blistered at the mere touch. He plucked the coals from the bowl in two tight, sizzling fists. The tentacles pulled his hands toward his face. A hiss of pain as the coals pressed into the bloody skin of his eyelids, pushing deeper into empty sockets. Blood and gore hissed and popped. His flesh melted around the coals, embracing them as blood bubbled on their red-hot surface. His own hissing gasp turned into a high-pitched scream.

He fell to the floor, smoke weighing heavy on him like dirt upon a grave. Consciousness faded as he writhed, hands cupped over his face. Smoke drifted from between his fingers as the coals burned deeper in his head. Hot, sticky blood oozed around his fingers.

"You've done well. I must say I am surprised. The eyes have not killed you." The stench of death drew closer. Almost overwhelming in its sickly-sweet foulness. "You may prove worthy of my blessing after all."

The coals in his head were beginning to cool, quenched in his blood. Talara's form towered above him. The rank stench was almost palpable. His smoldering eyes fell upon her, seeing her like a shimmering mirage of static color in the swirling black. His head swayed and then fell to the floor. He felt his body relax as unconsciousness dragged him further into the murky black.

"Rest well, my servant," Talara whispered. "You have much to do."

"What do you want?" he cried weakly, barely more than a mumble as he slipped deeper into unconsciousness.

"I want the girl." Talara's voice was quiet and gentle. "I want her to become the foundation of a new world. A world of gods and men. And you, ka-man, you will help me bring this dream to fruition. You will be my champion."

Talara's form dissipated in a swirling cloud of smoke. The darkness bled from the temple and Kunza-ka was alone and unconscious on the floor. His dimly glowing eyes stared blankly from a mess of melted flesh beneath his brows. The first human to receive a High God's blessing lay on the temple floor, covered in tears and blood.

CHAPTER 16

The ka-man returned to Kalaro sometime in the early morning, in time to lead the daily lamentation. By midday, the village was abuzz with activity. Odessa was watching from the window as a group of villagers left down the eastern road. Omari sat dragging the stone along the edge of his spear again and again to sharpen it. He had not slept in days. His body ached and his sores were fat and purple and malignant.

"A lot of commotion by the Elder's Lodge," Odessa said. Her voice was a bit hoarse. She had spent the entire morning wracked with coughing fits. Over the last few days, Omari had noticed she was radiating heat again. Walking past her was like brushing against a forge.

"Get away from that window," Mutumi snapped from a mat on the floor, where she sat weaving at the small loom she had brought inside ever since the village had become tense. She did not even slow her weaving, the wooden shuttle of red yarn sliding back and forth across the loom. Her tired and irritable eyes flashing at Odessa for an instant—the only time they left her work. "You're making me anxious with all your peeping."

Mutumi had returned from bringing a bedridden Ubiko a small breakfast of warm porridge a few hours earlier and since then, her demeanor had been especially grim and dour.

Odessa let the shutter drop. "What do you think they're doing?"

Mutumi said nothing and instead shot Odessa a disapproving glare as the girl began to pace, rubbing at her bandaged arm.

Omari spat on the stone and flipped the spearhead over to sharpen the other side. Mutumi rarely spoke more than a few words at a time since Kimi's death. When he asked her how Ubiko was feeling, she had given him little more than a dismissive, unenthusiastic grunt before sitting down and attending her weaving.

The strain between Omari and Mutumi had lessened in their shared grief, but he could still feel a distance between them. Holding her in his arms, her body collapsing into his, there was little warmth. Ayana came inside with a small handful of flowers, the last of the mountain lilies. "Did you see? The ka-man's already leaving!" She went to the shrine built for Kimi beneath the windowsill, a small shrine beside many others the Kusa family had lost.

"Going back up the mountain, I assume. While people are dying, our ka-man leaves us," Mutumi said, not looking up from her work at the loom.

Ayana sat down beside her mother while Odessa took a furtive peek out the window again. "Do you think Kimi will like the flowers?" Ayana asked.

Mutumi's sour disposition sweetened a bit. She glanced at the bundle of wildflowers on the shrine. "Of course she will. They're lovely."

Ayana beamed. "How was Uncle today?"

"Oh, he's feeling a bit better. But that boil on his neck continues to grow."

Ayana scratched at a lump growing on her own neck. "He'll be all right, won't he?"

"Of course! As long as he listens to his older sister." A wan smile brightened Mutumi's face.

Omari set the spear on the floor, took his knife from its sheath, and began sharpening it as well. He had honed the edges of his weapons twice already, but he had to busy his hands and his mind. There was something in the air today. Tension like a cord, frayed to its limits, about to snap. Ever since the ka-man left for the mountains, something in Kalaro had begun to shift and now it was at its limit.

Ayana looked at him but said nothing, instead staying close to her mother, almost hiding behind her as she worked.

She's afraid of me. The knife's edge rasped against the stone. *Or she resents me like her mother.*

He wiped the residue of iron shavings and spit from his blade onto the corner of his dashiki and began honing the other side. Odessa sat on the floor beside him, her feverish body making the hairs on his arm curl even at a distance. In her sleeveless tunic, he could see how thin she had become. The hollowness in her cheekbones and eyes. The rigidity of her slender arms, bones jutting beneath the skin, angular and harsh. She could barely eat anything without vomiting. Any solid food seemed too much for her fickle stomach. And now the coughing fits.

Both sides of the knife honed, he slid it in its sheath and set it on the ground beside the spear. Her bandaged hand, wrapped in linen like the mummies of Old Ebarria, idly skimmed along the spear's shaft.

Why did I do this to her? Why did I put her through all this? He'd known all along that Yakun's ritual would have ill effects. The human body was not made to withstand the rigors of divinity. To bind godsblood to mortal flesh was lunacy. *It was supposed to be me. It was always supposed to be me. Now she suffers because of my failure. The ritual did nothing but hurt her even further. She is no god of mankind. She's just a sick girl.*

He wanted to say something to her, to apologize for what he had done to her in the Arabako. But it was too late. What was done was done, irrevocably etched into the fabric of the universe. Instead, he took his quiver onto his lap and drew an arrow out, eyeing the shaft to make sure it had not warped. He checked the arrowhead, knapped flint unchipped and still sharp.

Yakun can fix her, he told himself. *He can drain the godsblood from her veins and take this curse from her. We can undo this.*

Yakun was the only person in the world who would know what to do about her affliction. He had formulated the ritual and sent Omari to the Arabako. He had to know of a way to unbind the godsblood for her body and soul. But Yakun lived on the northern edge of the Night Jungle, near Noyo. For days, Omari had ruminated over how he would convince Mutumi to join him. Day after day, he had envisioned taking his family and leaving Kalaro in the dead of night, but Mutumi would not go willingly. The Kusa family had been living in these mountains for generations.

He set an arrow in the growing pile on his lap and slid another from the quiver. *What I could I possibly say to her? She won't listen to a word I say. Not anymore.*

The hut was quiet for a long time, the air stagnant and stuffy. Midday was stretching into dusk when Mutumi set her loom work aside and took Ayana down to the river to wash some clothes. Omari tried to dissuade her, but she just glared at him and told him she would not be sequestered in the hut any longer. So he had let her leave without another word.

"Papa?" Odessa's voice came hesitantly, breaking the stale silence. Omari looked at her, sitting on the floor, knees pulled to her thin chest. Her eyes fell away from his and she opened her mouth, searching for the words to say. "Does Mama . . . " Her voice was thick and husky. She swallowed hard and wiped her eyes with a bandaged hand. "Does Mama hate me?"

The words struck him like a punch to the chest. "Of course not." He bent down next to her and her arms wrapped around him. He hugged her as she buried her face in his dashiki, noticing again how bony her body had become. And how much now heat radiated from her. "Your Mama would never hate you. You know that."

"But—" Odessa whimpered into his chest. "But I killed Kimi. It's my fault she got sick." A pained sob broke loose from deep within her chest, so much pent up suddenly released in a bout of ragged, heaving weeping.

"Oh, Dessa," he said, running a hand through her hair. "No, no that's not true." Her tears began to soak through his dashiki. His bare skin touching her began to scald, but he pressed her tighter to his chest. "Kimi was always a sick little baby. You know that. She was born with too much Gray in her lungs, that's all. It's not your fault. It's no one's fault."

"Mama thinks it is !" she cried into his chest.

"Your Mama is deep in grief," he said. "To lose another child . . . " His hand paused for a moment in her curls. "The bond between a mother and child is a bond of blood and soul. To have that bond broken . . . it's hurt her to the core. Grief is sometimes a potent drug. Whatever she says right now, she does not mean."

"It still hurts," she said quietly. "I loved Kimi too."

"I know," he said. "I know this all has been very hard on you. And I have not been there for you or Ayana or your Mama." He pulled away from her, his eyes wet. He thought of all the hours since Kimi had died, all the hours he spent wallowing in his grief while his daughter, all alone, dealt with an entire village turned against her. "I'm sorry. I'm sorry for everything."

She looked at him with eyes so filled with sadness and pain that his heart crumbled in his chest. This is what his selfish thirst for godsblood had wrought.

"Papa," she said, barely above a whisper. "In the forest, when I was hurt . . . did you do something to me?"

A lump began to rise in his throat, squeezing it shut.

"Because something isn't right," she continued. "I can feel it. And I don't think it's just from Egende bleeding on me."

Before he could even think of a response, footsteps pounded outside. Ubiko burst through the curtain, collapsing against the wall, gasping for breath. His eyes were sunken and his skin was ashen. He coughed, choking on his own ragged breaths, as he tried to speak. "Th-they're coming."

Omari's heart froze in his chest. "Who? Who's coming?"

"Obi. Everyone. They're all coming to get you two."

Fear poured through him, setting his nerves alight. "Where's Mutumi and Ayana? They were down at the river."

"They're with Mama. Mutumi . . . " Ubiko paused. "She knew this was coming." Ubiko glanced behind him, peeking through the curtain and then letting it drop. "Obi and his men mean to get you both by surprise, but I heard Mutumi and Mama talking. Must have thought I was too sick to do anything, they did. But I snuck out." A half-pained, half-delirious smile spread over his thin, angular face and then faded just as fast. He peeked out the curtain again. "You two need to go. Now."

Omari's mind worked slowly, parsing out Ubiko's words as if they were in a language he did not know. "What do you mean she knew?"

"There's no time," Ubiko said. "You need to go now. I don't know how long I'm going to be able to keep them distracted."

"What are you talking about? Won't you come with us?"

A pained smile cracked over Ubiko's face. "I'm sick, Omari. I'm not going anywhere like this." His eyes swept over Omari and his daughter, taking them in for the last time. "Run far from here and live long lives."

Before Omari could stop him, Ubiko had stumbled back out the curtain into the liminal world of dusk.

CHAPTER 17

Omari boosted Odessa over the wattle fence behind the hut and followed her over, taking her hand and dragging her behind him as he slipped between huts and threaded his way through the abandoned quarter of Kalaro. Ubiko's strained shouts rang in the air, each one a splinter rammed into his heart.

"Obi! Obi! Come face me like a man, you stoneless rat! Are you afraid to face a sick man now, you fat bastard?"

Odessa's feet dragged as he hauled her through the outer ring of huts and into the stubbly fields. Shouts and chanting soon replaced Ubiko's taunts. They ran, letting the sounds of the village fade from their ears. When they were halfway up the hill to the north of the village, a horn sounded, brash and abrasive in the twilight quiet.

They bounded up the hill. Omari cast a single glance back toward his home for the last twenty years. Where their home had been now stood a fire lashing at the night air. Torches bustled around the village like will-o-wisps. Carried on the wind came the faint whispers of unintelligible shouting.

"What's going on?" Odessa asked, turning to look behind them at the crest of the hill.

"Keep moving," he said, jerking her arm and pulling her down the other side of the hill. She stumbled a bit, her feet clumsy.

"What's going on?" she repeated, panic blooming in her voice.

He squeezed her arm hard, his fingers digging into her bandages. "Quiet!" he hissed.

Odessa was lagging and he wrenched her forward. *Does she not understand the danger we're in?* He looked back. Even in the twilit dark, he could see she was lost in her emotions. Her blank eyes were downcast as they ran. He turned back, still dragging her along. There was no time for gentle consolation.

Running parallel to the road out of the Kalaro, they crested another slight rise. Omari flattened himself to the ground, yanking Odessa down with him.

Below them, two torches flickered at the mouth of the bridge spanning the river. Across the river and beyond a few slight ridges, he could see the stakewall bridging the gap between the mountains and the steep hills of the basin. Torchlight haloed the gate leading out of the basin and into the Night Jungle.

Omari grimaced, but there was no avoiding this. Had he been alone, he would have scaled the stakewall and vaulted over the sharpened timbers. But he could not risk Odessa getting hurt again. Not as long as he lived.

There was only one way he could think of to get through the gate. Shock and brutality.

They slowed and moved away from the stakewall into the low brush. Moving in the torchlight were the silhouettes of four men and one woman. Some of Kalaro's best warriors no doubt. Some of the Kusa bloodline even, perhaps.

Omari strangled the emotion aching in his chest in a fist of cold, merciless detachment. The figures in front of the gate were enemy warriors and nothing more. Hostile men and women undeserving of his pity. It had been nearly two decades since he had last felt the icy fury of his hate. It was exhilarating.

A simple hunter had no chance against five of Kalaro's best warriors.

But Omari was no simple hunter.

He was a godkiller. He was an enemy to all gods and all those that would follow them. And for his daughter, he would kill anyone and everyone.

They crossed the river upstream, away from the torchlit figures on the bridge, and scaled the hardscrabble bank and ran, half-crouched, until they reached the stakewall. Night had sunk its claws deep into the landscape. Shadow surrounded them, giving him a modicum of comfort as they skirted the wall toward the gate. He told Odessa to stay hidden in a cluster of brush not far from the wall and left her to her scared protests.

Behind a half-rotten stump, only a few spans away from the gate and the five figures casting long, wavering shadows on the walls, he crouched and one by one stuck five arrows point-first in the dirt beside him. When he was done, he ran a hand over them, fingers grazing the coarse fletchings. He plucked one from the ground, nocked it upon his bowstring, and drew the string back easily. Boils and blisters chafed in his armpit as he sighted along the arrow's shaft a spear-wielding silhouette standing in front of one of the braziers. His wet clothes clung to his aching body.

His breath paused in his chest. His muscles tightened and froze. For just a fleeting moment, the world was suspended in a tranquil stillness. Just overwhelming darkness and shifting shapes in the firelight.

The arrow streaked through the dark like a gust of wind. The figure spun back and fell, clutching the shaft sticking out from beneath his ribs. The brazier came clattering to the ground, spilling coals as the figure slumped against the wall.

Omari let another arrow fly. And another. A second figure fell with an arrow in his groin. He screamed and tried to staunch the blood as it poured between his fingers, scarlet rivers twinkling in the firelight.

The remaining three figures readied themselves for battle. Long spears and wickedly curved swords bared in the firelight. Leather-wrapped wooden shields rose, bearing the spiraling shape of the Serpent. Battle-hardened warriors such as they were not easily daunted. They scattered along the gate, at the periphery of the fire's light. They were looking in his direction. Omari had no time to consider his next action. He slung the bow over his shoulder, picked up his spear, and charged the gate.

Frigid hate ran like ice water through his veins. Only the hot blood of his enemies would soothe him.

The three warriors charged to meet his advance. He feinted a thrust to the closest warrior's face. The woman raised her shield; Omari stabbed at their exposed shin. The edge of the shield knocked the spearhead away before it could draw blood.

Another warrior came. A sword flashed in a thrust toward his chest. Omari sidestepped. The sword swung down toward his legs. He knocked the blade away with his spear shaft and, with a twist of his hips, opened a wide gash in the warrior's arm. The warrior fell back a few paces, giving Omari enough space to swing around and deflect an incoming spear.

He kept the three warriors at bay with short thrusts and feints. Two spears and one sword assailing him, he knocked their blades away before they could skewer him or cut him down. But their shields kept him from delivering a killing blow. The warrior with the slashed arm was slowing, at least. His attacks were weak. But the other two warriors would not allow Omari to finish him off.

The wounded warrior was slow to raise his shield after a feint and Omari went in for a thrust toward his unprotected groin when a loud blaring horn filled the air. The man Omari had wounded with an arrow to the groin was on the ground, a kudu horn to his lips. Another bleating horn blast.

A spear flashed toward Omari. Distracted, he could only deflect it enough to keep from being stabbed in the chest. A jolt of pain as the spearhead pierced his shoulder. He grunted and stumbled back as the spear drew back for another thrust. Blood ran down his chest and along his ribs.

Panting like a beast, Omari sidestepped the slashing sword. The blade nicked his hip. The spear that pierced him flashed forward.

Omari parried the incoming thrust, knocking the spearhead aside. His own spear darted past the warrior's shield and into her gut. He wrenched the spearhead from her belly and fell back. Her spear slashed weakly across the back of his arm as he leaped away.

He turned in time to avoid being decapitated. He ducked and the sword whistled over his head. He swung his spear and caught the swordsman with the ironwood shaft in the shin. The warrior stumbled back.

Omari took his opportunity and followed through. He lunged forward, the spear snapping forward and plunging deep into the swordsman's neck. The spear-point ground against the the swordsman's vertebrae. The warrior stumbled back, dropping his shield and clutching at his neck. Blood as black as ink in the dark poured through his fingers. He fell, gurgling and choking on wet coughs.

The last warrior came from Omari's left side and thrust. Hearing the warrior's boots against the dirt, Omari spun and leaped back. The spear caught him in the side, plunging deep. He gasped and swung his spear wildly as he lurched back. The spearman pranced away from the swing, the bronze of his spear slick with blood.

The pain burned just below his ribs. His every ragged breath bolstered the hellfire swelling to the forefront of his mind. His vision blurred for a moment. The spearman circled warily. Omari swayed, the spear suddenly leaden in his hands.

"You kill gods and now you kill your wife's people. You truly are a miserable bastard," the spearman said. He feinted a low thrust and Omari jerked to attention. "Where is the girl, Omari?"

His mind still clouded with bloodlust and now obscured by pain, Omari could not even recognize the man before him. Omari blinked the pain away and steadied himself. *Don't listen*, he told himself. *Just kill.*

In one jerking motion, Omari flung his spear. It arced in the air and glanced off the spearman's raised shield with a loud clatter of iron on wood.

Before the shield had been lowered, Omari was on the warrior. The shield crashed against his chin as they tumbled to the dirt. He shoved the shield away with a hand and brought his knife down into the man's neck. He stabbed over and over again, screaming curses into the air until they devolved into guttural howls. The blade plunged into the man's face, neck, and chest. Blood splattered on Omari's dashiki, and a misting of droplets spattered his arms and face.

The man with the arrow in his groin blew on the horn again, his eyes widening and the bellowing of the horn growing louder when he saw Omari approaching.

Omari sheathed his knife and raised his spear with both hands. The warrior dropped the kudu horn and scrambled for his spear lying in the dirt.

Omari plunged the spearhead into the warrior's back with a strong overhead thrust. The warrior's arms flailed, fingers clawing at the dirt. Omari put his full weight onto the shaft. The spear point sunk to the cross guard, scraping against ribs and pinning the warrior to the ground.

The warrior gasped, mouth agape and eyes wide so the whites shone. His body was rigid, his arms and legs scrabbling in the dirt as if he could crawl from the spearpoint buried in his chest.

Omari twisted the blade against the man's ribs once more, then wrenched it free. The man tried to crawl, but his limbs only kicked in spastic spurts of desperation.

The stench of voided bowels drifted to Omari's nostrils, stinging them as the stink grew. He turned from the dead man and, leaning against his spear with a hand pressed to the gaping hole in his side, peered out from the torchlight and into the dark.

"Odessa!" he called. "Come to the gate!"

If they left now, they would be able to disappear in the Night Jungle before more villagers came. But the element of surprise was dissipating quickly. Like morning dew in the brash sunlight of the old world.

Far in the distance, torches swarmed in the dark. Distant shouts echoed in the valley.

He backed up, a hand pressed to his blood-soaked side, watching the swollen darkness at the periphery of the firelight. The tipped-over brazier and its scattered embers guttered in the dirt at the feet of the dead spearman still holding the arrow in his chest.

"Odessa!"

No reply came from the dark. With a roar, he kicked the second brazier to the ground. A cloud of cinders rose. Embers flew into the night upon the gentle summer's breeze. The diminished fire let the cover of night flow around him, obscuring his crouched, tense figure. He swallowed back fear swelling up his throat.

"Odessa! Now!" With one arm he lifted the gate's drawbar and flung it to the ground, then shouldered the heavy gate ajar. "It's time to go!"

Panic tightened its grasp around his throat. He opened his mouth to call out again when he heard footsteps approaching. The muscles in his shoulders and arms were taut and tense.

Odessa's figure emerged from the shadows. Her eyes were fixed on the dead warriors splayed out in front of the gate. "They're dead." Her voice was small and quiet.

He grabbed her by the arm and dragged her toward the gate. "And we will be dead too if you do not hurry!"

She pulled away, her arm covered in blood where his blood-slick hand had held her. She looked up. "You're covered in blood."

"It's not mine," he lied.

She stared at him blankly then back at the corpses. "You killed them."

Omari scowled and took her by the arm again. His fingers had an iron grip around her bicep. "They all want you dead! You're a smart girl. What don't you understand? We either kill them or they kill us." He tugged her arm. "Now *move!*" He hauled her toward the gate, a bright pain burning in his side. His side was wet with blood that ran down into his boots. She followed him, her hesitant feet scuffing the dirt.

He shouldered the heavy timber gate wide open. Odessa was staring at the warrior who had collapsed against the wall with an arrow stuck between his ribs. He pulled her through the gateway, leaving the gate open behind them. If denizens of the Night Jungle made it through the gateway into Kalaro, all the better for them to make their escape.

In the silvery pool of his imagination, he saw Mutumi and Ayana in the jaws of horrific beasts, their limbs torn from their bodies and their entrails strewn upon the ground in heaps. Despite his best efforts to crush the feeling swelling in his chest, his heart ached like it would rip in two at any moment. His bloody fingers found Odessa's and she took his hand as she had when she was just a small child. A little girl with a beaming grin of sunshine following her papa wherever he went.

I'm doing what must be done, he told himself. *I do this for her.*

An overgrown path ran from the gate through a clear-cut field of stumps and burned brush. Past the sparse clearing, a tangle of dense forest swallowed the road. Bare branches like skeletal fingers among the few still alive. Those fingers extended toward the leafed trees as if jealous of their vitality.

The wall of gnarled trees was still. Not even the slightest breeze played through the dull leaves and bare branches. As if the world held bated breath in this place. The heart of the forest was as black as the darkest night.

Odessa's hand was clammy. He squeezed it and they ran down the path into the cursed jungle.

Far behind them, a raucous clamor grew, shouts and horns blaring. But Omari paid it little mind. When they reached the wall of dying jungle, he veered left as his feet guided them along the path he had scouted through the treacherous forest. His mind was elsewhere.

Is Mutumi's betrayal any more craven than mine? We both have forsaken a daughter. His hand squeezed Odessa's for reassurance as they tripped and stumbled through the pitch-black forest. *Does this mean I love Ayana less?*

He pressed his spear-filled fist against the wound in his side to staunch the blood. Pain clouded his mind and he was thankful for it. He did not have the heart to dwell on his shortcomings any longer. Getting Odessa to Yakun was the only thing that mattered.

CHAPTER 18

Fear choked Odessa, crushing her windpipe in its strangling grip. Scattered thoughts droned in her mind like a swarm of locusts. Stumbling in the dark, she tried to focus on her father's silhouette, framed against the pitch-blackness in front of her. He lurched ahead of her, using his spear as a walking stick. A bundle of moss was packed into a wound on his side, a crude bandage held in place with his elbow. His other hand took hers and pulled her along. Her hand tightened around his, the blood slick on their skin beginning to dry. The blood of people she had lived and laughed with her entire life.

She still could not believe the village was hunting them. Denial was the only thing she had to hold onto, the only salve she had to numb the hurt, but it was slipping from her grasp with every stumbling step she took.

She tripped in the dark, her foot tangled in some twisted jungle plant. Her father's hand yanked her upright before she fell. She wanted nothing more than to stop.

"Where are we going?" she asked.

Her father was quiet for a while. "There is a wise man in the north. Past the Night Jungle." They continued for a bit, cutting through dense jungle. "He can cure you. I'm sure he can."

They ran through the jungle for hours, her father leading her through the dark while she languished in a numbed stupor. Images of bloodied corpses floated in her mind. Crushed and mangled by the boar god or gutted by her father's spear. All their eyes had the same terror and agony glazing them. Nausea seethed in her stomach and no matter how she tried, the images would not leave her. Blood. So much blood.

The Night Jungle, even this far in the highlands, came to life at night. Howls and screeches rang through the trees. All manner of nocturnal beasts and monsters called the Night Jungle home. Staggering through the dark surrounded by shrieks and screams, the fear of being caught by warriors seemed insignificant compared to the danger all around her.

Odessa and her father had gone on many hunts in the Night Jungle when Egende barred their entry and kept them from poaching in the Arabako. But they had never gone with just the two of them, and they never stayed through the night when they could avoid it.

Ahead of them, a shallow stream babbled. Her father pulled her along at a brisk, bouncing pace. The nearer they came to the stream, the more Odessa noticed the dim blue light of glowworms hidden among the leaf litter and undergrowth.

"Careful," her father whispered as he picked his way down the slight stream banks. "It's slippery."

Odessa followed him into the water. The gently flowing water came halfway up her shins, but it was nothing like the frigid water of the basin. It seemed heavier and denser. Alive somehow.

They followed the stream for a few steps and then her father turned. "Your trousers are tucked in your boots, yes?"

Odessa nodded then realized it was too dark for him to see it. "Yes."

"Good. Leeches can gnaw you to the bone." He turned back and they were back to splashing their way downstream. "Be careful still," he said. "The stream is shallow, but not too shallow for some nasty creatures to live in it."

They followed the stream for a short time, having to duck and crawl beneath overhanging vines and branches. Her father's spear jabbed the water in front of them as they hurried through it. Every waterlogged branch and slick aquatic plant rubbing against her leg sent tremors of anxiety jolting up her spine.

An inhuman scream tore through the night. They stopped in their tracks. The stream lapped at the back of their legs. It sounded as if the source of the scream was nearby, but the Night Jungle had a way of deceiving the human ear and eye. All sorts of spirits lived in the jungle's shadowy depths and had little love from humans.

"Come," her father said, pulling her to the opposite bank. He climbed ashore and scooped a handful of writhing glowworms from the rotten hollow of a fallen tree. "Take a handful and stay close."

As Odessa gathered a small handful of fat, squirming worms, her father bent over the bank and scooped more moss from the mud and packed it onto his wound.

"Is it bad?" Odessa asked, stepping to inspect the wound.

"Just a scrape," he said, dropping the hem of his dashiki and pressing his hand tight to his side. "Barely a trickle now."

Worry weighed heavy upon her chest, but before she could say anything, her father was moving, scooping a fresh handful of glowworms from beneath a rotten log for himself. Without him near, the darkness was heavier and more insidious. The light emanating from the wriggling worms in her fist was so paltry in comparison. She hurried to follow him.

He took her bandaged hand and they ran, guided only by the faint blue glow of the worms cupped in their hands. The glow afforded them a meager bit of comfort by allowing them to see a little more than an armlength away.

Odessa's limbs ached, atrophied from weeks of bedrest, and she could barely lift her feet. Exhaustion seeped into her body and weighed heavily on her eyelids. Her father stumbled ahead of her, leaning on his spear to keep himself moving. His panting breath was beleaguered and pained.

"Are you well?" she whispered, but her voice was overwhelmed by the shrill hooting of a monkey in the treetops above.

After an interminable amount of time, her father slowed and veered to the right. He held his handful of glowworms to the widespread tangle of roots of a fallen tree. The glow filled the space where the earth had risen. Between the twisting shapes of thick roots, there was an empty hole large enough for two.

"Come now," he said, ushering Odessa into the depression beneath the upturned roots. "We've gone far enough. We'll stay until dawn."

Odessa lowered herself into the hollow without another word, relieved to be hidden from view. Her aching muscles rejoiced as she settled into the damp dirt. Her father dragged a few broken limbs from the tree and obscured the hollow before crawling in beside her. The base of the roots above their heads gave Odessa strange comfort—as if having a roof of any sort above her head was a reassuring consolation.

Her father dug a small hole in the dirt between them and dropped his handful of glowworms inside. She did the same, although some of the glowworms had inadvertently been crushed in her anxiousness. Bits of worm guts clung to her palm, the luminescence fading quickly.

"Try to get some sleep. We have much land to cover at dawn. You will need your strength."

Odessa shook her head. Despite the heaviness of her eyelids, she knew sleep would not come. "What if something comes in the night?"

Her father took something from around his neck, cupped her hands, and put something warm and metallic in her palm. In the dim blue light, she saw it was a copper disc in the shape of a sun on a loop of rawhide. She had never seen her father wear it before. She turned it over and the amulet looked back at her. An eye of lapis lazuli bore into her with a piercing gaze. Her heart lurched in her chest. The evil eye.

"What is this?" she asked.

"Put it on. It will protect you like a ward."

Hesitantly, she slipped the rawhide around her head.

"It's a nazar. The wise man we're going to see, he gave it to me when I left for Kalaro. It will keep you safe as it for did me." He saw the uncertainty on her face and a forced smile came to his lips. "You probably think the evil eye is just the superstition of the old, no? But do you know where the evil eye comes from?"

Odessa shook her head. She knew it scared off evil spirits and could also be used to curse people, but she had never heard anyone speak of its origin. No one liked to talk about the evil eye, choosing instead to wordlessly use it as if naming it could earn the eye's ire.

"One of the oldest gods, almost as old as the forgotten gods, is Nazakh. Not long after the High Gods were born, Nazakh emerged from the horizon like a second sun. As tall as a mountain, with hundreds of fiery eyes that strike fear in the hearts of gods and freeze mortals like stone, Nazakh laid claim to the world. Nazakh is a cruel and gruesome god, more terrible than any other, they say. In the new world grown from the corpses of forgotten gods, he ripped apart any god that dared challenge him. It took all five of the High Gods of those early days to banish Nazakh to the badlands, but that was all they could do. Even the High Gods could not kill him. He is that terrible.

"That is why you must always wear the evil eye, Odessa. No god can touch you as long as you have Nazakh's eye. Nazakh has no love for men, but he spares no love for the gods either. All gods and monsters and spirits know to fear the eye. All this Forsaken business, it means little. The gods are not all there is, they are not all-powerful, they are not supreme above all. Nazakh is proof of that."

Odessa said nothing, only looked at the disc in her palm.

Her father grew quiet for a moment, staring out of their hole into the dark jungle. A distant howl came from far in the lowland jungle. "Have I told you why I pray to Ogé and Ogé alone? Despite all your mother's protests, why I spurn the other gods?"

"Because Ogé's the god of the hunt and you're a hunter," she said

"I'm a hunter because I am good at it. I pray to Ogé because Ogé is the only god that favors mankind. He was put in exile, not due to hubris or wretchedness like the ka-man will tell you. No, he was exiled because he favored man over the gods. He gave us life with his own blood and when asked who he favored more, he chose his children—mankind. He favored those born of the earth over his own brothers and sisters." He shook his head. "No other god would do that. High or Low, none of them save Ogé."

He lay back and pressed a hand to his side, wincing. "One day, Ogé will return to his former strength and save us. He will retake the scattered remnants of his power and bring down the betrayers who cast him to the earth. One day."

As he spoke, her eyes had drifted from his face and the ghastly pallor of his skin in the blue glow to his side. His dashiki was soaked with blood. Fresh, wet blood.

* * *

Odessa wanted to cry but she blinked the tears away. She unwrapped the dirty bandage from her arm. As he peered into the darkness, she lifted her father's bloody hand, lifted his dashiki and wound the wad of linen around his chest. He let her bandage him, tying the linen in a loose knot that would surely come undone later. Feebly, she tried to help, but there was so much blood.

CHAPTER 19

A branch cracked in the jungle. Omari jerked awake, ripped from a dreamless sleep. Despite his best intentions, sleep had dragged him into its pitch-black embrace. Leaves crunched somewhere nearby. He flattened himself against the dirt of the hollow, his spear clutched close.

Dawn's gray light had begun filtering through the leaves, thin and barely perceptible. Omari held his breath. There was only the chirruping screeches of the jungle's denizens. He waited, his body tensed and his breath bated, but he heard only the sinister music of the Night Jungle.

He shook Odessa awake. Her eyes fluttered open, stirring her from restless dreams to a grim reality. "We're going," he whispered. "Now."

Warily, he crawled out of the hollow beneath the tree's roots like a bear from hibernation. Rising to a half crouch, he paused. Sudden dizziness clouded his mind and his limbs felt weak. He swayed and leaned on his spear until the world stopped spinning. Sweat dappled his brow, and his boils and sores chafed against his still damp clothes. A hand pressed to his wounded side sent a lance of pain that almost toppled him. Still applying pressure on the wound, he steadied himself, breathing slowly and with pained effort.

In the pre-dawn dimness, he could see nothing but thick jungle in all directions. At the mouth of the hole they spent the night in, he saw a few drops of blood smeared on the leaf litter. His empty stomach sank and twisted in knots. He tried to get his bearings and orient himself, but his mind was foggy and vacuous from a lack of blood.

Odessa crawled from the hollow and stood beside him, rubbing sleep from her eyes. His hand took hers and they set off, half-crouched, in the direction he thought was northwest.

She tripped as he dragged her through the undergrowth between two towering, sprawling kapok trees. Her legs were trembling. She paused and swallowed hard.

Omari grunted dismissively. He had to concentrate on his every step. His feet were heavy and clumsy, every step announcing their presence. It was growing hard to stay balanced, as if his insides had turned to liquid and were sloshing to and fro as he lumbered.

More faint morning light suffused the dimness of the jungle's depths. He led Odessa up a slight ridge, using his spear to haul himself up the gentle rise tangled with snarls of vine and fern.

As he climbed, his foot dragged and caught in the exposed root of a dead strangler fig. He tripped and spilled forward, dragging Odessa down with him. As he fell, he caught from the corner of his eye a glimpse of bronze flashing in the dim light.

An arrow cut through the air above them. With a hollow thud, it buried itself in the twisted trunk of the strangler fig. The shaft vibrated from the impact.

A horn sounded nearby. A long blaring blast followed by distant footsteps crashing through the undergrowth. Omari scrambled unsteadily to his feet and dragged Odessa to hers, shielding her with his body as they ran.

More horns blared from all directions. Shouts filled the air as bodies crashed through the dense jungle behind them. Omari's shambling pace was not fast enough.

A whirring noise. A sharp pain struck his shin. Something struck his knee and wrapped around his legs. Ensnared, he fell to the ground hard.

Thick cords wrapped around his legs. Hard balls of ironwood clattered and clacked as he tried to unwrap his legs. Bolas were a thing of the southern tribes. Only a few in the village were skilled enough to use them.

"Omari!" Obi's voice boomed. Omari's blood chilled.

He shoved Odessa forward, propelling her away. "Run!" he hissed. "Run and don't look back!"

She began to stop and turn, her face darkened by panic and confusion.

"Go! Go now, damn you!" She turned and ran, crashing through the brush and disappearing amidst the greenery.

He sliced the cords from his legs and kicked free of them.

Figures moved in the jungle around him as he rose with a hiss of pain. He spun in a slow circle, bloodshot eyes following the movement rushing between trees and through the undergrowth. His spearhead swinging loosely in front of him. Under his breath, he mouthed his mantras.

A deep sonorous voice came from the jungle. "You're surrounded, Omari."

Obi emerged from behind a drooping and withered palm. His sickle-curved sword cut through a curtain of thick vines and foliage. "Give up. You must atone for what you have done." His skin was obscured by a thick layer of ash, giving him a ghastly gray appearance. In the hollows of his eyes, black soot had been smeared. His chest was bare, half of it hidden behind the huge shield he gripped in his opposite hand.

More warriors emerged from the jungle around him. Six warriors surrounded him, all of them similarly ashen. A woman stepped forward, spear leveled at her side. "We take no pleasure in this, Omari."

Obi stepped toward him, slow and deliberate like a stalking jaguar. The warriors surrounding him closed in. Omari's grip tightened around the spear. His eyes narrowed and his body tensed. He opened his mouth to speak then stopped.

A girl's scream cut through the jungle. "Papa!" Odessa's voice called out in the distance before being muffled.

Omari turned toward her voice, making to run when Obi's blade slashed the back of his knee. He went down hard on the jungle floor and scrambled away. His only thoughts were of Odessa.

He spun onto his back, swinging his spear in a wild backhanded arc. Obi knocked the shaft away with his massive leather-bound shield.

Another warrior came and stomped his wrist into the mud, grinding their heel into the slash across his arm. The muddy boot tore the scabbed wound wide open. Omari winced, trying to pull away from the boot, but it remained firm.

Obi's boot came down on his head. The world brightened and then dimmed in an instant. His head swam. The spear left his loose grip and fell to the dirt.

Stunned, his eyes focused and unfocused. Obi's hulking frame towering above, doubling in his vision. A boot to his chest pinned him to the dirt.

"Don't struggle. There is no other way," Obi said. His massive frame bore down on Omari's chest as he leaned forward.

Omaris' sternum and ribs groaned, on the verge of snapping. The breath was forced from his lungs in a hacking gasp. The tip of Obi's sword hovered next to his throat. He sucked in a thin breath, his mind muddled. "Let her go," he mumbled.

Obi's eyes, peering out from the soot black smears, were hard and impassive.

"She had no part in the hunt!" He pleaded, his voice ragged and hoarse. "I killed the sow! I bled the bitch! It was all me!"

"And you will be punished for it," Obi said. "As will she."

"But she didn't do anything wrong!"

"She stole Egende's blood into her body."

"The fucking hog bled on her! She didn't steal a damned thing, you shit-headed prick!"

A rustling came from nearby. Two warriors dragged Odessa toward them. Blood welled from a gash above her eyebrow. When she saw him, she struggled in their grip.

"Papa!" Tears can down her cheeks. She screamed at Obi, "Let him go!"

"Bind her and take her home," Obi ordered.

"Let her go, you worthless pricks!" Omari screamed.

The warriors tied her hands and wrists and dragged Odessa back the way they came. She kicked and screamed and cried, but the warriors did not stop. Three of the warriors that had taken Omari down followed, their weapons bared. They disappeared into the jungle. Her screams and sobs grew quieter until they faded to join in the jungle's melody.

"Where are they taking her?"

"To meet the gods, my friend." Obi's face was blank. "They do not care to meet you."

"You are no friend of mine, you whoreson bastard!" he snarled. His hand leaped to the knife at his belt. When his fingers reached the handle, they grew limp and fumbled at the sheath.

Obi's foot rose and crashed down onto Omari's face. His heel ground into his nose.

He gurgled and coughed, blood spattering his face. Obi brought his foot down again. A burst of white pain behind his eyes. Blackness burned into his vision. The taste of blood filled his mouth. The void called to him. Cold oblivion seeped into him.

His last thought before he slipped away was of Mutumi.

He sank.

CHAPTER 20

A chill, dry breeze ran across Odessa's skin. Unclothed and with her hands bound in front of her, she tried her best to hide her nudity. It had taken most of the day since her capture for the warriors to drag her, kicking and screaming, back to the village where they had stripped and cleaned her. Her throat was raw and her body was on the verge of collapse. The rage within her had burned out hours ago. All that was left was numbed fear.

In the plaza, the village milled around her with torches, somber chants rising to the night's sky. Their shadows danced, stretching from the large fire roaring in the plaza's center. Where she stood in front of the Elder's Lodge, none of the fire's warmth reached her. The place where her father's nazar had hung was bare and cold. Her captors had tossed it into the flames and the fire had taken it greedily. There was no protection from the wrath of gods.

She shivered more from fear than cold. No one would answer her questions. Why were they doing this? Where was her father? The only answers she received were glum silence, pitying glances, or stern rebukes.

Three villagers in black robes, their faces white with ash, stood with her. A villager on either side of her held one of her arms while the third, Ajatunde, held a burning bundle of sage and cedar in front of her, letting the fragrant smoke waft into her face before she began to circle her. Ajatunde was a tall, slender woman. She had always been kind to Odessa and her family. Odessa had even played with her granddaughter before she died of plague. Now she looked at Odessa with hard, dispassionate eyes as she chanted to Talara and flicked the burning bundle. Thin, silken ribbons of smoke swirled around her to purify the evil that corrupted her.

Once the bundle had burned and Odessa's eyes were red and watery from smoke, Ajatunde took her by the chin. Odessa tried to pull free from her, but her fingers dug into her cheeks and held her firmly in place.

"Drink." Ajatunde pressed a cup to her lips. Odessa pressed her lips together and tried to turn away. Ajatunde pushed the cup against her lips until it ground against her teeth. "Drink. Or I make you drink."

Reluctantly, Odessa opened her mouth. Ajatunde's fingers pried her mouth open further and the cup tipped, pouring a sour, milky liquid into her mouth.

Odessa's gagged. The urge to spit the foul liquid into Ajatunde's face was overwhelming, but Ajatunde clamped a hand over her mouth and leaned in close. The smell of ash and sage and cedar was strong. "Swallow it," she said. "It is better this way."

The inside of her mouth tingled with a slight burning sensation, but she could not swallow. The very idea of the thick, milky liquid going down her throat made her retch. There was something in it her body refused. Something about it repulsed her in a way nothing had before. She shook her head. A bit of the liquid trickled through the Ajatunde's fingers.

Ajatunde's other hand gripped a chunk of Odessa's hair and jerked her head back. The hand over Odessa's mouth tightened, pinching her cheeks until her nails dug into her skin. "Do not resist so."

Odessa shook her head, trying to free herself from the woman's grip. The hand in her hair twisted, yanking at her scalp.

"Your body is not ready. Drink and make yourself worthy of Talara's purification." The hand twisted her hair further and she winced.

With concentrated effort, Odessa took the thick, sour milk in with a large gulp, gagging as it ran down her throat. Ajatunde's hand stayed clamped over her mouth until Odessa's gagging had subsided, then she let go and stepped back, wiping her hands on the front of her black robes. Held aloft by the two robed figures, Odessa dry heaved. Spittle struck the dirt beneath her and hung in strings from her mouth.

Ajatunde lifted Odessa's head with a daub of thick ochre paint on her fingertips. She rubbed her fingers back and forth across Odessa's lips until a smear of ruddy brown stained her mouth and chin. "Sins are dirt and dung. Bless Talara, who takes it all within herself so we may not drown in our own filth."

Odessa pulled her head away and paint smeared across her cheek. Ajatunde's ashen face turned to a scowl. She set the cup of paint down and examined Odessa with a probing and disapproving gaze.

"It will have to do," she said to the villagers holding her. "The gods grow impatient. We must not waste any more time." The woman walked toward the fire, a shadow trailing behind her, pulled from the darkness at the edge of the fire's light. Odessa's captors followed, hauling her forward as she dragged her feet.

At the woman's signal, a ram's horn blared. To Odessa's ears, it sounded too much like the enraged bellow of the boar god. After the horn's blast faded, a series of batá drums began tapping a pulsating, back-and-forth rhythm.

Another rope was tied to the rope binding her wrists, and she was led around the plaza. An entourage of warriors armed with spears and clubs surrounded her and the robed villagers with faces of ash. As they passed around the fire, more villagers came and joined the procession while the drummers followed behind them all, tapping away with stony faces.

They passed the wreck of the Kusa home, and Odessa tried to pull away from the procession, to run to the ruins of her house, but the hands on her arm and the ropes around her wrists were strong. The roof of the hut had collapsed, and through the windows and doorway she could see the inside was still burning, the flames sputtering as they consumed the remnants. Hunks of thatch and the ribs of the roof lay inside, smoldering. The hut with Ogé's shrine was destroyed, its earthen walls torn down and reduced to rubble. Odessa craned her neck as they passed, desperately searching the dark. Her mother and sister were nowhere to be seen.

The procession followed the eastern road out of the village, a mass of torches lighting the path in the growing dark. Odessa's stomach rolled and writhed as the milky liquid boiled in her guts. Threads of haze began to work into the soft channels of her mind, soon clouding her fear and shrouding her thoughts in numb detachment.

They passed the gateway into the Arabako and followed the path. Stripped of its sanctity, the hallowed forest seemed not much different from the Night Jungle. The only difference was in its silence. The Arabako Forest was lifeless; the only sound came from the procession's footsteps upon the stone path. Even the batá drums had given way to silence.

The torchlight of the procession seemed to dim in the presence of the deep forest dark. Odessa's feet dragged clumsily along the ancient stone path. All the bodies moved in the torchlight, shifting shades of orange, red, and dark shadows.

After the path had begun to rise into the foothills, the procession veered off along a path freshly hacked through the forest with machetes and trampled by many feet. A sense of unease prickled along Odessa's skin.

Eventually, they came upon a familiar ravine. At the bottom of the ravine were the remains of a massive funeral pyre. The procession wound its way down the ridge into the ravine and circled the remains of Egende and her children. Ajatunde stepped amid the charred bones and ash, pulling Odessa along with her.

She bent down and took a handful of ash. "This is your sin." She held it to Odessa's face. "Eat the ashes of your wickedness and become whole."

Odessa began to pull away, but Ajatunde's hand gripped the back of her neck before her addled body could react. She shoved the ashes into Odessa's mouth. Odessa recoiled and shook her head weakly. Flakes of ash stuck to her tongue and clogged her throat. She coughed but the woman's hand clamped over her mouth kept her from expelling the ashes. Fear and panic came through the milky haze like cold rain as she choked on the ashes.

Another villager in robes hurried to Ajatunde's side and handed her a cup. The woman tilted Odessa's head back and poured more milky liquid down her throat. Odessa coughed, milk and ash splattering on the ground. Ajatunde clamped her hand over her mouth once more. The milk mixed with the ash and Odessa swallowed the milky paste in gagging gulps.

When Ajatunde released Odessa, she stumbled and doubled over, hacking and gasping for breath. The two villagers that had held her now scooped up double handfuls of ash as the woman pulled Odessa upright.

"Anoint yourself in the ashes of your sin as Talara anoints herself in the sins of the world." The two villagers rubbed ash and soot on her naked body. Starting at her shoulders and moving down to her feet they, smeared handfuls upon handfuls of ash on her skin. As they covered her in ash, the touch of their hands on her nude body sent jolts of fear through her. Her eyes watered.

After they had thoroughly coated her, they made sure to pack ash into the bloody wounds of her burned arm. When they were done, Ajatunde stood in front of her and, with a gentle finger she wiped Odessa's tears from the corners of her eyes down her cheeks, cutting through the ash. "There is salvation in martyrdom. To sacrifice is to love in its purest form."

Odessa swayed as the haze grew thicker in her mind. Soon, other villagers came forward to the remains of the pyre. Villagers with clean skin. They stripped and anointed themselves in the ashes of gods.

The drums began their staccato rhythm again. The drumbeat pounded deep in her ears. The haze was so thick in her mind, it felt as if her skull was swollen with the milky fog. In its swirling whorls, fear crackled like electricity. Jolts of terror arced through her mind. Her bound hands clasped between her breasts, she shivered and stumbled in the middle of the solemn procession.

Morning light broke through the trees before they reached the foot of the mountains. A large camp had been made amid the stone pillars there. The camp was empty, save for four villagers in black robes who met the procession at the base of the massive flight of stairs climbing up the mountains.

The procession took to the campsite and rested on pillars or sat on the soft forest floor, rubbing sore muscles and blistered feet. Without a word, Ajatunde and the four other villagers in black robes started toward the Stairs of Ascension with Odessa in tow.

They led her to the stairs flanked by the giant stone boars. Odessa's stomach churned as she neared them. Her skin prickled and sweat dampened the ash on her skin. The statues were hulking beasts that stared down at her with silent fury. They passed between the boars and she was sure they would turn and gore her, but they remained, stoically keeping their vigil at the base of the mountains.

They climbed the stairs. Odessa was vaguely aware of her aching muscles. They climbed for hours, her feet often catching the lip of a stair and stumble. They climbed until the sun was high over the village below.

Whenever the effects of the milk began to fade, Ajatunde would make her drink more of the lukewarm mixture from a small gourd that swung from her shoulder. By the time they reached the flat plateau of stone where the stairs turned up the side of the Serpent's Peak, her stomach was a hard, molten lump and her mind was a foggy swamp of ill-defined thoughts and fears. The mountains stretched high above her and below her, the land extended to the faraway horizon—but to her, the scenery was a blur. An ever-changing tapestry of color and sensation.

The air grew colder, but the burning of the milk in her guts seemed to ward it away. Her feet on the icy stone stung and her fingers and toes were growing numb, yet that cold seemed just distant enough that it did not bother her. The sensations of her body were as remote as the village below.

As they climbed, she could make out a terraced pyramid at the peak. It grew larger and larger as the sun began to descend in the western sky. The light of torches and braziers flickered above.

The terraces of the pyramid were steps fit for gods, homage to the path the High Gods had taken in their ascension up this very mountain. They were almost to the peak of the pyramid when a cold dread permeated her mind. No longer did the haze crackle with fear—it now froze like storm clouds on the horizon. A lull before a hurricane.

As they climbed higher, they passed figures standing on the higher terraces, all dressed in black and covered in ash. Some held torches to light the way and others held spears. All of them looked at her with a mixture of disgust and pity.

They crested the flat top of the pyramid and brought her before a massive altar of black stone. A temple stood behind the altar, at the back of the stone mesa. It terrified her. From the carvings adorning its walls to the very stone it had been hewn from, it scared her.

Obi stood outside the temple's leather-curtained doorway, looming tall and imposing over the girl and her captors. Through the haze in her mind, Odessa focused on Obi. Narrowing her eyes, she stared at him, seeing only the image of him standing above her father, sword pointed at his throat. *Where is he? What did you do with my Papa?* she wanted to shout, but her mouth was too dry and her tongue too numb to form the words.

"Where is Kunza?" Ajatunde asked him.

"Inside," Obi said. "He is not to be disturbed."

"What should we do with her, then?"

"Leave her with me," he said, refusing to look at Odessa. "It shouldn't be long before all the offerings are prepared."

Ajatunde nodded and hauled Odessa over to Obi, where she unbound her and fitted a pair of iron shackles around her wrists. A chain dangled from between the cuffs and Ajatunde held it firmly as Obi took a knotted strip of cloth from his belt. He stuffed the knot in Odessa's mouth and tied the ends behind her head. Once Odessa was gagged, he took the chain of riveted link and yanked her toward the altar. Ajatunde and her other captors retreated down the stairs.

Without saying a word, he lifted Odessa off her feet. Limply, she kicked and squirmed in his arms before he dropped her onto the altar. Before she could orient herself, he yanked her arms forward, looped the chain through a stone ring rising from the edge of the altar, and pinned it in place with a thick spike, leaving only enough slack in the clattering chain for Odessa to raise her hands a few inches from the altar's surface.

Odessa's blurry vision focused on Obi's callously dispassionate face—as dispassionate as Ajatunde's had been—as he finished pulling the knot tight. She tried to mumble through the gag.

"Be quiet," Obi said, straightening and appraising her with a blank expression. "It will be easier."

She screamed through the gag but Obi ignored her She wanted to cry and scream, but she had nothing left to muster. Her father was gone. Her mother and sister were nowhere to be seen.

She looked out at the horizon, blood red spilling out over the distant hills. There was nothing left for her to do.

She was at the mercy of the gods now.

And the gods had no love for Forsaken girls.

CHAPTER 21

The open sky was the color of ash when the Elders mounted the summit of the pyramid. Behind them, the mountains rose into the mists of early morning.

Odessa awoke from where she had collapsed on the altar. The feeling had been strangled from her hands by the binds around her raw wrists. When she saw the old men and women in black kaftans, their skin untouched by ash, a flood of warmth rushed to her cheeks. She attempted to hide her nakedness, pulling her knees up to her chest and awkwardly crossing her legs.

"Pitiful thing," Elder Cuchal said. The old man's watery eyes lingered over her naked body. She wrapped her arms around herself tighter.

"May the gods have mercy on you, little one," Elder Kusa said flatly.

"What brings you to the temple?" Obi asked, walking around the altar.

Elder Cuchal stepped in front of the other Elders. "We've come to give our aid to the ka-man."

"Kunza is no longer our ka-man. He's Talara's emissary. Her Priest of Ashes." Obi said. The Elders exchanged nervous glances. "Do you wish to devote yourselves to Talara?"

"We devote ourselves to all the High Gods," Elder Kusa said with disapproval.

"Then your devotion is weak and shallow."

Elder Kusa scowled. "That's blasphemy."

"Not blasphemy. This is faith," Obi said. "True faith. Through Talara, there is salvation." She drew close to the Elders. "A great change is coming. The Gray is only a portent of things to come. Only Talara alone can save us."

"What foolishness is Kunza-ka spouting now?"

"Through his mouth come Talara's words. He is her divinely appointed."

"Men can't be divinely appointed! That's absurd," Elder Cuchal started. The other Elders joined in his protests.

Odessa's head spun, the last threads of milky fog dissipating and leaving her mind raw and sensitive. All this talk irritated her and filled her with deep, cold dread.

"Where is Kunza-ka?" Elder Cuchal said. "He must answer for this sacrilege."

"He is in the temple and in the temple he will stay until he is ready," Obi said, walking to stand and block the path of the Elders. He towered above them, wide chest bare except for the thick layer of ash. His sooty eyes glinted with a spark of savage menace as he glowered at the elderly group before him. "You should go back to camp," he said, his words flat and sharp.

The Elders huffed and blustered in protest. Ajatunde came up the stairs and tried to assuage their consternation before ushering them all down the steps. Obi returned to his post without even glancing in Odessa's direction.

Throughout the morning, people in black, some covered in ash and some not, came in intervals, up and down the stairs, bringing with them large bundles of wood to stack around the altar until logs and branches surrounded her to her waist. As they worked, they kept their eyes downcast, refusing to acknowledge Odessa.

After the altar had been covered in wood, the villagers began bringing charred bones, huge ribs and femurs, and the skulls of the slain boar god and her children. These were arranged by the ash-faced villagers, Ajatunde chief among them, carefully and fastidiously moving them back and forth before finally placing them on the pile of wood.

Egende's ribcage was placed behind Odessa, flaring around her like the wings of some massive bird of prey. Vertebrae circled her while the legs leaned against the altar like pillars.

Surrounded by bones—the bones of a god she had helped slaughter—the thought that her death was for the best kept resurfacing. That her death was necessary to right the wrong they had committed. But that thought was always dwarfed by her fear of death. She did not want to die. She would have done anything to live just a little bit longer. She hated it, but it was true. She was craven and weak, unwilling to sacrifice her already cursed life for the lives of the entire village.

This was her only chance to win back the favor of the gods. No Forsaken ever regained their favor once lost. As far as she knew, it was impossible. Yet here she was, the chance of salvation in front of her, and still she wanted nothing more than to jump down the mountainside and run away. To run away from her home and her gods and hide from the world.

I have no home. No gods. Death is all there is for me. And this is a good death. She told herself these things more to convince herself than out of genuine belief. If she did not tell herself these lies then she would break down on the altar, sobbing and thrashing and begging to be freed. And that would dishonorable in the face of the gods. To sully such a sacred place with such reproachful behavior would be unthinkable. She had to be strong even though she held on by a thread of self-control.

She allowed herself little self-pity. She had spent the last few weeks feeling sorry for herself and her predicament. Self-pity would do her no good at the altar of the gods, as they would give her no pity. She had to die on the altar to escape perdition. There was no other way.

Men in black robes hauled a large copper cauldron up the steps, straining and huffing as they brought it past the altar and into the temple behind her. A wooden lid sealed with a thick coat of wax covered the cauldron, but dried blood ran from the rim down its sides.

The sun was beginning to descend when villagers began climbing the stairs en masse. They lined the terrace below the pyramid's peak and stood, waiting. Odessa's heart pounded and her stomach wrenched, the urge to vomit clawing up her throat. The villagers tried to avoid looking at her but she saw them, glancing at her with pity and disgust and reproach and even hate.

The Elders crested the top of the pyramid once more, along with two ash-covered villagers. Something was wrong with the Elders. They were quiet as they approached the altar, and their eyes were watery. They glanced at her and then looked away before, finally, Elder Kusa spoke.

"Be strong, Odessa," she said before giving her a final, pitying look.

Then she saw her mother and Ayana mounting the steps. Her mother dressed in black, but not in the black of the others: hers was the black clothes of a mourning mother, the same clothes she had been wearing since Kimi died. Her mother's tearstained eyes met hers for a moment, then darted away as she pulled a sobbing Ayana along and went to join the Elders, who took them in a sympathetic embrace.

Odessa wanted to call out to her mother. To scream at her. But her eyes fell to her hands and the ropes that bound them. Tears she thought had run dry streamed down her cheeks and all the composure she had worked so tirelessly to keep now crumbled and broke away with each ragged, sobbing breath. She cried until she couldn't breathe, sucking in deep, whining breaths between sobs.

And then a hush fell over the mountaintop, a weighty silence that quieted even her muffled sobs. The thin air grew cold as the leather curtain of the temple flapped open.

CHAPTER 22

Soft footsteps padded on the stone, in time with the click of a staff. Odessa turned and her breath caught in her throat. Her teeth gnashed against the gag. Terror caused her to shrink away as Kunza approached.

In the dim twilight his eyes glowed, smoldering coals regarding her with malevolence. The glowing coals were nestled in pits of gore, melted flesh scabbed over and oozing, with gnarled scar tissue and reddened skin at the edges. Those eyes seemed to flare as she met their gaze. Unable to look away, she followed him as he walked around the altar. His countenance was grave. The demeanor of an executioner.

He wore a cloak of vulture feathers and a headdress of crow feathers radiated from his head. A thigh-length skirt of black was all he wore under the cloak despite the cold. Like the others, his bare skin was covered in a thick layer of ash. His walking stick rattled with the bones of vultures and crows, their skulls affixed to the top of the staff and chattering with each strike against the stone. He walked straight-backed, not hunched over the stick with arthritic feebleness.

Kunza looked over the villagers and over the land stretching out into growing darkness. In the torchlight, his mutilated face was a gruesome sight. Yet Odessa couldn't take her eyes off him. A terror, base and primal, told her to flee, to gnaw her hands from her wrists and run away as fast as she could. But her muscles were frozen and her heart was still, barely quivering in his terrible presence.

A darkness hung around him, rising from him like dank morning mist. A darkness that sapped the warmth from the air and stole the breath from her lungs.

"Gods above and gods below." His voice was sharp and gravelly, like the scraping of a tombstone on a mausoleum floor. "We give you this flesh and blood as penance. Take it, and with it, our sins." He walked farther on the platform, his face turned up to the clouded sky. "Mother of Sickness, Eater of Sin, Talara, take this offering so we may serve you. Heal us of our affliction. Take Egende's wrath from our bodies and use us to purify a world gone gray.

"To Talara, we offer the flesh of those that killed gods so that they may be punished. To Talara, we offer our souls to be purified of the grave sin we allowed to unfold." He walked aimlessly across the platform in front of her, speaking not to the congregants before him but to the sky above, as if they were not even there. But he could see. That much she knew. Those smoldering eyes had probed into her and seen her very soul. "Forgive us, Goddess, and let us serve you."

He stopped in front of the altar and turned to face the crowd. "Talara has spoken to me and through me she speaks to all." A few scattered murmurs rose and died in the crowd. "Talara has shown me the Cosmos and I have seen the true face of this world. The Gray is unnatural. It's an unholy aberration. It's a corruption, twisting the flesh and minds of those afflicted. And it's ever-growing, taking root and spreading like cancerous seeds sown across the world." The words had a resonant quality to them that lingered in Odessa's mind. His voice was powerful. "The other gods, High and Low alike, they do nothing to stop this cosmic plague. They are helpless against it. But Talara, my Goddess, sees the worth in humanity and she sees a world where the Gray can be eradicated." He stepped up to the cauldron and placed a hand on the lid. "A better world begins today, my friends."

With a sudden jerking motion, he pried the lid off the cauldron and tossed it to the floor. The stench of blood was so strong that Odessa, even through her gag, could taste it in the back of her throat.

He dipped a cup into the deep copper pot and raised it. Fat drops of dark red blood dripped down its side as he held it out for all to see. "Take Talara's gift to mankind and dedicate yourselves to the Goddess of Rot and Rebirth. By her grace, we will be eternal." He raised his arms further, the vulture feather cloak framing his skinny body. A body free of boils and sores. "Look at what Talara has done already. She ate the disease from my body and she will do the same for you. Come now, come and accept her blessing."

Murmurs rose from the villagers. Only the ash-faced ones moved to line up in front of the cauldron. One by one, they kneeled before Kunza and sipped from the cup. He dipped a thumb in it and put a red mark on each of their foreheads. "With this blood, your sins are washed clean," he said each time as he pressed a bloody thumb to a forehead.

Soon, other villagers sheepishly stepped forward, heads hung in shame until they kneeled before Kunza. Until they looked up into Kunza's smoldering eyes and sipped from the cup. Men, women, and children all eventually drank the blood he offered them. They had prepared themselves, it seemed. Steeled their hearts for this unspeakable trial.

Odessa's mother ushered a sobbing Ayana to the cauldron. Odessa cried out through her gag but her mother was resolute, her jaw set as Ayana kneeled before

Kunza. She recoiled from his touch as he placed a hand on her cheek and wiped the tears from her eyes. "Do not be afraid. A god's gift is a wonderful thing." He held the cup to her lips and tipped it. Ayana did not even gag at the taste of the blood. She drank deeply and was no longer afraid.

Odessa's mother drank the blood and took the mark on her forehead, no longer crying afterward. Soon, even the Elders had taken the blood.

Odessa wanted to vomit, but her empty stomach had nothing to yield. She looked away, not able to bear any more.

"Do not avert your gaze," Ajatunde said from where she stood beside the altar. "What you see is salvation."

She looked up as the last few villagers took their blessings. Through her tears, she watched two ashen villagers lead a nude Ubiko up the steps. Bound at the wrists as she had been, he stumbled, barely able to stand. His eyes were glazed over and unfocused. Large black lumps spread across his bony body.

"Uncle!" she screamed around the gag.

His eyes drifted over hers but did not pause with any sort of recognition. The villagers made him kneel before the altar, tying his wrists to the same stone hoop to which she was bound.

She began to hyperventilate as the two in black started back down the stairs and two others mounted them, another naked man held between them. *No, no, no, no.*

In the back of her mind, she had been hoping her father had somehow gotten away. She had kept hoping, in some small, hidden part of herself, that he would charge up those steps, spear in hand, to save her.

Instead, he was carried, legs dragging and head lolling. Bruises splotched around broken skin along his shoulder and a gruesome wound in his side, packed with linen, oozed blood. His father's nose was crushed and disjointed with dark bruises mottling his nose and eyes. One eye remained half open, swollen and dark. The hair on one side of his head was matted with dried blood.

He was pushed onto his knees beside Ubiko and tied to the stone hoop. Odessa's hands reached out for his, but the chain held her back. She pulled against the shackles, thrashing and screaming through the gag. Sorrow ran so deep within her, great cracks in the very foundation of her soul. Her impending demise was forgotten as the last tears she had to shed streamed down her face. She strained against her shackles and tore at the gag with her teeth.

"Why?" she screamed, her words muffled by the gag. "Why are you doing this?" Long and drawn out, she begged the villagers for an answer. She screamed into the heavens, her voice cracking, drawn thin with pain and strain.

"Talara demands it," Kunza said to her, voice thin and brittle. He stood by as two black-robed men lifted the cauldron and set it between Ubiko and her father. Kunza turned back to his congregants. "Through treachery and unholy magic, the likes of which no mortal should have, Odessa Kusa has become something altogether unprecedented. An abomination of human flesh and stolen godsblood. That godsblood has been bound to her and she has been made a vessel for the energies of the Cosmos."

Odessa stared into the cauldron, trying not to listen to his lies. Inside floated myriad bones and sodden hunks of wood among the blood. Her wrists twisted in the shackles, rubbing the raw skin bloody.

"We shall sanctify this perverted vessel by Talara's grace, and use as the foundation for our new world." He stepped in front of the cauldron, brushing against Ubiko, who lay slumped against the altar. "A cauldron fit for a god." His hand slipped beneath his cloak. "But cauldrons must be filled."

He moved faster than Odessa's eyes could follow. Before she realized it, he had Ubiko by the hair. His knife slashed Ubiko's throat and blood spilled down his chest. His glassy eyes bulged, the glazed stupor clearing for a moment of terror. Kunza shoved his bleeding throat over the rim of the cauldron and let the blood pour inside.

Stray drops of blood splattered her father's cheek, but he did not react. His eyes were vacant, insensible even as Kunza approached him.

Odessa screamed and begged but Kunza did not stop. He took her father by the hair and wrenched his head back.

"Don't! Please!" The last syllable hadn't left her lips before Kunza dragged the blade across her father's throat.

Something broke inside her. Something precious and irreparable shattered as she watched his blood pour from his open throat.

The world swirled around her, but she barely noticed. Her screams had tapered off by the time Ubiko and her father had been thrown onto the pyre. Ubiko's still bleeding corpse lay on her left and her father's lay on her right.

Obi lifted the cauldron and let its contents pour over Odessa's head. The stench of stale iron and faint decay struck her before the blood splashed onto her head. Some of the blood was warm still as it doused her hair and poured down her face. Trickles ran into her mouth and she gagged. Bones and wood clattered on the altar around her.

She blinked blood out of her eyes, thrashing and tugging against her chain. She shrieked in disgust and horror. Her skin began to tingle.

"In the name of Talara, Goddess of Rot and Rebirth, I baptize you in blood and flame."

A torch touched the pyre and the dry wood took the flame eagerly. Odessa yanked at her shackles as the fire grew, crawling along her father's body and curling around her to lap at Ubiko's. She coughed and choked, ensconced in a cloud of putrid smoke.

"Breathe," Kunza said over the crack of flames and Odessa's screams. "Those flames won't hurt you. Breathe and take in the essence."

As the fire grew, so too did the tingling of her skin. Her blood vibrated in her veins. Her burned arm thrummed as smoke swirled around it.

Her heart was beating so fast and so hard, it felt like punches to her chest. She could not hear anything Kunza said to the congregants. All she could hear was boiling blood pounding in her ears.

The fire lashed toward the sky around her, licking at her body. Flames surged toward her burned arm, leaping and arcing along her skin. She pulled against her shackles, screaming through frayed vocal cords. A rivet gave way and she jerked backwards, crashing into the fiery wood. Flames scorched her back as she tumbled from the altar in a plume of cinders.

Lying on the cold stone, tongues of flame guttered upon her skin, still dancing in the coils of her hair—but only scorching it slightly. But her right arm, that gruesome thing, was wreathed in golden fire, covered in gouts of flame lashing out from her marred flesh. An almost pleasant pain ached in her bones as the fire roared.

The pyre crackled and sent sparks soaring in the air above the mountain. Cinders spun and flashed in the plume of smoke rising to the overcast sky, like lightning flashes in thunderclouds.

The night air was tinged with smoke and blood. The villagers behind Odessa murmured and cried out in alarm as she rose. In the bedlam, among the shouts and cries and fleeing villagers, she saw Obi by the altar, his sword gliding from its sheath.

She heard Kunza command that she be caught, but she was already running past the temple toward the far edge of the platform. Her heart pounded unbelievably fast.

She was halfway to the steep drop-off of the back of the pyramid, when a woman leapt toward her, spear darting forward in the firelight. Odessa ripped the spear from her hands and tossed the woman aside, never losing stride. The wood of the spear's shaft charred as she ran the rest of the way to the edge, where Ogé had sheared the mountain away in his fall.

A few steps away, she felt Obi's hand wrapped around her unimmolated arm. He jerked her back and her feet skidded against the stone.

With a snarl, she pulled against him. Buoyed by the overwhelming thrumming in her veins, she grabbed his arm and pulled him with her.

They toppled over the edge and fell in to the night.

CHAPTER 23

The girl was gone. They combed the mountainside and the Arabako, but she had disappeared.

Obi had been found, mangled upon the rocks nearly thirty yards below the temple. Now he lay in Kunza's hut, nearly two days after the mountaintop ceremony. Purpled skin bulged from his crooked shin, tented by sharp bone. Obi coughed on the smoke in the hut and then winced, his soot-streaked eyes watery as he grimaced, showing teeth stained with red. Kunza had been able to coax him back from death, but his body was ruined. So many bones broken and organs burst, he was slowly rotting away.

Throaty coughs rattled his chest and he breathed in wheezing groans, wet with the blood collecting in his lungs. Occasionally, air whistled through a gash in his side. Kunza kneeled beside him and placed a hand on his arm.

"Be strong, Obi. Pain is Talara cleansing your soul for the trials ahead. Don't shy away from it." He gripped Obi's forearm. "Embrace it. This pain you feel is sacred."

Obi's eyes were half-open, mad with pain.

Kunza squeezed his arm and rose, going to Talara's altar and putting herbs in the fire. More smoke rose from the flames, filling the hut. From his table, he took a bundle of charred boar bones and a cup of blessed blood and kneeled beside Obi.

"You are broken," Kunza said. "I can make you whole again. But I need your consent."

Obi groaned a little and Kunza nodded. "You are strong enough to bear this burden, I think. But I need to know, Obi. Are you prepared to dedicate your heart, body, mind, and soul to the Martyred Goddess of Rot, Talara? Are you prepared to take upon the sins of the world for the betterment of all?"

Another moan. Kunza took a strip of leather and held it in front of Obi's face. "Bite onto this and stifle your cries. This will hurt. But to hurt is to love. And like all things, it is fleeting."

Obi hesitated, mouth slightly agape. Kunza stuffed the leather into his mouth and he bit down hard.

"Are you ready?"

Obi nodded, his eyes filled with fear and resolve. He stared at Kunza's glowing red eyes and swallowed. A sound came, muffled from the leather. Kunza took his obsidian blade from his belt and dipped it in the blessed blood. He smeared the blood along the edge of the blade, filling the knapped grooves with red.

"Close your eyes and open your heart."

Obi lay back, his eyes pressed shut. His hands tightened into fists at his sides.

Kunza looked up as the guards led a sway-backed goat into the hut, dragging it by the horns. His empty cauldron sat open, waiting.

Kunza began his work.

Obi's muffled screams could be heard through the village like the whining winds of a coming storm. He lay shivering beneath a blanket against the wall of the hut. His blood seeped through the blanket, and the dirt floor in the center of the room was stained with it. He murmured and groaned and toiled beneath his covers as he suffered the pains of his blessing.

The goat's body, decapitated and gutted, lay in the center of the room in a ring of blood and bone. Ritual and blood made for powerful magic.

Kunza knelt before Talara's altar, her smoky form wrapped loosely around him.

"Will the blessing take?" he whispered.

"I cannot see the future, ka-man," she said. "Mortal flesh is soft and weak. The human soul is frail and crumbles so easily. I cannot say if he will survive."

"If he doesn't, what will we do? My body is too aged to chase the girl."

"You don't need to chase her," Talara said. "I am not so powerless as to let an aberrant girl escape my grasp. Focus on the tasks ahead of you, Priest of Ashes. Azka must be placated for now."

"Of course not, my goddess. I exist as your servant due only to your mercy and grace."

"I enjoy your groveling." She sounded almost amused. "My eyes shall find her wherever she is. And then you will take her and use her to create my paradise."

"Yes, my goddess."

"My sister, she creates such bright and beautiful things only for them to end up withered and diseased," Talara said. "I take these things that she no longer cares for. When they breathe their last pained breath, I give them comfort and take their burden from them. Life is corruption, of the body and the soul. The moment of birth is the moment you start dying. That is the essence of mortality. Something other gods do not understand until it is much too late.

"That is why my sister gives life and I take it. Because she does not grasp the pain of living. She does not comprehend the suffering. Only I understand your pain. And only I can free you from those pains."

Before he could respond, Talara's tendrils tightened around his middle, almost delicately. "If your apostle wakes, send him after the girl, but do not kill her. She is much too important."

CHAPTER 24

Odessa awoke in the dark, nude and shivering. Her heart was heavy and aching. Despair immobilized her like poison in her veins.

Her body throbbed, a heaviness in her bones and a hot, hot throbbing pain in her cramped muscles. She was curled at the base of a moringa tree, also known as a tree of life due to its nourishing seeds and leaves. The tree was long dead, hollow, and rotten inside. Beneath a canopy of ferns and vines and thorns, her body was curled around a long spear shaft, the bloody spearhead clutched to her bleeding chest. A thick layer of dirt and mud was smeared across her bare skin. Blood was dried to a dark maroon all over her face and chest.

Time passed in an indefinite blur. She lay in the shadow of hulking fern fronds and thorned vines, half-awake as the night above turned to day. Scant traces of light pierced the undergrowth she sheltered in, slipping between the waking world and the unconscious.

Awake, she endured numbed misery. Memories of the night on the mountaintop would swell to the forefront of her mind then dissipate just as quickly against the scarred wall her mind had erected. Behind it, she cowered away from her own memories. Of her father's dead body, mutilated and bloodless. Of the ka-man's eyes smoldering with an ancient evil.

Behind the walls of her mind, she hid from the time missing from her memories. In the haziness, she relinquished her very existence. She had died on that mountaintop. As punishment for the sin of killing a god, she was damned to a life turned to stone beneath thorns and brush, in the forest of the god she had murdered.

As she lay frozen on the cold, stony dirt, she imagined all manner of vines and moss and lichen crawling on her extremities, entangling and swallowing her. It was a peaceful, almost pleasant thought, becoming one with the forest she had wounded so gravely. The forest now empty of sacred life, gnawed further by a cancerous grayness.

As the sun knelt below the western horizon, she felt as if she had existed in multitudes beneath the thicket. The muted light filtering through cloud cover and the canopy of undergrowth shifted with the setting sun, and with it came new memories not altogether her own. Images of lush, primeval jungle. Of mountain peaks of pure white. Peaks sparkling with the brash light of a brilliant, inextinguishable sun, unburdened and unhidden.

Yet delving deeper, there were no images. Just emotion and sensation. Muddled feelings. Pain and fear. Loneliness like an empty pit gaping in her chest. A pit that soon filled with rage, magmatic and vicious, lashing out at the walls of isolation. A rage growing and growing. From her heart came lava flows of wrath and vitriol, flowing to her exhausted body and oozing into the cracks of her splintered psyche. A hate so pure, it was almost ecstasy. It was not hers, and yet it was. She had taken it.

Memories of blood and smoldering coals in the black of night kept emerging, oozing through cracks in the chitinous wall of her trauma-wracked mind. The taste of blood was still thick in her mouth. Her eyes were half-closed, still adrift in the interstice of being. Her fingers wrapped around the spearhead until they lost sensation.

The sun rose and fell in a rhythm unbeknownst to her. Beneath the undergrowth, she was beyond the rhythm of the sun and stars. Out of tune with the syncopation of the world, she delved deeper within herself, lost in the rushing of pain, the hurt coming much too fast for her to comprehend. She wanted to scream. To cry. But she knew no one would hear her. And even if there was, she had no voice to cry out with.

The bluegale birds first sang to praise the gods and the glory of nature and so the early gods blessed them with beautiful song. But Odessa was divorced from the gods and all that was natural. Her voice was the gurgling of a slit throat or the hoarse cry of smoke-choked lungs. Her mouth, tainted with the taste of blood, was unfit to make a sound. A womb of silence developed beneath the thicket: a womb for the Forsaken girl and a thorny tomb for the girl she once was. Godsblood poured through her. She was made anew in the womb of the forest.

Days passed by, stretching to weeks spent hibernating in the heart of the forest, lying in the paths young boarlings had trodden. The great boar's den was only a few spans farther, a burrow dug in the side of the mountain covered with dense greenery. A den now empty and slowly falling apart, the life ebbing from each tree and each vine.

Over the span of three days, she emerged from her restless floating between dream and reality. Like driftwood cast onto the shore and then pulled back to sea by the tide. With each waking moment came more lucidity.

Thirst was the first thing she noticed upon waking. Her mouth was parched and felt full of ash. Then she felt hunger like a barbed rope knotting around her stomach. A faint throbbing lingered in her extremities, and her limbs felt heavy and unresponsive. She rolled onto her elbow and looked around her, her dry, glazed eyes finally taking in her surroundings for the first time in weeks.

The canopy of ferns and mountain palms towered high above. The brush and trees bent above her to form a tunnel for young boarlings to charge through as they went to traipse through the woods their mother made safe.

She sat up, her joints creaking and popping, her muscles tight and cramped.

The nazar was gone. She remembered Ajatunde yanking it from her neck, but still its absence was raw and stung. Sadness came swelling from deep within her, rising to fill a resounding emptiness in her chest. Her burned arm was a tableau of melted skin and blackened flesh. The scarred furrows were stained dark with dried blood. From between cracking scabs and from beneath peeling skin came fresh red seeping to the surface. More black streaks ran through her arm like veins, branching out from her elbow down to her fingertips like roots burrowing beneath her skin. The blackened veins were tender to the touch, but her wounds themselves only ached with a dull, almost pleasant pain. The pains of living. Pleasant, but so very painful.

Her feet were covered in many half-healed cuts and scrapes packed with dried mud and blood. Slowly, she rose to her feet, steadying herself against the spear until her head stopped swimming and her shaking legs could bear her weight. She weaved back and forth, half-crouching with the spear as a walking stick, as she followed the forest tunnel away from the den.

Gaps in the thicket soon began to appear, and the tunnel soon gave way to open forest, dense and tangled in all directions. The canopy far above her head was thick but gave enough daylight for her to see by. She stumbled forward, spear clasped loosely in one hand, and took a thick, rough vine hanging from an acacia branch and hacked at it with the spearhead until she had cut into the heart of the vine. She cupped her mouth around it and sucked the water seeping into the exposed flesh like blood. The scant bit of water from the vine did little more than wet her mouth. It barely slaked her thirst, but it was enough.

She took a handful of green seed pods from the acacia, split them open, and gnashed on the hard brown seeds inside. The little bit of sustenance in her stomach quelled the trembling in her hands and brought some solidity to her unmoored mind. Strength ebbed into her limbs, limbs that felt hollow and ruined. Her fingers tentatively prodded the wound in her chest and came away wet with blood. She tried to piece together what had happened on the mountaintop and how she had come to be in the boar's den, but her memory was a haze of smoke.

For a while, she was still too exhausted to think, let alone mourn and truly process what seemed to her like the night before. But as she chewed on bitter seeds, the wall in her mind softened as strength edified it enough to bear the reality.

She was alive. That she was sure of. For better or for worse, she was alive.

Her father was dead. Ubiko was dead. Her mother and Ayana were gone, taken up in Kunza's spell.

Kunza and his horrible eyes smoldering in her mind even now. The obsidian blade. How sharp it was.

She sat beneath the acacia, rocking herself back and forth like a mother does a distressed baby. The urge to throw up rose in her throat, a strong acidic bile gurgling from her stomach, but she held it back.

Odessa wanted to cry but her eyes were dry. She told herself it was her lack of water that dried them, but she was not so sure. There was something broken inside of her. Her fingers ran along her sternum and stopped short at the wound.

She didn't know what to do. She had never felt so alone before. Helpless. She didn't want to do anything. She wanted to sit beneath the acacia for eternity. Her dreams of woodland perpetuity came to her, vague remembrances of her weekslong hibernation quickly followed by a feeling of discontent. She had to do something.

Kunza would come for her.

Her father had mentioned a wise man to the north. But where in the north? She was swamped by the enormity of her helplessness. The forest above her made her feel so small. What was she to do? She wanted nothing more than to have her father here to guide her.

She sat beneath the acacia for hours, not knowing what to do. But eventually, she got up, her mind still ruminating over her situation and the loss of her life as she had known it. While chewing on acacia seeds and the starchy stems of palm leaves, she gathered more palm leaves into a stack and fashioned herself a skirt like the ones she and Ayana made on spring celebrations. With vines and bark, she made herself a pair of clumsy sandals and lashed them to her feet.

The wise man. Her thoughts began to center on and swirl around one point. The idea of the mystical wise man her father had spoken of was now the point around which her attention revolved. *I have to get to the wise man.*

So, deep in the forest with only dense woodland stretching in all directions, she set out away from the boar's den, unsure of where she was headed. In the end, it didn't matter. She was already lost. If she got any more lost, she would only starve to death. If the village caught her, she would be sacrificed again. She was already dead. She had died with the boar god. She had died again on the mountaintop. Her body was just not aware of it yet.

She came to a stream and knelt by the water and drank deeply, gulping the icy water as it flowed past her. She washed the dirt and blood from her body, shivering at the cold water but rejuvenated by its chill. She followed the stream until it joined with a stronger stream. The streams coming from the mountains gave her a vague sense of where she was: somewhere in the northern end of the forest.

She followed the stream through the foothills, and when she came upon a log fallen across the stream, she crossed it toward what she thought was the northern bank. She kept the stream in her sight as she climbed the foothills parallel to it.

Night came swiftly, her single-minded pursuit of an illusory wise man distracting her from the fading light in the forest. She ate roots and seeds that made her stomach ache and slept beneath a broad-leafed tree, the stream babbling softly in the night.

In the night, her eyes grew wet with tears she had not been able to shed in the day. She dreamed of her family's screams. Of her father's still beating heart held before her. His blood poured down her throat. She dreamed she was chased through a dark wood by eyes of flame and obsidian blades.

CHAPTER 25

The terrain was treacherous at the base of the mountains. Sharp scree stabbed through Odessa's flimsy sandals and the slopes were hard on her exhausted legs, but she followed the mountain's edge until she reached the end of the stakewall.

The stakes abutted a steep cliffside as the mountain loomed high above. She followed the stakewall for a long time, thinking of the night her father had led her to the gate. She thought of those he had killed. And how they had killed him in turn. In her mind, she saw his lifeless face and smelled burnt flesh. She rubbed her tender fingertips along the nazar's edge.

As she drew closer to the gate, she drifted from the wall into the brush. It was foolish to go so close to the gate—which was no doubt being guarded by people meaning to kill her—but it could not be avoided. She had tossed her bag when she was captured. If there was a chance it was still there in the jungle, she could not leave it. Dressed in a grass skirt and with only her hunger pangs to keep her alive, she would not survive long, Night Jungle or not.

Her atrophied muscles ached and throbbed. Nausea bubbled in her guts. A dull, incessant thrumming ran through her veins and reverberated through her body. Branches and thorns scratched at her and the hard dirt scraped the skin from her knees. Drops of blood daubed the dirt and brush behind her.

The stakewall was the only way she could get out of the basin without risking falling from some cliffside and breaking her neck. And everyone knew it. So why were there so few guards?

They must think I'm dead. The thought saddened her but also brought her a bit of assurance. She could run away with a clean break and start anew somewhere the Gray hadn't reached. Somewhere no one would know what she had done. Somewhere far from red coal eyes and blood.

Still, she wanted more than anything to go home. But there was no home left for her. Far in the valley, her family's hut was a ruin of heat-cracked mudbrick and ash. Her thoughts drifted to her mother and sister. She wondered if her mother and Ayana were in mourning. If they were sad she was gone. *If I could only talk to them*, she thought, but she knew it was foolish. There was nothing to say. The time for talk had long passed.

She wondered if her mother would remarry, and a spike of resentment pricked at her. Why had her mother allowed this all to happen? She could have done something. Anything. She could have at least looked like she cared that her husband was dead and her daughter was being murdered in front of her. The entire time, Odessa had been looking to her for something. Anything. But her mother had refused to even look at her.

Odessa wallowed in despair and anger. Anger at her mother and the village and herself. Frustrated tears came to her eyes and she did nothing to stop them. Clasped in her clammy hands, the spearhead was heavy and its iron was smooth. *I wonder if this was one of the spears that killed Papa.*

If she hadn't been caught, her father would have been deep in the Night Jungle before anyone knew he was gone. If she had been quieter or quicker, he would still be alive. If she hadn't gotten pinned by the boar god and cursed, he would still be alive. If she hadn't been born, he would still be alive.

The wise man, she reminded herself. *Get to the wise man. Nothing else matters.* Fulfilling her father's last request was more important than her self-pity, she told herself, but that was not entirely true. It was only a distraction from the hurt and horror.

Footsteps scraping the hard-packed dirt stopped her in a heartbeat.

In the open scrubland, the only cover she could hide in was the brush that clung to the dirt and withering yellow grass in clusters. She crouched in the brush, her body tense and taut like a fraying rope. She held the spear close to her side, poised to strike. Through the brush, she could see a figure walking along the wall, coming toward her, the brush she hid behind only a few yards from the wall.

I'll kill him. If he sees me, I'll kill him, Odessa told herself, although she did not believe the words. Her heart quivered in her chest and she was so afraid, her muscles began to seize up, freezing with fright. Her limbs turning to stone, she imagined the man stopping in front of her, her leaping to her feet, spearpoint aimed for his throat, and his spear piercing through her middle. She imagined holding her own guts while they came out in loops through her fingers and spilled onto the dirt.

The footsteps drew nearer. Her grip tightened on the charred shaft, ash and soot crumbling beneath her fingers. Her body crouched lower, flattening with her muscles tensed. Her legs felt planted in the dirt and she feared they would fail if the man caught sight of her. She would be found like a cornered rabbit trembling in the undergrowth, eyes wide with terror, mind blank.

She held her breath in her chest, too afraid to let it pass her lips. The footsteps were close. Through the gap beneath the bush, she could see a shadow on the ground. A shadow moving along the wall. Her stomach tightened and her insides lurched to a queasy halt. She saw hide shoes walking only yards away.

Her eyes refused to even blink as she watched the feet. She feared the raucous pounding in her chest would give her away. Sweat beaded at her hairline and collected at the rim of her upper lip. With the figure directly in front of her, all pretenses of a fight evaporated. If those feet stopped, if they turned in her direction , if the figure uttered a single word—she would run. She would run as fast as her leaden legs would take her.

The figure passed. A minute stretched after the figure had disappeared from view. The sound of hide shoes traipsing on the trodden dirt path along the wall grew distant. Odessa's body remained tensed, ready to flee in an instant. The footsteps receded and the quiet of the wall returned. Still, she waited a few more minutes that stretched over an eternity, and then her breath hissed through her teeth and her muscles relaxed.

She crawled slowly through the brush, glancing back the way the warrior had walked—only to see the bare wall, old timbers standing at attention, their tips bristling with bronze.

Odessa moved through the sparse clusters of brush until she saw a section of stakes that leaned slightly toward the Night Jungle, a few of the timbers sagging with age. To Odessa, they were a ladder out of the valley—and a way to escape the grief and the pain. To leave it all behind.

Crouched behind a thorny bush, she waited for the warrior walking the wall to pass by again. Her nerves sparked with impatience. She wanted to be over the wall and sprinting into the jungle already. Every second spent in the valley was another second spent as prey. Of being the naked girl on the altar.

After a few moments, she could take it no longer and crept out from the cover of thorns. She was a few strides away from the wall, only open scrubland and bare dirt between them. Far down the wall to her left, she could see the gate and its guards.

At the gate, two villagers stood with spears, occasionally taking turns scaling the ladder to the lookout at the top of the wall, watching the Night Jungle while their attention was mostly turned away from the forest toward the village.

Watching for me.

She looked both ways along the wall and saw nothing but an empty rut and spans of upright timbers. The stakewall towered above her, more than double her height, its logs sharpened at the top. She padded into the clearing along the wall, half-crouched, and ran her hand along the timbers. The wood was smooth. There was nothing to grasp and hoist herself up with.

She kicked the sandals from her feet, pressed her sole to the wood of the leaning timbers, and stuck the tip of the spear firmly in the wood. With a kick, she shoved off and propelled herself up. Her other foot slapped against the wood, and she felt herself rise again before she began to fall. Her feet slipped against the smooth wood, her knees scraping against the wall as she fell back to the dirt.

A shout came from the gate. She took two steps back from the wall and charged forward to scale the wall again, emboldened by desperation and fear.

She rammed the spearhead into the mortared gap between two timbers as her feet struck wood. Her toenails bit into the hardwood. She propelled herself upward, an arm outstretched toward the top of the wall.

A horn sounded, echoing throughout the valley.

An arrow streaked past her back as the shouts of guards grew louder. Her fingers curled in the gap between two sharpened stake points. Her feet slipped for a moment and then found purchase. Another arrow whistled through the air a hairsbreadth away from the back of her neck. She clambered, and with both hands she hauled herself upward, leaving the spear hanging from the wall beneath her.

The stakes scraped against her belly. A quick glance below and she saw two warriors rushing along the wall toward her. With all her strength, she swung over the wall. For a moment, she was weightless. The jungle stretched to the horizon.

Then gravity took hold of her again. She landed, her legs collapsing beneath her. Jarring pain swept through her shins and into her knees.

She ran as fast as she could into the jungle, leaving her pursuers far behind.

CHAPTER 26

Grief was an obsidian blade, twisted and grating against Odessa's ribs, gouging wounds that would never heal. Driven deep in her heart, slicing it asunder in slow, agonizing cuts.

The forest was dark and endless She had never been in the Night Jungle alone before, either. Her legs shaking with exhaustion, she stumbled forward in the dimness.

Her sense of direction was tangled in the dark foliage, useless in the maze of massive tree trunks and layers upon layers of plant life, all half-dead and gnawed by blight. As daylight slowly seeped through the canopy to the jungle floor, she could see how cancerous yellow and brown had eaten away at the greenery, at centuries-old trees, gnarled and gruesome, some as thick around as their hut in Kalaro.

Vague memories came, fleeting and ephemeral. Flames and shadows obscured her vision, but she could see the blood spraying into the air and onto the burning altar. Ash-faced men and women in the throes of death as she ran them through with a charred spear. Screaming and crying echoed from the mountaintop.

That wasn't me. I couldn't have done that.

Spear in hand, she stumbled forward, barely keeping upright. Pain dug deep into her flesh like talons. The weight of exhaustion grew heavier and heavier with every step. When the rushing of her blood had stilled, her strength had bled away, leaving her slow and disoriented. But she could not stop. Either the warriors would catch her, or some beast of the Night Jungle—some horrible, abominable monster—would catch her and rip her open and feast upon her innards.

Movement in the periphery of her vision had her glancing behind often, the spear raised to stab and slash. But only forest stood around her, stretching in all directions. Her imagination conjured up images of all the creatures lurking in the outer world. In this forest unloved by the gods, there was no telling what creatures lurked in the dark recesses untouched by the sun.

Odessa only had the vaguest sense as to the Night Jungle's true size. It stretched from the western hills to the edges of the lowland savannah to the south and to the sandy shores to the west. A jungle, mountainous in its own right, spread out to the horizon when viewed from the hillsides. Now, it was a labyrinth—and she was trapped in its belly.

In every shadow lay an ashen body, poised to strike. In every rustling leaf, the footstep of a killer after her head. Fear kept her lifeless limbs moving—a fear so total, it drowned out all sense in its mire and murk. Flashes in her mind of the horror on the mountaintop: her father's dead body, the boar tearing a hunter open, her father's heart squished in the ka-man's hand. Terrible memories flashed in quick succession. Unbidden they came like thunderclaps, overpowering exhaustion and clear thought.

Something wrapped around her ankle and she lurched forward, into ferns and sedges. She rolled onto her side, scrambling to free herself. She expected to see bolas wrapped around her ankles but found only a tangled cluster of woody liana vines hidden within a splaying sedge. Relief drained from her tense body as she lifted her foot from the tangle of vines and rubbed the soreness from her ankle.

Stupid girl. Scared of every shadow. She knew there was much to fear in the jungle, but she had run like dumb prey, too scared to think. Around her, the labyrinthian sprawl of dense jungle spread out in all directions. *Don't even know which way I'm going.*

It felt good to sit, her exhausted legs throbbing as sensation returned. A deep ache simmered in her muscles and her lungs breathed fire. *Can't run like a spooked rabbit. I must get to the wise man. Use your head, Dessa. Think.*

Thin trickles of murky light pricked through chinks in the dull canopy above. The thought of climbing one of the trees to use as a vantage point crossed her mind. But the mere thought tired her. *What would I hope to find? More trees as far as the eye can see.*

The trees were spans above Odessa, and in her current state, she would most likely fall to her death long before she breached the canopy. She wasn't even sure if she would be able to continue walking let alone climb the twisted trunks of such massive trees.

She drank stale water from a calabash taken from the warriors, the warm water filling the cracks in her dry throat. After an hour of sitting on the damp leaf litter beneath the wilted sedge, she forced herself to unsteady feet and continued, heading in an unknown direction.

As the darkness of the jungle deepened, Odessa stumbled upon a stream and followed it, its twists and turns vaguely familiar. After a while, she thought she found the muddy bank where she and her father had crawled. The mud was pocked with the footprints of small animals but, amid the mess of tracks, she thought she could make out old footprints made by boots.

Retracing steps taken in the dark, it was almost full dark when Odessa stumbled upon the fallen tree they had taken refuge in. Without thinking, she crawled into the hollow at its roots and curled up in the soft dirt. With darkness bearing down on her, swallowing her up in its pitch-black maw, she was truly and utterly alone.

It was late morning when she crawled out from the hole beneath the roots. Hunger wrung her stomach. She tried to remember the day she was captured. But jarred from sleep and dragged out of the hollow without warning back then, her memory was nebulous.

But the more she examined the path she thought they had taken, the more she noticed fat drops of dried blood. *Oh, Papa,* she thought, remembering his bloody hand holding hers.

She followed the path until she came to the spot where he had sent her away. The leaf litter was still disrupted, the earth stained with blood.

She paused, her breath stolen. Then she forced her gaze away and continued, skirting around the bloody ground.

The path she had fled was more well-defined in her mind. Adrenaline blurred some of it, but she could mostly remember. Snapped branches and a crushed fern marked the spot where the warrior had tackled her. Gouges dug in the dirt from her struggling feet. Scratches in the dirt where her fingers had clawed, vainly trying to pull free from the warrior as he dragged her away.

She tried to picture the bag and bow and quiver as it had sailed from her hands and into the undergrowth, but everything had happened so fast.

One of her arrows lay in the undergrowth, grown over with thin vines and roots that mostly obscured it from vision. *How long was I asleep?* she wondered as she pulled the arrow from the grasp of the greenery. She could remember indistinctly the pattern of night and day as she had slept, but she thought she had only been asleep for two days at most, so sick from exhaustion and terror as she had been. But the jungle had reclaimed her arrow in the time since she had been taken.

She continued, finding more arrows nearby until she came upon her quiver, more arrows scattered around it as it lay in the undergrowth, the leather damp and dotted with mildew. A dank scent lingered in the leather. Her bow was not far from the quiver, still strung. It was damp as she picked it up, and she hoped its lacquered wood and waxed string had let it resist the worst of the jungle's insidious moisture. She unstrung it slowly and carefully. Leaving a bow strung for so long weakened the wood.

Not far from the bow she found her sack and began rifling through it, her fingers grasping clothes and food as if they were trinkets of the gods.

Any food she had packed was rotten, shriveled black, and mottled with mold. While searching, her fingers scraped something wet and pulpy at the bottom of the sack. When she drew her hand out she gagged. The cloying, putrid stench of rotten fruit clung to the back of her throat. The brown sludge smeared in globs on her fingertips and packed beneath her nails threatened to make her vomit, but she bit back the urge and wiped her hand clean on the ground. She dumped out the sack and picked out a tunic and pair of trousers from among the pile of rotten food and stained clothes. Stripping out of her tattered palm skirt and putting on her wrinkled, fetid clothes was a great comfort. To have homespun cloth against her skin again made her feel safe again. Almost whole in some strange way.

Among the decaying fruit and rot-stained clothes, she found a water gourd and her skinning knife. She stuck the knife in the belt of her trousers before beginning to clean the inside of the empty sack. Despite her best efforts the festering stink of decay remained, having seeped deep into the hemp. Her clothes and blanket were soiled, but there was little she could do but wipe off the worst of the rotten stains with a handful of leaves and pack them away again. Tying the sack's drawstrings to the bow like a lopsided yoke, she slung the bow and sack over her shoulder and continued her trek to what she thought was north. Her gaze was focused on the forest floor, looking for the leaves of edible plants her father had taught her. But she did not tarry longer than necessary. She only glanced at the dull greenery around her as she made her way at a brisk pace. Her feet dragged along through the leaf litter and undergrowth, and she used the trunks of trees she passed to steady her gait.

Beneath the broad, triangular leaves of taro plants, she was able to dig up a handful of round tubers and resisted the urge to bite into the starchy bulbs raw. Everyone knew not to eat raw taro, but her nagging hunger urged her on. She put the tubers in her bag and saved herself the burning itch of mouth and throat that would refuse to leave for days.

She was grateful for the few taro plants and wild yams she was able to find—not only for the food, but for the excuse to sit and rest her legs. In her digging, her hands had been sullied with wet dirt and sweat and detritus. The wounds in her burnt arm were packed with dirt too.

The sounds of the forest were loud and incessant, a droning buzz underlying it all while mixed with the chattering and howling of monkeys high in the understory. But it was what Odessa did not hear that unnerved her. The silent predators skulking in the shadows or the malevolent spirits waiting for the cover of night. Giant mantises and flies almost as large as her palm skittered and darted from her. She was able to skewer a giant mantis as long as her forearm with a well-placed arrow and slung it over her shoulder, its thin translucent wings poking out from beneath its chitin and its clawed legs reaching to the forest floor.

When the light grew dim, she made a small fire beneath a wide teak tree and, in a miserly amount of water poured in a clay pot, she boiled the sliced taro and yam until it was soft. While she waited for the tubers to cook, she grilled the mantis on a stake held over the flames. Steam whistled from gaps in the brittle carapace. When it was done, she broke off a leg while it was still hot, the thin carapace snapping easily. She bit the arm and relished the crunch. It tasted faintly like mushrooms. She ate a few hunks of yam and taro while they were still hot, scalding her mouth. Her stomach churned but she forced herself to eat, chewing slowly and taking a deep breath before she swallowed to keep it all from coming back up. As the heat of the day dissipated from the jungle and a chill sank to the forest floor, she wrapped up the rest of her mantis and taro and yams in a few wide leaves. She smothered her warm, pleasant fire with wet dirt and drank the hot starchy water before clambering up the teak tree.

A dank, earthen smell like moss and rot grew stronger as the chill thawed of the night clung to the jungle floor.

On a high branch hidden from the ground by leafy limbs below, she laid a blanket on a wide limb nearly parallel to the ground and lashed herself to it with a thick hemp cord. The feeling of rope around her middle made her think of the binds around her wrists, but she shied away from such thoughts. In the dark, they seemed to swell and grow malicious. Not just bad memories any longer, they became hellish nightmares she relived over and over again.

In the crook of the tree, where limb met trunk, she placed the bag and bow and rested her head upon it like a lumpy pillow. Skinning knife clutched to her breast, the jungle grew oppressively dark. So dark, she could not differentiate between when she had her eyes open and when exhaustion had drawn them closed.

All through the night, terrible noises echoed through the trees. Howls and moans. Sudden high-pitched screams that made her heart skip and leap into her throat. Sleep came to her in short respites. Whenever she closed her eyes, it seemed some sound, a thud or a scream, immediately woke her.

As she slipped back into a tenuous sleep, the jungle quieted, the only sound a faraway chirruping. A presence gathered in the shadows at the base of the teak, a wet slithering against fibrous bark. The smell of moss and fungus and rot, almost sickly sweet in its rankness.

In the branches climbed tendrils of vines, slithering along the limbs, their ends flickering like the tongues of snakes tasting the night air. They crawled slowly toward the sleeping girl. Climbing up the trunk of the tree and dropping down from branches high above her, they surrounded her.

Odessa did not wake up until the vines tightened around her throat. She meant to lash out with the knife, only to find her arm pinned by the slimy vines constricting her, pinning her to the limb and crushing the life from her.

In the dark, she could not tell what was strangling her. She thrashed in its grasp, wriggling like a worm. A vine wrapping loops around her wrist slithered around her scarred thumb and in between her palm and the knife. Her grip tightened around the smooth bone handle. The vine squirmed, trying to pry the knife from her hand, to loosen her grip enough to disarm her. She stabbed and hacked at vines as best she could. Restrained by the forearm, she could only weakly slash at the woody vines they tightened.

Her head grew light as the vine around her throat strangled the thought from her mind. She thrashed more desperately, panic the only thing in her dimming mind. Straining with all her might, the vines did not waver. They continued constricting tighter and tighter.

Her weak stabs grew stronger and more frenzied as her heart raced with terror. She gasped in thin, strangled breaths, sucking barely any air into her lungs. Chips of wood hit her face as she hacked the vines. Her arm lifted higher and higher as she stabbed at the vine looped around her middle, pinning both her arms. The vine around her neck slithered tighter, and she couldn't breathe. A pulsing pressure building up in her temples as she struggled against the vines with her last breath. Slashing and stabbing, thrashing and straining.

A crack and the pressure around her chest slackened. The vine around her chest gave way a bit, giving her arm enough freedom to hack it in half. Her arms free, she clawed at the vine around her neck with her left hand. She pulled it from her neck enough to gasp a deep breath. The pounding in her skull poured away from her head. The point of the knife slipped between her neck and the vine, and with a great effort she sawed it in half.

More vines coiled around her limbs but she slashed at them wildly, trying to keep them at bay. She cut the rope around her middle as another vine took hold around the shoulder. Her left hand grabbed her sack while her right hand drove the knife into the vine at her shoulder until the point grazed her skin. It snapped and, shaking free of therest of the encroaching vines, Odessa dropped from the limb to the darkness below.

A jarring pain vibrated from her shins to her tailbone as she landed. She stumbled but stayed on her feet. Pins and needles pricked her legs as she turned, trying to peer through the darkness. She heard the wet scrape of the undulating vines but could not see a thing. She raised her knife and slowly began to back away.

At the base of the tree, a shadow moved. A large mass slid down the trunk. The stench of rotten moss filled her nostrils. In the darkness, she could barely make out the mass rising from the forest floor to the size of a goat.

More vines and plants clawed at her ankles. She kicked them away and ran into the night, bouncing off tree trunks and pulling free from the grasp of overhanging branches, unsure if they were reaching for her.

She ran for what seemed like hours, tripping and tumbling through the night at breakneck pace until a screeching howl stopped her. The buzz of the forest surrounded her. It had been silent when the vines attacked her. The droning and clamoring of the jungle relieved her but also terrified her. Predators skulked through the night all around. The back of her neck prickled. She could feel eyes on her. *Just your scared imagination*, she told herself, holding the spearhead close to her chest.

Feeling around in the dark, she pricked herself on a thorny bush and crawled beneath its prickly boughs, getting scratched all over. She curled at the base of the bush and stayed still, not even daring to take a full breath.

She waited for daylight, the overwhelming noise of the jungle all around her. Predators, beast and monster alike, prowled in the darkness. She did not sleep until the light of morning dawned on the deep recesses of the jungle.

CHAPTER 27

Odessa awoke, haunted by the horrors of her dreams. She had slept until the jungle floor was as bright as it would be and then crawled out from the spike-bush. Her arms and face were covered in scratches from a night huddled beneath the bush. With a splash of stale water from her gourd, she washed her arm and wrapped it with fresh linen she had stowed in her bag weeks earlier, in what felt like another lifetime.

Abrasions coiling her arms and neck told her the vines' assault had not just been a nightmare. She did not know what the mass beneath the tree had been. No one knew of each and every terror that considered the Night Jungle home. Monsters of all kinds slunk through the shadow of deep jungle, along with beasts that could kill a person before the brain could register its presence.

But the monster that stank of rot was different. The sensation Odessa felt had not been fear alone. It was similar to the sensation on the mountaintop, when she had first seen the Kunza's coal-red eyes. It was the terror of the soul.

She tried to shake the fear of the night from her thoughts. The forest around her was thick, and she had no idea which direction she had run during the night. If she was not careful, she could walk right back to Kalaro and into the hands of the ash-daubed warriors. But there was an undercurrent of primal satisfaction that disturbed her as well.

She tried to divine from the shadows which way the sun was rising, but she could only estimate because the daylight was diffused by the gray haze above so many layers of leaf and branch. She made her best guess and headed to what was hopefully away from the rising sun. Her goal was to lose her pursuers in the forest, emerge on the western plains skirting the Night Jungle, and arrive at Noyo to find the wise man. It was as good a plan as she had. It made sense to her sleep-deprived mind.

A deep hunger clawed at her ribs. A few pieces of yam and taro did little to satiate it. She crunched on the end of a mantis leg still bent in prayer. Her stomach churned uneasily. The gourd hanging at her hip swung, its contents sloshing. It was less than half full already. She drank only enough to wet her dry mouth.

Her body was heavy with an exhaustion that seemed to weigh upon her bones. Despite the stifling heat of the deep jungle, she was occasionally struck by intense chills like being hit by a sudden mountain gust.

She traversed the steep slopes of jungle hills, beating a path through the dense undergrowth with a thick, straight branch that she leaned on for support as she climbed. Most of the hills sloped down to the lowlands, but the occasional rise brought with it more exhaustion. Her eyelids were heavy and she found herself almost falling asleep as she walked along the flat stretches of jungle between slopes.

Soon, the land leveled out and she knew she had reached the lowland jungle. Relief came and went in the same instant. The jungle stretched far westward and even farther northward.

She took off at a loping pace toward what she hoped was west.

Lightheadedness dulled her vision and black dots burned along the periphery. The trees around her shifted up and down as her equilibrium failed her. A stitch pulled taut along her ribs, and she could not draw a full breath. Acid bubbled in the churning of her empty stomach.

It was still midday, but she could not go on any farther. She cut through the thick jungle until she found a low hollow surrounded by high palms and ferns where she could bed down for the night. Taking a few sips of tepid water left the gourd with little more than a quarter to slosh inside. She ate the rest of the mantis and yams. A little strength returned to her trembling limbs and beat back the headache that clouded her mind.

When she felt steady enough to stand, she gathered a few handfuls of supple twigs and palm fronds and spent the next remaining hours of daylight twisting twigs and branches into small effigies and charms to hang from the branches and bushes surrounding her makeshift camp. When daylight faded into night, she was surrounded by almost a dozen small charms to confound the evil that prowled the jungle night.

She sat waiting for night to come, anxiety growing with the dark. An hour before night had truly seeped into the jungle, she gave in to her fear and gathered enough dead wood, which was plentiful in the blighted jungle, to start a small fire. She would rather risk attracting warriors than spend another night in the dark with evil spirits and possessed vines and creatures that reeked of death. The fire would keep beasts at bay and hopefully monsters as well. But doubt remained and fear stuck in her chest like a spike of cold metal.

The last shreds of thin light drained from the jungle floor and Odessa fed the fire with her bow in hand and knife laid beside her. At her right, arrows sat with their tips stuck in the dirt, spaced out less than a handswidth apart. She fought the weighty urge to sleep, jerking awake whenever her eyelids fluttered closed.

The flickering firelight cast the fronds of ferns and palms as strange, ghoulish, dancing shadows that seemed to move of their own accord. The fire burned away only a small amount of the blackness around her, but she was grateful for it nonetheless.

The howls and screams of the jungle came in full force and in all directions. The uproar filled her ears and drowned out her thoughts. Her eyes peered into the inky black, afraid some monster would sneak up on her, the booming of its footfalls muted by the cacophony.

Hours passed with Odessa drifting in and out of thin sleep. A few times, she heard the rustling of leaves in the dark or the snapping of twigs, but nothing came for her. After a while, unable to keep her eyes open any longer, she slipped into a deeper sleep. She dreamed of home and family.

When she awoke, fatigue still lingered in Odessa's sore muscles and a twinge of pain irritated her neck—but her mind felt much clearer than the day before. She ate the last of her yams and, after burying the smoldering remains of her fire, continued on. Most of the morning was spent foraging and scrounging what potable water she could from surrounding plant life as she walked.

She chewed on palm shoots and sucked moisture from the starchy fibers. Some scant bit of strength returned to her body. The palm shoots helped assuage her nausea, and the act of chewing kept her from falling asleep as she walked.

She was halfway up a slight rise when she suddenly stopped. A ray of faint ambient light splashed upon the left side of her face. A tiny sliver of sunlight slipping through a tiny crack in the leaves above. The palm shoot hung from her lips as she looked up. Through that crack she caught a glimpse of the sun. But the sun was supposed to be on her right side this whole time. In the northern sky.

She spat out the end of the palm shoot and glanced back at the trail she had cut through the jungle. Oh no. Oh no, this can't be happening. Have I been going the wrong way? The jungle around her had become a blur of trees and bush. She could have been walking in circles this whole time and not even known. Her memory of the last few days was hazy and sporadic. Even if she had been walking in the right direction initially she could have veered off her path at any time since then. Threads of worry worked their way around her heart and began to squeeze.

But when she looked back up at the canopy the sun's faint light shone heaviest on the right side of her face. She stared at it for a while until the wind shifted and the branches above moved to swallow that tiny hole in the canopy.

Was it my imagination? The jungle was a strange, disquieting place and she wondered if it was messing with her mind now. With the assaulting vines and rotten monsters, she thought she could have been delirious from lack of sleep and overexertion. Or evil spirits, insidious in their machinations, were driving her mad.

Oh gods, I think I'm going mad. I'm sure of it. I've lost my mind somewhere in this jungle.

She reached the cliffs before the jungle lowlands by midday, and for a while she sat, staring out over the vast expanse of jungle . It stretched to the far horizon, an ocean of blighted brown and dull green.

CHAPTER 28

Obi howled in frustration. The jungle was a dense labyrinth, and he could barely find the girl's putrid scent amid the jungle's odors. But they were getting close. He was sure of it.

His new tongue lay cumbersome in his mouth and his cries of rage and agony came out as throaty howls. His bony knuckles were unfeeling no matter how hard he hammered the ground. His arms were thick and hairy, his skin pulled taut over muscles not his own—skin that was now stitched and scarred and turned to thick hair around his shoulders. The hair around his shoulders and down his back was dappled white and brown and matted with the blood of beast and man. Along his arms and chest, bones rose from his skin like knobs of stone rising from the earth. The horns atop his goat's head poked his scarred shoulders as he screamed out to the gray sky above. A guttural, strangled scream from cumbersome vocal cords that issued through a mouth full of sharpened, ill-fitting teeth.

Everything hurt. His entire body ached and burned and stunned in a never-ending rush of raw sensation.

Waves of rage broke upon him again and again. Some bulwark in his soul had broken in the process. A change had come over him from within. All his emotions were raw and overwhelming; each one crashed over him, nearly forcing him to his knees.

Obi dug his fists into the dirt he had packed down with his blows. Hunched over, his goat head swaying, tongue lolling out of his mouth, he panted, trying to calm himself and think—but his mind was too muddled, too addled by the procedure and the magics.

His thoughts moved slowly and Talara's voice whispered incessantly inside his head, an unintelligible nattering in the back of his mind. He tried to listen, but there seemed to be some kind of barrier muffling her voice. He wanted nothing more than to hear the rasp of her whispered words clearly.

"Obi?"

His muscular frame turned awkwardly to his second-in-command, his jagun, standing a distance behind him. He couldn't remember the man's name. The bravest among them, even he would not meet Obi's eyes. The rest of the warriors stood clustered farther back in the jungle, lined up and awaiting his orders. All their eyes were averted from his grotesque form.

Obi nodded, showing his rage had subsided, although it most assuredly had not.

His second-in-command ordered his men. Obi wanted to break something. *Why had Talara taken so much from him?*

He could not even speak. His own men could not stand to look at him. He had become a pariah.

There had been a mute in the village when Obi was a boy. Born soft in the brain, the man never grasped speech; he just gestured and groaned. Everyone had humored the man, but in the end, he had been little more than a nuisance in the village, at best an amusing oddity. Obi dismissed the reminiscence with a derisive snort and a shake of the head. The beads in the braided beard of his goat's head rattled. He was nothing like him. He was a servant of Talara. He was the goddess's chosen apostle, blessed with strength no man could rival. The sidelong glances and wary stares of the others meant nothing. If they spurned him, then their faith in the goddess was weak.

As his warriors conferred, the phantom whispers echoing in his mind urged him forward in their incomprehensible tongue. He could sense something guiding him. One of Talara's eyes beckoned him. Day and night, they called to him. A certain kinship they shared, those in Talara's service. He could see them all around in the night, spirits in the shadows and beasts in the woods. Dedicated to the one that awaited all living things: the Queen of Rot.

He noticed a warrior risk a furtive glance in his direction. Their eyes met. The warrior blanched and quickly averted their gaze. They were right to fear him. He was Talara's holy scourge, an instrument of purification and mortification for a festering world.

The resolve of the dogged warriors was fading as the day wore into night. Exhaustion sucked the strength from them like leeches. At the base of the sloping drop-off, they set up camp while Obi broke trail, led by the putrid stench of tainted blood, ephemeral and fleeting on the wind.

He was drawn by something prodding deep in his mind. The lowlands were a tangle of jungle and swamp. Even so close to the highlands, the ground grew wet and his heavy, bone clad feet sank into the soft dirt.

The shadows grew deeper as the sun dipped below the horizon. They spoke to him in a tongue he could not decipher. But he liked it. The susurrations made him feel at ease. They eased the disgust that his new, twisted form had wrought within himself. The isolation he had felt was now gone, among the voices of spirits and shades.

They urged him through the jungle. His new sword, larger and more like a cleaver, hacked through vines and greenery. His long, twisting horns scraped against trees and left gouges in the bark as he hurried past. His goat eyes peered into the growing darkness and it yielded a bit, revealing the secrets it sought to obscure.

Movement in the shadows drew his attention. His body tensed. Nothing would stop him from getting the girl. Anything that attempted to hinder Talara's will would die in darkness.

CHAPTER 29

Odessa had camped among a grove of withered begonias, sleeping close to a roaring fire. But as night ebbed and thin, pale wisps of morning softened the blackness, her fire shrank to flickering embers. As she began shifting between the interstice of wakefulness and dream, a sudden jerk upon her leg jolted her awake.

Her eyelids fluttered open. An unfamiliar jungle shrouded in early morning dimness overwhelmed her. Before her mind had fully been roused from the liminal spaces of restless dreams, something wrapped around her ankle tugged her with a jerk and she was dragged farther from the scant ambient moonlight filtering through the thin canopy above the begonias.

She lurched with a start and tried to sit up, but pain lanced through her body like a thousand knives grinding against her bones. A hoarse gasp escaped her dry lips, and she collapsed back onto the leafy jungle floor. Her exhausted muscles, still numb with sleep, were limp and totally unresponsive to her demands.

Another tug and she was dragged farther into the undergrowth. She tried to speak, to cry out, but could utter nothing but a choked croak. The stench of death and decay was thick in the air, a cloying and stifling miasma.

She raised her head, craning her pained neck enough to see lichenous vines wrapped around her leg from her ankle up to her knee. They dragged her into a dark hollow beneath a deadfall, where the damp moss and lichen had made a home. The vines ended in a mass of ooze like snot, half as tall as she was, with a circular mouth lined with rows and rows of needle teeth. Its throat and mouth undulated, flexing and relaxing as it dragged her toward its maw.

Odessa jerked, her body twisting a bit before pain shooting up her spine took the breath from her lungs and brought black spots to her vision.

Another tug. She raised her foot and gave the vines wrapped around her other leg a weak, pitiful kick. The vines dragged her farther. The ooze surged from its hiding place. Its mouth opened and puckered around her ankle. Its needle teeth pierced her hide boots and dug into her skin like giant nettle spines, all of them rippling in an undulating rhythm, digging farther into her flesh and drawing more of her leg into its body.

"Let go!" She kicked again. Her foot glanced off the vine. The blob was unfazed. Its teeth ripped into her calf and dragged her deeper into its sinkhole maw. A caustic burning sank into the flesh of her leg.

She dug her elbow in the dirt and attempted to drag herself away, but the vines held her fast.

Something fluttered in the treetops above. Another beast here to tear her to pieces, she was sure. All sorts of scavengers and carrion eaters must have gathered to feast upon her corpse. She kicked again and her foot struck ooze and meat with a wet, weak thud. Her fingers dug into the dirt. With all the strength she could muster in her battered body, she tried to haul herself away from the snotty blob, but the blob held her fast.

She kicked once more. A disjointed hand of bone and sinew and mucus slid from beneath its mass and took hold of her ankle. She tried to pull free, but the hand pinned her leg firmly to the dirt. Its teeth buried deeper into her, scraping against bone. Another more savage scream burst from her chest.

Something moved in the corner of her eye—a shape darting through the air. It streaked over her, toward the blob, a fine powder falling from the silvery shape as it passed. The powder fell onto her both leg and the blob and erupted in a burst of sunlight.

She shielded her face, white afterimages burned in her eyelids. The pressure around her legs slackened and she kicked away, scrambling as fast as she could from the shadows of the deadfall and the mass of ooze that lived there.

The blob hissed and shrunk away, slinking deeper into the darkness beneath the fallen tree. The shape flew by again, and another sunburst lit the dank hollow.

Odessa crawled, each movement bringing with it stabbing pains like her bones were made of splintered obsidian. Her legs dragged behind her as she returned to the faint light coming from the hole in the canopy. Her pantleg was shredded and the tatters were slick with the blob's viscous saliva and globs of stringy mucus. The leg the blob had swallowed was covered in pinprick punctures that bled like holes in a waterskin.

Her head fell back against soft leaf litter. She heard fluttering wings and rustling leaves. She closed her eyes and let her beleaguered body loosen, melting into the jungle floor. Lack of sleep and food and water finally caught up to her.

Something light and hard bounced off her forehead. She burst awake, arms whirling, striking out at what had struck her. Her eyes still bleary and crusted with sleep, she clawed at phantom creatures of slime and flesh with mouths like needle-lined sinkholes.

A snicker from above. A giggling, high and musical, came from the trees above. Sitting in the lower branches above her was a small pale person, a foot tall at most. Neither male nor female, it sat with a natural grace and poise, its legs crossed and dangling, swinging back and forth. Its face was like a child's but its eyes were black like a wasp's. It wore a gossamer silvery tunic that looked like it was made of spider's web, the shoulders adorned with thorny pauldrons. A wreath of grass was braided in its straight pale gold hair. Wings like a dragonfly's sprouted from its back and fluttered as it laughed. Its laugh tapered off and the tiny person looked down at her and smiled, bouncing a nut in its thin palm.

"Little jumpy, aren't we?" Its voice was like a songbird's trilling.

Odessa scowled. A fairy. It looked to be just a pixie, the lowest caste of fairy. There had been a time when she had wanted nothing more than to see a fairy in the flesh. Even in spite of their penchanct for tricks and beguiling. But that desire of bygone youth was gone now. Her legs stung and burned with the intensity of a hundred wasp stings, and she did not like this fairy's mocking tone. "Leave me alone," she said.

The fairy tossed the nut it held away and clutched its chest, swaying and feigning exaggerated hurt. "You wound me!" It straightened and snickered to itself. "Is that any way to treat your savior?"

"You are no savior of mine, bug," she said, sitting up and trying to stifle her wincing. "Why are you here?"

The fairy shrugged. "Curiosity." It stood, the thin branch barely swaying with the fairy's bouncing steps. "Humans never come out here. And for good reason too."

"What was that thing that took me?" she asked.

"Rotfiend. Nasty things. They never usually cross into fae territory though. It must have been curious about you too." The fairy bounded from the branch and fluttered to the forest floor a short distance away from her. "So what are you?"

Odessa narrowed her eyes. "What do you mean?" "You're no normal human."

"Yes, I am."

"No, you're not." The fairy sniffed the air. "I can smell it on you. There's something off about you." It skipped and fluttered around her, circling around to her other side. "I thought it was plain human wickedness but no, there's something wrong with you."

"Shut up, bug."

"That's what I thought at first, at least," the fairy continued. "But I stayed and I watched after I scared the rotfiend off. And you know what I saw?"

"I'm in no mood for your lies. Now leave me be."

The fairy stopped. "Fae don't lie. So don't lie to me. How did you do that?"

The fairy pointed to her legs. Odessa looked down. The leg in the shredded pantleg was covered in pinprick scars.

"The sun hasn't even reached the top of the sky yet. And that rotfiend spit, it's poison. It should have melted your skin. And it did, it started to. But you know what happened?" The fairy took a tentative step forward. "It scarred quicker than it could eat it away. And all this while you were sleeping. That's not normal." The fairy stopped in front of her, perfunctorily. "So what are you? One of those half-human devils?"

"I'm not a devil! I'm a human. Inside and out!"

The fairy crossed its slender arms across its chest. "If you were human, you'd be just as lost as those others out there. Fae territory is a labyrinth of magic and thorn to big dumb humans. But here you are, sleeping on our doorstep like north. How'd you do it?"

Odessa sat up. "Did you say others? Other humans?"

"Yeah. A bunch of them," the fairy said dismissively. "Are they friends of yours?"

"No," she said. It had to be warriors from Kalaro sent to drag her back to that godsdamned mountaintop and carve out her heart. "Not at all."

"That's good, because they won't make it much farther, I think. The jungle is hungry." The fairy stepped closer, inspecting her. "So tell me. How'd you do it? How did a big dumb human get here?"

Odessa frowned. The fairy continued to stare at her with ink black eyes, so she busied herself with tending to her half-healed wounds. She drew her knife and cut away her shredded pantleg to expose the reddened leg and its pinprick scars. "I'm not dumb," she said after a while, unable to ignore the fairy's provocation.

"Could have fooled me." The fairy giggled and flitted closer. "So—" Odessa stuck the point of the knife in the dirt in front of the approaching fairy. "What do you want? Why do you continue to pester me?"

The fairy shrugged, unfazed by the blade or her taut, iron-edged tone. It walked around the blade to look at her straight-on. "I'm just playing."

"Look at the state I'm in. Do you think I'm in any mood to play?"

The fairy shrugged again.

"Well I'm not," she said. "And I'm especially not in the mood to play with *fae*." She spat the word 'fae' as if it was an insult.

The fairy grinned. "I'm not a bug anymore?"

"No, you're worse than a bug."

"What's that supposed to mean? Are you saying bugs are bad? Because I'll have you know, I'm friends with a lot of bugs and they've been nothing but good to me."

Irritation pricked the base of Odessa's neck. She had tolerated the fairy long enough. Her voice rose, hard and sharp. "Leave me alone! Just go, damn you!"

The fairy crossed its arms, pouting with a frown. Odessa expected it to chide her or voice its indignation.

"You're no fun," was all it said before it took flight, flitting up into the leaves above and disappearing in the jungle.

She sighed, releasing her frustration. Alone, without the pestering distraction of the fairy, the lowland jungle was unnaturally quiet. Her eyes kept returning to the hollow beneath the deadfall where the rotfiend had fled. And her mind kept returning to the other humans lost in this jungle.

CHAPTER 30

The fairy came to Odessa hours later as she limped through corridors of walking palms and strangler figs. It came from behind her and landed on a palm frond a few paces in front of her.

"You're alive," the fairy said, surprised. Odessa stopped and frowned. "You sound disappointed."

"I expected you to be in pieces by now."

"You still sound disappointed."

"Just surprised is all." More fairies flitted in to view, landing on fronds and branches overhead and eyeing her curiously.

"What do you want?" Odessa asked warily, her eyes following the newcomers.

The fairy cleared their throat and spoke with an almost royal affectation. "Introductions must be made. I am Poko, of the Fae Court of Iskolo the Peerless One, and I am to extend the Fae Court's cordial invitation to you. No human has ever set foot in the court of Iskolo, and it is with the greatest of honors that they extend to you this invitation."

"Why?"

"What do you mean?"

"Why am I invited, then?"

The fairy blanched. "This is a big honor. Just be grateful."

"No."

"What do you mean 'no'?" Poko asked incredulously.

"I don't want to go," Odessa said, beginning to pack up her camp.

"I don't think you understand, human. You can't just turn down an invitation from the Fae Court."

"Why not?" Odessa knew the fairies in the Night Jungle were outcasts. They weren't aligned with the true Fae Lords, the Low Gods that ruled the isles far to the north. The fairies here were little more than bugs with a penchant for trickery.

Poko sighed with exasperation. "You just can't, alright? You have to come."

The other fairies in the trees snickered.

"Very persuasive, Poko," one fairy called from above.

"You have such a way with words," another sneered.

"Shut up!" Poko shouted, their voice shrill.

Before Odessa could walk away, a thump in the distance drew her attention. A few moments later, a crash. "What was that?" she asked.

The fairies exchanged glances.

"One of the others. Another human," Poko said. "Or at least partly."

"What do you mean partly? Partly what?"

Poko shifted uneasily but said nothing. Before Odessa could say something, another crash boomed, this time closer.

Odessa's heartbeat quickened and she found herself thinking of Kunza-ka on the mountain top, eyes blazing with hate. She swallowed hard. "Will I be safe in your Court? Those other humans won't be able to get to me, right?"

"Those humans won't reach the Court. I swear to you that," Poko said.

Odessa glanced back in the direction of the crashing and then turned back to the fairies. "I'll go."

"Come on, human! Hurry! Hurry!"

A branch whipped her cheek as she passed.

"Slow down!" she said, the words not much more than a gasp from her burning lungs. Weakness still lingered in her muscles like a viscous poison dissolving her vitality.

The fairy paused, wings beating, swaying back and forth in front of her. "We have lots of ground to cover, human! Hurry!"

It darted off again into the woods. Odessa groaned and chased after it. The sounds of her pursuers had faded away in the distance and her fear had somewhat abated.

The dank stench of moss and decomposition swelled around them. It permeated the air with a cold dampness that soaked into the skin.

Through the tangle of brush and bramble, they came upon a wide clearing with a steep bluff rising on the other side. A massive tree towered above the clearing, half dead. Its thick roots, wider than she was around the middle, twisted through the loamy face of the bluff, like a tangled cluster of snakes burrowing into the dirt, exposed where the bluff had been washed away.

"You wait here!" Poko darted up above the bluff, around the massive tree and into the woods beyond.

"Wait!" Odessa called after it. "Get back here!"

Silence. A heavy, suffocating silence. The forest was dark and motionless around her. The canopy above the clearing was filled with branches laden with withered, shriveling leaves. Odessa chased the fairy halfway across the clearing before slowing to a stop. From the dark space beneath the roots of the tree, amid mud and moss, came a deep, grumbling groan.

She drew the bow from her back and set to stringing it. The dark hollow at the bottom of the bluff was large and dark and seemed to breathe a foulness into the air.

Movement high in the trees drew her attention from the bluff. At the edge of the clearing, she saw silvery shapes fluttering among the branches. Like spirits emerging from shadowy nothingness they appeared, tittering in the air or lounging on bare branches. Dozens of fairies in the trees circling the clearing.

When the the bow strung, she nocked an arrow and paced backwards slowly.

"Where are you going, human?" a chirping voice called from behind her. "You just got here!"

Unease unraveled in Odessa's stomach.

A fluttering procession of pixies settled upon the lowest branches of the massive tree. The fairies that had brought her to the clearing were among them. The silver of their clothes was more gossamer and finer than that of the others clamoring in the trees. There, they wore translucent silver, tarnished like smog wrapped around them. On the massive tree, the fairies shimmered, resplendent in the dimness like sunlight caught in drops of morning dew.

"Welcome, human, to the High Court!" A voice like the peal of a bell called from across the clearing. A fairy nearly double the size of the others appeared, seeming to materialize in the center of the massive tree. The only true fairy among the pixies, its skin was a soft, almost shimmering alabaster. It wore a gown of moonlight and had thorny rose stems braided in its hair. And flapping slowly and deilcately upon its back was a pair of butterfly wings that looked as if they were carved from glimmering diamond and sapphire. It was beautiful. "It's a privilege to be guest of honor at our feast, is it not?"

Odessa backed up farther, bowstring tense. A rush of air at her nape and then pain. She whirled around to see a fairy retreating into the trees. Blood seeped to the surface of a scratch on the back of her neck.

Another fairy swooped down and tangled itself in her braids, tugging and biting. She swiped at the fairy, but it was too fast and fluttered out of arm's reach.

"Don't leave before the festivities have begun!" another splendid voice called from the tree. Two more fairies came from the trees and clawed at her, fluttering around her as she flailed away from their darting attacks. She stumbled farther into the clearing. The fairies retreated into the trees again.

"What do you want from me?" Odessa asked.

"To join in our feast, of course!" the beautiful fairy, Iskolo, said.

Odessa's stomach wound into a series of knots. The dank stench seeped into her bones. Another low groan from the roots of the tree. From the surrounding trees came chirruping laughter.

Two of the fairies on the tree let loose a high, ear-piercing whistle. The groan grew louder and more forceful.

"Come now!" the fairy called above the whistles and groaning. "Father of the Forest, come bless us fae with your presence!"

The groan rose into a howling scream. Movement amid the roots. A heavy footstep. A long-fingered hand, dark and coarse like furrowed bark, its nails packed with dirt, grasped a root. A lanky, hunched-over form emerged from the hollow. Elongated arms like an old man's stretched down to its shins. Two arms with thin cords of muscles stretched beneath pale, loose skin that thickened to a hide like tree bark at its elbow. A huge body rose from the hollow, propped on its long arms, covered in moss and lichen that hung from its bony shoulders and back in long strands that dragged on the ground as it drew its bare leg from the hollow. Tall and thin, it rose to the height of the lower branches, shoulders hunched forward, standing on dirty bark-covered feet, its hands flat on the dirt.

An antelope skull with two dark horns twisting high above it, the points stained a rusty brown. Beneath the skull, a human jaw covered with a ragged mossy beard opened wide, too wide, and let loose a deep throaty scream.

A chant from the trees, over and over again. "The Father eats meat! And fairies nibble gristle!"

Chirping, melodic laughter among the branches. With a moaning scream, the massive Bruka charged. Odessa let the arrow she held fly. It flew over the Bruka's head and buried itself in the mud.

In long, lumbering strides the Bruka had already crossed half the clearing by the time Odessa turned to run. Fairies swooped down from the trees and assailed her, biting and scratching as she ran for the tree line. Dank cold licked at her neck, and it grew worse as the giant beast gained on her.

A quick glance behind. A dirty hand sweeping toward her. She dove and rolled away. The Bruka rushed past her and she scrambled to her feet, slipping in the leaves and dirt. Fairies clung to her, tangled in her hair, pulling on the bag tied around her neck.

The tree line was only a short distance away. After slowing to turn, the Bruka was right behind her again. The ground seemed to cling to her leaden feet. The sound of her pounding heart filled her ears. Her bandaged arm burned with each swing.

A loud bark behind her quickened her pace. Feeling bled from her heavy legs as she forced them forward. In bounding strides, she reached the tree line and leaped. Her bandaged hand latched onto the branch and she hauled herself off the ground. The branch cracked. She propelled herself upward. Her other hand still clutching the bow, she took a higher branch in the crook of her elbow.

The Bruka's hand wrapped around her ankle. Crushing pressure nearly cracked her bones. She kicked and thrashed, but the hand did not budge. The

Bruka's other hand rose to take her other leg, intending to split her up the middle with a cracking of joints and snapping of tendons and rending of flesh. Her free leg kicked its hand away. With all her strength, she drew herself up, curling her body with a jerk, yanking her foot free from its barkskinned grip and leaving sheafs of skin behind.

Free, Odessa swung up from the branch, her bandaged hand grabbing another, higher branch. As she climbed, more fairies swarmed her. Straddling a thick branch out of the Bruka's considerable reach, she swatted at them. They darted away from her swiping hand and flitted back to assail her each time she tried to bat them away.

From below, the Bruka's outstretched hands reached for her. As fairies darted around her, she tore at the bandage wrapped around her fingers with her teeth and loosened the loops of bandage around her thumb and first two fingers. She drew another arrow from her hip quiver, her tender fingertips stinging. She loosed the arrow at the Bruka as fairies clawed at her face, tiny fingers scratching her squinting eyes. The arrow buried halfway down the shaft in its shoulder, but the Bruka showed no reaction. It gripped the tree trunk and pushed and pulled.

The branches around Odessa rustled and snapped, the treetop swaying and shaking wildly. She drew the bowstring back again, eyes narrowed against the raking nails of fairies and blinking away attempts to blind her.

Another arrow punched through the deer skull. The Bruka continued shaking the tree, long arms trying to hoist itself up farther.

Odessa's legs tightened around the branch as the tree shuddered. She nocked another arrow and drew the string to her cheek. Her arm ached and burned. She pulled the string a bit further, overdrawing just a bit—intending to send the arrow to sink fletching-deep in the beast's skull. Blood seeped through her bandages.

A loud crack and pain lashed at her face. She recoiled, flailing. Blood poured from her brow and into her eye. She reeled back, the fairies coming in droves now. And then weightlessness. Wind whipping past her ears. A sinking feeling in her stomach. Her heart stammered and skipped a beat.

She hit the ground and gasped, the air forced from her lungs. Shockwaves reverberated up her spine, the arrow still clutched in one hand and a broken bow in the other. The bottom limb of her bow had splintered. Sucking in a thin breath, she struggled onto her hands and knees.

The Bruka was upon her, raising both its fists above its horned head. She dove into a thicket as it brought its fist down. The ground shook. She crawled through the brambles and undergrowth. The cover of brush above her, a thick blanket of branch and leaf, its vines and thorns, a bulwark. Deep barks and screams drove her deeper into the thicket.

The Bruka's hand burst through the brush and gripped her by the knee. The forest belonged to the Bruka—of course it would betray her. Thorns and branches tore at her clothes and ripped her skin as the Bruka dragged her out of the brush by her leg. Her knee ached in its crushing grip. Stabbing pain shot up her thigh as she squirmed.

When it had dragged her out of the thicket, she twisted toward the hand crushing her knee. The knife flashed from her belt in a high arc and she buried the blade in its hand. The Bruka's powerful grip did not waver. She brought the knife down again and again. Its grasp did not weaken.

It dragged her farther into the clearing to a chorus of giggling cheers. With all her strength, she brought the knife down on its hand one last time. The blade snapped in the middle, a flash of bronze pinwheeling to the forest floor. She threw the hilt and its jagged half blade at the Bruka's body, where it glanced off ineffectually.

The grip around her knee tightened. Something popped in her leg. The Bruka's other hand rose in a massive, rough-barked fist. She closed her eyes as it came down.

CHAPTER 31

A tremendous weight like the world itself had fallen on Odessa. Images of the boar flashed in her mind. In the shifting shadows behind her eyelids, she saw the void to which she was destined. Cruel nothingness.

She opened her eyes, expecting to see the afterlife. Instead, she saw her bandaged arm braced before her face, soaked with blood. Her top half was embedded in the dirt. The Bruka's fist came down again. Her arm took the brunt of the force. Hot blood seeped through the bandages and dripped onto her face. Her forearm burned with pain. Her shoulder ached. Twice more, the Bruka's fist battered her arm, pounding her deeper in the dirt.

The bones of her knee ground together as the Bruka lifted her dazed body up like a hunter would his quarry. Her arms dangled uselessly. Another hand wrapped around her midsection. Constricting fingers causing her to vomit in her mouth. The fairies laughed and hollered at her. The Bruka's mouth opened, the thick lichenous beard parting as its mouth stretched wider. Teeth like jagged stones and a tongue of coarse moss awaited her. Cheers and heckling. The hands tightened. Blood pounded in her temples.

The Bruka held her sideways in two hands. She battered the hand gripping her midsection with weak punches, her bloody right hand beating at the wooden fingers. Leaving wet daubs of blood on the wood. The Bruka began to twist her body in different directions.

She thrashed within its grasp. Her wet punches grew frenzied. *This isn't fair!* Her arm and her fist burned with agony. She put all she had into her last few punches—all her fear and despair, all of her rage, in one last punch before the monster tore her in half.

Fire arced down her arm and engulfed her bloody fist. Upon impact, the Bruka's hand caught fire, brilliant gold flames blooming from where her bloodied knuckles had left their mark.

The Bruka screamed and recoiled. Fire spreading along its hand, it threw her across the clearing.

She hit the ground and rolled. A tree stopped her roll, bruising her ribs. She lay on her side, stunned. Her legs were askew and motionless.

Across the clearing the Bruka raged, beating its hand against the forest floor as flames crawled up its wrist. The groans of the Bruka were like a tree being felled. Above her, the fairies' jubilation turned to panic.

Her bandages had burned and fallen in her rolling. The flames had subsided. Her burned flesh was red and blistering around sections of peeling skin. The channel where the flames had run was charred. But the pain she felt was almost pleasant. Like massaging a terribly knotted muscle. An exquisite pain seared into her flesh.

Odessa urged her numb body into motion. She crawled, dragging her crushed leg behind her. Brutal lances of agony burrowed into her legs and back and side. Ahead of her spread a dense thicket into which she could disappear and escape these forest horrors. Her leg dragged lifeless behind her as he hurried forward.

Flames danced up the Bruka's shoulder. It plowed into the bluff from which it had emerged. It rubbed its flaming arm against the bluff's muddy face, but the flames would not yield.

The Bruka swung, its flaming arm casting embers to the forest floor and cinders high in the air. Odessa scrambled onto her hands and knees, racing heart pumping life into her limp leg. The Bruka charged with a thunderous bellow that rattled her bones and booming footfalls that shook the ground.

Guttering flames of gold surged to life along her forearm. She bounded from the reach of the giant beast. It crashed into the thicket behind her, slamming against a tree with its flame-wreathed shoulder. Drops of flame sputtered to life in the undergrowth. She straightened, strength trickling into her muscles. Her leg tingled, the pain only a distant throbbing lost in the torrent of her burning blood.

Frustration and pain ran together in a barking groan from the Bruka. It swung its arms and again tried to beat away the flames that crawled up its shoulder and neck. There was panic and desperation in its movements. In the air tinged with smoke, the scent of fear set Odessa's teeth on edge. She snarled, something primal rising within her. Her heart beat with a war drum's ferocity. She charged at the Bruka.

Soft leaves and clumps of dirt were flung into the air in her wake. Newfound strength bloomed within her. Her heart pumped fire into her veins.

The Bruka. The fairies. She would kill them all.

Flames rose in the charred channels of her arm, fluttering with its swing. Her dry mouth tasted smoke and blood in the air. Bloodlust darkened her vision. The world around her became shadow and light, predator and prey.

The Bruka turned in its desperate flailing to find her charging within arm's reach. It swung its flaming arm, a wall of scorching heat barreling toward her head. She ducked the wild swipe and leaped toward its chest. Her unlit fingers found the tangle of matted beard and she hoisted herself up, bracing her feet on its skeletal chest.

The Bruka jerked backward and tried to throw her off. Flames lit her face and filled her with savage delight. Fire had spread along its mossy back and around the skull. In the empty eye sockets of that skull, she saw fear. Odessa roared like a lioness, and with all her strength pummeled the skull with a fiery fist. The Bruka's hands gripped her middle, trying to pull her away, but her fingers had wrapped themselves deep within the thick, matted hair. She clung to the beast and attacked, each punch growing more vicious, her snarling cries growing less human as her blood grew hotter. Pain from a broken body spurred the flames of her fury even further. Shards of bone stuck in her knuckles, blackening and growing brittle in the fire.

The Bruka's empty eye socket became a gaping hole. Cracks ran down the center of the skull from the shattered eye. It stumbled and reeled backwards. Its flaming arm flailed, the other continued to wrench her away. The mossy beard in her hand ripped from its chin, and the Bruka threw her into the clearing, where she tumbled to the ground and rolled. Before she had stopped rolling, she scrambled to her feet, crouched and panting. Flames wrapped around her entire arm, climbing up her shoulder, singeing her tunic, and furiously lashing out toward the sky.

The Bruka thrashed on all fours, its massive frame covered in ravenous flames. Smoke and the scent of blood hung in the air. Odessa stumbled into a headlong sprint. The Bruka saw her charging and lunged, swinging its horned head, meaning to skewer her.

Odessa took a horn in each hand and stumbled a few steps before planting her feet in the dirt and straining. She stopped the Bruka's lunge, all her muscles taut and trembling. The Bruka's flaming body pushed to no avail then tried to pull away. Odessa jerked and pulled as well, spurs of white-hot pain shooting up her twisted spine. Her fingers tightened around the curving, fluted horn and she turned them to and fro against the desperate thrashing of the Bruka, twisting the skull back and forth.

A low bellow then a series of short groans emitted from the Bruka as it tried to yank itself free. Odessa's feet dragged through the dirt but she did not relent. She dug her heels deeper, her thighs and calves burning. She strained until her spine threatened to break and her tendons and muscles quivered on the verge of snapping.

A loud bleating cry came from the Bruka as its knee fell to the dirt. A swarm of fairies darted around her, clawing and biting at her. The flames on her arm surged as she strained. She closed her eyes and ground her teeth and pulled even harder, the taste of blood in her lungs and fire burning in her veins. The cry grew drawn out, a pitiful bawling wail amid the crackling of burning wood and flesh and the chirping protests of fairies. She pulled and twisted and strained until, with a crack and a terrible squelch, the skull came loose.

She tumbled backwards a few steps, skull in hand. Thin strands of flesh and mossy skin hung from it. A few paces in front of her, the Bruka's bottom jaw and an open throat twitched as if for one last breath. Its tongue lolled out of its mouth. Murky blood the color of swamp water poured out, and the leaves and mud beneath it grew dark. The flames spread along the Bruka's inert body. The mossy beard went up in flames like tarnished gold, the brilliance of the fire fading. The more it consumed, the flames grew an evil red.

Blood as dark as the jungle's depths poured from the skull and splashed on the ground in wide arcs as she threw it aside. The scorched, earthy stench of the immolated Bruka filled the air, acrid and foul. Odessa took a step away from the burning Bruka, eyes on the blood spilling onto the ground in ebbing pulses of murk. She stumbled, strength fleeing from her body. The flames wreathing her arm guttered out and left charred, bloody flesh. Her mind was blank, her legs numb and moving on their own. Blood burned in her veins, and pain, in all its white-hot and all-consuming fury, sank into her body.

As she watched the burning Bruka, pain undermining each step, her leg gave out beneath her and she splayed into the mud. The strength had left her like the blood pouring from the Bruka's gaping neck. Fire ringed the bloody mouth and charred flesh; the rendering fat had begun to cauterize the wound.

The ground was cold. The light of the fire splashed on her face, but she derived no warmth from it. Cold seeped in her skin while fire raged inside her. She dragged herself toward the flames and the pooling blood. The burning in her own blood grew hotter. Her heart writhed in her chest, spasming as it melted in the intense heat.

Her fingers dug in the blood-soaked mud and she pulled herself closer. Flames singed stray hairs as she put her lips to the trickling arteries and lapped up the fetid, copper-and-algae-tasting blood. It nourished her. Revived her.

When the encroaching flames forced her away, she rolled onto her back away from the pyre that was the Bruka's corpse. Murky blood covered her mouth and chin. The sky above was iron-gray, threads of smoke rising from the clearing to join the thick clouds above. She sighed. The burning of her blood had simmered to a pleasant heat. Like her family's hearth.

She knew she felt pain, but a strange numbness dulled it. Nothing more than a faint throbbing, a thready pulse running along her twisted spine. Her eyelids grew heavy, drooping under the weight of an exhaustion that ran deep. To the bone. To the very soul.

But amidst that exhaustion there was contentment. There was comfort in the blood and fire and smoke.

CHAPTER 32

The tree!"

The fairies fluttered to the forest floor or darted hysterically in the air before the massive tree. Flames crawled along the root system and leaped up its trunk. Fairies rushed to calm the fire with handfuls of dirt or thimble-sized pots of rainwater. Puddles of fire grew in the center of the clearing where the Bruka had tried to beat the flames away. Meanwhile, the Bruka's body had now grown into a huge bonfire at the base of the tree.

Poko landed on the ground by the human they themself had brought to the Court of the Fae. The human that had killed the Father of the Forest and set the Heartwood alight.

The fairy stepped closer to the girl. The heat of the Bruka's immolation singed the end of their delicate wings. Some fae had prostrated themselves around the pyre that was the Bruka. Others gathered around the girl lying in a heap in front of the burning Heartwood.

"Is she dead?" Poko asked. Despite all the fae would lose, they could at least fill their bellies.

Iskolo landed near them, thorned crown askew on their silken hair. Flickers of angry flame danced in the gossamer silver of their dress. Iskolo charged toward Poko, a finger held out like a brandished blade. "Look at what you've done! Look at the consequence of your foolishness!"

Iskolo's guards landed on either side of Poko and took them by the arms. "It's not my fault! How was I to know she was a monster?"

"That's why I sent you in the first place!" Iskolo shouted. "It was your job to know!"

"I just wanted to help! The forest is dying! We're starving!" Tears rolled down Poko's face. "We need to eat, don't we?"

"None of that matters now!" The Fae Lord gestured toward the Bruka's body and the Heartwood. "You've killed the jungle. You've killed us all."

Poko fell to their knees, dead weight in the grip of the guards. "I didn't mean to. I didn't! I did it for you!" They looked up at the glow of flames catching in all the resplendent, glassy colors of the Iskolo's butterfly wings. "We can still eat! We'll eat and move court! We'll be fine!"

"There is no 'we,' Poko." The Iskolo 's voice was like the iron of men, hard and sharp and unyielding. "You are no fae of mine."

The guards forced Poko face-first onto the ground. The fairy kicked pitifully beneath their strength. A soft crunch and Poko screamed and cried. The guards twisted and snapped the delicate membranes and spiderwebbed veins of their wings. Thin shards of papery membrane fell like ash around them. Then, each guard placed a foot on Poko's back and pulled a wing. Poko's shoulders rose with each yanking motion until, with a wet rip, the guards wrenched their wings free.

Poko screamed. They lay immobilized by searing pain. Blood ran down the hollow of their back.

"Get back!" a shrill voice yelled. "Get back!"

The two guards threw the remains of Poko's wings at them and rushed to the Iskolo's side. They took flight to the tree line. The girl stirred, groaning and rising onto her hands and knees to swat at the few opportunistic fairies trying to eat her. Blood leaked from a wound one of them had made on her neck. Her left arm swung wide while the scorched right arm hung limply.

"Get away from me!" she yelled. "Leave me alone!"

Poko struggled to their feet, stumbling away on shaky legs. Instinctively, with their mind clouded by pain and fear, they hopped to take flight—and floundered onto their belly.

Flames had spread throughout the clearing, crawling along damp leaf litter. Brush blossomed in horrible conflagrations, bare branches bloomed in roaring color. Leaves curled, edges turned to ash, and fell away. Smoke smothered the clearing. The canopy above burned, lit by plumes of cinders, as if the heavens had erupted in flames. The dead trees around the clearing caught fire easily and spread to the living. On the ground, staring up at the fiery canopy and swirling plumes of smoke, at least they could still breathe, not suffocating and blinded like the fairies they saw taking flight through the pall of thick, scorching smoke. A few unfortunate fairies tumbled from the air. Another fairy, flying too close to a tree, began to spin in midair as its wing burst into flame.

"You!" The girl's voice carried above the roaring of fire and the screams of fleeing fairies. "It's you!"

Poko scrambled away, but a hand wrapped around their belly and pulled them aloft. Poko scratched and clawed at the hand, twisting and thrashing to free themself.

"Got you now, bug !" the girl snarled through gritted teeth. Her eyes were glassy from pain and watering from the smoke.

"Let me go, devil! Let me go!" Poko cried, flailing.

The girl's eyes narrowed. The pressure around their middle did not let up. Poko dug their nails into her hand as the air was squeezed from their lungs. They squealed in fear and desperation and anger. Panic spurred them on as they tore scraps of skin from the girl's hand.

A loud crack and a flaming tree began to topple with a long groan. The girl's grip loosened enough for the fairy to suck in a gasping breath. The tree fell against another with a crash. Branches broke and crashed to the ground, spreading their flames. With scorching heat in the air, each breath singed their lungs.

Poko squirmed, almost freeing themself. Then the girl tightened her grip on them and ran. The world became a blur of red and orange and black. Every swing of the girl's arm as she ran made their brain rattle in their skull. Then the fiery reds and oranges and yellows faded, and all they saw were dark trees flashing past them. They closed their eyes as dizziness turned their stomach. They willed themself not to vomit.

Soon, the swinging slowed then stopped. The fist that held Poko was pressed against the girl's knee as she doubled over and panted ragged, gasping breaths. She coughed and heaved, spittle dribbling from her lips. She fell onto her rear and sat, Poko still clutched in her fist.

"If you're going to kill me, just do it already!" Poko cried, an edge of fear rising in their voice.

The girl leaned her back against a tree, her head tilted up toward the thin slivers of sky visible through the dark canopy. They were in the heart of the forest, thick with trees dead and dying. Far behind them, the conflagration roared and crashed and splintered, dulled by distance.

The girl looked down at the fairy, her unfocused eyes red and watery. "Get me out of this jungle, and you live."

"I'd rather die," they said. But the fairy's thin bravado quickly died as the girl gave them a few rough shakes. Dizziness returned, Poko's head swaying as they blinked the swirling vertigo away.

"The fire's coming . Which way do I go?"

The fairy narrowed its large eyes. "I should have let the rotfiend have you."

The girl's jaw set, and she squeezed Poko until they thought their head would burst. Then the fairy was falling. Landing on its back, the bloody stumps between its shoulder blades sent bolts of back-arching agony through its body.

"Let the fire have you, then!"

As Poko writhed on the ground, the girl ran with booming footfalls.

Far away, the fire crashed and roared in its indiscriminate fury. The jungle was loud with creatures small and large fleeing the inevitable.

All their life, Poko had been part of something larger. The fae were one and they were many. Now, with no wings on their back, they were alone and very small in an endless forest soon to be ash. On foot, there was no way a grounded fairy could escape the impending firestorm.

Poko chased after the girl through the path she had broken with her massive legs.

"Wait!" they called after her. The girl's strides were huge and the fairy's slender legs were ill-suited for such running. Every stride caused their shoulder blades to jostle the raw holes left by their stolen wings.

They caught up to the girl tangled in thick undergrowth, cursing and thrashing through a curtain of vines and brush.

"Wait!" Poko shouted, dashing through the bracken. "I'll take you! I'll take you out of here!"

The girl turned and regarded the fairy. "Truly? No lying?"

Poko nodded.

CHAPTER 33

Odessa ran, fairy on her shoulder, thinking of immolation.

She hoped the smoke would kill her before the flames did, but she thought that was unlikely. Images of the Bruka writhing beneath the fire and the pained screams it emitted came to mind. Her arm burned with the memory of that agony. She had survived fire once, but it would take her in the end, it seemed.

She had heard from someone during some drought she could not clearly remember that, once they got going and got the wind behind them, fires like this could move faster than a full-bred horse. She pictured a wall of flame higher than the trees moving like a tidal wave across the forest coming toward her— swallowing her up, her skin peeling and her eyes boiling in their sockets, fat sizzling off her still-living body, screams drowned out by the roar of flames.

The fairy yanked on her braids. "The right! The river's to the right!"

Odessa bounded over fallen trees and rose bushes, ducking under low-hanging branches and darting around trees still standing. She ran headlong, faster than she had ever run, the last dregs of strength within her burning. Her legs were numb, her entire body sore. Yet she ran through the woods like a breeze.

The roar of the fire grew louder as she went, building in her right ear. Faintly, she could see a demonic glow flashing between trees and ash falling lazily from a sky growing dark with smoke. She veered to the left, down a shallow embankment.

The gods were against her.

An easterly breeze rose at her back. Hot cinders spewing from the burning canopy rose high into the sky and fell onto branches behind her. Fire blossomed in the treetops around her. Embers fluttered to the ground in front of her. Flames burst from the undergrowth.

She leaped over burgeoning tongues of flame. Soon, the smoke would choke her, scalding the soft tissue of her lungs.

"We're almost there!" the fairy shouted in her ear, its tiny voice barely audible over the roar. "Over this ridge!"

Her legs pounded as she climbed the ridge. Fire all around her. Her lungs screamed. A blade-like pain in her raw throat dragged with every inhalation. Furious heat lashed at her back, the wall of flame swelling to meet the vanguard firebrands. The heels of her bare feet blistered as she charged up the ridge.

She crested the rise and bolted down the steep hillside. Gravity urged her on, her steps growing larger and her speed uncontrollable. Branches whipped at her with barbed fingers. Her feet barely touched the hillside as she flew downward. Ahead of her, all she could see was trees.

The fire raged at the top of the hill, roaring in frustration as it slowed, picking its way downhill not as a wall of flame, but as tendrils pouring through the undergrowth. Soon enough, the trees had gone up in flames.

She bounced against tree trunks, not slowing at all as she vaulted over a tangled deadfall. Not far ahead, she could make out a thinning in the trees. A clearing.

A tree cracked and fell not far behind her, throwing up cinders and firebrands in an explosion on impact.

Her feet carried her down the hill toward the tree line. In front of her, the ground disappeared. A sheer drop-off down to the river.

"Slow down!" the fairy cried, peering through the curtain of her braids.

She burst through the trees and leaped into the air. She held the fairy above her as she plummeted. With the wind rushing past her ears, she could not hear the fairy screaming.

The river was a sheet of black rising to meet them. Legs kicking as if she were still running, Odessa hit the water with an enormous splash. Frigid water swallowed her whole as she sank below the water's surface. A moment of panic and she began to thrash upwards. She kicked and flailed one arm as she punched through the water's surface, with the other still holding the fairy. Her head followed, breaking through with a gasp.

Bobbing up and down the surface of the water, she turned and looked back where she had leapt. The woods above the river were a wall of flame now spreading along the edge of the drop-off. Red flames lunged at a dark brown sky. A blanket of smoke blew over the river toward the mountains. The river carried Odessa and the fairy away from the wall of fire at a quick pace, ushering her to the unknown.

CHAPTER 34

Odessa had never been a strong swimmer. The relatively mild current battered her as she struggled to keep her head above the surface. Her legs were leaden and almost immovable now, stiff-legged kicks only barely keeping her mouth above water. Her soaked clothes were sodden anchors of cloth and leather dragging her down to the river bed, growing heavier and heavier. The fairy had crawled atop her head and held onto handfuls of her hair. Every time her head began to bob underwater, the fairy would yank her hair like reins.

Odessa opened her mouth to speak as her body bobbed in the river. Water rushed in. She kicked herself above the surface and spat the water out in a fountain's dribble.

Fighting against the current, she kicked and thrashed on the water with heavy, deadened limbs. They floated, Odessa barely keeping her head up high.

A submerged log struck her in the side, branches scraping her arm as she pushed away. A gasp as she glanced off the bulk of wood and sucked in a mouthful of water. She coughed and spat it out.

And interminable distance down the river, she kicked toward the steep, forested banks, where withered branches hung over the river like weary beasts bent over to drink.

Kicking with all the strength of an animal's death spasms, she swam to the riverbank until her feet found muck and then half-walked, half-crawled to the shelf of dirt and roots. The river came up to her chest still as she scrambled at the tangle of exposed roots. Trying to haul herself out of the water, the muck sucked at her water-logged boot.

The fairy had scrabbled from her head onto the riverbank and now sat in a crook of the root system, panting and shivering as Odessa's trembling arms strained, pulling her halfway out of the water before failing and letting her slip back into the current.

Her legs grew limp and her knees buckled. Her arms, wrapped around the thick mangrove roots, kept her from sinking.

"Come on! Get up!" the fairy's shrill voice urged.

Odessa's eyelids drooped, and it took all her ebbing strength to not slip beneath the water and fall asleep in the murk and mire.

"I can't," she mumbled, her lips barely moving to form the words.

The fairy's small form grabbed at her arm and yanked, barely rocking it. "Come on! Climb, damn you! This is not the time for a nap!"

When Odessa made no move to climb, a pouting scowl came to the fairy's tiny face. It uttered a frustrated groan, lilting and high like birdsong in the fairy's high register. The fairy bared its tiny, sharp teeth and sunk them into the meat of Odessa's arm.

Odessa lurched to life. "What are you doing?"

"Waking you up!" the fairy said. "Now get up here! There's all sorts of nasty things in the river."

With a groan, Odessa tried once again to haul herself up. Her sopping clothes rubbed against the wet roots as she squirmed upward. Her arms shook, threatening to give out. Her feet pulled free from the mud and scrabbled at the roots, propelling her up.

The fairy skittered aside as she pulled herself onto the tilted base of the tree, her waist laid over the swell of roots like laundry laid out to dry. She panted, her limbs dangling from where she sat, between tree and damp riverbank.

"What are you doing? We have to go!" the fairy said, but Odessa ignored its nattering. She closed her heavy eyes, letting the first thready mists of sleep mend the cracks in her spirit.

She awoke to the smell of smoke. Day had slipped from the sky, and night had begun to take its hold on the world. Odessa jerked away, trying to piece together where she was, blinking away dreams of home and family and taking in the grim reality.

Talons of panic dug into her chest as she floundered on the bank. Alone. She was alone again. Lost in the jungle beset with an inferno of her own creation.

"Feel better?"

She turned to see the fairy curled in a cluster of creepvine higher up the bank.

"You snore when you sleep, by the way."

"Smoke. Is the fire coming?"

"Still a ways away. The wind just shifted is all," the fairy said dismissively.

Where panic had dug into her tight chest, relief now spread like a meager salve. Odessa pulled herself upright and crawled up the riverbank, taking handfuls of undergrowth and root and hauling herself up until she could stand among the mangroves and vines. At the top of the riverbank, the river ran, unremitting and endless, a few spans below.

"Now what?" she asked the fairy as it struggled up the bank beside her.

"Oh, now you want to get going?" the fairy scoffed. "What we need to do is find some place to hide through the night."

Already, the din of the jungle was growing, shrieks and howls and chirruping filling the air. Odessa nodded.

"Pick me up and get away from the river. This is not the place you want to be when it gets dark," the fairy said, their blasé manner giving way to true urgency. Odessa lifted the fairy and placed them on her shoulder before taking off. She padded away from the river, keeping it to her right side as she moved deeper into the jungle.

"Stop!" the fairy directed amid a grove littered with tall shrubs bearing wilted heart-shaped leaves as large as her head. "Put something over your mouth," the fairy said. "And cover yourself well."

"What?"

"That's suicide nettle all around us. Don't touch it, you'll feel its burn for weeks. And step carefully. Those tiny needles on the leaves can break off and take to the air."

Odessa froze, studying the plants surrounding her on all sides. A fine fuzz lined the underside of the leaves, a layer of tiny needles waiting to stick her. She had heard of suicide nettle but had never actually seen it. If it touched her, she would not only be in agony for weeks, but still feel the sting occasionally for the rest of her life.

"Why did you bring me here? Is this another trick, you pesky bug?"

"No, this where we're going to camp, you oaf!" the fairy said, offended by her accusation. "If you can find a place to hunker down in these nettles, we should be safe from most beasties prowling around at night."

"Are you crazy?"

"Just hurry up and cover yourself! And put me somewhere safe. If one of them touch me, I'm done for."

Moving as if startling the plants around her would prompt an attack, she took a poncho from her bag and draped it over herself before covering her mouth and nose in layers of linen. The fairy clung to her beneath the poncho.

Peering through a gap in the linen around her head, she picked her way through the grove, skirting around the sprawling clusters of broad leaves. She made a den in the hollowed remains of a rotten tree. The interior of the trunk was wide enough for her to curl up on the soft floor of punky wood and detritus. Outside the cracked bark through which she had shimmied stood a squat stand of nettles like a guard outside her shelter. A water-logged poncho draped over jagged pieces of half-rotten wood obscured the open gap that split the decaying trunk down the middle. Above her, the trunk opened to the canopy above, the rest of the tree having fallen decades ago—making the perfect smoke had she dared light a fire. Instead, she sat curled in her sodden clothes.

The fairy perched across from her on a shelf of rotten wood, its slender legs swinging. Its shrewd eyes studied her. Appraising her.

After a long while sitting in tense silence, Odessa spoke. "Why didn't you leave me? On the riverbank. You could have been long gone."

"A grounded fairy isn't going to get far," the fairy said. "And I'd rather take my chances with the monster I know than risk it on my own."

"I'm not a monster," Odessa protested.

The fairy leaned forward on the shelf, its gaze hard. "Then what are you really, huh?"

"I'm just a girl."

"You're no girl. You're a liar!" the fairy said, its songbird voice growing shrill. "What human girl can burst into flame and rip a Bruka's head off its body like it's nothing? A no-good liar is what you are. All you humans do is lie. And now I'm all broken and alone because of it!"

Odessa bristled, anger trickling into her exhausted muscles. But it died away before she could respond. She had not the strength for this bickering. Her very bones were leaden, her muscles gelatin. Her very soul was worn ragged.

She sighed and said nothing. She was unwilling to give voice to the myriad thoughts echoing through her mind. To voice them would be to turn these vacuous, half-formed notions into tangible truths.

The sulking fairy watched her, bright eyes alight with accusatory resentment.

"I'm a cursed girl," she said, finally. "But a girl nonetheless."

"Being Forsaken by the gods doesn't make you a monster like that," the fairy said, not believing a word she said. "It makes you a pariah, not a devil."

Odessa raised her burned arm. River scum clung to the reddened skin. Blood and mud dried on her arm in equal proportions. The flames had reopened her wounds. "I might as well be a devil." The black lines faintly tracing their way beneath her skin had spread, working their way down her forearm. Her next words caught in her throat, choking her. "I'm a godkiller."

She could not raise her eyes to see the fairy's reaction. Her eyes only traced the dark lines of cursed blood in her veins. Her throat was tight and her mouth was unbearably dry. "I have godsblood burning through my veins. I stole it and now it festers within me."

"Stop lying," the fairy said.

"I wish I was lying." Her hand dropped to her lap. She hugged herself, her eyes still unable to meet the fairy's gaze. "As it died, its lifeblood mixed with mine."

"You would be dead."

"I nearly was." She thought of the void, that unfathomable blackness and the flames that had seared her to nothing. "I stole something from it and now it's burning up in me."

Silence filled the hollow within the tree. It was getting dark, but the fairy's silvery form was clear through the dim.

"Why?" it asked, its voice barely a whisper.

"I didn't want to," Odessa said. "Believe me, I wanted none of this."

At first, it had felt good to unburden herself of the tremendous weight of guilt. To bare her sins so openly was like airing out a festering wound. Once she had begun talking, a cathartic exhilaration kept the words tumbling out. But now they slowed, taking off in the unrelenting silence of the fairy's judgment. She wished she could take the words back. She would rather choke on them and die than give voice to them again.

"You're definitely no normal girl, then."

Odessa looked up to see the fairy watching her. Appraising her with suspicion and wariness, but also a childish curiosity on its small, cherubic face.

"Then what am I?" she asked without thinking.

"I don't have a clue," the fairy said, earnestly. "I don't have the foggiest clue."

Odessa looked back to the burned arm in her lap. She hoped the mud and scum in her wounds would become infected. She hoped the arm would blacken and shrivel up and fall off.

CHAPTER 35

As the jungle grew darker, Odessa and Poko settled upon a sort of precarious truce. She sat hugging her knees, her wet clothes chilling her to the bone as night sank deeper into the jungle. She nudged the poncho's hem aside and peeked through the crack into full dark.

"Get some rest. I'll wake you up if anything comes," Poko said.

Odessa let the poncho fall back in place. "No chance. You sleep first. I'm not closing my eyes while you're there being mischievous."

"First of all, I'm not being mischievous. Second of all, can you even see in the dark?" The fairy crossed its slender arms. "What good are you going to be if something comes in the night, huh? It'll be gnawing on your leg before you even see it coming."

"I'm sure you would be gnawing alongside it."

"Why would I want you dead?" Poko's voice raised again, shrill and offended. "Think about it! I've got no chance of surviving without you! Is that what you want to hear? Will that make you trust me? To know that I'm totally and utterly at your mercy?" The fairy snorted. "You know how hard for me it is to admit that? This isn't easy for me. A fairy's got their pride, you know!"

Odessa hugged her knees tight to her chest again. "I just don't like being tricked," she said like a pouting child.

"Well, I'm sorry." Poko sat down upon the rotten wood again, deflated. "No more tricks."

When Odessa said nothing, only stared blankly into the dark deepening between them, the fairy said, "But how was I supposed to know you were a god-killer? I thought you were just a regular stinking human!"

Odessa opened her mouth to retort but stopped short. She had been about to say that she did not stink, but she couldn't actually remember the last time she had bathed. *How long was I asleep for? Does a dip in the river count?*

"Go to sleep!" Poko said. "You look half-dead."

Odessa opened her mouth to say something, but her tongue was sluggish. She had nothing to say. The little pixie was right. Sitting as she was, she did not think she had the strength to rise even if Talara herself had come to claim her heart. Her throat was raw, and the taste of smoke and the Bruka's brackish blood itched in the back of her mouth. But the sharp hunger pains twisting in her guts had abated and she was warily grateful, unsure if it was a relief or a sign of some greater malady. Because a thrumming heat ran through her veins still, despite the chill of her sodden clothes. She did not think she was feverish, but nonetheless, a current of pulsing warmth surged and radiated through her extremities.

Her eyelids drooped as she contemplated her condition. Her beleaguered body made the decision for her, and she fell asleep under the watch of the duplicitous fairy.

Odessa awoke to a midmorning sky high above her, a thin gray darkened by a pall of smoke drifting on the wind. Poko sat at the top of the rotten stump the two refugees had sheltered in. Their legs swung nonchalantly as they hummed a tittering tune.

"You're still here." Odessa shifted to an upright sitting position, her aching body groaning with the movement. "I thought about leashing you, but it looks like that won't be necessary."

The fairy's song stopped abruptly. They stood up and looked down at her, their hands on their hips. "You sleep the whole day away and the first thing you do is antagonize me?"

"It's barely morning," Odessa said as she rose to her feet and stretched, her joints cracking and popping with relief. She stood almost at eye level with the fairy on its perch. "And I thought fairies liked jokes."

"Jokes are supposed to be funny." Poko frowned. "That wasn't funny."

Odessa shrugged and then pulled the poncho down from across the gap in the trunk. She began wrapping herself as she had done the night before, careful to leave no bit of ankle or arm exposed for the nettles to sting.

She felt good. No nausea. No chills. Her muscles were a little sore, but she felt rejuvinated.

"What are you doing?" Poko asked, walking along the rim of the hollowed stump to stand in front of her. "Don't humans eat in the morning?"

Odessa paused, peering through the bandages she had begun to wrap around her head. "Does it look like I have anything to eat?"

"You don't have anything?"

"You and your friends tore my bag apart! What little food I had is ash now." With that, she finished loosely wrapping her head. "I wonder if the fire's died out by now," she wondered out loud, the bandage over her mouth puffing out with each word.

"You look so foolish like that," the fairy snickered.

"You said I had to do this!"

"It's the smart thing to do, yes. That doesn't mean it doesn't look stupid."

Odessa snatched the fairy and stuffed it beneath her poncho as she climbed out of the trunk and around the cluster of nettles standing outside their shelter. It was much easier picking her way through the grove of nettles in the daylight, yet she still took her time, careful to not disturb the heart-shaped leaves and their innumerable hairs like glass needles almost too small to see.

Once past the grove, Odessa stripped off her poncho and bandages, damp with sweat from the layers. Poko sat on her shoulder and led her back to the river. They followed the river's winding course through the jungle, walking atop the ridges and hills flanking it until the ground leveled out. In some places, the ground grew soft and swampy. Her feet would sink in the mud no matter where she stepped, and it was taking more effort to pull free from the suction of the mud's grip.

Despite the tension that hung in the back of their minds and the mutual resentment pricking at them, the fairy nattered in Odessa's ear throughout the day, taking Odessa's mind off the endless jungle around her.

For two days she walked, guided by the fairy perched on her shoulder. Two days of little food and what little potable water she still had in the calabash that had not shattered in her fall through the trees.

By the second day, the thrumming in her veins had subsided and hunger returned, leaving her weak and lightheaded. The jungle was thinning around them, and what trees surrounded them were half-bare and wilting. The fairy assured her they were almost at the edge of the Night Jungle, and Odessa believed them. She did not exactly know when or why she had begun to trust the fairy that had tried to kill her.

Perhaps all the chatter's worn me down, she thought, but she knew that was not quite it. The answer was simple—she just did not want to admit it. It was a relief to not be alone.

"Stop!" Poko hissed in her ear. They crouched on her shoulder, a small hand gripping a tangled coil of frizzy hair.

Odessa stopped, crouched down in the mud, and hid behind a wide mangrove tree. "What is it?" she whispered.

Poko said nothing. They just stayed crouched on her shoulder, peering out from beneath her hair.

With bated breath, Odessa sharpened her senses. Her eyes flicked back and forth from the ground to the canopy above, searching for movement. Her ears traced each rustling leaf around them. The air was humid and clung to her skin, heavy and thick. She could taste something in the air—a sort of musk.

A murmur of leaves brushed aside drew her attention. Slithering through the swampy plant life was a massive snake, its body as thick as a tree trunk. Its belly undulated over branches and leaves, scales scraping against the mud as it worked its way around the scattered mangroves.

It paused. Its tongue darted in and out, tasting the air. Only a few strides away, hidden among the dense ferns and palms, Odessa was frozen. The snake's cold eyes seemed to bore into her as it turned here and there, tasting the scents of the jungle.

Slowly, fighting against the cold paralysis in her body, she inched her knife from its sheath, daring not to move too quickly lest she attract the snake's attention. Her eyes stayed on the flicking tongue and the cold, impassive eyes scanning the placid swamp. If the snake wanted to kill her, she would be nearly powerless to stop it from wrapping around her and crushing the life from her body.

Unless I burn it, she thought. But she had no inkling as to how to make the fire bloom. And she really did not want to. The pain was too much; despite its almost pleasant agony, she did not know if she could bear those flames again. It took too much out of her, too much vitality drained from the bleeding flames. It was her life lashing out in gold tongues of fire, her lifeblood burning away. Vaguely and innately, she understood that much.

After a long, prolonged stretch of molasses-slow time, the snake began slithering again toward the river, which had widened and deepened in the wetlands. The snake's head slipped beneath the water's surface, and it slid its entire length underwater with barely a ripple. She watched its head surface again farther along the river. A tiny wake trailed behind it, barely noticeable in the river's rippling current.

I'm never going in that river again.

"Go," Poko whispered in her ear. "We need to get out of here."

"What do you mean? It's gone."

"It sensed you, though. The only reason it didn't go after you is because it already ate recently. Next time, I doubt we'll be so lucky."

Odessa closed her hand in a fist and began walking again, drifting farther away from the river. She thought of Obi's gruesome form and the roar of his frothing goat head. "Is there anything tracking us now?"

"I don't sense anything on our heels right now, but that's the best I can do."

Odessa sighed, a knot tightening in her stomach. "I can't live like this." Her feet splashed through water and muck as the swamp grew more treacherous. All manner of spiders and insects scrambled and flitted away from her footsteps. "I'm sick of being hunted. I'm sick of being cursed." *I just want my Papa.* The words came to her lips but she clenched her jaw shut before she could utter them. The wounds were still too fresh to air them out with flippant words. She had to pack them full of silence and neglect until they were nothing but gnarled, aching scars.

"We're almost out," Poko said, sensing her despair. "It'll be easier once we're clear of the jungle. There's a village downstream someplace."

Odessa nodded but said nothing.

They traveled in silence for a long while, the jungle's din swallowing the splashing and sucking of Odessa's footsteps. Both shared the same emptiness; each dwarfed by the enormity of their loneliness, they took comfort in the other's presence, whether they were conscious of it or not.

The swamp of mangroves and palms soon gave way to a dry and half-dead forest of acacia and thorn bushes. Boots caked with mud and clothes damp with sweat, Odessa skirted around tangled thickets as best she could— but still found herself being poked and snagged.

Through the patches of bare branches came the light of midday, gray and dull. The overbearing pressure of the jungle's density let up a bit and, no longer choked by dank greenery, Odessa felt she could breathe easier.

Poko felt none of her relief.

"The shadows," they warned. "Bad spirits in those shadows. The outskirts of the forest are full of them."

Odessa wanted to believe that their talk of bad spirits was little more than a result of the fairy's overactive imagination, the result of a shrinking homeland encroached by famine and disease. But she could not deny the way her hair would suddenly and without warning stand on end. Despite the heat, she had chills trickling down her spine like ice water sliding down each vertebra.

As the sun began to set, the chill worsened. At the base of her skull came a nagging itch. Silent whispers brushed against her skin.

"We need to hurry," Poko said, sensing the same chill in the otherwise humid air. "Spirits are drawn to you like flies to corpses and they pay no heed to your ward at all."

Spirits plied at her mind, the pressure growing as the sky darkened, trying to pry her soul loose and possess her body. She could feel them crowding around her, cold and malevolent shapes moving just beyond the veil of the physical.

"Odessa," her father's voice called. "Odessa!"

Other voices soon joined in. Ubiko's voice along with the other hunters, all of them shrieking in a ghastly chorus. Odessa stumbled and fell to her knees, her hands clamped over her ears.

"Stop it!" she cried. "Stop it!"

The voices swelled around her. "It's cold! Death is so cold!"

The voices burrowed deeper into her mind like icicle talons sinking into her soft, warm brain.

"Why didn't you just die? I'd be alive if you had just died," her father's voice echoed in her skull. "Why won't you just die?"

Odessa moaned, pressing her hands tighter against her ears. Images began flickering in her mind like shadows in candlelight. Images of gore and death. Her family, gutted, while crows and vultures ripped the flesh from their bones. Kimi was there, bloated and purple. A vulture dug into Ayana's guts, its snapping beak ripping and tearing at her insides. There was a sick squelching as it dug deeper, burying its whole head in her abdomen.

Then the gruesome image changed. Her father was on the mountaintop altar, wreathed in wicked flames. His face blackened and sizzled as he screamed at her in an inhuman tongue. Empty sockets cried tears of blood and viscera down his charred, peeling cheeks. His guttural screams warped into words.

"I hate you! I've always hated you!"

His arms, gnawed to the bone by flames, stretched out as he lurched from the altar. His burning hands wrapped around her throat, the bones digging into her soft skin. She clawed at him, but his fingers continued digging into her flesh, choking the life from her.

A sudden burst of light and it was all gone. Odessa blinked, kaleidoscopic afterimages swimming in her vision. She lay on her side, her fingers scrabbling at the dirt in front of her. Poko stood a few paces from where she lay, stooping to the ground and rolling something between their hands.

Too stunned to move, Odessa could only watch as the fairy picked up the ball of leaves and mud it had rolled and threw it toward her. In mid-air, the ball began to glow and burst in a shower of sun rays. The voices that had continued to whisper in hushed tones dissipated in the sunburst.

Odessa sucked in a shallow breath and struggled to move. She crawled onto her hands and knees. Poko rushed to her side.

"Get up! Get up!" They helped steady her as much as their tiny body allowed.

She tottered to her feet feeling sick and clammy. The chill began to return to the air, and the fairy began forming another ball of leaf and dirt.

"It shouldn't be that easy for them to get to you!" Poko said as they rolled the ball between their hands, a dusting of fine powder sticking to the dirt and leaves. They held the ball to their chest and looked at Odessa, who was swaying drunkenly. "Pick me up! We need to get out of here now! Run!"

Odessa shook her head and rattled her mind to attention. The voices were worming their way back. She could feel their icy fingers digging into her brain again. She scooped Poko up and took off running.

"Wrong way!" Poko shouted, pointing in the opposite direction. "That way! That way!"

Odessa skidded to a halt and ran back in the direction the fairy was pointing. Her mother's voice called her a burden. Her mother said she would rather Odessa had been stillborn. Kimi's choked shrieks rose and fell.

The faster she ran and the harder her heart beat, the more heat surged through her veins and kept the chill of spirits from entering deeper into her mind. All the while, the voices continued assailing her with horrible insults. Her teeth ground together as she ran, bearing the insults and the curses.

It's not real. It's not real, she told herself, but it did not matter. The voices were shallow facsimiles and cruel recreations, but the spirits invading her mind and trying to dislodge her soul were very much real.

Soon, the trees began to thin and she leaned forward, her tired legs forced to continue out of sheer momentum. Night was sinking into the forest but through the trees, she could make out the faint glow of sunset, purple like a bruise on the sky.

Her heart swelled with joy, then was quickly deflated by a blood-chilling scream. Ayana cried in agony in the back of her mind. Begging for her big sister. Crying out for her Dessa over and over again.

Odessa burst from the tree line with a grand sunburst at her back as Poko threw the last ball behind them. The spirits dissipated, but she didn't stop running. She ran through tall grasses, dry and sharp as sickles. She sprinted past low acacias and clusters of spike bushes. She ran until her legs were going to give out, then she stopped and doubled over, panting in ragged, pained gasps.

When she caught her breath, she straightened and wiped the tears from her eyes. A sniffle and then she said, in a choked voice, "Let's go."

CHAPTER 36

Ash-white skin scorched red by flames, Obi trudged through the mangroves with his wide, muscular frame slouched forward. Mud caked his blistering feet. His tongue lolled out from his frothing mouth. He panted through a throat scarred by smoke. Tears still spilled from the rims of his smoke-reddened eyes. A torrent of tears swelled within him, but his goat eyes could only grow moist with his sadness and no more.

All his men were dead. Through the night, they had fought bravely and fended off the night beasts, but there had been nothing they could do against the flames. They had been so close to the girl. Her presence had been so clear to him. So very near. So near his grasp.

By the time they heard the roar of flames, it had been too late. Cinders spiraled down from the canopy above them like hornets. The branches above them quickly burst into flame and became a ceiling of fire. Obi raised his shield to shelter the few warriors around him as they took flight, but as embers rained down on them, it quickly caught flame.

They ran, but the fire—spurred on by dry winds—barreled over them like a tidal wave, scorching the air in their very lungs before swallowing them entirely in a roaring inferno. Helplessly, Obi had watched his warriors, his friends, fall and writhe on the ground, screaming through flame-frayed vocal cords. The fastest among them fell, choking on smoke and coughing up spittle and snot as cinders fell upon them and ignited.

Blinded by thick curtains of smoke pouring through the trees, Obi had taken two of those closest to him and dragged them along in his flight. There was nothing else he could do. He thought he could at least save two of his warriors despite their struggling.

He did not stop until he reached the steep face of the highlands. The wall of heat that had seared the skin off his back had been left behind, but smoke still clogged his lungs. With a warrior slung on each shoulder, he had climbed halfway up the steep slope before setting them down.

They were dead, but he could not be sure whether the smoke had killed them or he had crushed the life from them in their escape.

He stayed on that hill with his lost warriors until the approaching fire forced him farther upward. For a while, he carried his comrades hoisted upon his shoulders, but as the fire began creeping up the base of the slope, he set them down. *Let this wretched forest be your pyre,* he thought grimly as he left their bodies on the side of that hill. They deserved much better, but this was all that he could give them.

In the swamp, the stench of smoke seeped into his every pore, and he carried the burden of their deaths upon his hunched shoulders. Despite their misgivings about the goddess's blessing, they had followed him without compunction or complaint. They had been his brothers and sisters in arms since he first picked up a spear. Now, their bodies lay lost amid the ashes of a cursed forest, far from the grace of the gods or the guidance of their ancestors.

He tried to count how many friends and comrades he had lost because of this girl, but it was growing harder and harder to think. Thirst dried his brain and a headache was splitting his skull like a machete splits a dry gourd.

Don't let their deaths be in vain, he chanted mentally. Those words kept him upright and plodding forward. He had not slept since the fire. He spurned food and drink. His grief and his rage were sustenance enough.

A thin snake curled loosely on a mangrove branch quickly slithered away as he neared. His huge sword, held in a massive fist of blistered skin and grafted bone, cleaved through ferns and palms and wilting flowers like a machete. The blade dulled upon the undergrowth, and palm bark left nicks in the metal. The sword was immaterial. His muddled mind focused on the Kusa girl and nothing else.

The Kusa girl's tracks were nearby but Obi eschewed them, as he had food and water. Her foul presence ahead was like a foreboding omen of a star in the sky of his youth. A star spelling doom and destruction. An unholy constellation he would set course for unwaveringly.

The mangroves soon gave way to wilting palms and withered acacias. Obi strode through the dying stretch of forest, a cool sensation on his raw and tender skin.

Ethereal forms brushed against him, spirits of all kinds guiding him through the forest. They congregated in this blighted land, as if mourning what had been lost already.

Spirits swirled around him and he caught glimpses of movement like shimmering mirages in the periphery of his vision. They whispered to him in a tongue he could not understand. His ears flicked and flitted as their whispered words tickled the back of his neck.

In the shade and shadows, the spirits swarmed him. Talara's voice became clear in his mind.

"You are close," she whispered through the trees as he trudged through thick thorns. "So very close. All those that you have lost, let their spirits guide you. Bring her to me."

Obi hurried through the forest, the spirits ushering him onward like a caressing wind at his back. He let his thoughts slip away, no longer resisting the primal rage that muddied his mind. All he could think of was slaughter. He could feel his ancestors and his comrades with him, all of them grasping his sword arm. His friends and family, they all thirsted for the Kusa girl's blood.

There was no capturing her alive. No matter what she whispered in his ear, the goddess would have to content herself with the girl's heart.

Kill her. Gut her. Kill her. Kill her. Kill her.

CHAPTER 37

I t's over there!" Poko stood on Odessa's shoulder and pointed. "See?"

Odessa cupped a hand over her eyes and squinted. Around her spread wide-open grassland, yellows and browns melting into the dark, cottony gray above. On the horizon, she could make out a cluster of shapes flanking the banks of the river.

"I think I see it," she said slowly.

"Are you blind? It's right up there!"

Odessa dropped her hand. "How am I supposed to see that far?"

"I dunno, I do it. Just look harder!"

She sighed and continued walking, making sure to stay a few armlengths away from the river's edge. She took a glance behind her at the shrinking jungle: the mountains, her home, and all she had ever known seemed a world away now, obscured in a shroud of smoke still rising from the heart of the jungle. It was discomforting, seeing the mountains from a distance. Looming over the horizon, their peaks were like shards of knapped obsidian tearing at the sky above. Only now could she begin to comprehend the enormity of the Serpent's corpse, which she had spent her entire life upon. From north to south as far as she could see, the mountains dominated the eastern sky.

The emptiness inside her yawned wide as she walked away. The savannah was an alien place, disquieting in its endless flatness. The sky seemed as if it would fall upon her without the mountain's bolstering to hold it aloft. There was just so much nothing, it unsettled her.

They continued along the river's edge, sweltering heat slowing Odessa to a plodding pace. She felt she could afford that small comfort. Behind them, nothing but grassland rippling in the wind like waves on the Saltseer. No monsters. No ash-gray warriors. Just the disquieting barrenness of the open plain.

Earthen and thatch-built walls came into view as they drew closer to the village on the river. But even in the distance, the village seemed eerily placid.

They camped for the night beneath a twisted, half-dead acacia, eating from what few hard seed pods remained on its branches. They gave little satiation and seemed only to make them more cognizant of their hunger.

They lit no fire that night. Odessa had lost her flint and iron. They huddled in the dark against the gnarled acacia, swaddled in quiet stillness. The only sound was the rustling of coarse grass in the night breeze.

Again, Odessa slept and Poko stood guard as had become their routine. The fairy was able to sneak the few hours of rest they needed during the day while Odessa walked. As she slept, Poko kept a small pile of balls made of braided strips of grass beside them. Each ball was the size of Odessa's thumbnail and infused with what little fairy dust Poko could produce. All throughout the night, spirits circled in the distance, seething with malevolence.

In the jungle, something had happened to Odessa's soul. Some flaw in her soul had been exploited and spirits swarmed to the breach like a pack of hounds following the scent of bleeding prey.

A flash of light awoke Odessa, jolting her from sleep with a startled cry. Dreams of home burst in a brief blast of sunlight.

Her eyes, struggling to adjust, caught a glimpse of shadow shifting in the air. Afterimages burned into her vision and obscured the wisps of shade as they retreated to the dark.

"What happened?" she asked.

"These things really like you," Poko said with a touch of derision. "Now go back to sleep. There's not many hours left until morning."

Odessa tried to peer through the dark, searching for movement. Whether she was looking for the movement of spirits or of more worldly threats, she wasn't sure. The flare of sunlight would have been like a signal for anyone searching for her. *Is Obi out there?*

"We should move camp."

"It's fine," Poko said. "They're not going to get you while I'm here. I take my duty very seriously."

"It's not the spirits I'm worried about," she said despite the goosebumps dotting her arms. What the spirits had done to her in the outskirts of the jungle, how they had violated the sanctity of her very soul, had scarred her. Her heart raced just knowing they were out there, circling in the night. But it was broad, faceless fear that she felt. The fear that urged her to move camp and hide, that fear had a goat's face. A body marred with scars and bunches of muscle bulging beneath ash-gray skin. "Do you sense anything out there?"

In the dark, she could faintly see the silvery fairy turn to face her. She could almost see Poko's brow furrow. "Like what?"

"Anything like me?"

"Like you as in human or like you as in . . . " Poko's words trailed off.

Odessa's silence was an answer in itself.

"Ah," Poko said after a moment of quiet. The fairy turned and stayed facing the open plain for a while. "Nothing but spirits," they said after a few minutes. "Lots and lots of bad spirits."

Odessa sat back against the tree, tense and fully awake. "I still think we should move camp. Your light was like a great big signal fire to everything from here to the horizon."

"Are you worried about the other humans from the jungle?" Poko said. "There's no way they could be on your trail still. You burned half the jungle. You're fine now."

She fiddled with the muddied hem of her dingy poncho. "Yes, you're probably right," she said, not believing the words as she said them.

"Quit worrying and get to sleep," Poko said. "We're moving at first light."

"You say that because you're not the one walking."

"But I'm starving! I want to be at that village for breakfast. They'll feed us, won't they?"

Odessa licked her dry lips. "Yeah," she said. "Probably." If the people in that village weren't able to sense that she was Forsaken, there was a chance she could beg someone for a meal. But she was not confident

It was only a few hours before the first light of dawn would begin to seep into the skyline when she was finally able to slip into a fitful sleep. Poko woke her when the sun was high above the mountain peaks of the east.

The village was less than a half day's walk, but as they drew closer, Odessa's uneasiness grew to a nagging itch at the nape of her neck. The river ambled by the still village, past the half-submerged remains of a latticed wood grille that had once spanned the river's considerable width. The middle portion of the grille had fallen beneath the water, leaving a jagged mess of broken logs to sag above the meandering current. Upright logs rammed into the riverbed had been broken in half or shoved aside in the middle portion's destruction. The snapped ends of logs poked from the water's surface, bright as bone against the murky river.

The nagging itch grew more persistent. On either side of the grille was a wall of rammed earth that wrapped around the village, blocking Odessa's view save for a few thatched roofs poking above the top of the wall.

She stopped suddenly, only a few strides away from the wall. The sight of the destroyed grille across the river had jarred some thoughts loose in her head. "There wasn't any smoke," she muttered.

"What?"

"There hasn't been any smoke all day. There should be smoke. A hearth fire or something. But there hasn't been anything."

"There is something off about this place," Poko said from atop her shoulder. "Something weird."

"It's way too quiet."

"Plague? Famine?" Poko suggested.

"What about that?" she pointed to the snapped logs jutting out from the water. "Plague didn't do that."

"Logjam built up and broke it down, maybe?"

Odessa stared at the wall for a moment longer, her face impassive. "We'll go around and see what's going on."

"But it's right there!" Poko gestured wildly toward the wall. "Just hop over the wall! Even if everybody's dead, there might be food left."

Despite the fairy's protests, Odessa turned from the river and skirted around the circular wall until she reached the latticed grille on the other side. The lattice of thick logs and hemp rope was intact, the river flowing around the grille with barely a ripple.

"No log jam," she said aloud, more to herself than to the fairy.

"It was just an idea."

Whatever broke the other one could still be inside then. She went back the way she came and stopped at a wooden gate set in the earthen wall. The gate stood open far enough for her to peek inside.

"Be careful," the fairy whispered in her ear.

"I thought it was just a logjam," Odessa said with a smirk.

Poko frowned.

Through the open gate, she could see a few mud brick huts along the river's edge, but nothing looked amiss. Good sense told her to leave the village behind, but her empty stomach's grumblings were too much for her to ignore. She inched the gate open farther and slid through the gap. The skin on the back of her neck prickled with unease.

A path led through the huts to the riverbank, where half a bridge stood over the water. On the other side of the river, another half extended a short distance from the bank. Some of the logs that had held the bridge aloft rose from the water still, the tops sheared off in a mess of splinters. The huts closest to the river had been reduced to rubble, their walls standing half-demolished with crumbling mudbrick and thatch strewn in heaps along the bank.

She crept along the wall's edge, dry grass rustling and crunching beneath her calloused feet until she came to a hut only a few strides from the wall.

Around the huts, loose feathers and bones were scattered about, grown over by grass. She rounded the front of the hut, creeping like a hare in a jaguar's den. A door of wood and reeds and mud was splintered, pieces of the door's frame still hanging from the hinges. Poko flattened against her shoulder as she took a tentative step into the doorway.

The interior of the hut was a mess. Carpets that would have hung on the walls were torn and thrown about the floor. A table against one wall and rattan shelves and baskets against another had been snapped, splintered, and crushed. A clay stove stood at the other end of the hut, the top smashed in and crumbling. Shards of shattered pottery were strewn around the stove, the bottoms of jars and bowls all that remained of the potter's handiwork.

A piece of the wall had collapsed, sheared off by some force to fall atop the splintered table. A section of the roof had caved in and lay in a heap in the middle of the floor. Odessa stepped over it, her eyes floating over the debris and destruction, eyes almost glazed in her bewilderment.

She came to a tangle of shredded blankets. Dried into the fabric was the unmistakable maroon of old blood. The maroon was sprayed across the blankets in fine, misting dots and in thick splattered drops.

"That's not good," Poko whispered.

Odessa took a handful of blanket. Dust rose in a thin cloud as she tossed it aside. "No," she said. "Not good at all."

She was surprised by how little her heart was racing. The sight of old blood elicited little emotion. Unease brushed her skin, but there was no stirring in her heart. She found that odd.

Among the wreckage, she found a short machete. The iron was weathered and pitted, but it held a halfway sharp edge.

"What do you think happened?" Poko asked.

"I don't want to find out." Around the stove, she found rice and rotten vegetables and rancid meat. She did her best to salvage what she could into a make-shift sack and left the ransacked hut.

She crept to the other huts, searching each one but coming no closer to discerning what sort of terrible fate had befallen the village. All she found were ruined homes and old blood stains.

CHAPTER 38

Few huts stood totally intact, and those that did were missing large sections of roof. Most of them were missing sections of wall or had been almost entirely reduced to rubble. One of the last huts Odessa searched was a half-toppled wreck of crumbling mudbrick and thatch. She tucked her machete in the belt of a dusty tunic she had salvaged from the other huts and began sifting through the wreckage, kicking at chunks of broken brick with salvaged sandals on her feet. In a small, two-wheeled handcart lay two sacks of looted goods and a skinny fishing spear. Her stinking poncho was draped over her salvage, drying.

Poko wandered outside the hut, having had their fill of empty ruins. "Are you almost done?" they called to Odessa as she flipped aside a piece of thatch and mudbrick. When Odessa did not respond, Poko paused and turned to find her staring at the ground where the brick had been. "What is it? What did you find?"

For a moment, she said nothing. Poko approached hesitantly, scrabbling over the debris until they stood beside her. The smell of faint decay grew as they neared. Lying amid the dirt and debris was the desiccated corpse of an infant, its tiny form misshapen by decay and the weight of the wreckage on top of it. Its skin was shriveled and dark like a dried date. Ants crawled on the infant's face, scurrying along the rim of its sunken eye sockets and from its half-open mouth. The baby's hands were still curled in tiny fists at its deflated chest.

"Oh," Poko said, unsure how to respond. They looked up at Odessa, trying to read her stony expression. "Are you okay?"

Odessa nodded and looked away from the corpse. "Yeah. Yeah, I'm good."

She laid a sheaf of thatch over the infant and left the ruined hut without another word. It had been easy to steel herself against the death lingering in the dead river village when there had been no corpses, just faded bloodstains. Whatever numbness she had felt while walking through the empty village bled away and she felt the raw sting of death again. She hoisted the handcart's crossbar.

Poko scrambled up the side of the cart and onto the poncho. Odessa hauled the cart forward over piles of debris and around the spilled walls of huts.

She hadn't thought of Kimi since that night on the mountain; but now, Kimi's face would not leave her mind. Swollen and purple where the corpse in the hut had been shriveled and ashen, she only saw Kimi as she had been on the day of her funeral. It shamed her, but Odessa could barely remember a time when Kimi had been well. She only remembered Kimi as a sickly babe, mewling and listless. It was a cruel world where innocent infants died and godsforsaken monsters such as her were allowed to live.

The cart rattled over the ribs of a collapsed roof that had fallen into the path between huts, jostling the fairy in the cart's bed. "Are we leaving?" Poko asked.

"I don't want to be here when it gets dark," Odessa said flatly. "Too much death here."

Poko looked up at the sun high above them, punching through the gray pall. "Yeah, that's a good idea," they said.

"We're on the wrong side of the river," Odessa said, speaking only to keep her thoughts of Kimi and corpses at bay. "We'll have to cross the river somewhere downstream."

She turned the cart down the path toward the gate and stopped. Poko jolted forward as the cart's handlebars dropped. The crossbar bounced to a halt on the dusty ground. Odessa pulled the machete from her belt.

Obi stood in the gateway, his hunched shoulders heaving as he panted. His eyes were wide and whirling in their sockets.

Odessa raised the machete. Her insides sloshed inside her. Her heart raced, unrestrained. "Stay back!" Her voice wavered, tremulously.

Obi swayed, the point of his massive sword dragging in the dirt as he staggered forward.

"I said stay back!" Her voice was taut and wavering like a frayed rope about to snap.

Obi was monstrous. Even hunched over, he was still taller than any man she had ever seen. His goat's head sagged, the huge, twisting horns curving out beyond his broad shoulders. The long hair about his head and neck was singed and his skin was mottled with blistering sores.

He raised his head and bared his sharpened teeth. A guttural scream burst from his throat with a spray of spittle. Obi charged forward with inhuman speed.

"Run!" Odessa cried as she leaped away from the cart. The sword crashed into the cart in an explosion of splinters. Poko tumbled over the side and scrambled away from Obi.

Odessa sprinted through the maze of ruined huts. Behind her, Obi crashed through mudbrick and thatch like they were nothing to him. She darted between half-collapsed walls and over heaps of rubble, making her way toward the river.

If she could get to the other side, she would be safe, she hoped. It was all that she had.

Obi's sword smashed through a wall a stride behind her. Bits of brick struck her back like wasps, and she stumbled forward.

Another bestial scream sent her scrambling away as the sword swung again, meaning to cleave her in two. She darted to the right and took off straight to the river bank. She raced past decimated huts, bounding over crumbling walls and collapsed roofs. The river was only a few strides ahead. Past the last remnants of huts, the ground sloped down to the riverbank.

Obi's sword sliced through the air behind her, sending another explosion of rubble to batter her legs. She stumbled, and pain dug into her left shoulder. Obi's skeletal fingers pierced the flesh around her collarbone and jerked her backward.

She cried out and tried to pull away, but he had her by the bone and would not let go. She spun in his grasp, his fingers digging deeper in her flesh. The massive sword raised above his monstrous head. Yellowed teeth bared, he snarled. The sword point streaked toward her.

Her machete knocked the point aside, and with a backhanded slash she hacked at the hand that held her. The blade glanced off the bones of his wrist.

She thrashed in his grasp, his fingers sinking deeper into her flesh. Blood trickled down her side. His sword raised again.

Her machete slashed and hacked at any part of Obi it could reach, but there was too much bone and hard hide.

As his sword came down again, an explosion of white light blinded them. In the flash of light, his sword jerked off course and opened a long gash down her arm instead of skewering her through the chest. Odessa twisted and pulled free from Obi's slackened grip as another burst of light lit the area around them.

She crawled away, kaleidoscopic shapes burned in her vision. Obi screamed in rage, clutching his eyes.

"Come here!" Poko's voice came from her right, and she staggered to her feet toward it. By the time she reached Poko, the burned spots in her vision had faded enough for her to see. Obi was hunched over, thrashing on the ground and slamming the dirt with his fist as his sword slashed the air indiscriminately. He tried to blink the blindness away. Poko threw another fairy-dusted ball, and Odessa shielded her eyes. Obi screamed again as Odessa scooped the fairy up and started toward the river.

The water rippled as she neared. She skidded to a halt at the edge of the riverbank. A slick serpentine head broke the water. Another soon followed. And another. The water broke in a furious splashing; beneath the surface writhed what looked to be a mass of snakes. Heads like eels rose from the water, too many of them to count. They rose on necks as thick as tree trunks and their mouths snapped, opening wide enough to swallow her whole. Fangs like spearpoints lined each snapping maw.

Odessa stumbled backward as the mass of heads rose high above her, the necks coming together to a singular serpentine form that slithered toward the riverbank. A head snapped forward and she slashed at it with her machete. It recoiled, a gash in its snout.

She clutched Poko to her chest and slashed at another head. And then another. The fang-lined maws rained down upon her. Her arm snapped back and forth, cutting hunks of scale and flesh from them.

She continued backing away as the mass of serpentine forms slithered up the riverbank. Behind her, she could hear Obi roaring as he rose to his feet.

"Run!" Poko cried.

Odessa slashed the snout of an incoming serpentine head. Another head sank its teeth into her forearm. She ripped free and stumbled away. Caustic saliva sizzled in the bloody mess of her arm. Without warning, fire blossomed from the fresh blood pouring from the bite. She grimaced and tightened her grip on the machete as flames crept down her forearm to her wrist.

The heads recoiled for a moment. Obi roared as he charged her.

Odessa turned and ran.

CHAPTER 39

She ducked below the brutal swing of Obi's sword. His great bulk plowed into her, knocking her to the ground in a cloud of dust. The machete tumbled into the brush. Poko scrambled from her grip and into the brush as a serpent's mouth snapped at her ankle, taking a hunk of flesh and leaving a simmering sheen of caustic saliva behind.

Obi was on top of her before she could even raise her head from the dry brush and dusty dirt.

She caught his sword hand by the wrist as it came to plunge the blade into her chest. The point wavered above her throat, his inhuman strength bearing down on her arm and inching the blade closer. She pummeled him with her fist wreathed in flame, but he was unfazed. His skin was scorched red by her battering fist, but he did not relent.

His other hand gripped her throat, plunging a bony thumb into her neck. Blood welled around his knuckle as he squeezed. He drew himself closer, his entire body weight behind the blade now a hair's breadth from her throat.

His slobbering head was inches from her own, snapping and growling at her. His teeth gnashed in rage. His eyes bulged with effort. His singed hair brushed against her, the stink of smoke and death filling her nostrils and stinging her eyes.

A serpent's mouth clamped onto his shoulder and jerked. Another took his thigh. Obi roared and thrashed against the hydra's grasp. Odessa shoved his sword arm aside and squirmed, trying to wriggle out from beneath his massive body.

The hand at her throat tightened and pinned her where she lay. She gasped and coughed, her windpipe crunching beneath his weight.

He swung his massive blade at the myriad serpent heads tearing into his flesh. Blood ran in thick streams down his body and dripped onto Odessa. His scarred back was drenched in blood with large chunks of flesh ripped from him.

He cleaved a serpent's neck in two, and the head fell to the ground beside them. Blood sprayed in the air from the flailing neck.

Another head took Obi's sword arm, fangs plunging into the underside of his arm. He jerked, trying to swing again, but the serpents yanked him backward. Odessa scrambled out from under him as he thrashed. Multiple heads tore into him. He pulled his sword arm free and began hacking at the hydra.

Odessa clambered for the machete just a few strides away. A few hydra heads lunged for her as she leapt on all fours toward the machete.

Fangs sunk into her thigh. Acid burned in her flesh. Her skin peeled away as the serpent dug deeper, fangs scraping against her bones.

Odessa's frantic hands grabbed the machete and she twisted in the serpent's maw. Flames eating at the machete's corded handle and creeping along the iron blade, she hacked at the hydra's head, slashing until the blade sank into the center of its skull.

The neck and head grew slack. She wrenched the blade from its skull and pried its jaws open. The flesh of her thigh was slick with blood, and the punctures from its fangs were sizzling pits of blood and flesh.

She scrambled to her feet, her wounded thigh refusing to bear her weight. Another head came lunging toward her. She swung her flaming blade and hacked through its skull like knotted wood.

The wounded neck recoiled, its stunned head lolling back and forth on its flailing neck.

She stumbled backward, the flames around her forearm and machete-wielding fist sputtering weakly.

Obi had ripped free from the grasp of all but one of the serpent heads. He was hacking at the heads as they continued assailing him. The head still holding onto him had its fangs buried in his abdomen and jerked him back and forth, trying to drag him off his feet, but they were planted solidly in the dirt.

He swung his sword in brutally ferocious arcs. Several severed heads lay at his feet. The hydra's many heads were bloodied and growing more hesitant in their strikes. They reeled back and hissed in fury and only attacked en masse.

Obi finally cleaved the neck of the serpent holding onto his waist and freed himself, stumbling back as the severed head fell, its bloody jaws slack and limp.

"Odessa!" Poko yelled over the hiss and howl of the fight. "Let's go!"

Her fist tightened around the machete's handle, charred pieces of cord falling to the ground in embers. The flames rising from her bloodied arm surged as she watched Obi struggle and bleed.

Obi swung his large sword at the nexus of the writhing necks, where the thick serpentine trunk branched out in a tangle of snapping jaws. The blade bit deep into the snake's scaled flesh. The hydra jerked away from the blow. Obi wrenched the blade free as the hydra's many heads came down on him from all directions. All hesitance forgotten with the swing of his blade, they tore at him. Obi slashed and hacked with a speed that made his arms and sword a blur of dizzying motion. Odessa began to take a step toward Obi, arm ablaze, when Poko grabbed her pantsleg and tugged.

"Odessa!" they shouted. "We have to go now!"

She cast one last glance at the Obi and the hydra. She wanted to kill him. She needed to kill him. Poko was screaming her name, but she heard none of it. All she could hear was the screams of the man that hurt her Papa. Inhuman wailing that she had not caused. Her teeth ground together as the flames crawled up her arm to her shoulder.

With a growl, she was running, her sandals kicking up puffs of sandy dirt as she charged at the hydra.

"He's mine!" The words burst from her mouth like a jaguar's snarl. A head darted to intercept her, and she buried the machete's blade in its jaws so deep, she could not wrench it free. As the head recoiled, she let go of the flaming machete and cleared the last few strides to the hydra's trunk.

"He's mine!" she shouted. "His screams are mine!"

With all the hate she harbored and the pain burdened on her, she plunged her fiery fist into the gaping wound Obi's sword left in the hydra's trunk. She rammed it into the hydra's body, sinking to her elbow in sizzling blood and oozing viscera. The hydra jerked with a chorus of pained hisses. Odessa dug deep within her soul and dredged up all the tar-black vitriol that had accumulated since her Forsaking. All the rage and pain and hate. She took it all into herself again, feeling it all as if it were happening to her again. Loss, grief, and guilt fueled the flames that poured from the wound. Blood boiled from around her arm. Threads of smoke rose from the scorching flesh as the hydra writhed. Heads snapped at her. Fangs raked her flesh, but she only forced her arm deeper inside the hydra.

The hydra began to slither toward the river. Odessa dug her feet into the dirt, but she was carried along with the hydra, sandals scraping against the mud. As soon as she began splashing in the shallows, she jerked her arm out from the hydra and leaped back from the water as the hydra's long body slid into the river. She landed at the edge of the river and sat, watching the hydra's body slither past until its tail disappeared beneath the water's surface. The water around her right arm bubbled and frothed. Her fiery arm was extinguished, quenched in the river. The infernal heat that radiated from her godsblooded body bled into the cool water. Her heart pounded magma through her veins and she felt lightheaded. She wanted to stay in the water forever, to enjoy the pleasant reprieve, the lapping relief of the gentle current.

Steam rolled from her right arm. She staggered to her feet. *He's mine,* she reminded herself. *I'll kill him. He's mine to kill.*

She strode out of the river onto the riverbank, shaking the water from her smoldering arm. She breathed deeply, trying desperately to keep from being swept away in the swells of molten wrath that flooded her mind like a drug. Jaw clenched, she forced herself to become cold and unfeeling despite the roiling rage pumping through her veins. A maelstrom of emotion held by thin restraints of forced composure.

Obi was staggering onto ravaged legs. Sword planted in the dirt, he leaned on it, his goat head hanging low. A wide gash ran along his brow, a scrap of skin hanging loose with bloody hanks of hair. Half of his head was soaked with blood. Amid the tangle of blood-matted hair, his eye was half-closed and bloodied. He was panting, his broken ribs rising and falling in whistling gasps.

"Obi!" Odessa's voice boomed.

Poko shrunk back into the brush at the viciousness in her shout.

Obi raised his head. His unsteady body stiffened and in his open eye radiated unfettered, irrepressible hate. She wondered how much of the man that had beaten her Papa so badly was actually left inside that monstrous form.

"Obi! I killed you once and I'll do it again, you bastard!"

From Obi's raw throat came a sound between a growl and a groan. He staggered forward.

Odessa strode to meet him.

Obi's staggering stride quickened to a headlong spring. Odessa charged at him with a scream.

Obi's sword came flashing in the midday gloom. Odessa ducked the blade and darted close, thinking only of her father's lifeless face and his open throat. Hate and rage surged through her arm like lava pouring through her veins. Her fist struck his chest with a loud cracking of splintering ribs. Her other fist came, high and wide, and slammed into his side, sending him sprawling to the ground.

She kicked him and stomped on his head until his horns snapped in half. Blood trickled from the broken horns. He dropped the sword and grasped her leg, sinking his bony fingers into her thigh. She pulled herself free, stomped on his arm, and then fell on top of him. She pinned his arm down with her knee and pummeled his head, screaming in inhuman tongues, letting her rage and wrath loose in guttural cries.

Her fists striking his hairy hide became wet thuds as she beat his head into a pulp of blood and gore. Blood and hair and strands of viscera clung to her knuckles. "I hate you! I hate you! I hate you!"

Obi's hand raked at her side, tearing swathes of skin from her arms but doing nothing to allay her fury.

"Obi! I'll kill you! I'll kill you a hundred times!" The walls of her composure crumbled with each strike of her fists. The blackness of her hate swallowed her up and her thoughts were incinerated in the molten flows of her wrath.

"Die!" she howled. "Die! Die! Die!

All restraint gone, her burned fist burst into flame once more. Obi screamed and clawed at her as his blood-soaked hair caught flame. His bleating screams were music to her ears. The thud of her punches punctuated the melodious cries like a war drum's beat.

She punched through the flames as they swallowed up Obi's entire head and chest. She continued pummeling the pulp of his split skull, fire enveloping his face and pouring from the crack in his skull. She screamed until her voice was hoarse.

When the flames singeing Obi's head and neck began sputtering and guttering upon his charred flesh, Odessa let her weary fists fall to her sides. Her hoarse screams had turned to weak, pitiful sobs. Her head tilted back to face the solemn gray sky. Blood was splattered across her face and in her hair.

The hate and the rage that had burned so violently in her chest had receded, leaving an overwhelming emptiness behind.

Her tears cut through the drying blood on her cheeks as they fell down her upturned face.

CHAPTER 40

They spent one last night in the village, taking refuge in the hut. Odessa was fast asleep when Poko's voice broke through the night's silence.

"Get up!"

Odessa awoke with a start, bolting upright with a gasp of pain. Her bleary eyes were wild with alarm.

"What is it?" she mumbled, voice still thick with sleep.

Poko was beside her. "Something's here."

Muddled by the last vestiges of slumber, her thoughts came jumbled and indistinct. Feverish veins of infection spread through her body and mired her mind in a balmy fog of confusion and disorientation.

"What's here?" she asked, the hydra coming immediately to mind. Could there be another one?

"Something bad. Really, really bad." Through all the strife she and Poko had been through since they had met, the fairy had never been this scared. There was pure terror in their eyes. A primal fear.

The numbness of sleep beginning to recede, Odessa could feel it too. She could feel it seeping into her skin. A chill permeating her to the bone. Her heart began to pound in her chest and her palms grew damp, but she did not know why. She could guess, though: It was the atmosphere. Like the low pressure before a massive storm. As if something catastrophic was roiling on the horizon.

Odessa scrambled to her feet and shoved a piece of thatch from the barricaded doorway. In the dark, she could see the vague outlines of spirits darting through the air, like mirages in the periphery of her vision. But that was all she could see. Full dark and the fleeting shimmer of illusory spirits. She replaced the section of thatch and turned, almost stepping on Poko as they struggled at her feet, pulling at the mudbricks and rubble that made their barricade.

"What are you doing?" she asked, stepping over Poko. Growing panic weakened her words, a twinge of anxious worry making them sound almost pathetically feeble. The cold pressure made her want to curl up and hide, but she resisted the fear, finding some mettle within herself and clinging to it.

"We need to get out! We're trapped! We need to leave now!" The fairy was hysterical, clawing at the rubble with animalistic fervor.

"There's nothing out there but bad spirits!" Odessa said, her own words sounding false to her ears. "Let's just build the fire up and wait it out. Morning will be here before you know it."

"We'll be dead long before morning!" Poko stopped their frantic clawing and faced her. Their face was gaunt and pallid with fright. Their fingers trembled, the tips of which were raw and bleeding, stark red on the pale silver of their skin.

"You have to feel it!" They approached her and took hold of her pant legs in quivering fists. "It's like a mountain walking toward us and this is just the rumbling of its steps. It's coming, Odessa! And we need to get out of its way now!"

Odessa took a step back, but Poko did not let go of her pant legs. They were right.

There was something in that chill that caused her skin to break out in goosebumps. There was a reason for the racing of her heart. A sort of static filled the air. A tension in the atmosphere. A vaguely familiar sensation, only multiplied a hundredfold. Whatever was approaching radiated a foul power.

For a moment, Odessa faltered, unsure of what to do. In her indecision, the chilling pressure only grew. In the light of their guttering fire, she found her bow and quiver and Obi's bronze sword. She tied the quiver to her waist with a hurried knot.

"Let's go, then," she said, her weapons in one hand and in the other, a crude torch of driftwood, reeds, and rancid animal fat. She tipped the head of the torch into the fire and it bloomed in flame. "We'll come back in the morning for the rest."

With a few kicks, Odessa brought the barricade down enough for her to duck through the doorway. She held the torch aloft, dripping fat onto the rubble as she half-crawled, half-stepped over it. Poko clung to her shoulder, nestling themself into her frizzy hair.

Outside the hut, she stopped abruptly as if she had struck a wall. The pressure was overwhelming.

"Too late," Poko whispered in her ear.

Toward the river, in the dark, there was a shadow moving closer. Darker than black, it looked as if the shape of a figure had been scraped from existence. Its shape fluttered and flickered like a mirage. It was the foul power radiating from it. She could feel it. She could feel each flutter pulse through her bones.

"Run," Odessa said. Her mouth was dry. She had to force the word from her mouth to overcome the muzzling pressure. Like a gag in her mouth. "Run for the gate."

Poko stayed frozen on her shoulder, eyes transfixed. Odessa found her own legs immobilized, as if the earth had risen and encased them in stone. In her hand, the torchlight wavered, shrinking away from the profound blackness that approached so slowly. She dropped the torch onto a cluster of dry brush and grass. The flame guttered for a moment before finding the strength to crawl along the stems of brittle grass and the edges of wilted leaves.

She took Poko and tossed them to the ground behind her. "Run!" she shouted, unable to turn and see if they had listened to her. Her eyes could not leave the shadowy figure.

As it came closer, she could begin to see through the darkness that shrouded the figure. The fire beside her shrank back in the presence of such darkness, but still it continued to emit enough light to see by.

A dozen strides away, a stumbling figure approached. One leg dragged behind the other. Its goat's head hung awkwardly askew, hair bloody and matted. Two broken horns curved from its half-caved-in skull. In its sunken face, there were two pits of dried gore. Twin chasms where a soul used to reside. Something in those deflated eye sockets glared out at her through the dark.

Odessa's legs shook like leaves in the wind. She rammed the sword point into the dirt and fumbled an arrow out of her quiver. Her trembling hands struggled to nock the arrow, and when she drew the bowstring back, she worried her clammy fingers would let the arrow slip.

Obi staggered toward her, arms hanging limply. With each step, it seemed as if he would totter over and fall, but he continued plodding toward her.

Odessa screamed in her mind but her mouth gave no voice to her terror. Why won't you die?

The aura filling the atmosphere was the same as on the mountaintop: dank and pervasive and poisonous. That same helplessness threatened to drown her. Her jaw set, and she focused her sight down the shaft of the quivering arrow. With a quavering exhalation, she let the arrow fly.

The arrow sailed high over Obi's head and into the darkness beyond. Odessa's hand fumbled for another arrow when a voice filled the air. A cold, malevolent voice. A voice like the howling wind over barren tundra.

"Odessa Kusa of Kalaro. You stand in the presence of a High God. You stand before Talara, the Sin Eater. Talara, the Goddess of Death and Decay. I suggest you do not send another arrow in my direction. Since I deign to speak to you in the flesh, I expect deference."

Talara's voice came from every direction, surrounding Odessa with spiteful words. The fire beside Odessa sputtered. Obi's reanimated corpse continued forward, the dim light illuminating its desiccated skin peeling and sloughing away. The body was shriveled and falling apart. Maggots writhed in open wounds.

Odessa nocked another arrow and drew the bowstring back. Her whole body twitched. Every muscle urged her to run away. She felt as if she couldn't catch her breath. She wet her lips. "What do you want?" she croaked.

Obi's body stopped. Its mouth hung slack, a black, swollen tongue lolling out. It did not move with Talara's words. "For now, I only wish to speak to you."

"Speak? You want to speak to me?" The words came from Odessa's throat, raw and rough. "This is your fault! You lied to the ka-man and had my father killed! You tried to kill me! You turned Obi into that awful thing and chased me down! And now you want to talk?" She panted, fear driving her to hyperventilation. Obi's corpse stared back at her blankly. Gritting her teeth, she let the arrow loose and it sunk halfway into Obi's caved-in face. "I don't talk to corpses!"

She was reaching for another arrow when an astounding pressure brought her to her knees. Collapsing onto her hands and knees, she gasped, unable to draw a breath. It felt as if a mountain was laid on top of her.

"I said I wish to speak to you. What you have to say is of no import." The scraping of Obi's dragging footsteps returned, drawing closer. "And do not waste any more arrows. This is a mere conduit. My true form exists in a plane far from your comprehension. Your arrows could not hope to strike me." Obi's monstrous feet, half-foot and half-hoof, came to a stop before her. "But I can still crush you like a bug, Odessa Kusa. As distant as I am, I can kill you in an instant. I could lay unimaginable torments upon you. You have managed to survive thus far, but do not overestimate your abilities. You are still so very mortal." Talara's pressure swelled, forcing Odessa to the dirt. "I wish to talk to you. But if you resist, I will simply rip the heart from your chest and be done with this. Do you understand?"

Odessa twisted her neck and turned her head to look at the grotesque corpse standing above her. Her throat was tight, strangled in the grip of terror. She averted her gaze from the looming corpse and instead stared into the pitch black, where not even spirits roamed. Nothing remained other than the overwhelming aura of dank decay and death. "You've been trying to kill me this whole time. Why should I believe you won't kill me now?"

"I still might," Talara said, the words dragging like a blade along Odessa's spine. "It all depends on how useful you prove yourself to be. Will you be of more use to me dead or alive? That is what I wish to find out."

Odessa fought against the pressure, pushing up with all her strength, but she remained flattened on the dirt, barely able to rise a handsbreadth. Spittle spattered on the dirt as she pushed, groaning against the weight of a god's power. Blood soaked through her bandages as she strained and struggled.

"You don't need to be a mere vessel," Talara said, placing a foot upon Odessa's back and forcing her to the dirt again. "Within you lies infinite potential. Humans are resistant to the rigors of the cosmic. You will continue to absorb life. You will need it. You will hunger for it. And you will grow ever stronger."

The pressure swelled again. Odessa struggled to take a single breath.

The hoofed foot ground upon her spine. The stench of rot and decay was unbearable.

"Join me and you may become unstoppable. You will be above all that is holy upon this planet. Without rival, this world can be yours."

The hoofed foot rose and let her free. Obi's bony fingers weaved through her hair and hoisted her onto her knees. Odessa clawed at his hand, her fingernails tearing at rotten flesh. The corpse's grip did not waver.

"My brother always had such a love for his creations. Like they were his children. He even loved them more than his true children, I believe. I never quite understood why he loved you humans so. So weak. So insignificant. Your life span is over in the time it takes for me to blink. I thought you were only fodder, useful only en masse to feed the Gray and keep it at bay. To keep it contained. But now I believe I do. Now I understand."

Obi's corpse raised her higher, lifting her by the hair until her toes scraped the ground. Her scalp was pulled taut and the roots of her hair strained with the weight. Her hands gripped the corpse's arm, taking some of the weight. Odessa jerked and thrashed as much as the tremendous pressure weighing down upon her would allow.

She spat in the goat's head's face.

She kicked at Obi's rotten, sunken chest. Spit spattered the matted hair along its nose. The pits of gore that were Obi's eyes stared at her pitilessly. It stood totally impassive as its bony fingers raked deep gouges from its swollen chest. Meanwhile, Talara said nothing. Its fingers sunk between ribs and scooped out stringy clumps of clotted blood. Maggots writhed in its palm, fat and ghastly white in the dimness.

The fingers in her hair tightened, gripping the hair close to her scalp and holding her fast. The cupped hand of gore and maggots rushed toward her lips.

Odessa screamed, a pathetic howl of disgust and despair. Desperate fire burst from her arm and she swung a fiery fist at Obi's corpse. Her fist hit the goat's broken muzzle and she felt bone crack and splinter. Scorched hair caught flame again as she brought her fist back for another swing. The other hand let go of her hair, and she tumbled to the ground in a heap. The flames along her forearm sputtered and died, the little strength she had gone.

The corpse stood impassive as fire engulfed its head again. The pressure surrounding Odessa lessened.

"Live," Talara's faint voice echoed. "Live and feed. Become stronger, for this whole world will be against you. Beasts and spirits will be drawn to your tainted scent. Other gods will come for you. But you must survive. Rip the hearts from your enemy's chest and consume all that they are. Do this and you will be redeemed, Odessa. Do this and you will be whole. Do this and you will be with your mother and sister again."

Obi's corpse collapsed to the ground as the pitch-black presence eased away. The fire grew a bit bolder.

"In time you will see I am your salvation," Talara's voice came, softer now and a bit more distant. "If you survive your trials, I will come to you again, Odessa."

And then, Talara was gone.

CHAPTER 41

The next day, they crossed the river further downstream, leaving behind the wrecked cart. By the end of the day, the ruined village beside the river was still within her vision, its earthen walls a brown smear against the coal-stained gray of the darkening sky.

Odessa carried a sack over her shoulder, a portion of what they had scavenged from the village: a bundle of food and clothes, a calabash filled with water, and a dull copper knife. The rest sat in the ruined cart, too cumbersome to take.

Days blurred together. The farther north they traveled, the more they veered toward the jungle. They skirted the jungle's edge for a day before entering it. Their food ran out and Odessa and Poko had to stop to forage, venturing through the barren outer reaches of the forest into the wilting green interior. With her stomach empty for two days, Odessa was able to find a large cluster of yams.

Two more rivers, trickling creeks in comparison to the river the village had sat upon, were all they had to cross on their trek north. At each river, she crossed with the bundle held above her head, the fairy nestled within it. She tried her hand at skewering some fish with a sharpened stick, but the fish were too few and scattered at the slightest disturbance. The image from the surface of the water was a lie that she had trouble seeing past. Fooled by the refraction, she thrust, and after the cloud of silt and sediment had dissipated, she would see nothing but muck at the end of her spear and that every small fish she had spotted had disappeared.

Eventually, her aim improved enough to compensate for the refraction and, staying on the banks of those rivers for a day or two at most, she was able to impale at least two or three. All day, she would stand, motionless in water up to her knees. The current splashed upon her bare skin, her spear arm cocked back, swaying back and forth, searching for prey to spring toward and pierce them through the middle.

Along the rivers, they could leave the shadow of the Night Jungle, using driftwood dried upon the banks as firewood. A small reprieve from the worst of the Night Jungle's influence.

With each passing night, Odessa's body grew wearier. Fatigue seeped into her muscles and into the very marrow of her bones. She lost count of how many days and nights had passed since leaving the village on the river. As the days of walking wore on, even Poko's nattering tapered away to leave them in an all-encompassing silence.

Soon, the flat ground began to roll, slight hills rising and falling off toward the western horizon. Staying close to the forest, they continued north. As the land grew drier and became more scrubland than savannah, Odessa kept watch on the skies. Whenever she caught a glimpse of any movement among the clouds, she would dart into the outskirts of the jungle and hide among dead palms and ferns. They were nearing Azka's lands. His Blessed Ones were in the sky, on wings of bronze. Their eagle eyes could see for miles, and they would not refuse giving chase upon finding a Forsaken girl.

To kill a Forsaken was an honor. It was an achievement worthy of recognition from their patron God, and the children of Azka were hungry for their father's approval.

Along the edge of the jungle, she and Poko trudged. She kept her knife in hand at all times, as if it would do any good against Azka's Chosen. A Blessed One would open her belly and take her head off her shoulders before she even saw them. And if Azka himself were to find her, nothing would be left of her body to be given to the earth in recompense. She would be obliterated, utterly and totally.

It was morning when she first saw the city of Noyo rise from the northern horizon, the early morning sun glinting off bronze roofs rising like spear points above walls of dusty white stone. Even on the horizon, Odessa could make out the tiered pyramid rising above the city, a wide palace sitting atop it all.

The palace of Azka. A palace of gold and bronze.

Her hair was a matted mess of curls, her body, thin and starved. Odessa stumbled toward the opulence of Noyo, a Forsaken wretch sneaking in the shadow of a god.

A road, faded with disuse, began to run an hour's walk from the edge of the jungle. Odessa saw no one on the road, but still, she avoided it like the plague. She wrapped her arm in thick linen and sweated beneath a poncho to hide her cursed limb. As if it would do anything to mask the darkness roiling from her skin like noxious vapor wafting from her every pore.

As she drew closer to the city, she slunk deeper into the jungle. Through the thick foliage, she could make out the shapes of men, women, and children toiling in the fields alongside lesser beings and beasts of burden. Harvesting what

stunted food they could coax from the dry, lifeless soil. Most of the humans were
naked, save for loincloths wrapped around their bony waists. Humanoid creatures with a single eye and a slavering mouth of fangs carried huge baskets, half-
full of squash, yams, maize, beans, potatoes, cassava, and millet. These creatures
had pale, pudgy flesh, reddened by the sun. Their limbs were thick with muscle.
They hunched forward carrying their loads, a certain looseness in their shuffling
gait, an aura of resignation in their steps.

A Blessed One streaked through the sky, wings of bronze blades shining in
the muddled light. Winged lions the size of elephants with wings of bronze, the
Blessed Ones were Azka's own children of diluted divinity.

Odessa pressed her belly to the jungle floor and hid. Poko curled up beneath
her. The Blessed One was out of sight. Odessa stayed prone for a long time,
breath held bated in her chest. Her body was tense and motionless.

Eventually, she let the air hiss from her lips. After a long while, she rose to
a low crouch, her eyes scanning the surrounding jungle and the fields beyond.
Everything was as it had been before the Blessed One had appeared. She continued on through the edge of the jungle, slower and with more caution.

So close to Noyo, she did not dare light a fire when night came. Instead,
she slept in the waning hours of daylight and awoke in the twilight. By midday, they reached the northern edge of the jungle. Across the plains of sickly
yellow grass and coarse fields of wilting plants—across a wide, placid river
that slithered down from the mountains—stood Noyo in all its majesty and
opulence.

"Where do we go from here?" asked Poko from their perch on her shoulder.

Odessa scratched at the linen around her arm. "I don't know." The wise man
was east of Noyo. That was all she knew. But there was a lot of land between
Noyo and the mountain's slopes. They had much too little food and water to
wander aimlessly. And Odessa did not know how many more nights she could
last. Each night was a chance to die. One wrong move and the undead would tear
her apart. She could not keep doing this.

This is my punishment. A life of being hunted. Running forever.

"So what are we going to do?" the fairy asked.

Odessa picked at the linen even more. She didn't have the heart to speak the
words swelling up her throat like vomit. I don't know. I'm lost.

She thought of venturing out into the outskirts of Noyo, but she could not
bring herself to do it. It was much too brazen. Forsaken did not have such luxu-
ries. She would be killed as soon as she set foot out in the open.

Instead, she crept back into the deeper parts of the jungle to think. As she did
so, she heard the rustling of leaves. Footsteps.

She crouched, knife drawn. Multiple pairs of feet sneaked through the jungle, a few spans away from the edge of the jungle. Coming from Noyo.

Poko hid within the tangle of her hair. Odessa remained motionless, listening.

Voices came from the edge of the jungle, whispers barely audible. Human voices. The first human voice Odessa had heard since leaving Kalaro. How many days had passed since then, she did not know. At the sound of those voices, a pang of loneliness twisted deep in her chest. The voices sounded like home. A slightly different dialect, one of haughty lowlanders, but a familiar sound nonetheless.

She followed the sound of their footsteps. Through the jungle, she caught a glimpse of them, three men with bows and spears, creeping through the palms. They were not dressed in loincloths like the slaves in the fields—they wore tunics of supple leather and sported bright feathers woven in their hair. Their skin was a shade lighter than her own., They reminded her of her father.

She followed them from a distance, trying to build up the courage to call out to them. To beg for help. To cry to them and tell them all the ill that had befallen her. But as she was doing that, a branch cracked beneath her foot.

Her stomach dropped. She froze. The hunters turned, their weapons raised.

"What is that?" one asked.

Her heart skipped a beat. In her hesitation, she had gotten too close.

The hunters spread out from each other, moving lithely like jaguars. They soon saw her. Their countenances darkened. They approached slowly and then stopped a fair few strides away.

"Drop the bow!" one of the hunters said. She did as she was told and then held her hands up, empty palms out for them to see. "Who are you?"

Odessa's mouth went dry. She opened it, willing sound to come out, but she was too stunned to speak. At last, she forced a raspy reply out. "I need help."

The hunters looked at each other. One of them looked back at her. "What's wrong?"

She nodded. "I've come to see the wise man."

"The wise man?"

The look in the hunter's eyes made Odessa uneasy. "Can you tell me where to find him?"

The hunters glanced at each other again. Another hunter spoke. "Are you sick?"

Odessa shook her head.

"Why are you following us?" the third hunter asked.

"I'm lost." Odessa tried to dull the edge of desperation in her voice. "I need help."

"There's something wrong with her," the second hunter said. "I do not like the look of her."

The first hunter stepped forward. Odessa tensed. "There's nothing wrong with her," he said. There was no kindness in his voice. He stepped closer, hand outstretched in placation. Like she were a wild animal. "I will take you to the wise man, girl."

His body language was tense. He moved like a predator on the hunt, stalking. The other two hunters glanced at each other, their eyes speaking in a language she was not privy to. Odessa watched the hunter approach, her heart sinking lower with each quiet step. He held his hand out for her to take, as if she were a child, and all she could think about was the warrior that had chased her and tackled her and hit her. She had lived all her life in the same village as him and he had dragged her up those mountain steps all the same.

Another step. His hand was almost close enough to touch her. I don't know these men. They'll make me a slave. Or they'll take my head to Azka. And they'll do worse things to me. The bad sorts of things that happen to girls. She didn't know where these thoughts came from but she couldn't get them out of her head. They buzzed and droned until she couldn't think anymore.

"Come, let's go," he said. His hand rested upon her shoulder. Before he could utter another false word, she drove her fist into his throat. His windpipe cracked and he crumpled with a wet wheeze, clutching at his crushed throat with the same hand he had reached out to her with. He choked on his lying breath and Odessa jerked the spear from his hand as he fell. She lunged toward the other two as they raised their bows.

She ran the spear through the belly of the second hunter, pinning him to a tree before he could nock an arrow.

The third hunter tried to run. Odessa left the second hunter pinned to the tree and chased after him. In a few strides, she caught up to him. She tackled him. He twisted beneath her, hands reaching out to shove her away. They hit the ground. Odessa took an arm and bent it until the bones snapped and ripped through the skin.

She clamped a bandaged hand around his throat and squeezed. His eyes were wide with terror. Odessa's teeth ground together. "Where is the wise man?"

The young hunter was blubbering, gibberish spilling in quick succession from his lips. Pain-addled eyes whirled in his head. She squeezed his throat a bit more and then relaxed her grip.

"Where is he?"

The hunter coughed and spittle splattered on his chin. "In the sacred grove." His words were wheezing, choked syllables.

Odessa squeezed the word from his throat again. "How do I get there?"

When she released, he gasped and fell into a fit of wet coughs. "There's a trail east out of Noyo. It runs into the foothills. The grove is surrounded by mountains. I don't know how to get in." Tears were filling his eyes. "I don't know anything else. Please let me go."

It took surprisingly little effort to squeeze the life from the hunter's throat. A slight bit of weight and he began thrashing beneath her, clawing at her hands. Her face was harsh and unyielding as she crushed his windpipe in her grip.

She stripped the hunters of a bow, a sturdy lacquered bow, and their arrows and set about out with the hunter's directions in mind. Poko was quiet for a long time. Odessa did not notice. She was only thinking about the wise man now. She didn't think she would ever actually reach him. The goal had always been a diversion from the inevitable. Now it seemed attainable.

After a long while, the fairy's voice broke her rumination. "Why did you do that?"

"What do you mean?" she asked, not breaking stride.

"Kill them," they said. "They were going to help you."

"What? No, they weren't. They were trying to trick me."

The fairy was quiet for a moment. "I didn't sense that."

Odessa stopped. "They were doing the same thing you did. He said he was going to take me to the wise man, but he wasn't." She continued walking. "I saw the look in their eyes. I know what they were going to do. I'm not stupid."

Poko said no more, but she could feel the fairy's judgmental gaze on her skin, like needles prodding at her.

She had done what she had to. She had seen their ill intention. The man's hand as it had come for her was the hand of a bad man. The kind of hand that would strip her and bind her. Men like that had no right to live. There was no reason to doubt that.

They continued their journey in silence, sneaking through the edge of the jungle until they could make out the eastern road in the distance.

"I will take you to the wise man," he said. *He was lying, right?* she thought. Of course, he was lying. Everybody does.

CHAPTER 42

The forest stretched at the foothills of the mountains east of Noyo, thinning into streaks of sparse jungle and montane woodland along the base of the mountains. From a distance, Odessa followed the faded road from Noyo leading east into a small hamlet built into the foothills. The hillsides were marked with scattered, terraced fields. Standing in the scant shade of a cluster of half-bare copperwood trees, she was reminded of Kalaro. A dull ache swelled in her chest. Like her heart was swollen and about to burst. Absentmindedly, she picked at the peeling red bark of the copperwood, staring at the few figures moving about the terrace fields. More thin, emaciated forms in loincloths toiling in the dirt. Seeing the world as it was outside of the insular glade of Kalaro was appalling. Her thoughts drifted back to the hunters. Her father had told her humans were of one blood. How could they do that to her?

Her own people had done worse to her. For years, long before she was born in better days, Kalaro had raided the lowland tribes with zealous abandon. She should not have been surprised. No one could be trusted. God or human, everyone was against her.

Yet the wise man remained a singular hope, a guiding star in the dark despondency she found herself adrift in. Her father's last command. She had to put her trust in that. Or else why go on living at all?

She hung back, far from the mountain hamlet, and circled around to the surrounding foothills of the south. Thighs burning on their upward climb, the slopes soon grew steep and she had to scale the forest peaks on all fours, grabbing hold of any trunk she could use to haul herself up.

It was a relief to be in the forest again, hidden in thickets. The trek across the open plain had been nerve-wracking. She had tried to only travel at twilight, when the spirits were still in their hovels and holes. But she had gained too little ground. The time was too fleeting.

It was almost dark by the time she found the trail leading from behind the village up to the greater foothills at the base of the mountains. It was little more than an overgrown footpath through the brush. It snaked up on high ridges bristling with trees and down into steep ravines filled with thickets of spikebush, switching back and forth on its upward climb up the slopes.

The foot of the mountains proper. The mountainside stretched upward, taller than the highest reaches of the most ancient heart trees at the center of the jungle.

Odessa turned around in a slow circle, eyes darting back from where she had come, searching for some branching of the path that she had missed. But there was none. It simply ended where the tree line did at the foot of the bare slope.

At the base of the cliff was a blanket of scree, on the ground from which sparse grass and woody shrubs sprouted. There was no indication of where to go.

That bastard lied to me, she thought. She paced at the end of the path, mind racing in circles. Going over all that had happened since she left Kalaro. All the pain and loss, all of it for nothing. To have come so far for it to end here was maddening. Disheartened frustration boiled inside her, waves of rage radiating off her as she stomped along the cliff side, eyes running over the craggy stone again and again.

Poko had climbed down from her shoulder and inspected the cliff on their own, wandering on the mossy slope of talus, refusing to acknowledge Odessa's frantic pacing. Their hand ran along the rock, slender fingers tracing the myriad crags and nooks.

Odessa groaned, exasperated and infuriated. "I suppose we'll have to walk up and down this whole cliff until we find a way through. That will give the Blessed Ones plenty of time to catch wind of me. Perfect. Just perfect."

Poko said nothing as they wandered farther away, to where the cliff face grew mossy and slick with lichen. Strands of moss hanging from a ridge above them brushed against their hand. Lichen clung to the rock, a thick crust of pale yellow and green.

Their hand ran through a curtain of hanging moss, fingers bouncing along the rock. And then, behind the thick curtain of moss, their hand no longer felt the cliff face. They stopped in the middle of a depression in front of the cliff, a dry creek bed, pushing their hand farther through the strands, finding no resistance.

"Odessa," they said, flatly, hand still moving through the air behind the moss. Odessa turned to see the fairy's arm halfway in the cliff. She rushed forward, slipping on the slope of scree.

She parted the curtain of moss. A triangular cleft cut through the cliff, the walls dripping with condensation as a trickle of spring water still ran along the bottom of the pass. The top of the cleft was tall enough that even Obi in his monstrous form would have been able to enter if he filed down his horns. She took a step inside, acutely aware that the entire cliff was above her head.

Poko followed as she ventured deeper into the pass. Heading up the diminished creek, their feet began splashing more with each step. The walls occasionally brushed her shoulders on either side. A slight twinge of claustrophobia caught in her chest but was easily quelled.

Light came faintly from the other side, bouncing off the slick walls like sunlight reflected off the waves of the ocean.

They emerged at the bottom of a ravine in the saddle of two mountains. Mossy forest stretched all around them, a landscape of green. She followed the trickling creek to the spring it came burbling out from and then continued up the slight, lightly forested slope of the saddle, through the immensity of green around them. So many different shades, from the pale green of lichen on the flat, worn stones at the bottom of the ravine to the soft green of moss on the trees to the deep, verdant green of the broadleaves above.

A crow perched on a branch squawked at her, its head cocked so that its black eye bored into her. As they passed beneath the branch it perched upon, the crow's gaze followed them, taking in their every step with silent reproach.

Odessa's heart began to flutter as she walked, not fully cognizant of where she was going. Her feet carried her upward but her mind was elsewhere. Back in Kalaro. On the mountaintop. In the Night Jungle. Retracing her path here, to this mossy grove. Since passing through the curtain of moss, she had found herself in a sort of transient out-of-body experience. Some part of her still didn't believe it. The wise man had been some vague, distant goal still just a few minutes before; now, she was walking in his hidden grove.

The forest around her was cool, and the air smelled of wet earth and life. A comforting sense of safety lifted the weight from her chest. She could breathe in this forest. Deep breaths. Every exhalation carried with it the soot and smoke of pain and grief and rage out from her clogged lungs. The chill in her chest warmed like the plains after sunrise.

A placid quiet filled the forest, their footsteps and the creaking of old trees the only noise. Relief moistened her eyes. She thought of her past life. She thought of her sisters and mother. She thought of her father, and tears began slipping down her cheeks.

They came upon a path beaten through the brush and followed it up to a clearing at the top of the saddle. The path ran up the slope, to a sod house sitting at the base of the high mountains. Drooping flowers of yellow and orange grew along the front of the house, a building embedded in a wide hump of sod, as if someone had pried the earth up and shoved a house beneath it.

Odessa stopped at the edge of the clearing, her feet suddenly heavy. Her stomach twisted in knots. Air left her lungs as she realized she did not know what to say or what to do. She hadn't truly believed she would get this far.

What if he doesn't believe me? Or he sends me away? Her hand reached and cradled her bandaged arm. What if all this was for nothing?

A crow swooped from the forest nearby to land atop the sod roof. It squawked, flapping its wings and ruffling its feathers before it settled on its perch. Odessa began to notice other shapes moving in the thin strip of forest behind the house. A llama appeared from behind the house and watched her, chewing its cud impassively before it moved on to inspect a cluster of tall, pale pink orchids.

The door of the sod house opened. A tall man stepped out, his skin as white as cream. He wore a red tunic with no sleeves, exposing pale, wrinkled skin adorned with tattoos of faded indigo spiraling up his arms. Elaborate patterns of spidery runes wrapped around his arms and each finger. His hair was long and wild, and he sported a tangled beard, all of it a warm, yellowed gray like the sun shining through the clouds above.

Stepping out of the doorway, he raised a hand in the air and waved. The crow fluttered down, and at the sound of its flapping wings, the old man paused and turned, allowing the bird to land on his shoulder. The crow flapped its wings once and squawked again. The wise man's eyes, an intensely icy blue, fell upon her again. "Do you need something, young lady?"

Odessa's feet moved sluggishly against the heaviness she felt all around her now. Anxiety bubbled in her knotted stomach like the tar pits of the wastelands far to the south. She opened her mouth, unsure if any sound would come out.

Odessa stopped a few strides away. Her hand suddenly went to her tangled hair, feeling the snarls and mats. Then she waved and smiled as tears of joy streaked down her cheeks.

"My father sent me."

CHAPTER 43

The death of your apostle changes nothing, Kunza. I am not so weak as to rely entirely on a human," Talara boomed in Kunza's hut. "Let me assure of that fact. What you see before you is a mere sliver of my ethereal form. I am so much more than smoke and shadow and it would behoove you to devote this to your memory. I am beyond your understanding. I am a cosmic force like no other. I am the unavoidable. I am the unending. All life ends with me!"

Her voice rang in Kunza's ears. "I offer you salvation and you dare question me? I offer to save your people from starvation and sickness and even the Gray, and you insult me like this?"

Kunza could say nothing. The air had been swept from his lungs. A tremendous pressure kept him pinned to the floor, unable to raise his head as the shadows and smoke gathered at the altar.

"I am not idle. There is a war being waged. The Gray ravages both your world and mine. Annihilation closes in and you are blissfully ignorant of it all. Gods die each day while you whinge and whine. We scratch and claw at the precipice of destruction and I alone can save us. And still, you have the gall to question me!"

Who is we? God or man? The thought came unbidden. But Kunza's reflexive obstinance was immediately destroyed before the presence of the Goddess of Rot and Ruin. Of course, he knew the answer. Blessed as he was, he was still a human.

Blood pounded in his ears as the pressure grew, flattening him even farther to the dirt. As if the sky had fallen on top of him. Or a massive boot was grinding him beneath its heel. It seemed an eternity. Then without warning, the pressure eased away. He gasped and coughed and his lungs filled with smoke.

"Perhaps I did burden you too heavily," Talara said, her voice oddly calm now. Her cold voice unnerved him. He had never been as scared as when she had shown him her fury then. But this cold composure rattled him to his core in a very different fashion. In a way he could not put into words. "Continue your work, my Priest of Ashes. I have others that can find the girl. We will have our vessel."

"Are you sure?" The words tumbled from his mouth.

"You question me again?" She said, a twinge of sardonic mirth twined along with warning in her tone.

The presence within the smoke dissipated, and the smoke itself began filtering upward, toward the hole in the roof. The overwhelming curtain of shadow that had darkened the hut receded. The crackling fire's glow surged from atop the altar to reclaim the hut. Kunza kept his head on the floor for a long while. Motionless, like a sulking child. He worried Talara would abandon him and his people for his foolish words. A part of him wished she would. He hated that part of himself. The obstinate part. Like a sliver of flint in his heart, stony and sharp.

I thought my faith was stronger now. Yet I still cannot restrain my foolish tongue. His forehead rose and dropped to strike the packed earth with a flat smack. *To speak like that to a god. My arrogance will kill us all!*

After a while he rose, unaided by his walking stick which now leaned against his table, gathering dust. On the table sat the cauldron, its bronze darkened with so much blood. A crust of dried blood along the rim of its wide mouth. He removed the lid and reached inside. His fingers scraped against the bottom. He scooped up a small puddle of congealed blood and slurped. His head leaned back with a gob of blood on his bottom lip. His eyes smoldered as blessed blood began to seep into his core. Her strength permeated his frail form, edifying his body and soul. He needed to kill that weak, faithless part of himself. To dig out the shard of stubborn hubris from his chest and cast it away.

"Priest of Ashes," he whispered softly to himself. "I am the Priest of Ashes. Talara's chosen servant."

He breathed in a deep breath. His coal-bright eyes flared.

When he left his hut, he did not don his cloak. Corded muscle rippled beneath his ashen skin. There was a litheness in his gait now. No longer did he shamble and limp along like an invalid; he moved like a jaguar among the huts. The village was almost entirely empty—only infants and the elderly remained to mind the hearths and homes. The rest of the villagers were deep in the withering forest, constructing a massive temple at the foot of the mountains. The warriors not out searching for the girl were raiding the lowland villages, gathering slaves for the construction of the temple and soldiers to fill Talara's ranks. But most importantly, they were collecting the blood of their enemies. Talara could not purify Kalaro without blood. An ocean of blood to cleanse the taint from their souls.

With Talara's blessing, he would create more apostles. More warriors of flesh and bone.

He left the hut, morning barely streaking the horizon, and made his way to the gate to meet the delegation from Noyo.

On his way along the road, he saw the familiar glint of bronze in the sky. He felt none of the dread he had once associated with the Chosen. It landed a few dozen feet ahead of him and waited, expecting him to come and prostrate himself at its feet. He did not.

"Is this the delegation?" Kunza asked. "A bit smaller than I expected."

The Chosen bared its fangs, low growl in its throat. "What did you do?"

"I've been blessed. You stand before Talara's Chosen. My name is Kunza, the Priest of Ashes. And I wish to speak to Azka. My Goddess has need of him."

ACKNOWLEDGMENTS

The writing of this novel, my first full novel, has been a long time coming. As such, there are so many people deserving of my sincerest thanks. Writing this at the very last moment, as I am wont to do, I am sure there will be people who have slipped my mind. For that I preemptively apologize. To those people I do mention, just know that no words could truly capture the depth of my gratitude.

Thank you to my mom and dad, and to my brother, Tony. Thank you for putting up with me all this time. I know it wasn't always easy.

Thank you to my wonderful wife, Ashley, for coming into my life when I was at my lowest. Without your support, I wouldn't have been able to do this. I love you.

Thank you to all the people who read All That Is Holy on Royal Road, and to everyone who left a comment or a review. Without your feedback I would have abandoned this story halfway through. You all gave me the motivation to keep going through burnout and hiatus.

Thank you to everyone at Podium who has helped me turn a very rough manuscript into something I can be proud of. To Julie for reaching out to me, and to Cass for keeping me on track. I know it was stressful at times, but I'm grateful to both of you from the bottom of my heart.

A special thank-you to my patrons for being the first ones to support me. Thank you, Sean Fletcher, Kite7, and Graham Kinnear. You're the best.

And one final thank-you to everyone who reads this novel. I never thought I'd write anything worthy of readership. So thank you, dear reader. Thank you for giving this little story of mine your attention.

ABOUT THE AUTHOR

Jeremy Knop is the author of All That Is Holy, a series that began on Royal Road as an experiment with serial fiction. He spent many years honing his craft, but it wasn't until after a yearlong battle with cancer that he truly pursued publication. Knop lives on a small farm in Michigan with his beautiful wife, Ashley, and their two dogs. Visit his website at www.jeremyknop.com.

DISCOVER
STORIES UNBOUND

PodiumAudio.com

Printed in the USA
CPSIA information can be obtained
at www.ICGtesting.com
JSHW021940080724
66057JS00007B/43